ILLUSIONS

Matt poured some of the fifty-year-old Napoleon brandy into the glasses, handed one to Willie, then sat in his favorite chair facing the fire. For a long time he watched the flames crackle and dance.

"You seem preoccupied," Willie said. "Court business?"

Matt smiled, but his eyes were serious. It was a while before he spoke. "I had a remarkable experience today, Willie. Strangely exhilarating . . . and, at the same time, disconcerting." He looked away, as though reluctant to meet her eyes.

She waited for him to continue.

"Jealousy," he sighed. "For the first time in years, I've been feeling jealous as hell. I thought I'd outgrown jealousy. I don't want to feel it, but there it is." He turned to her at last, his face youthful in its perplexity.

He got up from his chair and sat beside her. "Tell me, Willie, do I have reason to be jealous? Is that handsome young man I met today someone you could love?"

Willie threw her arms around Matt and hugged him fiercely. His revelation awed and delighted her. This brilliant, distinguished man was saying he cared for her as a man cares for a woman. Not for a minute would she lie to him – though his question didn't have a simple answer.

Illusions

Jessica March

NEW ENGLISH LIBRARY
Hodder and Stoughton

Printed and bound in Great Britain by
Cox & Wyman Ltd, Reading, Berkshire

Hodder and Stoughton Ltd
A Division of Hodder Headline PLC
47 Bedford Square
London WC1B 3DP

BOOK I

Success

1

Willa Dellahaye gazed through the plane window at the endless stretch of barren sand, remembering the ancient phrase the Arabs used to describe this part of the world – *Rub-al-Khali*, "The Empty Quarter." All the vast wealth that had come to this region through the fateful discovery of oil had not been enough to transform the trackless waste into a place of green. Even wealth and luck together, Willie thought, could not be the answer for everything.

Today the vista of emptiness stretching to the horizon struck a chord deep within her. There was a part of her that remained barren, a part where nothing grew. For all her success, she had not been able to change her own "empty quarter."

A voice jarred Willie from her reflection. "Miss Dellahaye, the captain has informed me that we'll be landing in twenty minutes."

She turned from the window and thanked the uniformed steward.

He lingered, a deferential smile on his dark face. "Has everything been satisfactory?"

"Yes, of course, thank you." How could it fail to be? The personal Boeing 727 of Seif al-Rahman was outfitted no less luxuriously than her own penthouse at the Pierre. She had slept on silk sheets in the plane's private bedroom, had dined last night and again this morning on meals served on Wedgwood china, prepared by a chef who worked exclusively aboard the private jet. The flight from New York had taken twelve hours, but the relief from her hectic schedule had made Willie feel the trip was more a vacation than an ordeal.

The steward was still hovering, his eyes scanning her body. For a moment Willie thought he might be on the brink of a pass. But accustomed as she was to the casual arousals sparked by her beauty, she could scarcely believe that an employee of the client who had arranged to fly her halfway around the world would dare such an indiscretion.

"Forgive me," the steward said, "but may I suggest you consider changing into something cooler? The plane is, of course, air-conditioned. But our advance weather report gives the ground temperature at one hundred fourteen degrees Fahrenheit."

She thanked him for the suggestion, and the man discreetly disappeared.

Willie took a Missoni shift of ivory linen and a makeup case from her overnight bag and walked back to the dressing room. As she shed her wool suit and slipped into her dress, she noticed the place on her wrist where the handcuff had chafed. Taking some aloe cream from the makeup case, she rubbed it into the irritated skin. She paused before the mirror in the opulent dressing room to run a brush through her shoulder-length strawberry blond hair, and to check again that she hadn't overdone the liner and mascara that emphasized the luxurious lashes of her enormous aquamarine eyes. She was not a vain woman. There had been a time when she underplayed her attractiveness, as if it were something to be ashamed of. But she had learned since that beauty – knowledgeably used – could be a valuable weapon in the arsenal of power.

The whine of engines throttling down, the rumble of landing gear being lowered, signaled Willie that the descent had begun. She hurried back to the forward lounge. Just before she resumed her seat, she collected the black morocco case that had been stored in a cabinet. Locked to its handle was a pair of handcuffs. Balancing the case in her lap, she snapped the second cuff around her wrist, then buckled herself in for the landing.

As soon as the steward opened the plane door, hot desert air rushed in like the breath of a dragon. Willie paused, looking out across the asphalt runways to the outline of a

8

strange city shimmering in the distance. Then she put on a white hat she'd bought yesterday and arranged the layers of veiling to conceal her face. When in Rome, she thought as she descended the ramp.

"On behalf of Al-sayyed Seif al-Rahman," the steward said as Wille went past him, "welcome to Jeddah."

A short distance from the ramp a white Mercedes stretch limousine was waiting. A dark, slender man with a mustache barely wider than a razor's edge emerged quickly as Willie's feet touched the ground. He hurried up to her and bowed slightly.

"*Ahlan wa sahlan*. Welcome, Miss Dellahaye. I am Salim Fawzi, personal assistant to Mr. al-Rahman. Did you have a comfortable journey?"

"Yes, thank you."

"I will be at your service whenever you require me." He held open the door of the Mercedes. "Please . . ."

Eager for the cool air that reached out from the limousine, Willie stepped in. As Fawzi sat down beside her, she could see the flash of gun metal beneath his well tailored jacket. The majordomo evidently doubled as a bodyguard.

"We will make one stop for customs," he said. "I expect it will be a quick one, but the formality is necessary. May I have your assurance," he asked, "that you are not carrying liquor, narcotics, or copies of magazines which would violate the tenets of our Muslim society?"

The way Fawzi's black eyes twinkled, Willie suspected he might have been joking, but about such delicate matters it was best not to take chances.

"Word of honor," she said, lifting her hand, as if to take an oath – until the handcuff restrained her.

Fawzi glanced at the morocco case. "Perhaps you'd be more comfortable if I put that with the rest of the luggage?"

"No, thank you," Willie said with a smile. "I think I'm most comfortable just as I am."

He nodded. "As you wish."

The limousine stopped at the terminal. As Fawzi escorted her through the arrivals section, Willie was aware of dozens of staring eyes, belonging to the clusters of airport loungers in search of entertainment, gossip, or perhaps the occasional odd job for a few *riyals*. In the insular, inbred world of Saudi, a woman in western clothes was still an object of curiosity.

Fawzi presented his card, along with Willie's passport, to a khaki-clad official, who administered the required stamp after a perfunctory glance. In Arabic, Fawzi explained that the western woman was a guest of Madame Seif al-Rahman. The official nodded and waved Willie's luggage through, evoking more stares, this time from the business-men who were busy turning their suitcases inside out to convince the customs inspectors that they had committed no violation of strict Muslim law.

After resettling Willie in the limousine, Fawzi took the seat next to the chauffeur. The tradition of purdah would be in force for the drive to the city, Willie concluded.

The journey into the old port city on the Red Sea told the recent story of the Saudi economy, of the Royals' attempt to venture selectively into the twentieth century. Factories puffing gray smoke cluttered the desert landscape, which had once resembled the craters of the moon in its silent majesty. Here and there stood naked girders, skeletons of abandoned projects, reflecting the sharp drop in oil prices and dramatically shrunken revenues. Along one strip of roadway, a crew of sweating expatriate laborers, Yemenis and Baluchis from the makeshift shanty-towns, poured hot tar.

A chauffeured Cadillac pulled alongside the Mercedes, as if to pass. From its back seat, three pairs of eyes, shrouded in black veiling, stared intently at Willie. She smiled, prompting a flurry of head-bobbing by the women, and a sudden burst of speed from the man at the wheel.

The traffic in Jeddah was a maddening jumble of noise and disorder. The drivers – all men, for women were forbidden by law to operate automobiles – maneuvered their cars with as much abandon as they had once ridden their camels.

Then suddenly, overriding the insistent blare of horns

10

came the high, keening voices of the muezzins, calling the faithful to prayer. Once the muezzins had climbed the towering minarets to send forth their holy message, but now there were only tape recordings, blasted through loudspeakers from atop the city's mosques.

The Mercedes came to a quick stop. Fawzi and the chauffeur stepped out, carrying small mats which they spread on the ground. Around them, other cars had also frozen in traffic, their drivers behaving in a similar fashion. Before Willie could ask what was happening, she saw men everywhere, all kneeling toward the east, beginning the prayer ritual. She sighed, took a chilled Perrier from the limousine's refrigerated bar and poured it into one of the crystal goblets perched in a mahogany rack. The prayer ritual would last awhile, but at least the chauffeur had left the air-conditioning on.

After a sip of her drink, Willie turned the Morocco case so its heavy latch was facing her. For the first time since she'd left New York, she dialed the combination known only to her and lifted the lid. At first glance, there appeared only a couple of books – a traveler's light reading – and some brochures from auction houses in New York. But when she touched a tiny button concealed in the hinge, the false bottom sprang up, revealing an inner drawer.

Against its black velvet lining shimmered a cornucopia of jewels: a pigeon's-blood ruby pendant; an emerald bracelet of contemporary design; an antique Deco lavaliere, set with a massive old mine diamond and dozens of faceted sapphires. A small chamois bag held a magnificent double rope of pearls, and in a niche at one side was a neatly aligned assortment of rings, set with diamonds and other gems, all original designs, all one of a kind.

Close up, and in such profusion, they might have been a jumble of costume trinkets. But there was no doubt about the true worth of the case's contents. Yesterday, when she'd signed the receipt at Harry Winston's, Willie had seen that the collection was appraised at nearly three million dollars. She smiled at the thought that this case,

11

these gems, were in a way the most expensive disguise she'd ever been asked to wear.

Once more she heard the call of the muezzins, and when she glanced up, she saw men everywhere, rising from their knees, rolling up their prayer mats and moving toward their cars. Quickly she closed the case. Perhaps Fawzi knew about her mission, but it was best to be discreet.

The men got back into the car, as casually as if their stop had been occasioned by nothing more than a traffic light. Soon it seemed they were driving away from the city.

"Will it be much longer?" she asked. The smallest tingle of alarm went through her. Could the wrong people have learned about the jewels, duped her into going with them as a prelude to theft?

"Not long now, Miss Dellahaye," Fawzi replied. "Madame al-Rahman is at the Creek for the weekend. She thought you'd enjoy the cool air."

Willie relaxed. She knew that the best of Saudi society kept retreats on the Red Sea inlet which they'd dubbed "the Creek." With most of the property owned by Royals, a beach house there was the ultimate status symbol. At the Creek, the wives of princes and businessmen alike could enjoy the breezes and relax in Parisian sportswear and Cote d'Azure bikinis, away from the strictures of Muslim custom.

Leaning back in the cool, whispering luxury of the limousine, watching the unchanging desert landscape pass by, Willie thought again that this mission she'd undertaken, the request she'd obliged, must surely be one of the quirkiest of her entire career.

It had begun with a phone call to her office last Monday, from a man who identified himself only as Harry Baldwin. He had refused to explain his business on the phone, insisting on seeing her and promising to make his visit worthwhile. His mysterious manner, rather than the hint of money, had persuaded Willie to find a spot in her already crowded schedule on Wednesday morning.

Precisely at the appointed time, the tall blond Baldwin had appeared in Willie's office. Good-looking and well dressed, though a shade too slick and flashy for her taste,

Baldwin had marched straight from the door to stand in front of her desk.

"Is it true that no one does it better than you do?" he asked cryptically.

"In my profession, Mr. Baldwin," Willie said, her blue eyes frosted with such disapproval that he wilted into a chair, "it's important to speak precisely. I can't answer your question until I know what you're asking."

"Divorce, counselor. Getting people divorced, and getting them what they deserve. That's what you do best, isn't it?"

She gave him the ironic answer she had often used before. "I do it well," she said, "when my heart is in it. But that's only under certain conditions . . ."

"I know all about that. Women – you always fight for the women. Right? Then I need you. Or rather, my sister does."

"Why doesn't your sister come to see me herself?"

Without answering, Baldwin reached inside his jacket and extracted a slip of paper. "She can't come. She's . . . in a kind of prison. But if you will go to see her, this will be the first installment on your fee."

He reached over and laid the paper in front of Willie. It was a check made out to her, in the amount of $50,000.

But money alone was not enough. It had never been enough to move Willa Dellahaye. Now, as always, it was the story that made the difference. When Harry Baldwin finished telling about his sister's marriage, and the reason she was so desperate for help, Willie had wasted no time canceling her appointments for the remainder of the week.

She had spent half a morning in the Fifth Avenue showrooms of Harry Winston, being coached on the descriptions and pedigrees of the jewels she would carry. Although it seemed to her that Baldwin was going to extreme lengths to conceal the real purpose of her trip, Willie couldn't help being caught up in the intrigue – and curious to discover if it had all been necessary.

The limousine had been traveling the desert road for almost an hour when Willie saw the sparkle of the ocean, and the march of expensive villas lining the road. Soon the

Mercedes turned into a driveway that led through a miniature park, a sure sign of wealth in this parched country. The desert could always be made to bloom, she reflected, for those who had the money to buy water and technology. Too bad the remedies weren't so simple for human hearts that were barren of hope and innocence.

The car stopped in front of a sprawling, classically simple California-style villa. Willie followed Fawzi up three steps and waited until the massive cedar doors were opened by a servant. Her high heels clicking rhythmically on the fawn-colored marble floor, Willie trailed the servant through an open gallery filled with masses of green plants and fresh flowers, to an enormous living room dominated by a bank of windows facing the water. On the walls hung paintings by Alexander Calder and Jasper Johns, a suite of Chagall lithographs and a Renoir that seemed misplaced among the moderns, which in turn contrasted with the museum-quality Islamic tapestries and antique brass trays. The scent of sandalwood – the traditional desert air freshener – hung over the room. The servant smiled, indicating that Willie should sit on one of the plump pink silk sofas that curved around the room.

For a minute, Willie waited with Fawzi. Surrounded by the trappings of great wealth, she mused over Baldwin's description of this place as "a kind of prison," and reflected once more on how little she knew about Seif al-Rahman.

Until the oil boom of the early seventies, his name had been unknown, unheard. But then, by virtue of his family connections to the Royals, he had become a middleman in every kind of major deal, from the sale of arms to the construction of hotels. The legendary fortune amassed in the process made him one of the world's richest men, with a net worth estimated as high as five or six billion dollars.

And his wife – his current wife – was Harry Baldwin's sister.

Amidst the rustle of fabric, on a cloud of Bal à Versailles she made her entrance. She was one of the most beautiful women Willie had ever seen. A perfect oval face, cream white skin accented by emerald eyes and vivid red lips, a

14

mass of jet-black curls rising from a classic widow's peak and cascading to her shoulders. She was wearing a turquoise Egyptian-style *galabiya* of gossamer cotton, embroidered with pearls. As the woman drew closer, extending her hand, Willie could see that the eyes were flat, devoid of warmth or animation. "Miss Dellahaye," she said, with just the hint of a quiver in her voice.

Standing to grasp her hand, Willie thought she could feel a faint trembling, the hint of a more powerful turbulence in the woman's soul. "Mrs. al-Rahman . . . I'm happy to meet you."

"Please – call me Sofia," the woman said, with forced brightness. "I'm simply dying to see what you've brought me from New York." She licked her lips in mock anticipation and took a seat next to Willie, exposing a slender well-curved leg.

For the next few minutes, with Fawzi hovering in the background, Willie cooperated in the ruse that had been so carefully prepared at such great expense. She opened the Morocco case and showed the jewels to Sofia, one at a time, describing the pieces knowledgeably, using the information given her by one of Winston's best salesmen.

A young boy in native dress offered tiny white cups of desert coffee flavored with cardamom, while a maid wheeled in a rack of gowns, against which Sofia could match the jewels.

For a few minutes she handled the pieces casually, then looked over at the bodyguard, who was plainly growing bored with the talk of jewels and fashion. "There's no need for you to stay, Fawzi. I may want to change my clothes as I make my selection. I'm sure we'll be quite safe," she added unnecessarily, for theft was virtually unknown in the desert kingdom.

Fawzi bowed and left the room. As the door clicked shut behind him, Sofia let out a sigh of relief. "We can talk now," she said quietly. "But leave the jewels on the couch. The servants don't speak English, but still – the show should go on."

Willie emptied the contents of the two trays, arranging

rubies, emeralds, diamonds, sapphires, and pearls on the silk upholstery. It felt a little like playing store, and she smiled.

"Yes," Sofia sighed, "after a while, it doesn't matter. I have collections like this brought in every few months. Seif allows me one million dollars in jewels every year . . . and I'd be a fool to take less."

"Would it have been so hard for you to see me – without this charade?" Willie asked.

Sofia responded with a sad smile. "My situation is hard to imagine, I'm sure. My husband is very generous about sending one of his planes – he has five – to fly any friend of mine here, whenever I choose. But there seem to be fewer friends as time goes on. So it's mainly the merchants I still see. Representatives from the European designers, or the jewelers." Her voice dropped. "On the other hand, yes, if he knew the truth of why I've brought you here, there's no telling what he might do to me . . . or to you."

"You think your husband wouldn't allow you to divorce him?"

Sofia gave another sad smile, then reached into the pocket of her gown and produced a folded document. "Read this," she said, "and tell me what you think."

Willie skimmed the paper, which resembled a lease in its wording. But it wasn't a lease. It was a prenuptial contract, dated seven years ago. By its terms, Sofia Baldwin, age nineteen, agreed to marry Seif al-Rahman for a period of ten years. During each of these years, she would receive a clothing allowance, a jewelry allowance, and a personal expense allowance of $1 million. At the end of the specified period, Seif had the option to divorce Sofia, without prejudice, and to settle on her a lump sum of $25 million. If, however, Sofia left the marriage, she received nothing.

"Well?" she asked, when Willie looked up.

"This document was drawn up in New York. Were you married there?"

"Yes. We keep an apartment in the city. We visit whenever Seif has business in the States."

"That's good . . . if you intend to file in New York."

16

"Look, Miss Dellahaye," Sofia said, a hard edge in her voice. "I thought you understood. I'm not going to file anything, anywhere, unless you tell me I can break this agreement and still come out ahead. I'm not going to walk away from a twenty-five-million-dollar payment, not with only three years to go."

A servant entered to refill their coffee cups. Sofia picked up a ring and pretended to admire it until the boy left.

It was Willie's turn to respond with impatience. "If you're content to regard your marriage as nothing more than a business arrangement, then perhaps you don't need me."

Sofia's green eyes showed panic. "I'm sorry," she apologized. "You were kind to come so far. And I do need you. But . . . well, if someone had told me seven years ago that I'd be talking to someone like you, I'd have said he was crazy. When Seif wanted to marry me, I felt like the luckiest woman in the world. I was just a kid then . . . I'd only been modeling a few months and I wasn't making much money.

"When Seif took over an entire disco for our first date – just because I said I liked to dance – I was dazzled. I'd never met anyone like him before . . . Seif can be charming when he likes, and he has a strange kind of magnetism. It's like those jewels, you see. The first time he gave me a gift, it was a diamond bracelet, and it cost more than anything my family had ever owned. That was real – and it was exciting. Like Seif. He was rich and he was powerful, and I thought if I married him, I'd have everything I ever wanted." She reached for the package of Dunhill cigarettes and the malachite lighter on the inlaid coffee table. She put a cigarette to her lips and lit it with long scarlet-tipped fingers that shook ever so slightly.

Sofia's words, the expression on her face, reminded Willie of her mother. But at times like this, didn't they all remind her of Mama?

"So it didn't live up to your dreams?" Willie prodded.

Sofia shook her head miserably. "I remembered seeing

your picture in *People* magazine. The story said you always win."

"The story was almost right. Most divorce cases are lost by one side. Sloppy preparation. Mistakes."

"I can't count on mistakes. Seif owns an army of lawyers."

"Let me worry about that. Just give me as much ammunition as you can. Seif doesn't let you go anywhere on your own, keeps you a kind of prisoner. But I just don't know how much sympathy we can generate from a lifestyle like this, even if you are always watched . . ."

Sofia gave Willie a long hard look, then jammed her cigarette into an ashtray. "There's more," she said, standing abruptly. "Come . . . I'll show you."

She led Willie up a marble staircase, down a long carpeted corridor to an enormous bedroom scented with perfume and hashish. The decor bore no resemblance to the serene, tasteful furnishings downstairs. On thick white wall-to-wall carpeting stood a huge circular bed covered with quilted red satin. Facing the bed was floor-to-ceiling Chinese cabinetry. As Sofia opened the doors, Willie saw a giant television screen, a well-stocked bar, and a collection of drug paraphernalia.

"Sit here." Sofia patted the bed. "It's the best seat in the house."

She slid a cassette into a video player and pressed some buttons. An image of the bedroom lit up the screen, as a strident passage from a Beethoven symphony played on the sound track. The bedroom door opened and Sofia entered, dressed from head to toe in sheer black veiling, her eyes heavily kohled. She was carrying a drink on a silver tray toward a heavyset man of about fifty, reclining, naked, on the bed. "My husband," Sofia whispered bitterly to Willie, "my leading man."

Pretending to stumble, the on-screen Sofia spilled the contents of the glass. The man drew back his arm and slapped her face, his eyes glittering with anticipation. She dropped to her knees, imploring forgiveness. He slapped her again and ripped the veil, exposing her body, which had

18

been oiled, the nipples rouged, the pubic hair shaved. Willie heard the intake of her own breath. She watched, fascinated and repelled, as the man forced Sofia to her knees, twining his fingers in her luxurious black hair, pressing his swollen penis into her mouth. His moans of pleasure rose and fell with the music, building to a violent climax of slaps and screams, as he pushed Sofia away, spattering her face with his semen.

He laughed and clapped his hands. Two young servants, a boy and a girl, no more than fourteen or fifteen, entered the room. Seif shouted something in Arabic, and the servants removed their clothes. He beckoned the girl closer, pulling her onto his lap, fondling her tiny breasts, as he watched the boy mount Sofia, who was lying on the floor, her eyes tightly shut. Laughing and shouting, he urged the boy to hurry, while his own fingers penetrated the girl, matching the rhythm of the penis that pounded Sofia's inert body. And when the boy was finished, Seif thrust the servant girl aside, reaching into the bed for a slender leather whip.

Pretending anger at Sofia, he flicked the lash across her breasts. She raised her hands, as if to protect herself, and he prodded her with his foot. Obediently she rolled over, raising herself on her hands and knees. Quickly he brought the whip down, once, twice, until she cried out. Laughing, he entered her roughly from the rear, ignoring her screams . . .

"No more," Willie said hoarsely, sickened by the scene she'd witnessed. "I've seen enough."

Sofia punched a button and the screen went dark. "That was one of our more tasteful cinematic productions," she said quietly. "There are more. Too many. One of me entertaining several of Seif's friends . . . gentlemen of, shall we say, exotic preferences. Seif even has one of . . . of me having the operation."

"Operation?"

Sofia bowed her head, but Willie saw the tears that fell onto her clenched hands. After a moment she spoke, her voice ragged. "That's what he really paid for, you see . . . to buy that . . . ."

19

"What?"

She looked up now, and Willie thought she'd never seen an expression of such inconsolable desolation. "He had me fixed, like a dog. I can't have children, and I . . . I can't feel anything."

Willie sat up straight. "You mean he had you sterilized against your will?"

"Not exactly." Sofia flushed under the intensity of Willie's eyes. "That was part of our . . . arrangement. What I didn't know was that when the doctor had me on the table, he'd slice off my clitoris . . . just to make sure I wouldn't enjoy any of my husband's games."

Willie bristled with fury. Now she understood the horror of Sofia's golden prison. Seif al-Rahman had bought himself a nineteen-year-old girl the way he'd purchase a piece of meat. Trimmed her to his liking, installed her here, to be his whore incarnate and private dirty-movie star. And because Saudi society frowned on resident mistresses, he'd gone through the charade of a marriage.

"I'll help you, Sofia," Willie said, with the force of an oath. "I'll take you with me today . . ."

"No! You don't understand. Seif's people, the staff, they all do what he says. I wouldn't get past the driveway. I'm not allowed to drive a car in this place. I'm not allowed to leave the country without his permission. He . . . he's threatened me. He said he would kill me if I tried to leave him. He can do it, you know. All he has to do is say I was running off to meet a lover. The law here would allow it. Just as they allowed . . ." she looked away. "The ancient sheikhs used to 'fix' their harem women the way Seif did me. To keep them from being unfaithful."

"And have you ever been unfaithful?" Willie had to ask the question.

Sofia laughed bitterly. "You mean off-camera? What would be the point? Maybe my heart could love another man, but my body is . . . dead."

Willie's heart went out to this beautiful woman. She had been seduced into hell by the lure of limitless wealth.

"I'll take your case," she said. "But you've got to get out

of here . . . to New York, where you can be protected. And where I can fight this through the courts. Western courts."

"Seif has a trip scheduled for next month. He plans to take me. Fawzi follows me everywhere, but I think I could lose him."

"How are your finances? Have you saved any money?"

Sofia nodded. "I can pay you . . . whatever it takes . . ."

"That's not why I asked. You'll need money to live on. This could be a long, dirty fight, and I want to make sure you can hold out."

"I'll hold out – if you can win."

"I'll win. *Nobody* has the right to do what your husband did."

Sofia smiled. "You don't sound like a lawyer. You sound like you're taking this personally."

Willie reached over and grasped the other woman's hand. "I always take it personally. That's why I'm so good. Now, if you have a guest room for me, I'd like to rest awhile."

Sofia settled her into a corner room, where she could hear the sound of the waves against the beach. Slipping off her shoes, Willie stretched out on the bed and closed her eyes, her mind already formulating strategies for what would surely be one of the biggest battles of her professional life.

Small wonder she found it hard to believe in the trappings of romantic love. All the women who came through her office door had whispered "I love you" to someone, believing no doubt that the words had meant "forever." Yet when they came to her, the words and passions had been twisted and distorted into a bitter struggle for money or revenge. In Willie's office, in the courtrooms where she battled, once bright dreams of love lost all their shine, beautiful vows of the heart soon revealed all their pitiful fragility.

As she drifted toward sleep, the sound of the surf outside her window became a whisper – the soft voice of the man who had made promises of forever to her. In her mind's eye she could see him, smiling as he took her into his arms, holding her, loving her. But just as she yielded to the warmth of his embrace, he disappeared, and all she could see as she hovered on the edge of consciousness was the barren endlessness of the Empty Quarter.

It had always been this way. The dream of love always faded just when she reached the brink of hope. It happened to all her clients, too, Willie thought. Like a mirage in the desert, the love they all sought shimmered in front of them, drawing them on. But as they drew nearer, the mirage vanished, just another of life's illusions.

2

The firm of Dellahaye, Crown and Belzer occupied the entire twenty-first floor of 375 Park Avenue. In addition to the three senior partners, it employed twenty-two secretaries, assorted clerks, twelve associates, and six junior partners. Willie had never intended this to happen. "I don't want to be part of a legal factory," she declared on the day she went into business for herself. She had changed her mind when she realized she was turning away as many cases as she accepted.

And being Willie, she made the change an exercise in principle. "The law is a damn men's club," she'd once complained to the one man who understood her principles. "Indeed it is," he'd replied evenly. "But if we can only get enough women like you, maybe we can change that."

So she had expanded with a purpose: to provide opportunities for outstanding young lawyers – outstanding female lawyers, though she'd taken on a few token men to avoid the possibility of a discrimination action. But it wasn't discrimination she practiced; it was affirmative action. The men, she reckoned, already had plenty of opportunities.

As the business press often noted, the firm of Dellahaye, Crown and Belzer was unique on two counts. It was a firm where a creative, dynamic female lawyer could count on becoming a partner in the traditional seven-year period. And it was a firm that specialized almost exclusively in "matrimonials," the polite term for divorce.

A half dozen years ago, there had been seven hundred divorce specialists in the United States. Now there were twelve thousand, with several of the best and brightest as Willie's associates. In her student days, divorce lawyers had been considered little better than ambulance chasers. When she returned, years later, to address a Harvard Law School graduating class, Willie spoke passionately about her chosen field. "You are what you think you are," she began. "If you see yourself as a practitioner of an honorable craft, you will ennoble that craft with your own sense of honor. Our constitution recognizes the individual's right to pursue happiness. When that right is abrogated through the loss of some physical function, our body of law provides compensatory damages. I believe the loss of love is one of the greatest losses a human being can suffer. And that is why I'm in the business of compensating that suffering through every means the law provides. Statistics tell us there is a divorce every twenty-seven seconds. I believe that this presents an urgent and compelling challenge to all of us engaged in the practice of matrimonial law. And that is why I have dedicated myself wholeheartedly to meeting that challenge . . ."

It was 9.40 a.m. when Willie strode past her receptionist, scattering greetings as she traveled the long corridor leading to her corner office. Though it was large, with a commanding view of the city – as befitted Willie's senior status – the office was somehow more personal and intimate than her apartment. The books on the shelves were old favorites, well read and well worn. The lithographs on the walls she had chosen herself: two Gormans, a Picasso, and a Klimt. And the massive partners' desk was one she'd found in London. When she traveled she bought things for her office as tourists buy souvenirs. Gifts from clients – an antique Russian samovar, the small Chinese carpet – these were displayed here, trophies for work well done.

As usual, her secretary had left a thermal carafe of coffee and a fresh bouquet of flowers – today it was tulips – on her desk. To one side was a stack of newspapers: the *New York Times,* the *Wall Street Journal* and the *Christian Science Monitor*, with major items circled in red. Documents awaiting her signature were set squarely in front of her chair, arranged in order of priority.

Willie poured herself some coffee and thumbed through the phone messages.

It jolted her suddenly . . . the power of a name on a small piece of paper. She stared at it, forgetting for a moment that she was the head of a large and powerful law firm, remembering only that she was a woman.

Then she put the paper aside. Later would be soon enough. After she'd done some work and quieted the excitement that had broken through her professional routine.

She buzzed her secretary on the intercom. "Lettie, I want you to call a Professor Zaki Hatem at Columbia University. His specialty is Islamic Law . . . try the Middle Eastern Studies Department first. Set up a consultation. Then have Research do an in-depth on Seif al-Rahman. Also on his current wife Sofia. Call Harry Baldwin and set up an appointment. Any time in the next couple of weeks will be okay."

"Right away."

"On this message from the New York Bar Association . . . I can't make it out . . ."

"Francis Aloysius Harrigan called twice . . . himself. In person. He said you were to call The Minute You Walked In." '

"Oh." Francis Aloysius Harrigan was everything Willie admired and rejected all rolled into one. He had taught her more about the gritty day-to-day business of practicing law than any single individual. And for what he taught her, she wasn't particularly grateful. "Call His Highness back," she said, "and let's see what he can do to make my day."

"Check."

A moment later, Harrigan's velvety baritone resonated

through the speakerphone. "Willa, darlin' – how good of you to call me back so promptly. And how is New York's champion of distressed women today?"

"I'm fine. What can I do for you?"

"All business are we? Well, that can be an admirable quality." Harrigan would not be rushed. Conversations with the dean of New York divorce lawyers ran on his timetable, or not at all. "I can't tell you how proud I am of the career you've made . . . how proud I am of my little protégée . . ."

Willie bristled, but she wouldn't give Francis the satisfaction of a rise. "Your 'little protégée' thanks you. Was there something you wanted?"

"Yes, dear Willa. The pleasure of your company for lunch. Today."

"Today? I already have—"

"Change it," he cut in. "I have a matter of some moment to discuss with you. I can promise you an interesting lunch . . . not to mention stimulating company . . ."

She laughed in spite of herself. "Francis, you have the soul of a snake oil salesman . . ."

"I'll take that as a compliment . . . and a 'yes.' The Four Seasons at twelve-thirty."

He hung up before she could say another word. Still smiling, Willie instructed her secretary to cancel her previous lunch appointment. Harrigan could be a pain. And a bastard. But if he had something to say, she wanted to hear it.

A tap on the door announced Pamela Belzer. Dark and sleek and impeccably groomed, Pamela would have adapted nicely to any corporate setting. She was the firm's resident expert on the economics of divorce, and she could readily quote, chapter and verse, statistics on alimony and child support in every state of the union.

"Sorry to barge in," she said, "but I'm at a crossroads, and I need another opinion, right away."

"Have a seat. Everybody seems to be in a hurry today."

"Take a look," Pam said, handing over a sheaf of papers. "Just the top page."

"What is this – the national debt?"

Pamela didn't smile. Money was one thing she never joked about. "These are the numbers I've worked out with Nina Blackman."

"Ah . . . ." The Blackman divorce was still in the early stages. When Rob Blackman, television's hottest anchorman, had informed his wife of fourteen years that he wanted a divorce, Nina had headed straight for Pamela Belzer. A wise choice. Blackman's latest three-million-dollar contract gave Pam the kind of numbers she liked to work with. The budget she'd drawn up would give Nina the Blackman duplex on Central Park South and provide her with a monthly allowance of $20,000. Willie scanned the breakdown:

Mortgage payments:	$2200
Utilities:	$ 240
Telephone:	$ 650
Domestic Help:	$ 980
Insurance:	$1200
Home Improvements:	$1500
Maintenance:	$1200
Food & Beverage:	$2100
Auto Expenses:	$ 600
Entertainment:	$2000
Travel:	$1100
Clothing:	$2500
Personal Care:	$ 800
Private Schools:	$2000
Miscellaneous:	$2500

"Let me guess," Willie said. "The husband doesn't want to pay."

"They never do," Pam pronounced soberly. "But that's not the only problem. He's threatening to contest custody. My client's hysterical, and I'm not sure what to advise her. I thought I'd better bounce this one off you . . ."

Willie frowned. The threat of a custody suit was a powerful one. When she'd started practicing, judges almost automatically awarded children to the mother, unless it could be proven she was unfit. Now judges were just as likely to award custody to fathers who had the money and resources for a court fight.

"Who's the attorney?" Willie asked.

"Ned Roman."

Her frown deepened. "I've been up against him. He wrote the book on winning through blackmail. He threatens to take the kids away, and the numbers drop. It stinks, but it works. Is there a chance Blackman really wants the children?"

"I'm not sure. There's another woman in the picture. It hasn't hit the gossip columns yet, but Nina tells me that Rob wants to marry Gloria Hacker – of the lumber-mill Hackers. I had Research run a check . . . she doesn't come out as the ideal stepmother, but Nina's still scared. She's afraid she'll lose a husband and two children if she doesn't make nice."

"Which is exactly what Roman wants her to think. Tell me, has Roman given you his 'you can't put a value on a father's relationship with his children' speech?"

Pam looked astonished. "How did you know?"

"He always makes that speech when he's ready to talk money. The man's not good in a courtroom. He counts on the 'Two S'es' – Starving out and Scaring – to force a settlement. On his terms. About these numbers" – Willie pointed to the sheet – "have we inflated them?"

"A little," Pam admitted. "But Nina's standard of living has been high for the past five or six years . . ."

"Trim the numbers, and then dig in. Roman will settle. Tell your client to count on it."

"Thanks, Willie. You know, I always tell my clients they'd be better off if they could see divorce as a business deal, if they'd stop worrying about being nice girls and let me negotiate. I've always said—"

"I remember."

The memory of Willie's first meeting with Pam was a sour one. "Divorce is big business. And it's going to get bigger," Pam had said, in answer to Willie's "Why do you want to work here?" That answer, and the prediction (which had proven exactly accurate), were wrong in Willie's book. But Pam had been superbly qualified – top five percent in her class at Yale, and *Law Review* as well.

I'd rather have this woman on my side, Willie had concluded, echoing a sentiment that had been directed at her years ago. Hiring Pam had been a good business decision. Still Willie wished that wasn't so.

"It may start out being about love, but it ends being about money. Period," Pam finished, quoting herself.

Willie had no sharp comeback for this. "Good luck with the case," she said as Pam left.

Alone again, Willie picked up the phone message she had put aside earlier. She dialed the number herself, counting the rings, as anxious as a teenager.

The familiar husky voice answered: "Hello?"

She tried to sound calm. "Jedd. It's Willie. I got your message. What a surprise to hear from you . . ."

"I'm glad I can surprise you . . . How have you been?"

"I've been . . . fine. And you?" How strange, she thought, to be making polite small talk with Jedd. After all that had been . . .

"Not as fine as I might be. I need to see you, Willie. Have dinner with me? Tonight?"

"Yes." The answer slipped out before she could debate the wisdom of it.

"I'll pick you up at seven. Same place?"

"No – I have an apartment at the Pierre now."

"Isn't that awfully 'establishment' for you, counselor?" he teased.

"Take that up with my accountant," she said pleasantly and hung up.

The Four Seasons ranked high on the list of places suitable for "Power Lunches," and that, no doubt, was why Francis had chosen it. Willie wasn't surprised when the maitre d' showed her to a choice table alongside the pool. Flamboyant Francis loved to be seen holding court in the city's finest restaurants and clubs. Nor was she surprised that she was the first to arrive. He was probably lurking in the men's room or the bar, just so he might make an entrance. There was no end to the silly games played in the name of power. She ordered a glass of white wine and decided she would give him ten minutes and no more.

"Willa, darlin'!" Harrigan greeted her effusively, right after her drink was served. "You're looking gorgeous, absolutely gorgeous."

"So are you," she said dryly. There was no denying that the Silver Fox (a nickname derived as much from his overblown rhetoric as from the curly mane that had gone prematurely gray years ago) had scarcely aged in the dozen or so years she'd known him. He looked fit in a stoutish way (probably good tailoring) that went with his florid complexion (maybe high blood pressure, but more likely alcohol, she thought maliciously). His nails were manicured and he wore the horn-rimmed spectacles he affected in the courtroom, or when other serious business was at hand. Harrigan, more than anyone she knew, was a creature shaped for dramatic effect – but knowing that didn't necessarily reduce the impact.

She almost laughed aloud as he leaned back in his chair and managed to summon a waiter with a lift of his bushy eyebrows and an anticipatory expression. I wonder what *that* bit of business cost him in tips? Willie mused.

Having ordered his drink, he turned his full attention to Willie. "No doubt you've been consumed with curiosity as to the purpose of this meeting." He smiled to soften the conceit of his statement.

"No doubt, as you intended." She smiled back.

"Ah, Willie, Willie . . . it was a sad day when you left my employ. How I've searched in vain for another protégée with your native intelligence, your tenacity and determination . . ."

"Thank you," she said, hoping to staunch the flow of Harrigan's rhetoric.

". . . your passion for the law. But" – he paused for effect –"there are some important things you might have learned, had you lingered longer with the firm of Harrigan and

29

Peale. Balance and proportion and a sense of the absurdity of it all. Here you are, as affluent and successful and, yes, as powerful in your own way, as any one of us. Yet you still have that fanatical gleam of the have-not. Why is that, darlin' Willa? Do you really have no use for the club that would have you?"

Harrigan's words touched a nerve. "Francis, *darlin'*," she said, slowly and with deliberate irony, "I'm sure you've heard the joke about the waiter who works in a mediocre restaurant: he serves the food, but he won't eat it. I love the principle of law, but the service of it gets pretty mediocre. And I won't swallow that whole."

"Well, if you feel that way," Harrigan crowed, undaunted, "you'll feel delighted with my invitation . . . to speak at the National Conference on Matrimonial Law in September. Naturally, I am program chairman of this event—"

"Naturally. Who else but you? A major architect of New York's so-called equitable distribution law, the man who's responsible for impoverishing thousands of women and children—"

"Now, now, Willa. Those blue eyes of yours are flashing wildly. Perhaps your blood sugar is low. Let's order some lunch." He hailed a waiter.

"I'm not undernourished, Francis. I'm simply speaking the truth."

"Ah, yes, the truth." He sighed. "Well, then, let's order lunch for the sake of civility. Which, I apparently failed to teach you, is often more valuable than truth." He studied his menu intently, and Willie knew he wouldn't say another word until he was good and ready. "I will have the grilled tuna with hoisin, and another Stolichnaya, straight up," he said to the waiter, who was hovering discreetly. "And you, Willa dear?"

"Salad and—"

"That's not a proper lunch at all. No wonder you're so nervous and tense. Bring the lady the snapper baked in lemon sauce. And the hazelnut layer cake for dessert."

Willie laughed and let the order stand. There were still moments when it was nice to have a man take care of her.

"Now," Harrigan said solemnly, staring into Willie's eyes. "Have you thought about what an opportunity this is? You and other – less able – female attorneys have criticized our matrimonial laws at length. In the press. Now I'm giving you the opportunity to offer constructive alternatives."

"What's the catch, Francis? Why would you do such a thing? The conference is big stuff. We'll get a lot of press coverage, and that means the legislators will have to pay attention."

He affected an air of injured innocence. "I don't apologize for the equitable distribution principle. It was a sincere attempt to recognize the changes which have taken place in our society. If, unfortunately, some segments of the female population have suffered, that's been largely due to interpretation. How could we know what the judges would do?"

"You knew," she said vehemently. "You knew, Francis. You made it sound like a step forward. But it wasn't. It was a way to make divorce financially easier for men. To dump women and children and come away with more disposable income than they had before. How can you sit there and tell me you didn't know?"

He smiled. "Let's say – off the record – that I'm not surprised. You asked for equality, you got it. Be careful of answered prayers, Willa darlin', the ladies got exactly what they asked for. If they weren't clever enough to be specific, is that my fault?"

She stood up abruptly, face flushed, blue eyes almost purple with rage. "All right, Francis. I'll speak at your conference. I'll give you and everyone else an earful. But I'll be damned if I'll eat lunch with you." She rushed out of the room, almost colliding with the waiter who was bringing their food.

"The lady's changed her mind," Harrigan explained smoothly. "You know how ladies are . . . but not to worry. I'm certain I'll do justice to this fine meal." He smiled and attacked his lunch with relish. Willa Dellahaye had reacted with all the fiery spirit and competitive drive he'd counted on, and walked neatly into the snare he'd prepared.

She ambled along Fifth Avenue, simply passing time, unwilling to return to the office. Harrigan had unsettled her, bringing to the surface all the restlessness and unease she'd been feeling lately. Years ago, when her dream had been young, she was so sure about what she meant to accomplish. He goals had stood like shining beacons, incandescent in their purity, pulling her forward, through the grinding mechanism of law school, through all the wearing rituals that stood between her and the coveted degree of Juris Doctor. Now she had the degree and all the recognition that went with it. Yet someone like Francis Aloysius Harrigan seemed much more comfortable in his skin than she did in hers. There was something wrong. Something. He had been laughing at her, as if he knew a secret that eluded her. She had lost her sense of certainty, yet she had no choice but to go on, as if it were still there.

She dawdled, uncharacteristically, in front of Saks Fifth Avenue, though she had no interest in buying anything. She normally shopped in the efficient way she did everything else, replacing and replenishing by list, rather than by impulse, twice a year. She had never experienced the restorative power of a shopping spree, the pleasure that came from extravagant self-indulgence. And yet she wasn't ready to return to the office.

There was something of spring in the city streets. Not flowers or green things, but a mood evoked by the renaissance of balmy weather after the cold, gray winter months. Hunched shoulders and heavy coats had given way to smiles and bright colors. Willie felt the change of atmosphere around her, and she yearned to respond to the optimism of spring.

"Can you spare a dollar for a drink, ma'am?" A youngish man with a heavy growth of beard held out a grimy hand. "I really need one . . ."

The candor charmed her, and she fumbled in her purse, but found nothing smaller than a five-dollar bill.

The beggar saw her dilemma. "I can't give you change

. . . but I'll remember you in my prayers," he smiled hopefully.

She handed over the money.

"God bless America. And rich people like you."

Rich people like me. How strange. Could Harrigan be right? She had crossed all kinds of boundaries, but little Willie Dellahaye still thought of the rich and powerful as "them".

Dinner with Jedd Fontana was no big deal. At least that's what Wilie told herself each time she checked her watch, willing the hours to fly away. But the restlessness that had brought her home early from the office made a lie of all her assurances. So did the new bottle of Guerlain's Naheema that she'd stopped to buy.

Her apartment was immaculately neat, as always, and smelled faintly of furniture polish. She'd bought the place because it came with a full range of hotel services, and because her accountant had insisted she "buy something, for God's sake – we need a tax write-off." The space was good, the view of Central Park from the terrace dazzling, and the place would, no doubt, turn out to be an excellent investment.

When interviewers from the women's magazines walked through the apartment, searching for clues to her personality, for the bits and pieces that would make her accessible to their readers, they came up empty. She had no decorating stories to tell, no cute or funny tales of how she'd searched long and hard for the perfect lamp or the wall hanging she couldn't live without. In truth, she had found a decorator whose portfolio she approved and handed over a large check. In return, she'd been provided with tasteful and amiable surroundings in a clean, undistracting contemporary style.

In response to questions about her home, she volunteered the name of her decorator and withheld the very piece of evidence that would reveal more than Willa Dellahaye's public personality. The fashionable magazines advised single women to make comfortable nests for

33

themselves because they, no less than their married sisters, deserved real homes. Willie's truth was unfashionable, and one she rarely admitted, even to herself. A professionally decorated hotel apartment was as far as she was willing to go, for, to her, the core and essence of a real home was a husband and a family. Instead she had chosen routine and efficiency, which were twinned in her mind. They eliminated clutter and freed her energies for the thing she cared most about: her work.

Her wall of closets was a case in point: neat rows of what the fashion press called "power suits," arranged in color groups. Complementary silk blouses lined up on racks below. Accessories grouped in clear Lucite boxes. A standing rack of shoes, dozens of pairs, chosen for comfort and suitability. Off to one side – and similarly arranged – were her "fun" clothes, cocktail dresses and gowns and sportswear.

Fashion should be functional, she often told interviewers. "I can dress or pack with my eyes closed. It's unproductive and a waste of time to make a fetish of clothes. The make a statement, and a woman, no less than a man, should be clear on the kind of statement she wants to make."

But now, as she contemplated the contents of her closet, she was far from clear on the kind of statement she wanted to make. Dresses were pulled out of the closet, frowned at, then flung carelessly on the bed. A black silk was too somber. A red chiffon, too flashy. Finally, she settled on a bronze silk.

Next she worked her way through the series of daily stretches she'd started eight years ago, on the day she turned thirty. Nature had blessed her with good bones and superb flesh. Now the maintenance was up to her. Her reward was a scented bubble bath, rather than the usual no-nonsense shower. A herbal facial to refresh and tighten, though her flawless golden skin needed no first aid.

She lined up her cosmetics, just as Mama used to do. A bronze blusher for her magnificent cheekbones. Charcoal shadow for her lids and a periwinkle blue liner to frame her enormous jewellike eyes. Two coats of jet mascara, a slick of lip gloss, and she was finished.

Vigorously she brushed her hair, until it shone, falling to her shoulders, thick and straight. She slipped into her dress and was searching for the right pair of earrings when the house phone rang.

Jedd had arrived.

She ran to the door, waiting for his knock.

And then . . . there he was. The lean aristocratic face, like a Goya painting. Smooth dark skin marred only by a tiny scar that looked like a dimple when he smiled. Coal black eyes that promised everything and gave away nothing. He wore a gray banker's suit and a white shirt, but he carried them with the grace and swagger of a matador.

"Hello again." The husky voice stirred layers of memories, as he grazed her hair with his lips, his arms circling her lightly, all too briefly.

"Hello, yourself." She stared openly, taking inventory of the familiar features. "You've cut your hair," she said accusingly.

He laughed. "I'm delighted you noticed. My barber tells me the highwayman look doesn't cut it in corporate boardrooms these days."

"Why not?" she shot back. "I'd think of it as truth in advertising."

"Ah, Willie," he smiled, though the black eyes were serious. "Let's not start . . . not yet. Let's just be a man and a woman for a little while. Offer me a drink, won't you?"

She opened the bottle of chilled Montrachet and filled two slender flutes. "Cheers," she said, lifting her glass.

"To love." The word hung in the air, daring Willie to respond. She didn't. Jedd looked around the spacious living room, appraising the decorator furnishings. "Very nice," he said, "but it isn't you."

"Oh?" Her voice rose. "Who is it, then?"

"It's image. Like my haircut. It's Willa Dellahaye, Esquire. It's success and it's money. But it doesn't say anything about you. My Willie . . ." There was the huskiness again, tugging at the memories she'd carefully sealed away.

" 'Your Willie' doesn't exist anymore," she said crisply,

35

"and thank goodness for that. As for this place . . . it suits me and it's convenient. I'm very busy . . . "

"Too busy for love?" There was that word again, seductive, enticing.

"Too busy for fairy tales."

In the dim light of a small Greenwich Village restaurant, they looked like storybook lovers lingering over a romantic dinner, accompanied by soft piano music from the bar. Two beautiful, elegant people, separated only by a small expanse of pink linen.

"This is nice," Willie said, "but I would have expected Lutece or Le Cirque from you."

"That's my Willie." The black eyes sparkled with amusement. "Still a snob . . . still putting people in neat pigeonholes, so you can handle them with neat, tidy clichés."

"A snob? Me? You're crazy, Jedd Fontana. You're the one . . . you and that smug Palm Springs rat pack . . . acting like you owned the world, like you were better than everyone else—"

"Maybe that's true," he interrupted, reaching across the table to take her hand. "Maybe we were thoughtless, spoiled kids. But what's your excuse? You shut people out because they don't think the way you do. How is that kind of snobbery better?"

The challenge went unanswered. Jedd managed to unbalance her, as no courtroom opponent could. "So what brings you to New York?" she asked, ignoring the pressure of his hand, the racing of her own pulse.

"You."

She envied his directness, but didn't trust it. "What else?"

"Business."

"Family business?"

"You make that sound like a crime," he said quietly, with more than a trace of bitterness.

"Search your conscience for the answer to that. If you have one," she added primly.

36

Jedd Fontana stared at the beautiful face that had bedeviled him for so many years, at the full lips made for kissing, pursed now in an expression that reeked of self-righteousness. He wanted to shake her, but he chose reason instead. "My conscience is in good order, counselor. But I'm surprised that after so many years in the law, yours sees only black and white. There are areas of gray, you know . . ."

She leaned over the table, unwilling to give an inch. "What I know – after years in law – is that you get gray by whitewashing black."

"I give up." He threw out his arms in a gesture of mock surrender. "No, that's not true. You know I'm never going to give up on you."

Quickly she changed the subject. "You still haven't told me what you're doing here."

"I'm looking for a small publishing house . . . thinking of buying it."

"I didn't know that Fontana interests included publishing."

"They don't. But I want to do something on my own. You ought to be able to understand that . . ."

"Yes. I . . . I just didn't realize you felt that way."

"There's still a lot you don't know about me, Willie. Maybe we could fix that. I'll be in New York for two more days . . . give us a chance to make a start . . ."

"We've had a start." She paused. "More than one . . ."

"People change," he said softly. "Love makes things possible." He gazed at her intently, silently taking an oath that his words were true.

But outside of her natural habitat, the courtroom, no oath seemed good enough. She had always wanted to believe him, and in the end what they called love never lasted more than a moment, a night.

She tore her eyes from his, and was glad when the waiter interrupted them to ask about the desserts.

They rode the elevator to Willie's apartment in a silence that was charged with unspokens. She struggled with the physical pull that was almost palpable, as they stood, shoulder to shoulder. Her body craved his touch desperately, but her mind told her that nothing had changed, that loving Jedd was as impossible as it had ever been.

When they reached her door, it took all of Willie's self-control to deliver the speech she'd rehearsed: "I'd invite you in, but I have an early appointment."

He smiled in that lazy, knowing way that made her temper rise and her heart lurch. "That's okay, Willie. All in good time." He lifted her chin for a long kiss that made her dizzy. And then he was gone.

The apartment seemed sad and unwelcoming. Two wineglasses stood on the coffee table, a reminder that Jedd had been there. Was not here now. She started to clear the glasses, clumsily broke one, and left the debris where it lay, a symbol of shattered hope.

In the bedroom, she dropped her clothes on the floor and crawled under the cool sheets of her big, solitary bed, her body restless with unfulfilled longings, her senses still full of him. The image of his face, the touch of his lips, the scent of his cologne mingled with the sharp masculine aroma of his body. Sleep would not come easily tonight, she knew.

If only she could believe the things he'd said . . . if only. But Willie knew far too much about Jedd Fontana.

And far too much about this thing the poets called love. Nights like this, when her body and heart longed for romance, when every fiber of her being cried out for completion, she asked herself when had she lost her innocence, her ability to believe . . . ? Had it been her success – being so goddamn good at cleaning up the mess left from other people's lost loves – that had taught her how fragile and treacherous and unreliable the dream could be?

Or was the disappointment and sadness only the inevitable, inescapable legacy of her beginnings?

BOOK II

Lessons

Prologue

The child sat up, shivering, rubbing the sleep from her eyes. The noises that had wakened her were getting louder: a man's angry voice, the bump and scrape of furniture on bare wood floors, a woman's voice crying and pleading. Through the walls she heard a scream that dissolved to a whimper. Mama and Papa argued a lot, but these sounds frightened Willie as nothing had before.

Still half asleep, she slid out of bed, feeling her way along the short darkened hallway, to the closed door of her parents' room. Just as her hands touched the door, it was wrenched open. A dark shadow swayed before her, a bogeyman, big and menacing and evil. She pulled back and saw past the giant, into the room. Mama . . . lying back curiously on the bed, legs open, head lolling. Mama . . . usually so angelically beautiful and clean . . . Now a dark bruise marred her perfect cheek, and blood trickled from her nose and mouth, coloring the wavy golden hair that strayed over her face. Even more frightening was the blood that stained her naked thighs and the snowy white sheets.

Too shocked to move or cry out, Willie looked up at the shadow still swaying in the doorway. She caught the faintly astringent smell of whiskey. In the dim light from the bedroom, she saw the giant's face. Papa.

He reached out clumsily to her. But when she recoiled, he stiffened with anger. "Goddamn!" he muttered. "Goddamn it all to hell!" He shoved Willie aside and stomped off, slamming his way out of the cabin and into the night.

Mama lifted herself up, as if to follow. But on seeing Willie, crying and confused, she wrapped herself in a sheet and sank back onto the bed. "It's all right, baby," she murmured hoarsely, "I'm all right."

41

Willie stared at the blood and the bruises. More than anything, she wanted her mother back, the way she'd always been, beautiful and clean. Finally she turned and went into the bathroom, returning with a wet washcloth. "Wash your face, Mama," she said, with a curious authority for one so young. "I'll help you make it better."

As she reached out to her mother, wiping the blood from her battered face, Willa Dellahaye left childhood behind forever.

1

Belle Fourche, South Dakota: 1959

"Hurry up, Willie, or you'll miss the bus."

"I'm ready, Mama . . . I'm just looking for my arithmetic book."

As the school bus sounded three short blasts on its horn, Willie ran out of her bedroom and grabbed the lunch her mother had prepared. "I bet I get a hundred on the test today," she said excitedly, "and then I'll have five gold stars."

"That's wonderful, honey." Ginny kissed her daughter and watched the child race out of the cabin. "Watch out for ice on the hill," she called after her. She sighed as she poured herself a second cup of coffee and contemplated the morning ahead. There were beds to be made and dishes to wash, a new movie magazine to read, but still the day felt empty and lonely. She felt the familiar lump in her throat, the rush of warm tears on her cheeks.

She spent a lot of time crying these days. Always when she was alone, in the cozy dream cabin that Perry had built for them on the riverbank, in the midst of a majestic stretch of wilderness near Spearfish. Even when she told herself how lucky she was to have a hard-working husband who didn't drink away too much of his weekly paycheck from the Lucky Nugget mines. And even when she thanked heaven for sending her such a good and beautiful daughter as eight-year-old Willie.

Virginia Dellahaye's life had turned out just the way she'd dreamed it, when she was the prettiest girl in the sophomore class at Belle Fourche High School and Perry the captain of the football team, and it seemed only right

43

that they would fall in love and marry. Yet nothing felt the way she'd thought it would, and she could hardly remember what it was like to be happy.

Once upon a time, she had vague but colorful fantasies about going to design school, or maybe selling beautiful things in a city department store. Now she made pretty clothes for Willie and dressed her small collection of dolls with "movie star" designs from her sketch pad. And the wilderness cabin – which stood on the very spot where she and Perry had parked and dreamed and whispered promises in high school – felt more and more like a prison.

She looked at herself in the mirror, then compared what she saw with the framed wedding photograph on the big maple dresser. She was every bit as pretty as she had been then, even prettier. She'd been perming her naturally blond hair. And she'd learned from the magazines how to highlight her big topaz eyes – "cat's eyes," Perry had called them – with bronze eyeliner and powdered shadow. Her figure was richer and lusher than it had been.

But the girl in the picture was smiling and happy, triumphant that she'd reached the only real goal she'd ever had – a church wedding, in a long white dress, to a handsome, athletic boy that half the girls in school had coveted. The woman in the mirror had lost her sparkle; her shine had been worn away by months and years of a predictable sameness.

She sighed again and went into the kitchen to pack Perry's lunch: a thermos of coffee, warmed-up meat loaf, a chunk of homemade bread with butter, a wedge of lettuce, and a slice of layer cake. She wrapped everything carefully, first in wax paper and then in a brown paper bag.

She bundled up against the biting March wind, in her imitation fur coat and wool muffler, and went outside, hoping the ten-year-old secondhand Ford would start easily. The day was sunny and bright, and the jagged rock formations of the Black Hills stood like towering statues against the clear blue South Dakota sky, but Ginny no longer noticed the beauty of her surroundings. She put the car in gear and drove slowly down the narrow driveway, watching out for lingering patches of ice.

She had made this ride to the Lucky Nugget mine hundreds of times, whenever the weather would allow, even when Willie was a tiny baby. Perry would be coming up for his lunch break in about fifteen minutes, and he'd be hungry as always.

Not so many years ago, when she was still in high school, she thought of the gold mines as dark secret places that held almost half of America's treasure. She would conjure up romantic adventure stories about the French trappers and traders – the first white men who settled the state – who left their mark on names she heard every day . . . names like Dellahaye and Belle Fourche, "Beautiful Fork." When she studied state history, she had thrilled to frontier tales about Wild Bill Hickok and Calamity Jane, who were buried in Boot Hill Cemetery in Deadwood; to stories of Sitting Bull's rebellion at Standing Rock reservation and the massacre at Wounded Knee Creek.

Now her imagination no longer responded to the history of rugged frontiersmen and daring outlaws who had ridden through the eerie, haunting buttes and gorges of the *Mauvaises Terres* – the Badlands. Not when the present was so colorless and flat and the future without promise of change.

As Ginny approached the mine, she saw that a dozen or so wives were already clustered near the entrance. In the days when she rode the school bus to Belle Fourche, she used to pass the mine and see the women waiting, just as they did now. She had thought that was romantic, too. Now she wondered if they were all as miserable as she was. She parked the car, greeted the other women with a collective "hi" and a wave, and took her place among them.

The Lucky Nugget was one of the largest gold mines in the western hemisphere, second only to the fabled Homestake. Its "lead," or gold-bearing ore deposit, had been discovered on a hillside in 1876, by a military expedition led by General Custer. Now, almost a hundred years later, the miners still followed the ore body, almost 8000 feet below the surface. They used jackhammers in place of the old-fashioned picks and shovels, and the gold-bearing rock was loaded mechanically, rather than by hand. A half dozen buildings housed the equipment that processed and refined the ore. But one thing was the same as it had been in the old days: it still took six or seven tons of hardrock ore to yield an ounce of the precious yellow metal. It wasn't so different from Ginny's life: a monotonous routine to be endured day in and day out, in the hope of a shining moment.

Since the first lode had been discovered, the Lucky Nugget had yielded hundreds of millions of dollars in gold. But to the men like Perry Dellahaye, the days of hard, gruelling work yielded, at best, about $150 a week, after taxes.

"Saw your little girl at school the other day, Ginny . . . she's just as sweet and as pretty as can be," said Elmer Hawkins's wife, Grace.

"Thanks, Grace . . . how's your arm today? Any better?"

"So-so. Doc Morris says he'll take the cast off Friday, in time for the union dance. I bought myself a new dress . . . how about you? Are you gonna wear that green satin?"

"I guess so . . . I fixed the top so it would look different from last year . . . "

The women broke rank as the first shift of men came up from the mine, grimy and tired and eager for some relief from the backbreaking business of digging gold. Out came the ear plugs that protected their hearing from the battering roar of the jackhammers. Then came the routine check of the miners' clothing, to make certain they weren't carrying away bits of ore.

In his plaid lumber jacket and dungarees, his body toughened by nine years of physical labor, Perry Dellahaye still stood out among the other men, even if his face had lost the cocky, dashing expression that Ginny had loved.

"Hey, Perry, over here!" she called.

A few long strides and he was beside her, dropping a perfunctory kiss on her hair. "What's for lunch? I'm starving!"

"Meat loaf . . . come on, let's go sit in the car."

"Meat loaf again? Didn't I tell you I was in the mood for fried chicken?"

"Didn't have any chicken in the freezer. I'll pick some up for supper. Hey," she said brightly, "how about I make the chicken and some potato salad and apple pie – and then we drive into town tonight and see a movie? It's been weeks and weeks since we went anywhere . . . "

"Can't," he said tersely, chewing his meat loaf. "Told Jack and Elmer I'd meet 'em after supper . . . "

"Again?" That meant he'd be gone for hours, and she'd be spending another evening at home alone with Willie. "Can't you change your mind? You go out with them more than you do with me . . . "

"Cut it out, Ginny. You're my wife. I come home every night. I'm taking you to that dance Friday night. Why can't you be satisfied like everybody else?"

She had no answer, but more than anything, she wanted to think of one.

That night Ginny was still asking herself what she could do to change her life, what would make her want to get up in the morning with something to look forward to, something other than getting older and waiting for grandchildren. After she bathed Willie and put her to bed, she doodled in her sketch pad, but she didn't have any good ideas for new designs. Besides, who would ever see them?

She pressed the green satin she'd altered by reshaping the sleeves and adding two rows of sequins to the bodice, hung the dress in the closet, and went to bed with a two-month-old copy of *Silver Screen* for company. All the women on the slick, glossy pages seemed to be smiling, and she wondered if they were as happy as they looked.

A few short years ago, her happiness began and ended with Perry Dellahaye, the most popular boy in the junior class. After he had given her his class ring, she had put aside her fantasies of doing "something" with her talent for sewing and design. Perry had been sure he'd get an athletic scholarship to college. She had gladly abandoned her own

47

tentative and unformed ambitions and shared instead in his dream of becoming a physical education teacher and coach.

But the athletic scholarship never came. Perry talked awhile about going to the state university, but nothing came of that. Instead he followed his father (and his grandfather before him) into the Lucky Nugget.

Though she never said anything to Perry, Ginny was almost relieved when he gave up the idea of college – and going away for four years to a place where he'd be meeting lots of other girls. She was thrilled when he proposed, when they set their wedding date for the week after her graduation.

With his first earnings, he'd bought the land near Spearfish, announcing that he meant to build them a proper home, with his own two hands. Every weekend, and in between eight-hour shifts in the mine, he worked on the cabin, with Ginny cheering him on, just as she did when he played football in high school.

The cabin was finished the last weekend in May. The day before their wedding they had stocked the refrigerator with their favorite foods and filled the rooms with bunches of wildflowers, in anticipation of their week-long honeymoon.

The honeymoon was everything Ginny had dreamed it would be. She and Perry were like two kids on school vacation, taking long walks in the woods, swimming naked in the clear icy blue waters of the river, and promising to love each other always.

All too soon it was time for Perry to go back to work, and time for Ginny to start acting like a wife. At first she had loved this snug little cabin. She had read all the homemaking magazines, searching for cute patterns, decorating ideas, and fancy recipes.

By the time she made her home as nice as any of the magazine pictures, she was pregnant. Perry had been so proud – and extra thoughtful of her during those months. Even when he came home dead tired, he'd insist that she put up her feet and rest awhile, before she did the supper dishes. Then he'd carry her to their big double bed and lay her down gently, telling her how beautiful she was and how happy she made him, just before they made love.

She knew Perry hoped the baby would be a boy, a son he could teach to hunt and fish and play ball. Her heart had gone out to him when he said "little girls are nicer," after the baby turned out to be a girl.

She'd named the baby Willa, after the woman who had written *My Antonia*, the book she had loved in English literature because it had made her smile and cry at the same time. Willie had been a beautiful baby, with gorgeous blue eyes and a serious manner. She hardly ever cried or fussed, even when she was teething. And when Ginny dressed her in pink cotton pinafores trimmed with white eyelet, she looked just like the baby dolls in the stores.

But something had happened to all those storybook days, and Ginny didn't know what it was. As the years passed, the honeymoon cabin came to feel more like a prison than a home, especially during the long winter months. With only her little girl and a console radio for company, Ginny found it harder to fill the hours until Perry came home. She stopped searching out new recipes to try, for he had stopped noticing the fancy dishes that took hours to make. And though she still fixed herself up every day, he had stopped noticing that, too. When she begged him to take her somewhere on the weekends, he said he was tired or busy with chores around the house. When she asked him to take a walk, he acted like she was crazy. Yet he found plenty of time to go hunting or drinking with "the boys" from the mine. And he expected her to cooperate, or at least acquiesce, when he came to bed, ready to take his own pleasure before he fell asleep. He didn't seem to under-stand – or care – that she felt lonely and bored and depressed. Or that she hated it when he used her body without giving her the sweet words and tender caresses she craved.

Worse yet, she didn't understand why these things had happened, or when they had stopped being friends and lovers and become strangers who shared a home, a child, and little else. When she told herself she was probably better off than most of the women she knew, she became even more depressed. There had to be more to life than just going through the motions and putting on a good face for the rest of the world to see.

She heard the door of the cabin open and slam shut. From the heavy thump of Perry's boots on the plank floor, she could tell he'd had a lot to drink. Quickly she put out the bedside lamp and slid under the covers, pretending to be asleep. She heard him clanking around in the kitchen before he came into the darkened bedroom. He bumped into the dresser, muttering curses as he pulled off his clothes and dropped them on the floor.

He climbed into bed, reeking of whiskey and stale cigarette smoke. Ginny stiffened and pulled away from the cold hand that clumsily foraged under her nightgown. "Leave me alone," she whispered when the hand pursued her.

"What the hell do you mean — 'leave me alone'?" Perry thundered. "That's a fine way to treat your husband!"

She sat up abruptly and turned on the light, facing him down, instead of retreating the way she usually did when he'd been drinking. "I mean you have to pay some attention to what I want, Perry. I keep telling you I'm not happy, and you don't seem to care . . . "

He stared at her, his eyes fogged with liquor and confusion. "What do you want from me, Ginny? You think what I do is fun? What's it gonna take for you to quit your griping and start acting like a real wife?"

"I want to get out of here." The answer was quick and unpremeditated. "I don't want to be stuck up here in this cabin, all by myself. I want to live in town, maybe get me a job. . . . "

"A job?" he echoed. "I'm breakin' my back every day so you don't have to work. Goddammit — do you want everybody to think Perry Dellahaye can't take care of his family?"

"It isn't the money, honest," she pleaded, willing him to understand. "I just want to do something besides cooking and cleaning and taking care of the house. I want to see people . . . I want to feel like I'm doing *something* with myself . . . "

He shook his head, as bewildered as if she'd been speaking a foreign language. "You're talking crazy, you know that? Leave this house . . . get a job . . . I never heard anything so crazy in my life." With that, he rolled over on his side and pulled up the covers, signaling that the conversation was over.

Ginny turned out the light, but she didn't sleep for a long time. Now that she saw a way out, she wasn't about to let go so easily.

The union hall was brightly lit, the institutional gray of its walls relieved by red and white crepe paper streamers and bunches of colored balloons. As they had done for the three previous years, Johnny Whiteside and his Mountain Boys serenaded the dancers with a mixture of country music and tinny adaptions of popular songs.

Ginny was almost having a good time. In her refurbished green satin, she was easily the prettiest woman in the room. And Perry had danced with her five times, without being asked.

"You look nice tonight," he said, when the music stopped.

"So do you," she answered automatically, though he did, in a starched white shirt and his good blue suit, his curly black hair clean and shining, his strong jaw freshly shaven. "Perry," she went on tentatively, "did you think about what I said the other night . . . about us moving into town and all?"

"Don't know what there is to think about. The cabin's our home, just the way we planned it. I've been thinkin' you just don't have enough to keep you busy . . . maybe it's time to have another baby . . . "

Ginny's topaz eyes opened wide. I can't go through that again, she thought, not after the heartbreaking seventh-month miscarriage that had nearly cost her life. And much as she loved Willie, another baby was the last thing in the world she wanted now. She felt suffocated by Perry's words and the idea of being chained even tighter to the monotony of life in the cabin. She took her handkerchief out of her purse and wiped her face.

51

"Want some more punch?" he asked. "You look kinda warm . . . "

"No," she said. "I've had enough. Maybe you have, too. Driving's gonna be rough tonight, with all the snow and ice. If we lived in town, we wouldn't have so far to go . . . "

The muscle in Perry's jaw tightened. "The day I can't handle my whiskey, I'll give it up altogether," he said, turning and heading for the open bar.

Twenty minutes later, she was still waiting for him to return, but he was busy drinking and trading jokes with Sheriff Jack Barney and a couple of men from the mine. When Elmer Hawkins asked her to dance, she answered: "Sure, why not." It was fun being admired, being around crowds of people for a change. As they danced past the bar, she noticed Perry looking at her and scowling. She told Elmer she would sit the next one out.

When Perry said he was ready to leave, she didn't protest. He'd had a lot to drink; besides, Polly Henderson, the widow who sat with Willie on special occasions, would be anxious to get home.

They didn't talk much in the car, and Ginny couldn't help remembering how different it used to be, when they took this same ride after the high school dances, when every minute they shared was special, and when it seemed like being together all the time would be heaven.

The lights from the cabin guided them up the last tricky turn of the road. As Perry pulled up beside Mrs. Henderson's truck, Ginny opened her door and ran to the house, shivering in her party dress and sheer stockings.

She paid the sitter and went into Willie's bedroom, cracking the door and listening, until she heard the sound of the child's even breathing. She kicked off her high heeled pumps and started to unfasten the hooks on the green satin.

"Here," Perry said, his voice husky with liquor and desire, "let me do that . . . no need to rush . . . we can sleep late tomorrow."

"Not tonight," Ginny said wearily. "I've got my period, and I'm tired . . . "

"You're always tired, goddammit!"

"Keep your voice down . . . you'll wake Willie."

"I won't keep my voice down! And I won't take this any more," he shouted, tearing the dress from Ginny's body. "You're not going to turn me away tonight!" He slapped her face with his open hand, sending her sprawling onto the bed . . .

2

When her husband didn't come home for a couple of days, Ginny was frantic. Perry had hurt her, but she'd never wished for life without him. Maybe he'd crashed his car somewhere on the mountain road and was lying in a ditch, half frozen or worse. Not knowing what else to do, she telephoned her in-laws. "Perry's here," his mother said, "but he don't have nothin' to say to you." Before Ginny could respond, her mother-in-law hung up. Now fear gave way to uneasiness. Perry had never stayed away from home, and as far as she knew, he'd never discussed their marriage with anyone else.

When she heard his car pull up late Sunday night, she was almost limp with relief. If he was ready to make up, she would do her part. Quickly she put the leftover pot roast in the oven and a welcoming smile on her face.

But Perry's face was closed against her. He grunted in response to her attempts at conversation. And when she served up chocolate cream pie – his favorite – for dessert, he muttered, "There's more to life than food."

The sentiment surprised her, for Perry had always seemed to care a lot about what was put on the table. She waited expectantly for him to say more, but nothing came.

Maybe, she thought, maybe he was talking about making love. If that was what he wanted, she'd go along. She'd had enough trouble for a while. But he stayed on his side of the

53

bed that night, and went to sleep without so much as a "good night."

In the days that followed, she tried to break through Perry's icy coldness, but he continued to talk to her in monosyllables, consuming the food that was put before him and keeping away from her in bed. She was used to his temper, but this was worse somehow.

She stayed away from the mine for a week, saying she was "too busy," hoping to provoke her husband into talking to her. But he only shrugged and said, "Suit yourself." She felt lonelier than ever, not knowing how her marriage had come to this.

On payday, Perry went drinking with the boys, as usual. And when he came home, Ginny was waiting for him, wearing a babydoll nightgown. One way or another, she meant to end the cold war. Perry's expression softened when he saw her, looking as pretty and loving as the day they'd been married.

"Come to bed, honey," she coaxed. "You must be tired . . . "

He reached for her. "God, I've missed you . . . "

"I missed you, too," she said. "I don't want to fight anymore, but you've gotta understand how I feel . . . "

He stiffened and pulled away. "What about how *I* feel?" he roared, his voice roughened with whiskey and anger. "How do you think I feel when nothing I do is good enough? When you turn away from me? When you won't give me a son?"

Ginny pulled up the covers, trying to hide from his anger.

"That's right," he said. "Run away from the truth. Get yourself tarted up, trying to make a fool of me. But I'm telling you for the last time – nobody makes a fool of Perry Dellahaye." He drew back his hand and smashed it into her face.

"No!" she screamed. "Don't you ever lay a hand on me again!"

He slapped her twice. "You're my wife and I'll do what I please. The sooner you learn that, the better off you'll be."

Shaking with outrage, Ginny waited until Perry had

fallen into a drunken sleep. She was grateful that Willie had slept through the quarrel this time, but she was going to fight back. Perry's words had battered her as much as his blows.

She went into the kitchen and dialed the sheriff's number. "Jack," she said, "this is Ginny Dellahaye. We've got some trouble, and I need you to come out here . . . "

She put on her robe, made an ice pack for her face, and sat at the kitchen table until she heard the sheriff's knock. "Perry did this," she said, pointing to the bruises on her face, "and I want you to do something about it."

"Now wait a minute, Ginny," Jack said. "Are you saying you got me out of bed because you and Perry had a fight?"

"It wasn't just a fight," she pressed on, though the expression on the sheriff's face wasn't encouraging.

"Perry hit me. Hard. More than once. It isn't right for a man to hit a woman, and there oughta be something you can do about it."

"What the hell's going on here?" Perry demanded, as he clumped into the kitchen, dressed only in his underwear.

Barney laughed sheepishly. "Your missus called me. I thought there musta been an accident or some emergency. Turns out she wants me to take you in . . . can you beat that?"

Perry scowled, clenching and unclenching his fists. For a minute Ginny thought he'd hit her again. "Sorry you made the trip, Jack," he growled. "Nothing I can't handle . . . "

The sheriff left, after warning Ginny that she'd better not waste his time again, or he'd have to run her in. She turned to face her husband, terrified at what she might see.

"You'll be sorry you did that," he spat out. "Tomorrow everybody's gonna say that Perry Dellahaye can't keep his wife in line, but I'll show them . . . "

Perry didn't come home from work the next day, or the day after that. Ginny bought a new lock for the cabin door, though she didn't really think it could keep him out. But she felt she had to do something. She explained to Willie that she and her daddy had been fighting, "the way married people do," and that she shouldn't worry about it.

But Ginny was worried. Her supply of groceries was dwindling and her tiny reserve of cash was almost gone. Much as she hated the idea, she knew she'd have to go to her sister Janet or her brother Ron for a loan.

It was a Saturday morning when Jack Barney drove up to the cabin, along with two of his deputies. "What's wrong?" she asked, when she saw the men. "Did something happen to Perry?"

"No, ma'am," Barney replied, producing a paper from his pocket. "I got this dispossess order here. Perry says you and your little girl . . . well, you have to vacate these premises . . . "

"What? What are you saying?" Ginny's anxiety escalated to terror. "Me and Perry . . . we're married . . . I'm his wife . . . you must've made a mistake . . . "

"No mistake," the sheriff said, staring her down. "Perry says he's gettin' a divorce, and the cabin's his legal property. Me and my men are here to help you get packed."

"You mean now? You're gonna put us out *now?*" This had to be a bad dream. Please let it be a bad dream, she prayed.

"Too bad you let it come to this, Ginny, but there's nothin' I can do about it. Perry says you can use the car to get wherever you're going . . . I'll have to come around and pick it up in a couple of days. Perry's name is on the title, just like it is on the deed to the cabin . . . Sorry," he said, but Ginny had the feeling he wasn't sorry at all.

Helplessly, she stood by, frozen by shock and confusion, watching the three men throw her belongings and Willie's into cardboard cartons, occasionally consulting a list that Perry had provided.

"What's happening, Mama?" Willie asked anxiously. "Why are they taking our things?"

"I . . . I don't know . . . " Ginny was too numb to think clearly. "Stop!" she cried out, as Barney carelessly flung her precious sewing machine to the ground. She rushed forward to stop him, but he pushed her away.

"Stand aside," he said roughly, "or we'll take you in."

A second later, Willie was all over the sheriff like a little tigress, biting and scratching. "Don't you touch my mama! Don't you dare touch my mama!"

It took both deputies to pull her off. "Like mother, like daughter," Barney muttered. "Better mind your manners, or you'll end up just like your mama."

When the men were finished, they put the cartons into the second-hand car which Ginny had thought was hers. She choked back a sob as the sheriff snapped a padlock on the door.

And then she watched them drive away, still trying to comprehend what had happened. A short hour or two ago, she had been a wife with problems. Now she was abandoned and homeless, along with her darling Willie, who stood clutching her hand and staring at the cabin that had been their home.

"What's gonna happen now, Mama?" she asked.

"We're goin' on a trip, honey," Ginny answered, wondering where they might find shelter, and who would take them, when they had no money to pay.

Her father couldn't help. He had moved into a trailer after Ginny's mother had died. And now Miss Ethel from the beauty parlor was living there with him.

Because she had to go somewhere, Ginny drove to her sister Janet's frame house in town. Janet started frowning the minute she saw Ginny and Willie, along with their boxes of belongings. And by the time Ginny finished explaining what had happened, Janet's plain face was unsympathetic. "I'm sorry, Ginny," she said. "I'm sorry you're in such a bad way. I don't know what you did to make Perry leave, and I don't want to know. That's between you and him. But I can't let you stay here. Frank's always had an eye for a pretty face, and I'd just be askin' for trouble. Maybe you oughta ask Ron," she added grudgingly.

As the door closed in Ginny's face, she felt like the world had come to an end, but only for her and Willie. She went back to the car and headed toward her brother Ron's house, praying that he and Sara wouldn't turn her away.

She drove down the narrow streets of Belle Fourche

feeling as if all the town knew of her shame. No one she knew had ever been in such a position. Sometimes Elmer Hawkins drank too much and cuffed his wife Grace around. But Reverend Watson or Grace's brothers always straightened him out. No decent woman had ever been turned out of her home like a criminal.

She rang the bell of Ron's house at the end of Sycamore Street. Her sister-in-law Sara opened the door, her belly swollen with her second pregnancy, her face flushed from the heat of her kitchen.

"Why, Ginny . . . what a nice surprise. And Willie's with you, too. Come in . . . I just made a fresh pot of coffee."

When Ginny described her plight, Sara's response was sure and immediate. "You poor thing . . . how awful for you and Willie. I'd like to give that Perry a piece of my mind. You'll stay with us, in the attic room, as long as you need to, honey."

"Maybe we oughta wait till Ron gets home . . . make sure it's okay with him."

"Why wouldn't it be?" Sara asked indignantly. "You're family."

"Well, Sara, I have to tell you . . . I asked Janet first, and she didn't want us . . . "

"Oh, Janet . . . she's always been jealous of you, honey. Ron's different . . . he'll want to help you. I bet he'll talk to Perry if you ask him. You just wait and see, Ginny . . . everything's gonna be okay."

Living in Sara's house, Ginny felt she had a refuge, rather than a home. Though she had grown up in this town, just as Perry did, most of its people seemed to feel that she was in the wrong, that she was a troublemaker who deserved whatever punishment her husband meted out.

As the months passed, it felt as if the attic room would be the only home she and Willie would ever have. More than once she wondered if this was to be the punishment for wanting more than a woman had a right to want. If she'd known what would happen to them, she'd have put her foolish ideas aside and promised to be a better wife. If only

58

she'd begged Perry's forgiveness before things had gone so far, they wouldn't be living on the charity of relatives. If only . . .

To pay her way and Willie's, Ginny tried to earn money by sewing, but there wasn't much call for dress-up clothes in Belle Fourche, and most of the women did their own simple alterations. She worked as a supermarket checker for a while, and then as a receptionist at the Chevrolet dealership. Her jobs didn't last long, for there was always a man in charge who pressured her to "be friendly," and who turned ugly when she wouldn't – just the way Perry did.

She tried to talk to Perry once, when he arrived at Ron's house demanding to see his daughter. He had dropped his divorce talk shortly after he'd gotten Ginny out of the cabin, and she had taken that to mean they might be a family again. But when she spoke to him about reconciliation, he was angry and belligerent. He blamed her for all the inconveniences he'd suffered since he threw her out. He swore he'd never give her a divorce or the chance to ruin his life again.

That night, Ron loaned her the money to hire a lawyer. She went to see Sam Reynolds, who took her money and promised to file for divorce on grounds of desertion.

Months later, Reynolds told her there couldn't be a divorce as long as Perry claimed he wanted a reconciliation. Ginny protested the lie, but Reynolds said it was the law.

When Willie came home from school, she found her mother crying. She listened intently while Ginny repeated the lawyer's explanation of why she had to go on living in limbo, with neither the privileges of marriage nor the freedom of divorce.

"That's not fair," Willie said passionately. "Papa doesn't take care of you, the way Uncle Ron takes care of Aunt Sara. He doesn't even want us in his house anymore."

"I know," Ginny answered brokenly. "But that's the way the law is."

"I don't think that's right," Willie insisted. "That's not right at all."

Eventually, after more than a year had passed, Reynolds

did manage to get Ginny a legal separation and twenty dollars a week in child support, along with a warning that she'd better be "as pure as the driven snow," if she didn't want to lose the money and her child. The warning only made her angry. Not because she had any yearning for a man right now, but because it was so unfair. Perry came and went as he pleased, and no one in town thought any less of him. Ginny had always thought of herself as a "nice girl" when she was single, and now people thought she was an easy target for insinuating remarks and cheap passes.

Her only friend was Sara, whose life wasn't any better than Ginny's had been. With three children, already feeling old beyond her years, Sara got up at six (after feeding the newest baby twice during the night) and worked her way through a repetitious succession of chores, well past sundown. She was grateful for Ginny's companionship and help and often expressed the wish that they could go on living together always, like sisters. Ginny tried not to say anything that would offend Sara, but the idea depressed her even more than the thought of growing old in Perry's cabin had. She didn't realize the power of emotion behind Sara's words until one morning in early March.

The day had started like any other. Ginny had fixed breakfast and helped get the children off to school, then she'd gone upstairs and made the big double bed she shared with Willie. The attic room was always neat and tidy, for unlike Sara's kids, Willie never left a mess for anyone else to clean up.

Her first round of chores finished, Ginny went into the bathroom, craving the hissing warmth of the radiator and the luxury of a little hot water to soften the chill of the cold winter morning. First she brushed her thick wavy hair over the basin, and then as she was cleaning the brush, she noticed a single renegade hair, gray and wiry, tangled in the bristles. She pulled it out and stared at her face in the mirror, looking for more signs of the wasted years, the time she'd spent in limbo, neither married nor single. Still frowning, she stepped into the shower, letting the warm water sluice away the knots in her shoulders. She tried to keep up a good front for Willie's sake, to be thankful for food and shelter, but she felt she carried a world of worries on those shoulders. As bad as all the real problems was the fear that if she ever dared to dream again, she'd only end up worse off. Just like she was now.

"Ginny?" Sara called out, as she came into the bathroom and sat down on the toilet cover. "You almost done? God, I just had to get off my feet . . . there's still a mountain of ironing in the basket."

"Leave it," Ginny said. "I'll finish up, just as soon as I dry off." She stepped out of the shower and reached for a towel.

"You're so lucky," Sara sighed, staring at her sister-in-law's naked body. "You still look like a girl . . . not like me," she said sadly, looking down at her own flaccid shape.

"Oh, Sara," Ginny soothed, wrapping herself in a towel. "You've had three babies, the last one just a couple of months ago. Besides, Ron just said last night how pretty you looked in that dress I made."

"Yeah, he always says stuff like that when he wants me to be nice to him, in bed, you know. The rest of the time he hardly notices, any more than he notices the Hoover in the closet."

Ginny almost laughed, but seeing the sadness of Sara's expression, she reached out and hugged her, the towel slipping to the floor. "Oh, Ginny," Sara murmured, her arms circling Ginny's waist, "I love you so much." As cool fingers stroked the warm of her back, Ginny was surprised by the answering response of her body, the stiffening of her nipples as they pressed against the coarse cotton of Sara's shift.

She didn't protest when Sara took her hand and led her into the attic room and onto the bed. She allowed the kisses and caresses and returned them in kind, welcoming the feelings of intimacy and warmth she'd almost forgotten.

For Ginny, the tentative exploration of that winter morning was more than a whim, yet less than a discovery. She had felt comforted by Sara's gentle loving. The physical pleasure was a reminder that her body could still

61

feel sexual, but Ginny had no interest in repeating it or making it a way of life.

For Sara, however, the opposite was true. Whenever she and Ginny were alone, she made remarks and gestures of invitation. Ginny didn't want to hurt her, so at first she tried to smile away the invitations. But Sara would not be put off.

One evening, while Ron and the children were downstairs in the kitchen, she cornered Ginny in the attic bedroom. "I need you," she pleaded, clinging to her sister-in-law in a desperate embrace. "I can't stand being around you and not touching you. Please, Ginny, please love me again . . . "

"We can't," Ginny said, her voice low as she struggled to disengage. "Pull yourself together, Sara . . . one of the kids might come in. We can't do what you want . . . it wouldn't be right." She took her sister-in-law's hand and led her to the bathroom. "Wash your face, and I'll go check on supper."

Ginny composed herself, smiling brightly as she bustled around the kitchen, trying to hide the conflict she felt, knowing she and Willie would have to leave this house before something terrible happened.

She tried to keep up a good front during supper, to avoid Sara's reproachful glances and Willie's questioning eyes. Preoccupied with his mashed potatoes and pot roast, Ron didn't seem to notice the tension, but Willie was always quick to pick up signals that something was wrong.

Somehow Ginny got through supper and the evening cleanup, but sleep was difficult that night. Where could she and Willie go? What would they live on while she waited for a court hearing? She'd put aside a few dollars for Mr. Reynolds, but that was all she had.

When morning came, she was still troubled, but she had an idea. Sara was stiff and formal during breakfast, but she accepted Ginny's offer to do that day's shopping with a curt "Okay, if that's what you want to do."

Ginny drove her sister-in-law's Chevy straight to Len Sharp's General Store. She made some small purchases, and as Sharp tallied up the bill, she searched through her purse. But all she had was a handful of change that didn't even add up to a dollar. "I . . . I seem to be a little short," she said, her cheeks flushed with embarrassment.

"I reckon your brother's good for it," the storekeeper said. "That is, if you're still livin' with him and Sara . . . "

"Thank you, Len," she said, hating the man's smirk and patronizing manner, knowing she couldn't afford to say anything that would alienate him. "I'll see that you get your money." Head bowed, she left the store, not noticing the man who followed her out.

"Hey, there . . . young woman," he called after her.

"You talkin' to me?" The man was about sixty, bearded and gray-haired, with the tanned leathery skin and the tight muscles that came from years of outdoor work.

"Aren't you John Barber's daughter Virginia?"

"Yes . . . "

"I'm Ben Cattow. Your daddy and I used to be friends . . . "

"I remember," she said. Ben had a ranch about twenty miles out of town, but no one had seen much of him since his wife had died.

"I hope you won't take this wrong, Virginia, but I'm sorry about the trouble you've been having." Like everyone else in Belle Fourche, Cattow knew all about Ginny's plight. He'd heard Perry badmouth his wife, painting her as a frivolous, headstrong woman who shirked her marital duties. But unlike most of the other men, he felt sorry for the pretty young woman who'd been thrown out of her home, who didn't even have enough money to pay for a few groceries.

Ginny smiled her gratitude for the kind words. "It's been hard," she admitted.

"Maybe you and I could help each other. Don't know if you've heard, but Mrs. Loomis left the ranch last week . . . she's gone to live with her son in Pierre. That leaves me without a housekeeper. I'm offering you the job, if you're interested . . . "

A job. The chance to move out of Sara's house and to be

on her own. "I'll take it," she said quickly, before he could change his mind.

"Whoa," Ben laughed, his gray eyes twinkling. "That's no way to do business. First you have to hear what I'm offering. The pay's fifty dollars a week, and room and board for you and your child. Have to warn you, though . . . it's pretty quiet on the ranch in the dead of winter . . . "

"I don't care," Ginny said. "Willie and me, we need a place to stay, and some extra money for . . . for the divorce."

Cattow nodded. He'd heard Jack Barney boast of how he'd helped Perry "teach his missus a lesson, just to show the other women around here that it doesn't pay to go against their husbands." He had remarked that it was a sorry day when a man called in the law against his own wife. "Job's yours," he said to Ginny. "You can move in whenever you want."

"Thanks, Ben. You won't be sorry. I'll work hard, I promise. I can start tomorrow, but I'll need a ride out—"

"I'll send one of the hands. 'Bout ten o'clock, after morning chores."

Reluctantly, Ginny returned to the house, avoiding Sara's eyes. "I bought some extra flour," she said. "Figured I'd bake a cake for dessert."

Sara said nothing, but Ginny could feel the anger and the unspoken questions. When the cake was in the oven, she took out a mop and bucket and washed the cracked kitchen linoleum.

She didn't sit down until the children came home from school. And not until the evening meal was on the table did she announce her plans. "By the way, Ron," she said casually, "Ben Cattow gave me a job today . . . housekeeper at his ranch. He'll pay fifty dollars and room and board for me and Willie. I appreciate your givin' us a home all this time, but now you have another baby, and I figure it's time for us to clear out . . . "

"Sounds good," Ron said, not caring much one way or the other. "I wish you luck."

"Kind of sudden, isn't it?" Sara asked, her cheeks flushed with emotion.

"Not really," Ginny answered evenly. "We've imposed long enough."

"That's a long way for Willie to travel every day," Sara persisted.

"It isn't too bad . . . the school bus makes a pickup at Watkins' Corner . . . that's only half a mile from Ben's place. Willie won't mind, will you, honey?"

Though this was the first Willie had heard of a job or a move, she reflexively supported her mother. "I don't mind," she said. "It might be fun, living on a ranch."

After the supper dishes were cleared and stacked at the sink, Ginny filled a basin with warm, soapy water and started to wash. The rest of the family went into the living room to watch television, so she worked slowly, marking time.

But just as she started the pots and pans, she heard Sara's angry voice behind her. "How could you, Ginny? How could you do this to me?"

She turned to face the accusation. "I'm not doing anything to you," she explained, trying to sound reasonable and calm. "It's just time for us to go . . . It'll be best for all of us."

"It isn't!" Sara hissed. "And it isn't fair! You showed me a little happiness, and now you're leaving me flat. You can go where you want, but I'm stuck here, and you don't care!"

"Hush, Sara, hush . . . I do care about you. I love you like a sister, but I can't do what you want. So it's better if I live somewhere else."

"You'll be sorry," Sara threatened, her face distorted with anger and misery. "You'll be sorry when you go to get that divorce. How would you like it if I told? What do you think would happen then? You'd better change your mind, or you're gonna lose your case and your daughter!"

"You wouldn't do that . . . you couldn't. Willie's all I have . . ." But Sara turned and left the room.

She repeated her threat the following morning, as Ginny gave back the key to the house. "Remember what I said last night," she warned. "Don't think you can just walk away from me!"

"I'm sorry," Ginny said, edging out the door. "I'm really sorry."

She felt an enormous sense of relief once she and Willie were in Cattow's truck. "Aunt Sara's upset because she's gonna miss us," she said, in answer to the questioning look on Willie's face. "But she'll be okay . . . "

She hoped that Sara would be okay, that time would soften her feelings of anger and betrayal. That Sara might tell what had happened between them didn't really seem anything to worry about. After all, she had children of her own . . .

3

As winter gave way to spring, Ginny started to feel almost happy. Her job at the ranch was demanding, but Ben was a fair man; more than that, he was a friend. He paid her regularly, and the room she and Willie shared was pleasant and cozy, furnished with good oak pieces and a pretty braided rug that Ben's late wife had made. He never minded if she needed time off to visit Willie's school or her lawyer in town.

When Willie came down with a bad throat infection, Ben drove twenty miles in the middle of the night to fetch the doctor, whose car had broken down. He waited till dawn, right at Ginny's side, until the antibiotic took hold and the fever broke. The next day he promised the child a trip to the summer rodeo in Deadwood, if she'd hurry up and get well. "We can't have you being sick," he said. "You and your mama brighten up this lonely place."

The three of them spent quiet, cozy evenings playing cards or eating popcorn and watching television on the big set in the living room. Ben taught Willie to play poker "like a cowboy," salting his instructions with tales of the gold rush days.

"Tell me about Wild Bill," Willie would often ask, knowing the story was one of Ben's favorites.

66

And he would clear his throat and begin: "It was August the second, in 1876. Wild Bill Hickok had come to Deadwood a couple of weeks before, to bring law and order, or so folks said. But Bill was a gambling man, and he had his own reasons for coming. Black Hills gold, that's what it was. And the gambling tables was where he did his mining.

"Anyway, there he was on that hot day in August, in the Number Ten saloon, holding two pair – black aces and eights. He had his back to the door, and young Jack McCall, an evil young man, shot Bill in the back of the head. Away he rode, though folks say that Calamity Jane chased him down . . .

"And," he would conclude with some satisfaction, "the moral of the story is that you'd best look out for an ambush whenever you're playing for high stakes."

Snug in the security of Ben's protection and care, Ginny could almost forget that she was his housekeeper. He never tired of telling her how much happier he was since she and Willie came to live at the ranch.

She, in turn, never counted the hours she worked or measured her pay against the task she performed. Ben was a true friend, and Ginny gave herself wholeheartedly to repaying his kindness. When his rheumatism flared up, she dosed him with aspirin and rubbed his shoulders with liniment.

When finally, after three years of legal separation Ginny's lawyer was able to file for divorce, she brought the news to Ben. They sat together, sharing a pot of chamomile tea in the big sunny kitchen.

"I'm scared, Ben," she said. "After all this time, it's gonna happen, and now I'm really scared."

Ben reached over and took her hand. He cleared his throat, a serious expression on his kind, weathered face. "I have another proposition for you, Virginia. I think you know that you and Willie have a home here as long as you want. But I'd like you to think about staying on here . . . as my wife."

Ginny's eyes widened with surprise. She was devoted to

Ben as a friend – yes, loved him almost as a father. But she had never imagined he believed otherwise.

"Don't say anything now," he continued. "Just think about what I've said. You and Willie would be taken care of, no matter what happens in court. And when I'm gone, this place and everything I own will be yours . . ."

"Thank you," she said softly. "I'll think about it." Though Ben was old enough to be her father, or even her grandfather, she trusted the promises he'd made.

She went upstairs to the room she shared with Willie. She sat by the window, staring into the starry night for what seemed like hours. If she married Ben, she would never have to be afraid. As Mrs. Ben Cattow, she would be beyond Perry's reach, above the gossip and worry that had tarnished her life for so many years. But she didn't love Ben the way a woman loves a man. She wondered how it would feel, living out her days on this ranch, with no more choices to be made.

"Mama . . . why aren't you asleep?" Willie sat up in bed, rubbing her eyes.

"Ben's just asked me to marry him," Ginny replied.

"Oh . . ." Willie, too, had come to love Ben, but her mother didn't sound too happy about the idea of becoming his wife. "Do you want to?"

Ginny sighed. "It's not that simple, honey. If I marry Ben after this divorce business is over, he'll take care of us both. You'll have nice things, and . . ."

Willie climbed out of bed and hugged her mother close. "Ben's a nice man, but don't marry him if you don't really want to. Don't do it for me. I just want you to be happy."

Ginny had never been inside the Belle Fourche courtroom. It was smaller and less grand than she'd expected, but being here felt like the most important thing in the world. After all these years of waiting, she'd have her chance to get some justice, to start a new chapter in her life, free of Perry and the anger that had outlived their love. And although she was still scared, she finally dared to hope again.

Ben sat where she could see him, dressed in his Sunday

suit and wearing his solemn churchgoing expression. When she had turned down his proposal, he had simply nodded and said, "The offer still stands, Virginia. I still want to help you, any way I can." He had spoken to her lawyer and volunteered to testify as a character witness. That would count for something, for Ben was well respected in Belle Fourche.

Willie was there, too, in spite of Ginny's objections that she was too young. "We're in this together," she said. "I want to see the judge do right by you."

But Ginny's confidence was tentative at best, and when Perry swaggered into the courtroom with his lawyer, throwing her a smirking salute, she felt cold with fear. "Mr. Reynolds," she said, tugging at her lawyer's sleeve, "are you sure we're gonna come out okay?"

"Leave it to me, Virginia. I told you before – we can't ever be sure in a divorce case . . . we don't have many of those around here. But if you've been a good girl, why, we can hope for the best. Your case is the last one on the docket today. That means the judge will want to finish up before the weekend."

Reynolds made a brief opening statement, asking the court to grant Ginny a divorce on grounds of desertion, to award her custody of Willie, maintenance payments, and child support. Then he called John Barber as his first witness. Ginny's father testified that she had been a good girl who only had eyes for Perry Dellahaye, the boy she'd planned to marry.

Perry's lawyer, Joshua Skidmore, got Ginny's father to admit he couldn't swear under oath that she had been "pure" before her marriage – and then dismissed him.

Reynold's next witness was Ben Cattow, who painted a picture of a young woman of good character who loved her daughter and mothered her well. He testified that Ginny worked hard and had no social life away from the ranch, that he'd "be proud to have a daughter like that."

Skidmore approached Cattow carefully. "Now, Ben," he said smoothly, "I wouldn't question your word for a minute. But isn't it possible, on a big spread like yours, with all the hands you employ, that Mrs. Dellahaye might have had a special friend . . . ?"

"No," Ben snapped, "it's not possible. You're fishing, Joshua, and you're out of line."

"No more questions."

Reynolds final witness was Ginny herself. "Now, Virginia," he said, "tell us what your days were like when you lived with your husband."

"Well," she began, "I got up at five-thirty during the week," and then went on to describe her daily routine of domestic chores and innocent recreations, like listening to the radio and reading her magazines.

"Would you say you were a good wife, to the best of your ability?"

She hesitated for a split second, over the question she'd asked herself over and over during the past years. "I . . . yes, I tried the best I could."

"Now tell us about your domestic problems."

Ginny had known this question was coming, and she dreaded it. Reynolds had warned her she'd get no sympathy for refusing Perry his conjugal rights, that her best chance lay in emphasizing the beatings he'd given her. Haltingly she told the court about the time they'd come home from the union dance, how Perry had been drinking heavily and how he wanted to make love.

"I wasn't feelin' well . . . it was . . . it was my time of the month," she said, blushing furiously, "but Perry got mad when I said I couldn't . . . He hit me and he made . . . you know. Willie woke up . . . I guess she heard him yelling and hitting me. Perry just walked out of the house. That wasn't the only time . . . "

With her lawyer's prodding, Ginny testified that she had no intention of ending her marriage, even after she'd been beaten again, that Perry's claims of reconciliation attempts were false. "So," Reynolds said, "Perry Dellahaye abandoned you and your child to fend for yourselves, with no assistance other than the twenty dollars weekly, which this court forced him to pay."

"Yes, that's right."

"Thank you, Virginia."

Ginny tensed as Skidmore rose and came forward to question her. "That's a sad story you've told," he said. "Now let me help you remember the rest of it. You say you were a good wife. Do you mean that you shared Perry's marriage bed willingly, except for those times when you were . . . unwell?"

"I . . . not exactly . . . sometimes I was tired."

"More tired than your husband was, after working long hours at the mine, to support his family?"

"Objection, your honor," Reynolds rose to his feet. "Counsel is badgering my client."

"Objection overruled," the judge responded. "Defendant's counter-complaint charges that the breakdown of this marriage was due to plaintiff's repeated refusal of conjugal rights. That's what we mean to find out today."

"Thank you, your honor," Skidmore smiled. "I'll rephrase my question. Isn't it true, Virginia, that for several years, you refused your husband often and without just cause?"

Ginny's eyes darted around the courtroom, searching for rescue, for a way to answer the question truthfully without destroying her case. "I did have reasons," she pleaded.

"Did your husband provide food and shelter, for you and your child?"

"Yes, but . . . "

"Did he beat you, prior to the incidents you described, which came after years of provocation?"

"No, but . . . "

"Then what were these *reasons,* Virginia?" he asked, as if he were humoring a retarded child.

"I wasn't happy . . . I was all alone in that cabin . . . there was no one to talk to . . . Perry wouldn't take me anywhere . . ." Ginny went on, desperate to make the judge understand how it was. And Skidmore let her ramble, smiling in an attitude of exaggerated patience.

"You weren't happy," he said finally, "though your

husband did everything a man can be expected to do, so you decided to make him unhappy, too. Is that right?"

"Leave her alone! You leave my mother alone!" Willie screamed. Heads turned as the child bolted from her seat and ran to Ginny's side.

"Order!" The judge rapped his gavel to silence the buzzing spectators. "Order," he repeated, glaring at Ginny. "The court won't tolerate this kind of disturbance. If you can't keep your own child quiet, I'm going to cite you for contempt."

"Sit down, honey," Ginny whispered, "quick, before we get into trouble."

"But Mama," Willie argued, loud enough so all could hear, "they're telling lies about you, and that's not right."

"Come on, child, you have to sit down." Reynolds pulled Willie away from her mother, and led her back to her seat. "We apologize, your honor," he said.

Willie did as she was told, silently raging against her father for making these men their enemies. Why didn't Mama do something about it, she wondered, why did she just sit there looking like she was ready to cry. Willie knew that nothing got done by just crying.

"Well, Virginia," Skidmore continued, smiling more broadly than ever, "that's certainly a willful child you've raised. In your suit, you've asked for custody of this minor child. *And* you've asked that my client, after all he's suffered, surrender his own flesh and blood – and give you money to keep her. Now that we've all had a demonstration of the upbringing you've provided, I submit that you're no better a mother than you were a wife . . . "

"Liar!" Willie shouted again, her face red with indignation and outrage. "She's a good mother! You don't care about her or me. All you care about is *his* side!" She pointed an accusing finger at her father.

"Order!" the judge rapped furiously. "Bailiff, remove this child from the courtroom. The court cites Virginia Dellahaye for contempt of court. Sentence to be passed following decision on the matter before us. Court will recess until Monday morning."

Reynolds took Ginny's arm and led her from the courtroom, out to the front steps, where Willie and Ben Cattow waited. "We're losing, aren't we?" she said, her face a study in misery and defeat.

The lawyer cleared his throat. "I wouldn't say that, Virginia. There's no denying that Perry has a solid case, as to the divorce being your fault. But unless he can prove you're unfit as well, there's every chance you'll have custody of your daughter, and maybe some child support too. Now about the final installment on my fee . . . "

"C'mon, Ginny," Cattow interrupted. "I'm taking you and Willie home now." His jaw twitched as he turned to Reynolds. "You'll get your money when you've done your job," he said tersely.

"What is it, Ben? Why did you talk to Mr. Reynolds like that?" Ginny asked, when they were settled in the truck.

"I don't want to scare you, and Lord knows I'm no lawyer, but it seems to me that Perry's lawyer is doing better by him than this fellow is by you. Looks to me he kept getting caught with his pants down, no offense. Looks to me he didn't have any kind of plan . . . "

"He's right, Mama," Willie agreed. "*His* lawyer was much smarter. How come you didn't hire him?"

Ginny hesitated. She hated to keep reminding Willie of how limited their choices were, but she answered truthfully. "Reynolds was all I could afford, honey. I guess you get what you pay for."

Willie persisted. "But if he isn't any good, why did you keep him?"

"I wish you had talked to me, Ginny," Ben said quickly. "Maybe it's not too late . . . I haven't had much use for lawyers, but I can drive into town tomorrow . . . talk to Seth Hollis. He did some work for me four, five years ago, when I bought that east parcel of pastureland from Jack Lonnigan. Maybe he can do something for you . . . "

"But what if he can't?" Willie asked. "Nobody in that court seems to care about us, Mama. What if the judge says I have to live with *him*? We can't let them split us up . . . we just can't! It'd be like ripping a branch off a tree."

73

"What else can we do, honey? The judge says we have to come back on Monday."

"We can run away! We can leave this place and go somewhere far away . . . please, Mama, please say we can . . ."

"Oh, honey, I don't know . . ."

"Maybe the child's thinking straight," Ben said. "I don't hold with breaking the law or running away. But the law in this town seems to be on Perry's side, and that's not right either. I'd hate to lose you, Ginny, but if Seth can't come up with anything more than lawyer talk, maybe we'd best make some plans . . ."

Saturday morning dawned bright and sunny, the deep blue western sky streaked with gauzy ribbons of clouds. Outside Ginny's window, the air was cool and clean, pungent with the freshness of newly cut grass.

Though her day in court had gone badly, she felt a little better today, what with Ben's promise of help and the strength of his support behind her. She yawned and stretched and looked fondly at her sleeping daughter. Willie lay on her side, brows furrowed, the long, slender fingers on her hands curled into twin fists, resting protectively against her mouth. Her breathing was quiet and even, but when Ginny leaned over to kiss her, she tensed.

"What? What's wrong?" she asked sleepily.

"Nothing, honey . . . you can sleep a little longer." Ginny rubbed her daughter's back, watching the muscles relax as she drifted back to sleep. Not for the first time, she contrasted Willie's childhood with her own, mourning the years that should have been spent in carefree play, but it had passed instead in day-to-day survival. She would make it up to her, she vowed. But today she couldn't imagine how or when that would happen.

She took a long, warm shower, grateful for Ben's steady supply of hot water, careful to keep her hair from getting wet. She toweled the moisture from her body and looked at herself in the full-length mirror. She was trim and youthful, just as Sara had said. Now that Willie had shot up so quickly, the two of them looked more like sisters than mother and daughter. But what good was that when they both lived like old-maid aunts?

As she brushed her hair, she smelled the aroma of coffee percolating and hurried her pace. It was her job to start breakfast, not Ben's. Quickly she applied her lipstick and slipped into her jeans and a denim shirt. "Better get up," she called to Willie as she ran downstairs.

Willie went into the steamy bathroom, took off her nightgown and folded it neatly. She turned on the taps in the shower and tested the water before she stepped in. Quickly and efficiently, she washed "all over," just as Ginny had taught her years ago, starting with her face, working down, brushing past the breasts that had appeared on her tall, slender body. Mama had talked to her, blushing and embarrassed, about "becoming a woman," but Willie had cut her off, declaring airily that she knew "all about that stuff." She had no wish to dwell on those dark, secret mysteries. And she was in no hurry to "become a woman," for she had seen firsthand how precarious a woman's lot was.

Once Papa had loved them both. The memory was now so clouded and tarnished that she sometimes wondered if that time had really existed. But she did remember his hearty, booming laughter when he had called her his Princess, when he had taken her for long walks and taught her the names of animals and trees and flowers. He had loved Mama, too, before the fights had gotten fiercer and the laughter had disappeared. Before the night he'd left them forever, taking away his affection and all the protection they'd had from the cruelties that unloved women had to face. Before he'd turned into the stranger who'd come to court, ready to hurt Mama any way he could. She hated that stranger, and she wished she had the chance to hurt him as bad as he'd hurt them.

Downstairs, Ginny and Ben had just finished sharing their morning coffee. "You want the usual for breakfast?" she asked. "Eggs, sausage, hotcakes?"

"Later, honey. Foreman asked me to go out to the barn and have a look at the new foal . . . thinks she isn't feeding right. I want to see if she needs Doc Wilson before I drive to town. You and Willie start without me, keep me a plate in the oven."

"Whatever you say." She took a fat roll of sausage meat from the refrigerator, sliced off a dozen patties and arranged them in a heavy cast-iron skillet. Next, she mixed flour, eggs, milk, and baking powder in a big china bowl, set it aside and turned the flame under the griddle high. She heard the sound of a car crunching through the gravel behind the house and wondered who could be calling so early in the day.

She parted the white cambric curtains over the sink and peeked out. It was Ron, slamming the door of his Ford like he wanted to kill it, and marching resolutely toward the house. She turned off the gas jets and ran to the door. "Hi!" she called out, then stopped in her tracks. His eyes were red and swollen, and his clothes looked as if he'd slept in them.

"What's wrong?" she asked. "What's happened?"

"You!" he spat out. "You happened! Sara told me what you did, how you forced yourself on her and made her do unnatural things. Here I was feeling sorry for you, after I heard how the judge said you were a bad wife and a bad mother. Then Sara told me . . . she said that's why she didn't want anything to do with me. You made my wife go queer, Ginny, and you're gonna pay for it! I'm going into that court on Monday and tell the judge all about you . . . "

"No, Ron, no . . . you've gotta listen to me. It wasn't the way Sara said, honest it wasn't. It was just . . . "

"You callin' my wife a liar?" He drew back his arm as if to strike her.

A scream of rage froze the arm in midair. It was Willie, still in her nightgown, eyes blazing, pointing Ben's double-barreled shotgun at her uncle. "No!" she shouted. "You lay a hand on my Mama and I'll kill you!"

"Now, Willie, you put that thing down before somebody gets hurt," Ron coaxed. "Me and your mama are having a private talk, and it doesn't concern you none."

"Yes it does! You want to make trouble for us . . . I heard you!"

"Do what he says, sweetheart . . . please," Ginny intervened, ready to face the consequences of Ron's anger, rather than jeopardize Willie's welfare.

"Give me the gun," Ron insisted, "or I'll have the sheriff on you!"

"I'm not afraid of you!" Willie pointed the gun downward and pulled one trigger. The blast blew a hole in the floor and filled the air with smoke. "I've still got another shell in there," she warned, "so you better get out of here."

"What the hell is going on?" Ben rushed into the kitchen, armed with an old six-shooter. "You having some trouble, Ginny?"

"He's making trouble!" Willie nodded toward her uncle. "I heard him yelling at Mama, so I got your shotgun from the closet. He was going to hit her, and I made him stop . . . "

"Is that right, young fella?" Ben asked quietly. "That makes you a trespasser . . . now get the hell off my land before I call the law."

"I'm going," Ron said sullenly, "but the law's gonna hear about this . . . and some other things, too. You're finished in this town, Ginny, and that's a promise." He turned on his heel and stomped off to his car.

Ben turned to Willie. "Put the gun back in the closet, child," he said firmly, "and don't ever touch one again until you're old enough to know better."

"But, Ben . . ." Willie started to explain why she'd run for the gun, how scared she'd been by the shouting and the mean, ugly words, how she only wanted to protect her mother from being hurt again.

"I understand," he said softly. "See this piece here?" He held out the six-shooter for her to examine. "My father gave it to me when I was sixteen. He taught me how to use it – and when. I keep it clean and ready. Last time I fired it was maybe six, seven years ago . . . killed an old rattler sleeping in the shade, out by the barn."

Willie put the gun away and returned to the kitchen. "I'm sorry about the hole in the floor. I just wanted to show him I meant business."

"So you did." Ben gave her a small smile. "Floor can be

77

fixed . . . just you remember people can't be fixed so easily. So it's best to use other ways to protect the people you care about."

"What ways?"

"Good sense, keepin' 'em from hurtin' themselves. The power of persuasion. And maybe even – sometimes, when it can be made to work right – goin' to the law . . . "

Willie fell silent, thinking about it. How could Ben talk about using the law to protect anything after what it had done to Mama? All the law had ever done was hurt her, threaten her, take away her home and even her reputation, and now it was threatening to split them apart. But she was afraid to ask Ben about it. They had already agreed they might want to break the law, and hearing that it could sometimes be a good thing might make it harder to break.

Ginny had returned to the stove and was going through the motions of fixing breakfast, though food was the last thing she wanted. She laid the meal on the big trestle table and sat down with Ben and Willie.

The three of them picked quietly at the food. Ben's face was sad as he spoke what was on everyone's mind. "No point going to see Seth now, Ginny, not if your own brother's going to speak against you. Doesn't matter what he's going to say . . . Perry's lawyer is smart enough to use it."

"We have to run, Mama," Willie pleaded, "we have to. Please, please, let's go today."

Ginny remained silent, paralyzed by fear and doubt and indecisions. She knew that Ben and Willie were right, but she couldn't think of a single place to go to.

"You have any relatives in some other state?" Ben asked. "Anybody who can put you up for a while?"

Ginny shook her head. Perry had an uncle in Wyoming, but that wasn't going to help her any.

"We could go to a big city," Willie urged, reaching for a plan, anything that would mobilize her mother and get her away from Belle Fourche, where everyone seemed to be on Perry's side. "You could make your clothes and sell them, Mama. You're always saying how people in big cities spend money on clothes. Please, Mama, say yes."

Willie's words reprised a long dormant fantasy. "Do you think I could?" she asked, turning to Ben for affirmation. "Do you really think I could?"

The old rancher struggled to find words of encouragement, words that would send away the two people who had brightened his life. "Never lived in a big city myself, but I hear there's all kinds of opportunities. One thing's certain, you'll be together. And that's what counts."

"Okay," Ginny said. "We'll go."

Ben reached into his pocket and put a set of keys on the table. "Take the pickup . . . it'll save you bus fare and get you out of here before anyone notices. I've been meaning to trade her in, but I figure she'll get you wherever you're going."

Within two hours, Ginny and Willie were packed and ready to go. Their clothes were few, their personal effects meager. They had no suitcases, but Ben had supplied them with a couple of duffel bags. They stood together in front of the truck, Willie scanning the road for signs of trouble, Ben shuffling his boots in the dirt, Ginny holding onto the man who had been their only true friend.

"Go on now," he said, his voice furry with emotion. "Make as many miles as you can get before it gets dark." He embraced mother and daughter and helped them into the truck.

Ginny turned the key and started the motor, shifting into first gear as she waved goodbye to Ben – and to the town she'd called home all her life.

Two hours later, they had traveled farther away from Belle Fourche than Ginny had ever gone. The sun beat down mercilessly on the battered old Dodge pickup, though the sound of distant thunder promised rain many miles away. But in spite of the heat, the fugitives made a breathtaking picture. Willie, with her high, sharply defined cheekbones and the strong, clean jawline of her curiously adult face, contrasting with her mother's perfect features and golden-brown eyes, her soft and delicate childlike beauty. Even Willie's coloring – the tawny shadings of her skin, the

79

copper and silver streaks in her thick, straight hair – seemed to come from a bolder palette than that which had created Ginny's peaches-and-cream beauty.

When Ginny complained of the heat, Willie unscrewed the cap on the gallon bottle of water on the floor and half-filled a small tin cup. "Do you want a drink, Mama, to cool you off?"

Ginny accepted the cup gratefully. She sipped the water, then poured the remaining few drops over her head, patting them on to her cheeks as they trickled down her face. She ran her fingers through the fluffy blond hair she'd been perming ever since someone had told her she resembled Marilyn Monroe. "Why don't you play with your dolls, honey? It'll help you pass the time."

"Yes, Mama." Dutifully, Willie sifted through one of the duffel bags, until she found Marlene and Laura, the two dolls Ginny had bought at the five and dime. She had said they were for Willie, but Mama was the one who played with them, dressing them in glamorous movie star clothes she made with scraps of material and the sequins and beads she bought at the notions counter. She loved to make up stories about where they'd go in their beautiful clothes, about the handsome movie star men who'd take them to glittering restaurants and glamorous clubs, on romantic trips to Paris or Monte Carlo.

Willie never had much use for dolls, even when she was younger, but she enjoyed Mama's pleasure in them. Topaz eyes shining, lips parted, her excitement would build with each new detail, endowing brunette Marlene and blond Laura with all the glamour and excitement she'd never seen firsthand in a South Dakota mining town. Men who wore tuxedos and shaved every day, who smelled of fine cologne and bore no resemblance to anyone in Belle Fourche.

Willie went along with the pretense that the dolls were for her, though she preferred books and games you could play because you are smart. She sat Laura on her lap and patted the doll's blond wig. "She's not as pretty as you are . . . she just looks nice in the clothes you made. Someday you'll have beautiful clothes, too."

"Wouldn't that be swell," Ginny said, glad for the distraction from reality. "Laura's new boyfriend is a producer, and he fixed it so she had a screen test. Of course, it was wonderful, and . . . " The truck sputtered and pinged, lurched roughly, and then went on. "Oh darn it, Willie, we sure don't need any trouble now. What if we get stuck here? What if . . . "

"Don't worry," Willie soothed. "We'll be okay, and you'll sell your clothes, just like I said. We can go to Hollywood, too, if that's what you want . . . "

"Wouldn't that be nice," Ginny sighed, brushing a damp curl from her forehead. Willie's words and the heat of the day made her think of a picture she'd seen in *Modern Screen*: Tab Hunter sitting near a kidney-shaped sky blue swimming pool, surrounded by a bunch of starlets sipping beautiful sophisticated drinks that looked like colored ice cream sodas.

She wasn't sure she believed in Willie's idea, but she didn't have any of her own. All she knew was that they had to get as far away from South Dakota as Ben's old truck would take them. She tried to concentrate on the doll fantasies, but as the miles and the past slipped away, a new kind of fear took hold of Ginny.

She hadn't been happy in a long time, but her unhappiness had been ground in familiarity, in faces and places she'd seen every day of her life. Now, she saw road signs, with names like Laramie and Sundance and Cody, names that might have evoked colorful stories in her mind when she was snug and safe in Perry's wilderness cabin. But now the names were just streaks of black paint on cold slivers of metal. They held no magic, no welcoming refuge for a woman with a child, with nothing but an old truck and two hundred dollars standing between her and God knows what.

She swallowed hard as the truck passed a sign saying "Welcome to Wyoming," and she drove on. When the mountain road widened into a T formation, Ginny looked to the left and then the right, her eyes scanning the twin banks of arrows and the choices they offered.

Suddenly she jammed on the brakes and brought the truck to a grinding stop. Slumping over the steering wheel, she began to cry.

"This is crazy," she sobbed. "Where are we gonna go? I can't do this, Willie, I just can't . . . . "

"Yes, you can, Mama," Willie said urgently, gripping her mother's hand, willing her for once to be strong and not so afraid. " . . . *we can*. We've just got to . . . because maybe it's the only way we can stay together. And," she added after a second, "I want to see what's at the end of that road."

"But where?" Ginny looked up at her daughter through eyes fogged with tears and confusion. "Where do we go?"

The sun was setting, laying down a path of gold in the distance. "That way, Mama," she said, with a certainty that seemed to come from some reservoir of hope she had never tapped before. "Let's go toward the sun."

4

The man at the Las Vegas gas station was kind, but the news he gave them was all bad. "Transmission's a goner, ma'am. And that ain't all . . . " After listing parts and repairs that were needed, he offered them $50 for the truck.

Tears welled up in Ginny's eyes. It had seemed like a good idea to stop here on the way to Hollywood, to get the truck repaired and see what such a glamorous place looked like. "But we were thinkin' about going to California . . . and we don't have the money to go any other way . . . "

The mechanic took pity on the young woman and her daughter. Pretty as a picture, both of them, one so sad, the other so serious. "Listen," he said. "We get a lot of truckers passing through here . . . I bet I can find one who'd be glad to take you, just for the company."

"Oh, gosh, thanks . . . that'd be swell." Ginny smiled

through her tears, grateful for the prospect of rescue. "But what are we gonna do in the meantime?"

"No problem. My mom runs a motel just down the road. It's kinda slow right now. I can get you a room real cheap . . . I bet you'll have a ride by tomorrow. Meantime, you can try your luck at one of the casinos, maybe hit a jackpot on one of the slots . . ." He smiled encouragingly.

Their nine-dollar room at the Sunset View Motel smelled of Lysol and mildew, but Ginny was too excited by the prospect of adventure to notice. With the extra $50 in her purse and the promise of a ride, she had already forgotten how precarious their situation was. While Willie unpacked their things, storing them neatly in a battered pine dresser, her mother headed straight for the shower.

She unwrapped a tiny bar of soap and lathered away the day's grime and fatigue. Then she worked the lather through the thick blond hair, rinsing thoroughly, and wishing she had some lemon juice to add shine and "highlights."

Refreshed and revived, she wrapped herself in a frayed grayish towel and chose an outfit for her night on the town: a pink angora sweater – Perry's last Christmas gift – and a white gathered skirt she'd made herself. "All set," she smiled. "Now we'd better have our sandwiches and that Coke we bought, before it gets all warm and yucky. If I win tonight, we'll have something nice tomorrow . . . in a real restaurant."

"I don't know if this is such a good idea, Mama. What if you lose? Maybe we could use some of the money from the truck for bus tickets . . . "

"But maybe I'll win," Ginny countered, reaching for the hope of something that would signal a break in the years of bad luck. Never that practical or careful, she needed the hope more than she needed the certainty of $50.

Willie couldn't understand this sudden excitement over a slender "maybe" any more than she could understand her mother's ready acceptance of defeat. But, out of habit more than conviction, she bit back any words that would spoil Ginny's enthusiasm.

As they consumed their simple meal, Ginny chattered on, her imagination now in full swing, fed by the prospect of good luck, good fortune, all those things which had been in such short supply. Anything was possible – for weren't they here now, in a glamorous and fabled place? Never mind that the room was dismal, the sandwiches stale and dry. Ginny Dellahaye, who had never been out of South Dakota, was here – in Las Vegas. And tomorrow they'd be on their way to California.

Later, as Ginny dressed, Willie sat cross-legged on the bed. She always enjoyed watching this ritual, though she usually resisted her mother's attempts to draw her into it. First Ginny brushed her hair vigorously, making it shine with golden lights. Then she "teased" it into a fluffy crown before smoothing it out, artfully arranging wisps and tendrils around her face.

She spread her small but precious cache of five-and-dime cosmetics on the dresser: one jar of all-purpose cream, an apricot blusher, a worn cake of golden eyeshadow, a stubby brown eyeliner, and a tube of mascara. One by one, she applied them carefully, checking the results in the cloudy mirror.

Willie thought her mother was prettier without all the makeup, but there was no denying she looked more glamorous when she was finished, just like the movie stars on the cover of *Modern Screen*.

"How do I look?" she asked, pirouetting for Willie's inspection.

"Beautiful, Mama. Like always."

"Thanks, baby." She gave her hair a final pat. "Wish me luck," she called out over her shoulder. "And don't forget to lock the door."

Ginny's first glimpse of Las Vegas had been disappointing. But now, at night, the town had come to life, the dull, flat daytime colors transformed, as if by magic, by miles of bright neon, into a mammoth playland. It reminded her of a giant carnival, the lights and the noise, the chance to ride

84

a roller coaster and forget your troubles, the chance to spin a wheel and win a prize.

Ginny hitched a ride to the Sands hotel, which the mechanic had assured her was "a classy place." A huge sign in front announced that Dionne Warwick and Red Buttons were appearing, two shows nightly. She walked up the driveway, which was lined with cars and limousines, past a liveried doorman, hoping she didn't look too out of place in such a grand hotel. A bellboy directed her to the casino, which was bigger and noisier than anything she'd ever seen in the movies. So many people, so much cigarette smoke.

She stopped in front of a brightly colored slot machine, dropped a quarter in and pulled the lever. Nothing. She tried once more and moved to the roulette wheels, which had always seemed so glamorous in the movies. "Excuse me," she whispered to a gray-haired man who had a large pile of chips in front of him. "Could you tell me how to play?"

"Shush," he muttered, without even looking at her. "This ain't no kindergarten, lady."

Ginny blushed and stepped back, embarrassed and flustered, quickly losing her place.

"That wasn't nice," a deep voice drawled. She turned to see a tall, deeply tanned man with clear gray eyes and dark wavy hair, dressed in a white western suit and a cream-colored Stetson. Thinking he meant her, Ginny started to apologize.

"Heck, no," he laughed, his eyes crinkling with amusement. "I meant him, that jerk by the table. No gentleman would talk to a lady like that. Especially such a pretty lady."

Ginny blushed again, this time with pleasure. The stranger looked handsome and rich enough to come straight from one of her fantasy stories.

"My name is Harley T. Bonne, but you can call me Hank. If you're still lookin' for gambling lessons, I'd like to show you around . . ."

And he did. With what seemed like an endless supply of hundred-dollar chips, Hank showed Ginny how to play roulette, how to sip the fancy drinks the house served its high rollers, and best of all, how to enjoy the kind of carefree good time she hadn't known for years.

The hours flew by, though there were no clocks in the casino, nor any windows to show the passage of time. Ginny declared she wasn't tired at all because she was having so much fun.

"Yeah," Hank agreed, "but I think we're gonna have to call it a night, darlin' . . . got to catch me a plane in four or five hours . . . How 'bout we have a bite of supper in my room?"

Ginny hesitated, but just for a moment. She felt like Cinderella, and she didn't want her evening to end. Besides, she was curious to see what a room in such a fancy place looked like.

She wasn't disappointed. She oohed and aahed, while Hank gave her the "ten-cent tour" of his suite, starting with the well-furnished, thickly carpeted sitting-room, moving to the sparkling bathroom with its colored tiles and fixtures, and the bedroom with its king-size bed and big screen television.

"I'll bet this costs the world," she said.

"Don't cost a cent," he explained. "Compliments of the management. " 'Course I couldn't tell you how much I leave behind every time I come to this place, so they get their money one way or another."

"My goodness," she said, not really comprehending the kind of wealth that allowed you to lose so carelessly.

"This time I got the best deal of all . . . meetin' you downstairs."

Hank called room service, and Ginny discovered she was hungry enough to order a steak. The meal, complete with champagne, was brought by a white-jacketed waiter, who set the table in front of the windows, with their picture-postcard view of bright lights and the city below.

After they finished eating, Hank took the single rose from the slender green vase and handed it to Ginny. "Not as pretty as you . . . "

The compliment brought tears to her eyes. It had been

such a long time since a man had ever said sweet words to her. Hank got up and put his arms around her, kissed her mouth, and stroked her cheek. She felt all warm and cozy, here in this elegant room, with this rich, handsome man. A hotel full of women, and he had picked her. Just like Cinderella. And she didn't have to go back to that dismal motel. Not yet.

She wasn't sure what to do next, so she kissed him back. He took her hand and led her into the bedroom. "I'd be a happy man if you let me unwrap this pretty package, Ginny darlin'."

She nodded, and he slipped off her sweater and skirt. She wished she had prettier underwear, but Hank didn't seem to notice, as he exclaimed over the creaminess of her skin, the soft curve of her breasts. He turned out the light and took his clothes off, but Ginny could see that his body was lean and hard.

Compared with Perry, Hank was a storybook lover, kissing her all over and saying sweet things. His hands were sure but gentle when he parted her legs and stroked her rhythmically, until she was warm and wet and ready for him. When her breathing quickened, he entered her. "Oh, darlin'," he whispered against her neck, "you are so beautiful . . . so beautiful." He moved inside her, first slowly, then hard, then slowly again. When she began to moan with pleasure, he matched the rhythm of her hips and stroked her steadily. "There you go now, sweet thing," he encouraged, "there you go now," he murmured, nuzzling her breasts, his hands cupping her buttocks, until he felt her back arch and her body stiffen. "Yahoo!" he yelled, coming in a great warm rush, and falling against her.

"Beautiful Ginny," he mumbled, his face in the pillow, his arm thrown around her.

She lay still for a while, until she realized he was asleep. Gently, she moved his arm and went into the bathroom to fix her hair and makeup. When she came back to find her clothes, he opened his eyes and asked sleepily:

"Where you goin', pretty lady?"

"I have to get back . . . before my daughter wakes up. She'll be worried."

"Tell you what," he drawled. "You keep me company while I get ready, and I'll drop you off on my way to the airport. I'll call for the limo right now . . . "

The ride back to the Sunset View Motel was a short one, but it was like being carried from one world into another. Ginny's first limousine ride made her feel like a movie star, but it was over all too soon. "Take care of yourself, darlin'." Hank kissed her lightly on the cheek and pressed some folded bills into her hand. "Here," he said, "this is your share of our winnings."

"Gosh . . . thanks . . . thanks for everything."

"My pleasure," he said, waving as the sleek black limousine pulled away.

Ginny turned the key in the door of Cabin 2 and tiptoed inside quietly.

"Mama? Mama, is that you?" Willie called out.

"Yes, baby . . . go back to sleep."

Willie sat up in bed. She had hardly slept all night. "Where were you?" she asked accusingly. "I was scared you might be hurt."

"I'm sorry, honey." She sat down on the bed and hugged Willie. "But wait till you see . . ." she chattered on, spreading the money Hank had given her over the blanket, counting as she went along. "Three hundred dollars . . . isn't that great? You get back to sleep now, and we'll talk later."

Willie was full of questions about the money and the long hours unaccounted for. But more than that, she was angry with her mother for forgetting she was here. She wanted to cry out words of blame. How could her mother be so careless? But knowing how fragile Ginny was, Willie kept silent and slipped back under the covers. Ginny stripped off her clothes, crawled into bed beside her daughter, and fell promptly asleep.

They slept so late that they missed checkout time at the motel by hours. But Ginny didn't seem to care. She insisted

88

on taking Willie back to the Sands, so she could see for herself how luxurious the place was, while they both enjoyed a late breakfast of fresh orange juice, waffles, and sausage at the hotel coffee shop.

"I still think we should go and buy some bus tickets now, Mama," Willie said. "We don't have to wait for a ride, and I don't think we should spend any more money here. We're going to need it, when we get to California."

"Don't you worry about money, baby. There's so much money around here, and I'm goin' to get us some more. We're paying for the room anyway. If I can get us another couple of hundred tonight, we'll be that much better off. We'll buy the tickets first thing in the morning, I promise."

"But Mama . . . "

"No buts, honey . . . now finish that waffle. I want to get back to the room and fix myself up."

Ginny stared down at her last twenty dollars in chips, her panic building as she faced the enormity of what she had done. She had tried to remember everything Hank had taught her last night, and she had even won a few times. But the more careful she had tried to be, the more she'd lost. Desperately she looked around. There must be someone in the casino who was as nice as Hank. She spotted a lone man ordering a drink.

"Hi," she said brightly. "Do you need any company for luck?"

The man's expression was unsmiling as he studied Ginny, his eyes raking her body. "Whatsa matter," he asked, "lose all your money?"

"I guess I did," she admitted, wondering if she'd made a mistake in talking to this man. He didn't seem friendly or kind.

"Okay," he said abruptly, pushing a hundred dollars' worth of chips at her. "You got yourself a deal."

Relieved, Ginny smiled a thank-you. Everything was going to be all right. She would win back the money she'd lost and then go back to the motel.

But her luck seemed to have disappeared, along with

Hank. She and the stranger had lots of free drinks, but that was all the casino gave them. He was a moody player, and the more he lost, the angrier he got. When Ginny's stake disappeared, he said, "If you want any more, it's gonna have to be a party."

She nodded, thinking he didn't seem to be in a party mood.

He laughed triumphantly when he won a few big bets, but Ginny's luck didn't change at all. After the last of her chips disappeared, she looked expectantly at her companion.

"That's enough," he said. "Now we go pick up my friends, and you're gonna show us a real good time." He slid his hand down her back and squeezed her flesh possessively. "And you better make sure I get my money's worth."

She pulled away, frightened by his words, the expression on his face. "Don't do that . . . I don't want to go to any party . . . I have to leave—"

"The hell you will," he snarled, his voice rising. "You took my money, you little tramp, and now you're gonna pay up."

"Something wrong, sir?" one of the casino floor men asked quietly.

"You bet something's wrong. If you're gonna let hookers in this place, you better make sure they're honest. This bimbo hustled me for a couple of hundred bucks, and now she wants to cut out . . . "

"But I'm not a hooker," Ginny protested, tears streaming down her face. "I'm not, honest, I just came here to gamble. . . "

"Yeah," the man shouted, "with my money!"

"I'm very sorry this happened, sir," the floorman said smoothly. "The house will make it up to you. Please step into my office . . ." He signaled discreetly, and two burly security guards appeared, dragging Ginny out of the casino.

"Don't show your face here again or we'll have you arrested," one of them threatened, shoving her roughly into the street.

Still sobbing, Ginny sat down on the curb, forgetting that she was wearing her best skirt. Dazed and bewildered, she tried to figure out what had happened, what she had done to be treated so badly. What was she going to do now, with no money and no chance to get any? And how was she going to tell Willie that she'd lost everything?

"What were you doing with a creep like that?"

Ginny looked up and saw a tall, rangy man dressed in jeans and a denim jacket. He had an outdoorsman's face, tanned and leathery, rugged features, and watery blue eyes framed by short grizzled hair. He was smiling at her.

She shook her head. "I don't know . . . I was just tryin' to win some money, but he thought . . . "

"I know what he thought. I was in there. Thought I'd come out and make sure you were all right. Buy you a cup of coffee?"

Ginny accepted gratefully, though she'd just made one bad mistake with a stranger. Kindness had been in such short supply and she needed it so badly.

"My name's Webb Foley," he said, after they were seated across a small table in an all-night cafeteria. "I fly high rollers from California to Vegas. I'm on my own while my passengers are losing their money . . . Want to tell me what you were doing with that lowlife?"

Ginny looked up from her coffee, her eyes still shiny with tears. In the bright light of the cafeteria, Webb's face looked open and honest, almost boyish with concern. There was something about him that reminded her of Ben. Slowly, haltingly, she told him about Perry and Willie, about their flight from South Dakota and the past two days in Las Vegas. "Now all that extra money's gone . . . I don't know what to do . . ." she finished desolately.

Webb's response was prompt and decisive. "First thing you'd better do is get out of this godforsaken town. Vegas is no place for a lady like you . . . or a kid."

She nodded. "I know, but . . . "

"I'll give you a ride. No strings," he added quickly. "Only one passenger on this run, so there's room for you

91

and your daughter. You'll like Palm Springs . . . it's a nice place."

"But I was thinkin' about Hollywood. Willie said I could sell my clothes to the rich people there . . . "

"No shortage of rich folks in Palm Springs. Lots of movie people, too. Try it, Ginny . . . Looks to me like you and your kid could use a friend. I'm volunteering. What've you got to lose?"

Ginny agreed there was nothing to lose. At this point she was only too glad to let someone else take charge, if just for a little while.

5

"Here we are, folks . . . Palm Springs below."

Ginny and Willie pressed their faces against the plane's window, eager for a glimpse of what would be their new home. Surrounded by great stretches of desert, sheltered by gray and purple mountains, Palm Springs seemed as perfect and unreal as any of Ginny's fantasies: a man-made confection of white stucco palazzos with red tile roofs and aquamarine swimming pools, bordered by lush green lawns and graceful palm trees.

"Ooh," Ginny sighed, "it's gorgeous."

"Ain't it, though," Foley agreed. "When I was a boy, most of this desert was still Indian country. Outside folks came to take the cure at the sanatorium. Then a couple of movie people – Charlie Farrell and Ralph Bellamy – they came out and started their own private playground, a place called the Racquet Club. Told all their Hollywood buddies, and the rest, as they say, is history. Indians still own about half the land, but the sanatorium's a fancy hotel now – the Desert Inn. Lots of hotels . . . fancy shops, too, down there on Palm Canyon Drive."

"Gosh," Ginny said, "that sounds good to me."

"No free rides, though," Foley warned, "no more than

92

anywhere else. All you get for free is fresh air and a good climate. Find yourself a job, maybe a new husband, and you'll be okay. After we land, I'll take you to see my girlfriend. Laura works at one of the country clubs, and she has a house in town. Her spare room should do you fine, till you get yourselves settled."

Turning toward his single paying passenger, Webb raised his voice. "End of the line, Mr. Caldwell . . . time to get up."

After an expert landing, Foley taxied down the field toward his regular hangar. He helped his passengers from the small plane, unloaded a large, heavy sack, and gave some instructions to a waiting mechanic. "This way, ladies," he said pointing toward a small parking lot on the fringes of the airfield.

He piled their belongings into his Jeep and drove toward town, pointing out landmarks along the way. "Up in the mountains there you can see Bob Hope's place . . . over here on the left is the Gene Autry Hotel . . . the Desert Inn's a couple of miles south . . . that's where they have those big golf tournaments, with all the movie stars . . . "

Willie was less interested in what Webb was saying than in the impressions of her own senses. This was a different world from any she'd known. Shiny new cars, sleek, well-groomed people who didn't seem to have a care in the world. She glanced at Ginny, who was completely caught up in their new friend's narrative.

Webb seemed to be what Ben would've called a "straightshooter," and Willie was inclined to trust him. As for this new place, she'd wait and see. It had been too long since she'd felt safe and secure anywhere.

"Now you're really gonna see something," Webb announced, turning the Jeep off the main road, driving up to a high wrought-iron gate manned by a squadron of blue-suited men. "Delivery for Mr. Fontana," he said. "The name's Webb Foley."

One of the men consulted a list. "You can go in, but the ladies will have to wait."

"Ah, come on," Webb coaxed. "At least let me take the

kid . . . she's my niece," he improvised. "Ten minutes and we're out."

The man scrutinized Willie, then nodded his head. "Ten minutes. The other lady stays here."

Reluctantly, Ginny got out of the Jeep, and Webb continued along a meandering driveway lined with palm trees, to a massive structure of stone and glass and redwood. It was a house of sweeping curves and dramatic angles, its colors and textures in perfect harmony with the natural setting, surrounded by rich green foliage and banks of brilliantly blooming flowers carefully nourished by two gardeners and an excellent sprinkler system.

"What is this place?" Willie whispered, overwhelmed by what she saw.

"Thought you'd get a kick out of it," Webb said with a laugh. "This spread belongs to Sam Fontana. His family uses it for vacations and such. Big wedding going on today . . . one of the daughters is marrying a fella from around here. And that," he pointed to the sack, "is full of party favors. Have a peek." He untied the bag. It was full of twenty-dollar gold pieces.

Willie had never seen so much money. "You mean he's gonna give those away?"

"Yup. Ten thousand bucks' worth. Bank in Vegas got them, special for the occasion. Whatever Mr. Fontana wants, he gets. C'mon . . . can't keep the man waiting."

Webb identified himself to another cluster of blue-suited men and was sent to the back of the house. Willie had never seen anything like this in her whole life. A red-and-white striped tent that could have sheltered an entire circus stood on the manicured back lawn. Underneath were dozens of tables covered in pink linen, decorated with cut flowers and set with china and crystal and silver.

The assembly of wedding guests was equally dazzling. Men in black tie, women adorned with expensive fashions and elaborate hairdos, their jewels shimmering in the late after-noon sun, as they sipped cocktails around a sparkling blue swimming pool. "Look," Willie said excitedly, "there's Paul Newman! And the man next to him . . . isn't that . . .?"

"Yup . . . the vice-president of these United States, in the flesh. Keep looking, Willie, you'll see a lot more before we leave."

What kind of man was this Sam Fontana, Willie wondered, that such important people would come to his house? She kept looking, as Webb told her to.

Tucked neatly in a glass-sheltered grove of bougainvillea and hibiscus were a dozen white-jacketed musicians, playing lush romantic melodies. Mingled with the sound of music was the clinking of glasses and the tinkle of laughter, new sounds to Willie's ears. People enjoying themselves. Here was one of Mama's fantasy stories come to life, and Willie found this revelation, the discovery that such people did exist, more awesome than the lavish display of wealth.

Webb spoke to a uniformed maid, and a few minutes later, a tall, heavyset man with wavy steel-gray hair and a trimmed mustache appeared. "You're late," he said, scowling, before Webb could utter a word. "I wanted this stuff before my guests arrived."

"I'm sorry, Mr. Fontana, but the bank didn't have it all yesterday. I had to go back this morning . . . "

"Never mind," he said. "Sam Fontana can make allowances on his daughter's wedding day." Noticing Willie, he plucked a gold piece from the sack and handed it to her. "Here, young lady . . . in honor of the bride."

"Thank you," she said solemnly, transfixed by all the wonders she'd seen.

"You're welcome." He smiled at her, and without knowing why, she felt relieved that Sam Fontana's mood had shifted. "Come on, Foley," he said expansively, "I'm just about to toast the bride. Take a glass and drink my daughter's health." He ordered one of his men to take care of the gold pieces and walked to the bandstand.

As if by magic, the party noises hushed. "Welcome," he began, in a resonant baritone that needed no microphone. "Family and friends, I give you my beloved daughter, Lisa."

On cue, a slender brunette gowned in antique Alençon lace, her dark curls caught up in a gossamer mantilla bordered with seed pearls, appeared at her father's side. "To the bride." Sam raised his glass and drank. Then he embraced his daughter, and Willie was surprised by the tears on his face.

"This is a happy day for the Fontana family," he continued, his voice drenched with emotion, "and I only wish my dear Amelia had lived to see it. Now I want to welcome my new son, Charles, into the family. From today on, Charlie's one of us. That means he takes the good with the good . . . because there's *nothing* bad about being a Fontana!" He paused for the laughter and applause that followed. "Now Lisa's brother, my son Jaime Esteban Diego Domingo – you all know him as Jedd – wants to say a few words to the happy couple."

Willie stared as Jedd Fontana, lean and handsome in his formal suit, took the stage with the easy grace of a natural athlete. His skin was burnished dark by the desert sun, his jet black hair was long and straight, combed dramatically back like a matador's. To Willie, he looked dashing and sophisticated as he raised his glass in a salute. "To Lisa," he said. "I forgive you for all the big-sister stuff you ever did. Charlie . . . make her happy, or you'll answer to me." His voice cracked with the passion of his sentiment, but no one laughed. Young as he was, Jedd Fontana carried a certain authority; the prospect of having to "answer to" him didn't seem a mere empty threat. With a courtly bow, he invited the bride to dance.

Willie watched, fascinated by this gorgeous creature with the flashing black eyes and heart-stopping smile, by the tenderness and affection he showed his sister. These people really like each other, she thought, marveling at the kind of family that was bound together with loyalty and devotion. Her eyes followed Jedd, as he danced past, laughing at some private joke he shared with his sister.

The groom cut in, and as Jedd turned, his eyes met Willie's. He smiled, and for a moment it seemed as if he might speak to her. "Jedd!" his father called, and then he was gone.

"We'd better go," Webb said. "Your mama's waiting for

96

us." Willie left reluctantly, for she'd felt a real-life kind of magic in this place, at this wedding, in this family, which seemed to her everything a family should be.

Webb drove them to a modest stucco bungalow behind a gas station and honked his horn twice. A tiny redhead in a pink sundress came running out, throwing her arms around Webb and planting noisy kisses on his face.

"Whoa," he laughed. "I've only been gone for two days."

"Two days too long," she declared. "I always worry when you fly that crate." She pulled away and studied his companions speculatively, hands on hips, a possessive gleam in her green eyes.

Webb caught the look and laughed again. "Innocent, Laura, honest. You know I'm a one-woman man. This is Ginny Dellahaye and her daughter, Willie. They were stranded in Vegas and I gave them a ride. Ginny needs a job and a place to stay. I volunteered your spare room till she finds work. Ginny, Willie . . . this is my girlfriend Laura, my one and only . . . or she'd bust my head with a tire iron. But don't you worry, Laura's got a big and generous heart." He ruffled the woman's short red hair affectionately.

"He's right," Laura said, extending a hand to Ginny. "You're welcome to stay. Webb'll bring your stuff inside."

The house was furnished haphazardly, as if by someone who had better things to do, but it was neat and clean. "Make yourselves comfortable," Laura said. "Webb and I'll run out and get us all a bucket of chicken for supper. Help yourselves to anything you need."

"They seem like real nice people," Ginny said when they were alone. "I think we'll be okay here."

"I think you're right, Mama. You rest while I unpack."

Visions of the Fontana wedding, the handsome boy who'd almost said "hello," were still vivid in Willie's mind as she emptied the duffel bags. The spare room was furnished with a convertible sofa, a small chest of drawers, a radio, and a lamp made from petrified wood. She cleared

97

a small space in the closet for their clothes, and carefully arranged their remaining belongings in two empty drawers. Years of living in other people's homes had taught her to take up as little space as possible, to be quiet and neat and ever mindful that hospitality could be withdrawn at any time.

When she was finished, she went into the kitchen and filled two glasses with cold water. She handed one to her mother.

"Here, Mama," she said solemnly. "You're gonna be happy here . . . or somebody's gonna answer to me."

"Sorry, we're not hiring."

"The buyer's not in today."

"We don't deal with individuals, only with established firms."

In the past three hours, Ginny had heard every variety of "no." It didn't matter how the words were delivered – with sympathy, irritation or condescension – they still added up to no work and no income.

Last night Laura had offered to introduce her to the manager of the country club where she worked. Ginny had been about to accept when Willie had interrupted. "What about selling your designs? You have to try," she'd urged. "You've been thinking about it for such a long time . . . "

But no one here seemed to be interested. Ginny paused in front of yet another of the chichi boutiques that lined Palm Canyon Drive. The window display was simple: a single bored-looking mannequin wearing a black dress and a fox coat (why anyone needed a fox coat in this climate, Ginny couldn't figure out). A gold-lettered sign on the door said CUSTOM DESIGN AND DRESSMAKING. This might be a place where they could use her skills as a seamstress, her flair for design. She took a deep breath and walked inside.

A smart-looking saleswoman glanced briefly at Ginny and turned her attention back to her customer. "This is an original design, Mrs. Collins," she said persuasively, "so you won't see another one like it at the country club gala . . . "

Ginny sat down on the edge of a gilt and needlepoint chair and waited until the customer had made her purchase and left the shop

"Yes?" the saleswoman asked, omitting the customary "May I help you?"

"I'm lookin' for work," Ginny explained. "I'm a good seamstress, and I design dresses . . . "

The woman stared, as if unable to believe what she was hearing.

"Here, I can show you." Ginny pressed on, fumbling in her bag for the assortment of doll clothes she'd brought as samples of her work. "These are some of the dressy numbers, and this one . . . this is a sporty outfit . . . "

The woman's mouth twitched. "Wait here," she said, taking the doll clothes into the back of the store.

Ginny's hopes soared. Someone was actually looking at her things. She tiptoed toward the curtain to listen.

". . . it must be a joke."

"No, I think she was serious. 'Dressy numbers' . . . isn't that priceless?"

To Ginny's horror, the two women started to giggle. She peeked through a sliver between the curtains and saw each one holding up one of the miniature designs for the other to mock. Blinded by tears and hurt and humiliation, she ran out of the store, leaving her precious creations behind. She didn't stop running until she reached Laura's house.

"What happened, Mama?" Willie asked anxiously, when she saw Ginny's face. "What happened? Couldn't you find any work?"

"No, baby . . . nobody wants my clothes. They just . . . laughed." She started to sob softly, like a little girl with a broken toy.

Guilt washed over Willie as she watched her mother cry. She had sent her out to be ridiculed. Then came anger, strong and hot. "Never you mind," Willie said fiercely. "They must be stupid . . . and mean. They'll be sorry . . . just wait . . ." She hugged Ginny close until the sobbing stopped. "You lie down and take a rest, and I'll start supper."

Ginny curled up on the convertible couch and closed her eyes, trying to erase the day's humiliation, wondering if she was doomed to fail here, just as she had done in Belle Fourche.

For a long time Willie hovered protectively over her mother until she heard the even breathing that came with sleep. She covered her with a light blanket, and gently wiped away the last traces of tears.

Don't you worry, Mama, we're going to make it, she vowed silently. *No matter what, we're going to make it.*

6

"Miss . . . you there . . . !"

Ginny hurried around the club's terrazzo-bordered swimming pool and across the redwood deck toward the teenager who was languidly beckoning to her from a chaise. The young girl wore heart-shaped sunglasses and a skimpy bikini that Brigitte Bardot had made all the rage.

"Can I get you something?" Ginny asked, smiling dutifully just as she'd been taught on her first day of work, two years ago.

"I'll have a lemon coke with lots of ice. And a bag of potato chips."

"Right away." As Ginny headed back to the snack bar to fill the order, she was stopped by one of the club's older members.

"What can I do for you, Mr. Cornell?" she asked.

"Ah, Ginny," he smiled, "you could do a lot for me, if only you would . . . but I'll settle for a fresh towel."

"One towel, coming up."

In the years since she'd come to Palm Springs, she never stopped marvelling at how many ways the rich were different from anyone else. On them, even old age was kinder, later in arriving and much more attractive. Randolph Cornell was at least seventy, old enough to be her father – or her grandfather. In Belle Fourche, he'd be an "old-timer," waiting out his days watching television or talking about the "good old days." But here he was, tan and fit, decked out in a snappy cabana outfit, flirting and teasing just like the younger men did. Ginny didn't mind. The men didn't get mean or ugly when she deflected their passes with a smile. And their attentions made her feel desirable and much younger than her thirty-four years.

But she never took any of them seriously. Laura had warned her about that when she got her the job. "Cabana girl's pay isn't much, but with your looks, and that great smile, you'll make it up in tips," she'd said. "But don't even think about taking up with one of the members. Especially the married ones. You might have fun for a while, maybe even get a couple of presents. But when they get bored, you're out of a job, and they go on to the next one. Get it?"

Ginny got it. She wasn't about to do anything to jeopardize her job. The work was boring and routine, but it wasn't hard. She enjoyed being outdoors. The sunshine and fresh air had brought a healthy glow to her creamy skin, and the exercise had tightened her muscles, adding tone and definition to the contours of her body. In her work clothes – a pair of white shorts and a T-shirt bearing the club logo – Ginny looked great, and she knew it.

When she reached the snack bar, she called out her order and waited for the counterman to fill it. Then she swung by the linen supply room to pick up Cornell's towel.

Laura was inside, checking the stacks of monogrammed towels against the numbers in her notebook. "Paperwork again?" Ginny teased. "That's what you get for joining up with management."

"Yeah," Laura laughed. "It's a dirty, rotten job, but someone has to do it." She had been promoted recently to manager of the pool concession, and while she enjoyed flashing her new badge of office – gold braid on her short white jacket – she was full of mock complaints about the longer hours and new responsibilities. "Say, Ginny, did you ask Willie about working an extra shift on Saturday?

Two of my regular girls are out, so I need all the part-timers I can get . . . "

"Count on Willie," Ginny said. "She never says 'no' to extra work. Sometimes I feel bad about that, though. All she does is study and worry about saving money for college. That doesn't seem right, Laura. When I was her age, I was interested in parties and boys, but Willie . . . she's so *serious*."

"Nothing wrong with that, Ginny. Be grateful she has a good head on her shoulders. She'll make something of herself, you wait and see."

Ginny was grateful for her daughter's common sense. But it didn't seem normal to be so wrapped up in studies and plans for the future. When Laura had offered Willie part-time work around the club, filling in for waitresses and towel girls, Ginny had been pleased.

Now sixteen, Willie had developed into a real stunner, with a cover-girl face and figure. Ginny had hoped her daughter would catch the eye of one of the wealthy boys who frequented the club. She was beautiful and smart, and she was going to have an education. In Ginny's eyes, that made her more than good enough to be the wife of some young heir to a fortune. Now *that* would be a secure future, the chance to be well fixed, with never a day's worry about where the next dollar was coming from. But though several boys had asked Willie out, she had turned every one down. When Ginny asked why, Willie always dismissed the boys as "spoiled," or "too rich," or "airheads" as if all these qualities were somehow interchangeable.

"I hate trigonometry," Willie declared vehemently.

"Me, too," her best friend Cheryl agreed. "And I hate Margo Williams and her deb clique."

"Me, too. And I hate brussels sprouts."

"Not fair, Willie . . . no food . . . you know I don't hate anything about food!"

"Okay, I'm sorry . . . we'll start again tomorrow. I have to go now," Willie said, jumping out of the Mustang covertible Malcolm Vinnaver had given his daughter for her sixteenth birthday. "I'd ask you in, but I have a lot to do."

"Gee, Willie," Cheryl pouted, "if you don't keep me company today, I *know* I'm going to cheat on my diet. I bet I go home and eat a pound of chocolate chip cookies before supper. And it'll be your fault if I can't fit into my blue dress Friday night. Bad enough I *have* to go out with Robbie Mason, the drip . . . but if I end up *bursting* out of my dress, too, I'll just die of embarrassment. Do you want *that* on your conscience?"

Willie laughed. She knew Cheryl well enough not to take her theatrics seriously. "Not on my conscience . . . you don't have to eat the cookies, and you don't have to date Robbie Mason. But I do have to do the laundry today, and then I have to study so I can ace the history exam tomorrow."

"Very well, then," Cheryl sighed, "you leave me no choice but to go home to my *miserably* empty house. Adieu . . . "

Willie waved, smiling as the Mustang pulled away. Cheryl was a good kid, even if she was a little wacky. And who could blame her for that, what with her weird father and his parade of wives and girlfriends.

Willie walked up the flagstone path that led to the whitewashed cottage, checked the mailbox and let herself in. The aroma of breakfast coffee and biscuits still lingered in the air. Thanks to Mama's constant efforts, the cottage Webb had found for them looked and smelled like a real home.

The cottage had been part of a rambling estate, which one of Webb's regular clients had bought with a plan to subdivide it into residential parcels. He had persuaded the developer to sell the cottage to Ginny, to take back a mortgage with Webb as co-signer. Though the place had been run down after years of disuse, Willie had fallen in love with it: the beamed ceilings, the stone fireplace, and the sunny kitchen, two cozy bedrooms and a pretty tiled bath. With two attractive gardens, front and back, it was the nicest place Willie had ever lived in. She and Ginny had combed the second-hand shops for old wicker furniture, which they'd spray painted white and fitted with brightly colored cushions they'd sewn by hand.

In fact, everything had worked out better than she could have hoped. They always had enough to eat and money for an occasional movie. And with good friends like Webb and Laura, Willie hardly ever thought about the people they'd left behind in Belle Fourche. Palm Springs High was okay, too, even if Cheryl was the only real friend she'd made there. "Oddballs," someone had called them, and they'd adopted the name proudly, defiantly, setting themselves apart from the other kids.

Though Ginny urged her to "have more fun," or to "splurge on a little something," Willie rarely craved either. Sometimes she felt restless, though she couldn't put her finger on exactly what it was she was missing. Still, when she contrasted her life with Cheryl's she felt lucky by comparison. Cheryl's mother was an Italian actress whose pictures sometimes showed up on late-night television. After the divorce, she'd gone back to her home in Tuscany, assuring Cheryl – who'd been five at the time – that she'd be much better off growing up in America and living with Papa.

"Papa" was a moderately successful Hollywood director at the time, dedicated equally to the advancement of his career and his own pleasures. Though his career had faltered, Malcolm Vinnaver's priorities hadn't altered with the passage of years. To his daughter, he was either cruelly neglectful or inappropriately indulgent. Once, when Willie had been invited for dinner, Malcolm had spent one of his rare evenings at home. He'd complimented Willie lavishly, exclaiming over her exquisite coloring and bone structure. Cheryl had been seized with a fit of coughing. Malcolm had turned a sardonic glance in her direction. "Ah, yes," he remarked, "my Cheryl also has a classic bone structure – her mother's, actually – but Nature and gluttony have seen fit to obscure it with an unsightly camouflage of fat."

Cheryl had bolted from the table, with Willie close behind, wondering why people had children if they were going to treat them so badly.

Though Cheryl always had plenty of pocket money, Willie never envied her. She and Mama loved each other; there was never any doubt about that. They had stuck together and with help from their friends, they'd made a new life.

Willie still worried about her mother. She saw how Ginny looked at Laura and Webb when they were together. She saw the longing and the loneliness in her mother's eyes, and she wanted Ginny to find a nice man for herself. But what would happen if she did? Once, when Willie tried to bring up the subject of divorce, Mama had said they were never to talk about it again.

Willie went into the bathroom, emptied the contents of the hamper on the floor, and sorted the clothes. She scooped up one pile and dumped it into the combination washer-dryer in the small pantry off the kitchen.

Next she took a neatly labeled package of hamburger from the freezer and set it out on the counter to defrost. She washed five medium-size potatoes and sliced them neatly into a casserole dish. A splash of milk, a covering of chopped onions and a few dabs of butter, and the casserole went into the oven to bake slowly.

She shredded and washed a head of lettuce, cut a tomato into four neat sections and returned the salad fixings to the refrigerator. Dinner underway, Willie spread her history notes on the living-room floor. She knew she could do well on tomorrow's test, even without studying. But she had a dream, and simply doing well wasn't the way to make it come true. Willie couldn't remember exactly how the dream had taken shape. But when the kids at school talked about the future, she knew she wanted to be a kind of person that hadn't existed when Ginny was in need. She wanted to be someone who could have saved her mother from the years of struggle and pain.

The counselor at school had agreed that Willie was "scholarship material." But Mrs. Windham raised an eyebrow when she'd asked about law school. "Willa, dear," she said, "don't you think you'd be better off with a more . . . realistic goal? Teaching, for example. Now *that's* a fine career for a woman . . . "

Willie had shaken her head stubbornly. "I don't want to teach, Mrs. Windham. That might be all right for other people, but I want to go to law school."

"Yes, dear," the counselor said patiently. "But perhaps you don't realize what's involved. Law schools don't accept many women. But let's say, for the sake of argument, that you are accepted. Where will you get the money for tuition? And if you somehow manage to do that, what then? Do you have any family connections that will enable you to find work? It's all family in that field – who you know, who your parents know. Have you heard of a single female lawyer in this town? You're a good student, Willa. Why not pursue avenues that are open to you? If not a teaching career . . . perhaps journalism. Your English teachers say you're a talented writer."

"But what's the good of having talent if you can't use it the way you want to?" Willie argued. "I want to help people who've gotten a bad deal. People like my mother. I think I could do that with the law, if I made it work right. I know it won't be easy, but I don't care. I'll do it, Mrs. Windham, I will . . . "

The counselor smiled. "I believe you might at that. All right, Willa, I'll assist you any way I can. Letters of recommendation and so forth. Keep your grades up, and you'll certainly qualify for a scholarship at the state university. As for the rest . . . well, I wish you luck."

Willie had no intention of depending on luck. She would stay at the top of her class. She would find a way around every obstacle Mrs. Windham had mentioned – and anything else that stood in her way.

As she reviewed the Articles of the Constitution, she heard her mother's key in the door. "Hi, baby," Ginny called out. "Smells awfully good in here . . . "

"Hamburgers, potato casserole and salad. I'll start a fire in the grill and we can eat outside."

"I'll do that, honey, you go on with your schoolwork. By

106

the way . . . Laura asked again about your working the extra shift Saturday night. I told her you would."

"That's fine, Mama." Willie went back to her notes until the aroma of barbecued burgers told her that dinner was ready.

They served their simple meal on the wicker and glass table on the back patio, surrounded by the flowers they'd planted together. The quiet was broken only by the chirping and humming of insects. The cool desert air was scented with honeysuckle, the mountains purpled by the last rays of sun against the darkening sky. On evenings like this, Willie was almost happy.

Saturday afternoon was unseasonably warm, but Willie looked cool in her uniform of white shorts and matching shirt. Her long sunstreaked hair was skimmed back into a ponytail, and her face shone from hours of nonstop waitressing. The crowd at the club was larger than usual, swelled by the teenagers home on spring break. Occasionally she glanced longingly at the pool, which was filled with young people splashing and enjoying the sunshine and warm breeze.

Later, she told herself. When the pool closed at six o'clock, she'd have a chance for a swim and a light supper at the snack bar, before it was time to set up for the evening dance. Though Ginny fretted about the extra shifts, Willie didn't mind. There was nothing else she'd rather do, and the extra money would fatten the bank account she'd earmarked for college.

A burst of laughter announced the arrival of Jedd Fontana, along with his usual entourage of buddies and adoring girls. Though she'd neatly categorized Jedd as "just another rich airhead," she couldn't ignore him. Whenever he made one of his holiday or weekend appearances at the club, she reacted as she had the first time she'd seen him. She followed him with her eyes, hoping he'd sit at one of her tables. These past few years his face had lost some of its boyishness, and the classical Spanish features had taken on a refined, aristocratic quality. Taller than

Willie, tightly muscled, he had the grace of a natural athlete. He still wore his black hair long and combed back, accenting the high forehead and the straight aquiline nose. He was taller than Willie now, but he had lost none of his pantherlike grace. But it wasn't simply his physical appeal that magnetized her. It was the spirit she could see in his eyes, deepset coal-black smudges that sparkled or smouldered but were never still. And it was his manner, a way of carrying himself that both infuriated and enchanted her. Life had been good to Jedd Fontana, and he acted at all times with the easy confidence of someone who expects his prayers to be answered. All of them.

When he asked Willie to bring something, when he smiled his appreciation, she felt strange new stirrings. She had a crush on Jedd Fontana, and she'd rather die than admit it. She saw her feelings as a weakness, a disorder, like a cold or a rash. She was ashamed when she eavesdropped in the women's locker room, listening for giggly, whispered mentions of his name, for girls exchanging tidbits of gossip about his current "flame," information that she could use to persuade herself that he was just another bad-news playboy, spoiled and arrogant and lacking in substance.

Her heart gave an unruly thump when Jedd and his friends seated themselves at one of her tables. Quickly she positioned herself behind him. "Will you be ordering lunch?"

"Yes" – he shot her a dazzling smile – "if we can see some menus first."

The girl to his right giggled. "Oh, Jedd, you're too much . . . "

Yeah, Willie thought, too much of everything, as she walked off to get the menus. When she returned, the same girl was arguing heatedly: "But the man was a criminal. My father says he broke the law and he deserves to go to jail . . . "

"Maybe it's a bad law," Jedd said quietly. "As I see it, Dr. Fisher helped girls in trouble . . . instead of forcing them to go over the border to some Mexican clinic – or worse."

Willie stood quietly with her pad poised, listening to the conversation. She had read the story they were discussing in yesterday's paper. The town had been buzzing with news of the doctor's arrest. She had felt sympathy for the man, who charged only nominal fees for the abortions he performed – and she was surprised to hear Jedd defend him.

"Hey, Fontana," one of the boys teased. "How come you're sticking up for the guy? Could be he helps *you* out every once in a while?"

Looking for an excuse to hear more of this conversation, Willie picked up the water pitcher and walked slowly around the table, filling each glass.

"Shut up, Benson," Jedd snapped. "And get your mind out of the gutter for a minute. I'm talking about principles here. I'm saying it isn't fair to put a man in jail because he stands up for what he believes in."

"Watch it! Now look what you've done," Jennifer shrieked at Willie, who had been so enthralled by Jedd's answer that she'd continued pouring water into an already full glass. "Clumsy stupid girl," Jennifer ranted, dabbing furiously at her silk slacks with a napkin.

"I'm sorry," Willie apologized, her face crimson with embarrassment.

"It's okay," Jedd intervened, "accidents happen."

"Yeah, Jen," one of the other girls piped up, "maybe the waitress lost her water because she was too busy trying to find out where to go when she gets into trouble . . . We'd better order lunch before she drowns us all . . . "

Willie stood her ground through the peals of laughter, knowing she couldn't afford the luxury of telling these brats where they could go. When the laughter subsided, she took the orders and hurried to the snack bar, where she slammed the slip down with a bang that shook the counter.

"Whatsa matter, kid?" the counterman asked. "Rough day?"

"Yeah," she said, wishing that someone else could serve lunch to Jedd's crowd, that she could become invisible for the rest of the afternoon.

But no such rescue was in sight, and when the food was ready, she delivered it carefully, not wanting to make a single mistake that would make them notice her again. Once she caught Jedd's eye. He smiled sympathetically and winked, following her movements, though all three girls at the table were vying for his attention.

Neal Corcoran was at his usual place, a table off the far end of the pool. He was one of Ginny's regulars, but she would have noticed him anyway. He was more reserved than most of the other men, though she thought him attractive in an old-fashioned matinee idol kind of way. He was unfailingly polite, almost courtly, and he was rich. Old money, by local standards.

His father, Terrence, had been a good friend to Phil Boyd, the man who, in the 1920s, had helped "sell" Palm Springs as a resort. When the place was incorporated as a city in 1938, Boyd became its first mayor – and soon brought in Terry Corcoran and his brother Kevin as carpenters to build houses. The Corcoran brothers shrewdly used their earnings to buy small desert tracts. Some they sold later, at enormous profits. The property they kept – lots that were now part of Palm Canyon Drive – had become even more valuable. Through prudent investments, mainly in small local radio and television stations in California and the Southwest, Neal Corcoran had multiplied his inheritance many times over.

Gosh, he's elegant, Ginny thought as she approached Corcoran's table. He was wearing white linen pants and a blazer. A white Panama hat. He looked like Ronald Colman. Or John Barrymore.

"Afternoon, Mr. Corcoran. Can I get you some lunch? We have that seafood salad you like today. It looks real good . . . "

"How thoughtful of you to remember, Virginia. I will have the seafood salad, on your recommendation. And a bottle of chablis, please. Your daughter's quite a lovely young woman," he said, as Willie rushed past. "You must be very proud . . . "

"I sure am." Ginny was pleased and flattered by Corcoran's words. Most of the members didn't know – or care – that she had a life away from the club. She returned the gesture. "How's Mrs. Corcoran? I hope she's not sick or anything . . . "

He shook his head, and Ginny could almost feel his sadness. "Mrs. Corcoran is . . . indisposed." He looked into Ginny's eyes. "You really *are* a thoughtful and very remarkable woman. We must have a cup of tea and a nice chat one day . . . "

Did he mean that? Ginny wondered as she walked away. Corcoran wasn't being fresh; he was too much of a gentleman for that. A cup of tea and a chat didn't sound like a pass. He was probably just lonely and unhappy, and Ginny was sure that had to do with his second wife, a diminutive brunette he'd married three months after his first wife's sudden death.

They lunched at the club almost every weekend. Sharon Corcoran rarely smiled, in spite of the expensive clothes she wore, the fine home she lived in, and the attentions her husband lavished on her. She must be weird, Ginny concluded. Or too spoiled to know a good thing. And he must be awfully nice to put up with such an unappreciative woman.

"Aren't you just the luckiest person," Cheryl raved, munching her way through a double cheeseburger. "All this food, whenever you want it." Paying guests weren't allowed in the snack bar kitchen, but Laura had said it was okay for Willie to share her meals with Cheryl.

As Cheryl reached for a frozen candy bar, Willie said sternly, "That's at least a million calories . . . you told me to stop you, remember?"

"That was last week," Cheryl sighed. "When I believed I had a date for the dance tonight. Robbie *claims* he's visiting his aunt for the weekend. Really! Even a drip like him doesn't want to be seen with me. But I do expect a more original excuse . . . "

111

"Maybe it's not an excuse. Why do you do that, Cheryl? Why do you always put yourself down?"

Cheryl raised one eyebrow, her chubby face a parody of Malcolm's expression of disdain. "My shrink says it's obvious . . . but I'll give you one guess."

"Oh, come on, Cheryl . . . so your father is mean to you. Are you going to let that ruin your whole life? Lots of fathers are awful. My father . . . " Her voice caught.

Cheryl stopped chewing. All Willie had ever told her was that her father hadn't lived with them for years. "What about him?" she asked eagerly. "We're supposed to be best friends, and you've never told me *anything* . . . "

My father is a rotten sonofabitch, she said in her mind. But she couldn't speak the words out loud. "I don't want to talk about him. It was a long time ago . . . "

"He vanished – poof – like my mother? Is that it, Willie?"

"Something like that," Willie conceded, just so Cheryl would drop the subject.

"That's just as well, then. When love dies, living together becomes legitimized bondage . . . " Cheryl concluded dramatically.

Willie stared at her friend, struck by the words that seemed strangely true. "Where did you hear that?"

"Malcolm Vinnaver, the world's greatest authority on love. That's what he said when he divorced Sheila. My father takes turns, he's very democratic. First somebody leaves, then he leaves somebody." Cheryl attacked her candy bar with new relish. "I keep waiting for my turn. But all everyone does is leave me."

"I won't leave you," Willie promised. "We're best friends."

Cheryl smiled sadly. "I know you mean that now. But everybody leaves. That's life . . . "

They were interrupted by a male voice. "Excuse me . . . " It was Jedd Fontana.

"Guests aren't allowed in here," Willie said.

"I know. But could I talk to you for a minute, Miss . . . ?"

"My name's Willie. And I'm on my supper break. The club's closed until seven . . . "

112

"I know your name." He smiled. "I found out the first day I saw you here. I just didn't want to get familiar. Come outside with me . . . please?"

Willie glared at Cheryl, who was pinching her leg furiously under the table. "Okay . . . but just for a minute."

"Now . . . what do you want?" she asked when they were outside.

"Can I introduce myself first? I'm Jedd Fontana . . . "

"I know who you are."

He smiled as if he'd known that all along, and she felt like slapping him. "Look," he said softly, "I don't blame you for being mad, Willie. I'm really sorry for what happened before . . . Jennie had no business talking to you like that. I told her she should apologize, but . . . "

"But Jennie doesn't think the hired help is worth an apology . . . "

"Sometimes Jennie doesn't think, period," he said, still smiling. "That's no excuse, but I'd like to make it up to you . . . " He held out a folded ten-dollar bill.

She looked at the bill. Ten dollars was a lot of money, and she needed every penny, but she couldn't let Jedd buy her that way. "No," she said coldly. "If you think money can fix everything, you're no better than your girlfriend. I work here, and that means I have to take a lot of garbage from people like your friends. But my feelings count as much as yours; they're not for sale."

"Good for you," he said, his black eyes sparkling with admiration. "I knew you were beautiful, Willie . . . but now I can see how special you are. I'm sorry I offered you money. I didn't mean what you thought. Let me make it up to you some other way . . . please?"

She had run out of steam. And now she was feeling those strange flutterings she got whenever he was around. She nodded because her throat was tight and she didn't have any more words to throw at him.

"Friends?" He took her hand and squeezed it, and she felt like she was blushing all over. "I'm going back to school tomorrow, but you'll be seeing me again. That's a promise."

*　　　*　　　*

113

"You never told me you knew Jedd Fontana," Cheryl said accusingly, when she caught Willie later.

"I don't. This is the first time he talked to me – if you don't count 'Bring me a club sandwich.' "

"I forgive you then. Now tell," Cheryl leaned forward. "Did he ask you for a date? Oh, Willie, he's such a *magnificent* specimen."

"No, Cheryl, he didn't ask me for a date. What would Jedd Fontana want with me? No, don't answer that . . . I can guess. Case closed."

"Now you're doing it . . . what you told me not to. You're putting yourself down. You're gorgeous and you're smart . . . God, I'd give my soul to be either."

"I'm not putting myself down. I'm just being realistic. We're the oddballs – remember?"

Cheryl smiled sadly. "I never forget. But you . . . you don't have to be. Honest."

"I wait tables here. That doesn't exactly make me part of the jet set."

"It isn't about money, Willie. Look at me. I'm not exactly poor. And Malcolm used to be famous. But I'll always be an oddball. You're different. You have something special. Even *Malcolm* says so. Any boy would want you. Including Jedd Fontana."

7

You can see forever from here, Willie thought, looking down at the dazzling panorama that unfolded before her. But where does it all go? she wondered, shielding her eyes against the brilliant morning sun, trying to see past the miles of desert. All around her, the granite mountains were thick with towering evergreens and frosted with a deep layer of snow.

"Oh, Webb, it's beautiful," she said. "Thank you, thank you for bringing us here. This is the best Christmas present."

114

"Easy, too, " he smiled. "Last night, when you said it wasn't like Christmas without snow, I put in a call to Santa Claus. And he said: 'Webb Foley, you take those favorite girls of yours up the mountain, pronto.' Mother Nature did the rest."

"It's gorgeous," Ginny agreed. "But I thought I'd die coming up in that cable car. You didn't tell me it was going to be scary . . . "

"I wasn't scared," Willie said. "It was wonderful . . . riding straight up to the sky . . . "

"Almost six thousand feet up," Webb said. "I watched the crews building this tramway a few years back in '62 . . . they brought the cables up by helicopter . . . now that was a sight—"

"I hate to spoil your fun," Laura interrupted, "but I'm freezing. Do you suppose we could get to our Christmas dinner – and the presents?"

"That's right," Ginny said. "Gosh, we already have so much . . . Webb, you and Laura, you've been so good to us . . . " Her eyes misted, and she faltered. "I don't know what we would've done without you . . . "

"Same here," Webb said gruffly. "Never had any family till you came along . . . "

The cottage smelled of the holidays – ham glazed with fruit sauce and Ginny's special pound cake that took a half pound of butter and six eggs. Outside, the sun was shining and the temperature was seventy degrees, just right for hibiscus and honeysuckle, and a dramatic contrast to the little bit of winter they'd sampled just half an hour away.

Inside, the living room was festive with chains made of colored paper and the litter of discarded Christmas wrappings. In the center stood the Scotch pine Webb had brought on Christmas Eve, just as he'd done on their first holiday together, when he'd promised "a real tree, because real people like you deserve it." It twinkled with tiny white lights and red ribbons and candy canes, throwing off a crisp, woodsy fragrance.

Ginny was exclaiming over her present from Willie: a

necklace of rhinestone baguettes, cut to look like diamonds. "Oh, honey, it's gorgeous. But this must have cost a fortune . . . you shouldn't have . . . "

Willie had spent twenty-five dollars of her savings on the necklace, and her only regret was that the stones were paste. "Someday I'll get you real ones," she promised. "I will . . . "

"Open yours now, honey, I'm dying to see if you like it." Ginny had spent long hours late at night making the white sheer wool dress for her daughter.

Willie opened the package carefully, so that the paper and ribbon might be re-used. The dress was lovely, simpler and far more restrained than Ginny's usual creations. Willie was touched that her mother had instinctively known what would suit her. "It's beautiful . . . thank you, Mama." She threw her arms around Ginny and kissed her.

Just then the doorbell rang. It was a delivery boy carrying a long white box. Willie watched as her mother opened it, revealing a dozen red roses. "Where did they come from?"

Ginny read the card aloud: "Merry Christmas to a lovely lady. May I have the pleasure of your company for New Year's Eve?" It was signed "Neal Corcoran."

"Who's he?" Willie asked. Roses are serious flowers, and she had never heard mention of any man.

"Someone from the club . . . he seems real nice."

"Is he married?" Willie frowned. She had seen enough of club flirtations to be suspicious.

"His wife left him awhile back. New Year's Eve . . . gosh . . . wouldn't that be swell? Look, everybody, look what I got." Ginny showed off her flowers proudly. "Nobody ever sent me roses before."

"Good for you," Laura said. "Anything we should know about?"

"They're from Neal Corcoran . . . he wants me to go out with him on New Year's Eve. Do you think it would be okay, Laura? I mean, him being a member at the club and all?"

Laura started to repeat her rule about fraternizing with

the guests, but Ginny looked so pleased, and heaven knows she didn't have much of a social life . . .

"How well do you know this guy?" Webb interrupted. The women looked at him curiously, for he wasn't one to interfere.

"I . . . I talk to him on Saturdays. Once we had coffee together after the club closed. He never gets fresh, and he's . . . you know, kinda respectful. What's the matter, Webb? Don't you think I should go?" she asked, almost pleading.

His answer was a while in coming. "You have a good time," he said finally. "Just be careful . . . I hear that divorce of his was really messy. And promise you'll talk to me if anything serious develops . . . "

"I promise," Ginny agreed cheerfully, relieved that the matter was settled.

But Willie wasn't so sure. Ginny looked so happy about the flowers and the date. But how could she go out with a man when she was still married? There had to be a way to get her freedom. There just had to be . . . But before she could reflect on this latest development, Webb announced he had to leave.

"So soon?" Ginny protested. "But why?"

"Business," he answered.

"On Christmas Day? What kind of business?"

Before he could answer, Laura cut in heatedly, as if she'd argued the issue before, "Sam Fontana's business, that's what. He's got Webb flying God-knows-what to Mexico all hours of the day and night. I don't like it, Webb, I don't like it one bit. At least if you knew what you were doing—"

"Pay's good," Webb cut in. "I don't get good money to ask questions. I mind my own business, and that's why customers know they can trust Webb Foley." He gave Laura a reproving look that said the subject was closed.

But Willie's heart lurched at the mention of the name Fontana, and suddenly she remembered the first time she'd seen Jedd – and his mysterious father, surrounded by wealthy and powerful people who had come to pay homage to Sam.

Why was Laura so upset about Webb working for Sam?

117

Willie wondered. Did she believe that Sam was doing something wrong?

Willie gave Webb a hug and thanked him for making their Christmas so special. Then she went into the kitchen to wash the dishes and do some quiet thinking while Laura and Mama chatted in the living room.

Suddenly she heard tapping on the back door. It was Cheryl. "Merry Christmas," she said, handing Willie a box of candy.

"Merry Christmas," Willie responded quietly, noticing her friend's red and swollen eyes. She didn't ask why Cheryl was here, when she was supposed to be spending the day in Los Angeles with her father. "Would you like some cake? I can fix you a plate of ham if you're hungry . . . "

Cheryl shook her head and slumped into a kitchen chair. "He did it again, Willie. He called yesterday to wish me a Merry Christmas and to say he wasn't coming home. Business, he said," she added bitterly.

"I'm sorry." Willie put an arm around her friend's shoulder. "I wish you'd called me. You could have spent Christmas Eve with us . . . "

"I was too ashamed," Cheryl said, her face a study in loneliness and sadness. "I don't know why I let him surprise me. I should know by now that he doesn't care about me . . . "

Willie wanted to say Cheryl was wrong, but in truth, she doubted that Malcolm cared, either about his daughter or anyone else. "Come inside," she coaxed. "You can share my Christmas. After all, oddballs have to stick together . . . "

The club was decked out in full holiday regalia for the annual New Year's Eve gala – silver wreaths and artificial white trees glittering with red and green balls. The guests sparkled and glittered, too, as they danced to the music that would go on until dawn.

Willie had volunteered to work the late shift for double her usual wages. She had nothing special to do, and though she wouldn't admit it, she hoped for the chance to see Jedd again. It had been such a long time. He'd probably

118

forgotten their brief conversation, but she remembered every word, every gesture. As the hours passed, her disappointment grew. At least Mama was out tonight, dancing and having a good time.

Ginny had been so excited as she'd dressed for her first real date since high school. "Neal's gonna take me to the Racquet Club . . . isn't that the greatest? I thought he was kidding when he said I could pick any place I wanted. He didn't bat an eye when I said 'the Racquet Club.' Just imagine, Willie . . . *me* at a place like that. Spencer Tracy's gonna be there, and Henry Fonda and . . . "

She had jumped up and down like a child when Corcoran had arrived in his black Jaguar. He'd presented Ginny with a magnificent cluster of orchids. When she'd wondered out loud how to wear them, he'd explained smoothly: "They're for tomorrow, so you'll remember our time together. You don't need any adornments tonight, Virginia . . . you look ravishing."

He said their home was "charming," and he'd been polite to Willie. "I promise to have your mother home at a sensible hour," he smiled graciously.

Willie hadn't smiled back. There was something about him she didn't like, something she couldn't put her finger on. Still, Mama was probably having fun, and that was better than being here, filling drink orders and cleaning ashtrays.

As she ran back and forth to the bar, she kept scanning the room, willing every face to be Jedd's. At 11.45, he walked in, a beautiful young woman at his side. Her heart sank, but a moment later her spirits soared. The young woman was his sister, Nina.

Willie kept looking across the room. Over here, she repeated silently, over here. Look at me.

And then he did. Their eyes locked, just as they had the first time Willie had seen him. He smiled, said something to his sister, and made his way through the crowd. "Hello," he said.

"Hello, yourself."

"Dance with me."

119

"I can't . . . I'm working . . . "

"Just one dance . . . outside." He took her hand and led her into the cool starry night. "It's good to see you again," he said huskily.

"I didn't think you were coming," she blurted out, then blushed at what she'd admitted.

"I wasn't," he laughed. "There's a party at the house, but my sister wanted to meet some friends here. Her boyfriend's out of town, and I volunteered to bring her."

"What about you?" she asked. "Don't tell me *you* didn't have a date?"

He laughed again. "Let's just say you're my date . . ." He gathered her close, and she forgot that she was wearing a waiter's jacket and a serviceable black skirt, as they moved together to the music.

Suddenly the orchestra stopped and struck up "Auld Lang Syne," and the sound of horns and noisemakers surrounded them. "Happy New Year," he said. And before she could answer, he kissed her. One heart-stopping kiss that left her breathless and dizzy and hungry for more.

"I . . . I'd better get back to work," she said, moving away, frightened by the intensity of her own feelings.

"Not so fast." He held her wrist and drew her back to him, their eyes level, and she could feel his warm breath on her face. "We have some unfinished business . . . remember? I want you to come to Sunday brunch at my house, Willie. Say yes."

That's crazy, she thought. Her crush on Jedd was bad enough, but to go out with him when there were so many good reasons not to . . . "

"Yes," she said, because while she was looking into those coal black eyes, she lost the power to say "no."

A short distance away, Virginia Dellahaye had her hand kissed for the first time. "Happy New Year," Corcoran said, pressing her fingers to his lips. "I hope this is the first of many celebrations . . . "

"Gosh . . . thanks." Ginny could hardly believe her ears. Neal was saying he wanted to see her again. "I'm having a really swell time. I never thought I'd see the inside of this place."

Corcoran chuckled. "You're so refreshing, Virginia . . . so delightfully refreshing. It will be my pleasure to show you many new places . . . and new experiences . . . "

"Look . . . oh, look . . . isn't that Lucille Ball? Do you suppose . . . I mean, would it be all right if I asked for an autograph?"

"I have a better idea." Corcoran took Ginny by the hand and walked her across the crowded room. A moment later, he was introducing her to the glamorous movie star.

"I'm thrilled to meet you, Miss Ball," she said breathlessly. "I watch your television show all the time . . . "

"Tell that to my sponsor, and I'll buy you a drink," Lucy wisecracked. "Would you like to join us?"

Ginny was dying to sit down at the star's table, but Neal said: "Another time, Lucy, thank you. I want Virginia all to myself."

Though she was disappointed, Ginny was flattered by Neal's words. She was even more flattered when he gave the orchestra leader ten dollars and asked him to play "I Only Have Eyes for You." He was a smooth dancer, and Ginny felt as if she was living one of her made-up stories, only better.

"Have you ever been to Paris?" he murmured against her ear.

"No," she answered. "I haven't been anywhere, except . . . "

"It's cold in Paris now, but it's lovely in the spring. You'd like it, I think . . . "

Did he mean he wanted to take her? she wondered. But she was still married to Perry. Everything was happening so fast. Too fast. She felt lightheaded with champagne and excitement, but she knew she'd have to do something about a divorce. And soon.

"Did you have a nice time, Mama?" Willie sat cross-legged on Ginny's bed, sharing the breakfast she'd made for her mother.

121

"It was wonderful," Ginny sighed. "We danced and we drank champagne. Neal introduced me to Lucille Ball . . . can you imagine that? Me, with all those rich people. You know, Neal's not stuck up at all. He acted like I was one of them. And guess what? He kissed my hand, just like in the movies. He's gonna call me again, real soon, he said . . . "

"But Mama . . . if you like this man, we have to get you a divorce . . . "

"I know," Ginny sighed. "I know . . . I've been thinking about that ever since I woke up. I'm gonna call your grandfather soon . . . maybe things cooled down in Belle Fourche . . . How about you, honey . . . are you tired? I felt real bad about having a good time while you were working so hard."

"Don't feel bad, Mama. I'm not tired. And I'm going out on Sunday . . . with Jedd Fontana."

"Wow!" Ginny sat up straight, her own adventures forgotten in the thrill of hearing the Fontana name. This was exactly what she'd always wanted for Willie. A rich boyfriend. Security. "When did this happen? Honestly, honey, sometimes you're so close-mouthed . . . even with your own mother . . . "

"He just asked me last night. There's not much to tell," she said, though she could have gone on about how it felt when his breath whispered against her cheek. Or how his mouth twitched when he was just about to smile.

"I'll bet there is . . . I've seen that boy look at you. I knew he was interested. Play your cards right, honey . . . Jedd Fontana's a real catch . . . "

"Oh, *Mama* . . . " Willie hated it when her mother talked like that, making it sound like the most important thing in the world was to "catch" some man. She had seen the wedding picture that Ginny kept at the bottom of her dresser drawer. She had seen the happiness on her mother's face – and on her father's as well. Nothing she'd seen or heard told how or why that kind of happiness disappeared, leaving anger and bitterness in its place. And until she had the answers, Willie wasn't about to believe that a man was the biggest prize that life had to offer.

When Sunday came, she let Ginny fuss over her clothes and her hair. She told herself it was for Mama's sake that she was wearing the new dress – and the eye makeup. But when she looked in the mirror, she was glad that she looked as good as any of the girls Jedd brought to the club. "He'll sit up and take notice," Ginny predicted.

And Jedd did notice. "You're beautiful," he said, without sounding like a jerk. He was nice to Mama, too, without being patronizing or condescending.

"Wait'll you meet my father," he said, helping her into his white sports car. "He's a great guy."

"I've seen him a couple of times at the club . . . "

"Pop doesn't go there much. He's kind of . . . private. He doesn't like crowds, except at the house."

"Oh." In spite of herself, Willie wanted Jedd's family to like her. She thought they were special, not because they were rich, but because they seemed so solid and close. The rich part bothered her. It put Jedd in another world, made him the kind of person who didn't have to worry about saving enough money for a state college.

Jedd knew he'd be welcome at any college and in any career he chose. That made him suspect. Willie believed that anyone who had those kinds of choices without lifting a finger suffered serious character defects. She had to believe that, for if it weren't true, then life would be unbearably unfair.

The Fontana mansion was quiet outside, but as she and Jedd came through the front door, she heard the sounds of a large family. In the front entrance hall, reaching all the way up to the double-height ceiling, was an enormous Douglas fir, blazing with colored lights and laden with ornaments, some obviously expensive, others the work of childish hands.

"See that one?" Jedd laughingly pointed to a felt Santa with button eyes and a cotton puff beard. "A real work of art – right? I made it when I was six, and I haven't topped it since."

"It's very nice," Willie said politely, almost resenting Jedd for being so . . . normal.

"Hey, everybody," he called out, leading her into a huge family room.

Sam Fontana was seated in an oversize armchair in front of a big-screen television, watching a football game. He reminded Willie of a king, with all his children and their friends clustered in small groups around him.

"Pop, this is my friend, Willie Dellahaye . . . "

Sam extended his hand without rising. Like a king. His dark eyes, so much like Jedd's, but deeper and more piercing, appraised Willie. "Welcome to our home," he said, then resumed watching the game.

Jedd introduced her to the rest of his family. "Now let's get something to eat," he said, "Football Sundays are casual, so we'll have to help ourselves."

Jedd's idea of "casual" was a mammoth feast laid out on a dining table that seemed to stretch for miles. Silver warming trays held scrambled eggs and bacon and ham and sausage. Smoked salmon, sliced paper thin, was arranged on large oval platters. Willie counted at least seven different kinds of bread and muffins and sweet rolls in heaping baskets. Following Jedd's lead, she picked up a gold-bordered plate and some silverware wrapped in a white embroidered napkin – and tried to choose.

"Would you like a Mimosa?" He offered a pitcher filled with orange juice and champagne. "Or maybe you'd rather have a plain juice . . . "

"I've had champagne before," she said stiffly. "Lots of times."

"Okay." A smile tugged at the corner of his mouth, as he filled a crystal goblet for her.

They carried their meal back to the family room. As Willie ate, she noticed that conversation rose and fell according to Sam. As long as he was absorbed in the game, no one spoke. But when he shouted "way to go" or "damn, that was stupid," the talk and laughter resumed.

When half-time came around, all eyes were on Sam as he got up from his easy chair and sat down next to Willie and

Jedd. "You look familiar," he said to her. "Do I know you?"

"I work at the club, part-time and after school," she said, waiting for a reaction that would tell her she wasn't really welcome in this house.

But Sam simply nodded, satisfied that he'd placed her. "Your family lives around here?"

"It's just my mother and me . . . we live near Wayne Road."

"Your father . . . he passed away?"

She hesitated, then chose the lie that was closest to the truth. "My parents are divorced."

This time she saw the bushy brows come together in a frown. A moment later, it was gone. "Must be hard for the two of you, on your own."

"We manage." Though she cared what Sam thought of her, she wasn't willing to be pitied.

"You're a beautiful young lady," he said. "I suppose you're looking forward to getting married . . . "

"I'm looking forward to college."

He nodded again. "An education . . . that's a good thing. My Jedd goes to Brown University . . . like the Rockefellers. Summers, he works for me. I expect great things from my boy."

Willie smiled politely. Was Sam trying to tell her that Jedd – his crown prince – was too good for her?

"What about you?" he asked. "Do you have ambitions?"

"I want to go to law school."

"No," he responded, as if she'd asked his permission. "That's no job for a woman."

"Why not?" she challenged him, though she knew at the moment she said it that taking on Sam Fontana at anything, even on a "football Sunday," was stepping into an arena where she was overmatched.

"It's a rough-and-tumble business. Like that football game. It takes strong men to win."

"It takes a lot more than physical strength to win . . . even in football," she argued. She knew it was foolish, that she might be wrecking her friendship with Jedd . . . but

125

there was something about Sam that reminded her of the men in Belle Fourche, something that drove her to speak out. "It takes brains and determination, and I have those . . . "

"So you think you're pretty strong-minded?" he said with a smile.

"Yes, I do. What's more, I think the law needs women, to represent the needs of women. I think if we're going to—"

"I wish you luck in your chosen career." The smile was gone. Sam got up and returned to his chair, and Willie knew the battle was lost.

"Your father doesn't like me," she said to Jedd, as they were driving home in his car.

"That's silly," he said lightly, though he had seen the look on Sam's face when Willie had talked back. "He doesn't even know you. He just has strong opinions."

"Meaning no one else has a right to any?" she snapped. In spite of all the surface politeness, Willie had felt uncomfortable and unwanted at the Fontana house. She had been right to believe she wouldn't fit in with Jedd's world, but being right just made her more miserable.

"I didn't say that, Willie. Why do you jump on people that way? It's what you did with Pop. All I meant was that he's used to a little more respect than you showed him . . . "

"Respect?" Willie's voice rose with indignation. "Is that what you call it? Respect goes two ways, Jedd . . . " she went on and on, just as she had with Sam. We're fighting, she thought, and we hardly know each other, but she couldn't stop until her thoughts had poured out of her in a rush of words.

Jedd didn't speak for a long time. "You're a different kind of girl, Willie Dellahaye," he said finally, "but I think I like you anyway."

"Thanks a heap," she said sarcastically. "I suppose that means . . . "

"It means I like you, period. I just don't know what we'll do about that."

His easy confidence irritated and bedeviled her. As far as Willie was concerned, this date had been a disaster, yet

126

here was Jedd, using the word "we," just because he'd decided to like her. Big deal.

But when they arrived at her house, she lingered in the car a moment longer than she'd meant to. Long enough for Jedd to kiss her lightly on the mouth, to stroke her cheek. "See you," he said, just before he drove away.

She walked inside, her fingers pressed against the place where he had touched her, holding the warmth of him close to her.

She jumped, startled and embarrassed when she saw her mother standing at the window.

"Hi, baby . . . tell me all about it," Ginny said eagerly.

"There's nothing to tell. We had brunch, we watched a football game, and we came home."

"Nothing to tell? You got to meet the Fontana family on your first date, and you call that nothing? Honey, when a boy introduces you to his folks, that's serious."

"His folks don't think I'm good enough. At least his father doesn't, and that's all that counts in that family . . ."

"What? Why that stuck-up so-and-so! What did he say to you? I'll go over there and give him a piece of my mind!" For years Ginny had accepted second-class treatment for herself, but she'd do anything to make sure Willie got better than that.

"It's okay, Mama," Willie lied. "I wouldn't want to go out with him anyway."

When Jedd returned home, he found his father seated in his favourite armchair, smoking a cigar. The family room was empty, the television set turned off. Without being told, Jedd took the seat nearest his father and waited.

Sam got right to the point. "This new girl . . . what is she to you?"

"We're friends . . . "

"That's no answer, boy. When a man wants a friend, he goes to another man. From a woman, you want a good time or you want something serious. This girl . . . she's not just a good time. Am I right?"

"Yes, Pop, but . . . "

"She's not for you," Sam said sharply. Then, more softly: "I was young, too. I can see why you like her. She's beautiful and smart and she's got spirit. But she's not for you."

"Why, Pop?" Jedd rarely challenged his father. But then Sam had never said "no" to anything he really wanted, and right now Jedd wanted the right to see Willie again. "Is it because her family doesn't have money?"

Sam's expression darkened, and Jedd was afraid he'd gone too far. "That's stupid, boy. You know me better than that. Money counts. Plenty. But I don't hold being poor against anybody. A man needs a woman to stand behind him and to raise his children. This girl wasn't raised the right way . . . she doesn't know how to be a wife to a Fontana."

"That's not fair," Jedd persisted. "You're blaming Willie for something her parents did."

"Did I ever tell you life was fair? Only losers complain about that. I raised you to be a winner. You spend time with this girl now, you're going up against your father. I'm telling you she isn't right for you. Do you understand my meaning?"

"I understand." Jedd knew better than to argue any further. He had seen grown men, powerful men, back down when his father said "no." He only wished Willie could have done the same.

8

The sound of organ music filled the air as Willie sat silently and watched her mother commit bigamy. The wedding was taking place in the garden of Corcoran's estate, not in a church. The man performing the ceremony was a municipal judge, not an ordained minister. But to Willie it seemed a kind of sacrilege all the same.

I'm part of it, too, she thought, as she stood stiff and

128

uncomfortable in her organza dress, feeling more like an accomplice than a maid of honor. It was the best she could do, and she hated it – not being able to find a way for her mother to marry without defying the laws of religion and society.

When Neal had started turning up at the house regularly, bringing her gifts and flowery compliments, Willie had gone to the city library to search for clues, for something that would show her how to save her mother from committing a crime. Hours of fruitless research only convinced her that she was out of her depth, just as she'd been back in Belle Fourche. Passion and determination weren't enough. What she needed was a legal library – and the training to use it. But Ginny's chance for happiness would not wait.

As Ginny walked solemnly toward her intended groom, Willie searched her mother's face for signs of doubt, but found none. As a bride, she looked radiantly beautiful, as fair and fragile as a camellia in the peach-colored dress Neal had had flown in from Paris. Around her neck was a strand of lustrous matched pearls, his gift on their wedding day. Finally, after all the hard years, Ginny had everything she'd dreamed of, everything Willie wanted for her. But not like this, Willie thought, not like this.

"Dearly beloved," the judge intoned, "we are gathered today to unite this man and this woman . . . "

The words sounded accusingly familiar to Ginny, reminding her of the day she had promised herself to Perry, a pledge by which she was still bound. She had wanted to do this right. God knows she had tried.

Right at the beginning, she'd called her father, asking if the law had forgotten about her flight from South Dakota. But her thin thread of a hope had broken when he'd said her case was far from forgotten, that there was still an outstanding warrant for her arrest. He'd added that even after all this time, scarcely a week went by that Perry didn't get drunk in some saloon and curse Ginny out for running away and escaping his vengeance. She had hung up quickly when her father started asking questions about where she was and what she'd been doing.

After Neal had proposed, she'd had another idea. Money could fix almost anything, she believed, and a rich man's lawyer might fix the mess she'd left back home. She'd called and made an appointment with Greg McKenzie, one of the attorneys who frequented the club. A day later, Neal had said casually: "I understand you're seeing Greg next week . . . nothing serious, I hope?" She had canceled the appointment. She couldn't risk having her secret come out. She couldn't risk this chance. Neal was the first man who had approached her with serious intentions, and there might not be another.

Willie was a young woman now, and it was time she had better than a life of second-best and making do. She deserved to go to a good college, and she deserved a boy like Jedd Fontana.

Ginny only vaguely understood the urgency of her daughter's dream of law school, but she did understand Willie's pain when Jedd had called to say he wouldn't be seeing her for a while. "I told you – his father doesn't approve," Willie had announced grimly – and then refused to say another word. Ginny's heart had ached over the disappointment her daughter had tried to hide. And she had made up her mind to marry Neal, no matter what.

"If there be anyone present who can give just cause why this man and this woman may not be joined in lawful matrimony, let him speak now . . . "

I do, Ginny thought, I do. Her eyes met Willie's for a guilty instant. Quickly she looked away, at Laura, her lone bridesmaid – and remembered another broken promise, the one she'd made to Webb. She'd meant to keep that one, to let him know if the relationship with Neal became serious. She had called him the very night Neal first mentioned marriage. "Webb just left," Laura had said sleepily. "He's flying some rock-and-roll star to Vegas. He'll be back tomorrow."

But the next morning, as she'd been getting ready for work, she heard a news bulletin on the radio. "This just in

130

". . . singer Little Bobby Shaftoe is dead. Rescuers report that there were no survivors in the wreckage of the small plane that was carrying Shaftoe from Las Vegas to Palm Springs. Also dead in the crash is veteran pilot, Webb Foley. Authorities say that Foley radioed a 'Mayday' signal shortly before the plane went down in the San Andreas Canyon. An investigation is underway . . . "

The shock of losing Webb had all but pushed his warning from Ginny's mind. Strangely enough, it had been his death that had moved the wedding plans along with breathtaking speed. When Laura had been immobilized by shock and grief, Neal had insisted on taking care of the "arrangements." He had gone on making arrangements for Ginny ever since.

He had selected her bridal gown from sketches sent from Paris, and her trousseau during a whirlwind shopping trip in Beverly Hills. "Less is more," he'd said, very politely, each time she reached for the ruffles and sequins she favored. He'd taken her to Elizabeth Arden for a haircut and makeup lesson. And then he reminded her that she'd have to quit her job at the club. She'd agreed gladly.

In fact, she'd gotten into the habit of agreeing to everything Neal wanted. He never said "no" or "don't" straight out. He wrapped his "nos" in fancy words that made her feel funny and a little dumb, like she'd done something wrong without even knowing it. It was easier just to let him make all the decisions. She'd learned her lesson about what happened when you didn't let a man have his way.

" . . . I now pronounce you man and wife. You may kiss the bride."

"Now you belong to me," Neal said, taking her lips in a decorous kiss scented with peppermint. A second later, the organist reprised "Here Comes the Bride," and she was being showered with rice and confetti.

"All the best to you, Ginny." Laura was the first to offer her good wishes.

"Thanks – for everything. I hope this wasn't too hard for you, I mean being in the wedding and all . . . " Ginny looked anxiously at the redhead's tiny face, pale in spite of the makeup, and shadowed under the eyes.

Laura's lower lip trembled. "Webb would've wanted me to be here with you. He always wanted the best for you and Willie."

Ginny hugged her friend, feeling an unexpected tug of nostalgia. "I'm gonna miss seeing you at the club every day, Laura. I hope you'll come visit me every chance you get."

Laura looked around, at the big house and the carefully land-scaped grounds. "I expect you'll be pretty busy taking care of all this . . . "

"Oh . . . I don't know. Neal's kind of particular about how things are done."

Once, Ginny had asked her husband-to-be about his favorite dishes, so she might prepare them after they were married. "Dear heart," he'd answered, "I have a cook and three in help to keep the house and grounds in good order. But I'm sure we can find something suitable to fill your days."

Ginny moved through the ranks of wedding guests – most of whom were Neal's business associates – shaking hands and exchanging polite kisses. Under different circumstances, she would have preferred a huge affair, so that Willie might meet Palm Springs society as Neal Corcoran's stepdaughter. But a big society "do" that might make the papers outside of Palm Springs was much too dangerous. Timidly, she had asked Neal if they could keep it "small and you know, kinda tasteful." She had almost fainted with relief when he'd not only agreed, but also complimented her in that funny way of his. "I applaud your desire for restraint, Virginia dear. A man in my position . . . a third marriage would seem to call for a certain . . . understatement."

Though it was small, the wedding was lavish and luxurious beyond anything she had known before. Flowers enough to fill a greenhouse, pretty white chairs trimmed with ribbons set out in the garden, a real society orchestra, a staff of waiters, ready to serve the cases of French champagne and cute little canapés, a wedding supper prepared by Palm Springs's finest caterer.

132

But what mattered most to Ginny was that she was now mistress of this great rambling Spanish-style house, with its swimming pool and acres of grounds. She had a rich and influential husband. A stepfather for Willie, one who could give her the right kind of start in life. And he was good-looking, she reminded herself, as she watched him smoothly striding toward Willie, who sat alone on the edge of the patio, under the shade of a dogwood tree.

"May I have the pleasure of a dance with my new daughter?" Neal bowed, extending a manicured hand to Willie. She took it for Ginny's sake. It would have been selfish to tell her mother that something about Neal – underneath all those good manners – made her skin crawl. As she allowed him to lead her around the floor, she could smell the cloying muskiness of his cologne.

She caught a glimpse of Cheryl, who gave a jaunty thumbs-up salute as Willie danced by. Poor Cheryl. She looked fatter and dowdier than usual, after a failed attempt at straightening her frizzy brown hair, and a crash diet that had added six more pounds to her more than ample body. At her side was Robbie Mason, who wasn't at all bad looking in a suit and tie, though Cheryl persisted in calling him a jerk. A comment on herself, Willie thought, thanks to Malcolm.

"You've grown strikingly lovely, Willa," Neal murmured.

"Thank you."

"I suppose it will be my responsibility now to ward off armies of young men?"

"What? . . . Oh." Willie didn't like this assumption at all. She'd gotten used to the way things had always been, with her and Mama looking out for each other. If she'd cared about the luxuries Neal would provide, she might have felt he was owed a voice in her life. But she didn't. Still, she'd humor him for Mama's sake. "I don't have much to do with young men."

"Really?" He chuckled. "No doubt that will change, and soon, unless I miss my guess. There's nothing quite like the innocent sensuality of young love . . . "

Willie could hardly wait for the music to stop, for the opportunity to bolt from Neal's polite but stifling arms, and to join Cheryl, who was busy filling a plate with canapés.

"Isn't this all too beautiful for words?" Cheryl popped a shrimp into her mouth, a dreamy expression on her face. Her eyes were misty, almost reverential as they took in the wedding festivities.

"I guess." Willie couldn't manage wholehearted agreement. What's more, she couldn't understand why her friend had gone so sappy when she'd heard about the wedding. Cheryl, of all people.

"Your mother looks gorgeous," Cheryl said, adding wistfully, "and she certainly has the figure for that dress."

But Willie wasn't looking at the dress. She was watching Neal dance with his bride, noticing how his fingers slid possessively down Ginny's back. She knew all about sex, but she found it hard to imagine that her mother would welcome Neal's touches, his caresses. Though she couldn't bring herself to picture them in a carnal embrace, she understood that there was something about a man that Ginny seemed to need.

In the time that Neal had become her declared "boyfriend," it was as if Ginny had become part of a desirable club, the community of women who had men. Her step became more confident, her laughter more wholehearted. It helped, of course, that he was rich and important, a "catch" by Ginny's standards. But Willie believed it was his maleness, as much as his money, that made her mother seem more complete. That was an idea she couldn't welcome, but she accepted it as one more way she and Ginny were different.

"To my bride, Virginia," Neal toasted. "May she always be as fresh and lovely as she is today."

Ginny glowed in the light of his words, in the applause and attention of people she hardly knew. Important people, and now she would be one of them.

"Happy, my dear?" Neal asked solicitously.

"I can hardly believe it," she answered truthfully.

"Perhaps a little more champagne will convince you."

"Gosh, maybe I'd better not," she giggled. "I'm already kinda tipsy."

"Perhaps this is a good time to be tipsy," he said, his baritone voice layered with meaning. "We should be leaving soon . . . "

Ginny blushed like a teenager at this suggestion of what was to come. A few chaste kisses aside, Neal had hardly touched her at all. "All in good time," he'd said once, in answer to her questioning eyes. Still, she had started to wonder about a fiancé who never got fresh. If he hadn't been married twice before, she'd have worried he was queer. All that quiet reserve, with never a show of either passion or temper – it was hard and a little embarrassing to imagine honeymoon nights and "company manners" all at the same time.

"I think it's time to dispense with your bouquet, Virginia," Neal reminded her. "If you insist . . . "

She had insisted. Neal had vetoed the ritual throwing of the bridal garter as "inappropriate," but she wanted some of the fun of a regular wedding, even if she had married into society. She stepped into the center of the patio dance floor, and as the orchestra struck up a fanfare, she sent her bouquet of orchids and baby's breath sailing in a graceful arc that almost ended at Willie's fingertips. Instinctively Willie flicked it away. The flowers ricocheted squarely onto Cheryl's luxurious bosom, prompting a yelp of excitement.

"That means I'm next," Cheryl crowed triumphantly, casting a meaningful look in Robbie's direction.

"Good luck to you," Willie said dryly. She had no interest in catching a bouquet or anything remotely bridal.

In the master bedroom of Neal's home – her home now – Willie performed her final duties as maid of honor, helping Ginny change into her beige linen travel suit. In a little while, Ginny would be on her way to Los Angeles, to the Beverly Hills Hotel, where she and Neal would spend the first night of their honeymoon. Tomorrow they'd fly to Paris, for a week at the Georges V hotel. Then they'd drive to Juan-les-Pins, for a month in an oceanfront villa owned by one of Neal's friends.

For weeks, Ginny had been showing off pictures of the place, exclaiming over its graceful balconies overlooking the sea, the staff in attendance, the glamorous neighbors – an exiled Turkish princess and a French film star. Neither she nor Willie had mentioned the fact that this would be the first time they'd ever been separated.

But now, as Willie undid the pearl buttons of the bridal dress, Ginny said softly, "I'm gonna miss you, honey . . .I wish you were coming, too."

"I'll miss you, too, Mama. But I want you to have a good time. Just send me some postcards and let me know you're okay."

"You'll be okay, too, won't you, here in Neal's house – I mean our house?" Ginny asked anxiously.

"I'll be okay." Willie hadn't wanted to move in until Ginny came back from France, but Neal had insisted. Together they had packed their belongings and closed the little cottage that had sheltered them. Willie rarely cried – with a mother who cried so often, she felt the need to be always strong and in control. But as they said "good-bye" to the house and prepared for yet another new life, there was a lump in Willie's throat and a sadness in her heart.

Now, as she helped her mother out of her dress, she felt a rush of embarrassment. Ginny was wearing a new silk slip, part of the collection of underwear she'd taken to wearing lately, as if in rehearsal for her married life. "Mama," she began tentatively, "this is what you want, isn't it? You do love Neal, don't you?"

Did she? Ginny asked herself. She wasn't sure what that meant anymore. Back in Belle Fourche High School, whispering and giggling with her girlfriends, she thought she knew all about love. The excitement when Perry smiled at her, the dizzying warmth of his touch. That had been the love of her life – and look how that had turned out. With Neal it was different. He treated her like a lady, and that would have to be good enough. She took Willie's hand and sat down with her on the bed. "Neal's gonna give us a good

136

life, honey. You'll go to college and law school, too, just like you always wanted. You'll have your pick of all the nice boys in this town . . . why, I'll bet even that stuck-up Fontana bunch will sit up and take notice . . . "

With growing horror, Willie listened to her mother describe the good life that was ahead of them. It's for me, she realized, it's all for *me*. She threw her arms around Ginny and held her close, as if for the last time. Never had Willie's love for her mother been so fierce, so protective as it was now, at this moment when she realized the true motive behind her mother's marriage to Neal Corcoran. It wasn't really love, though perhaps there was some in the equation. It wasn't Ginny's own need for luxury. It was only to provide security for Willie, to give her the chances Ginny had never had. For this, more than anything else, Willie knew, her mother had committed herself to a marriage that only put her – put both of them – one step farther outside the law.

BOOK III

Cases

Prologue

She stood shivering in the cold evening air, her mind at war with her will, not wanting to take another step – and yet knowing she had no choice. The mountains loomed black and forbidding around her, the slopes draped with soaring pines that stood outlined against the starry night sky like dark sentinels guarding an enemy camp.

Why had she ever agreed to come here, to the last place in the world she ever wanted to see again? She had begged her mother to find another way. But Ginny had insisted there was none: He had found them, and now he was holding their future to ransom. It was up to Willie to face the past they had tried to outrun, to reason against the power of anger and hate. If she failed—

No, she thought, there was no room for failure.

She set her shoulders and forced herself to walk the weed-choked path. As she reached the rough-hewn oak door, she heard the sound of a television set from inside. She knocked and waited. After a few moments she knocked again, but still no one came. She turned the knob and walked in.

1

Berkeley, California, 1969

From her seat on the platform that had been set up in front of the university library, Willie looked out at the sea of faces illuminated by torchlight, the faces of young people assembled to hear whatever message of hope or promise of action she had brought them. In the brisk evening breeze, the brightly colored banners of "Students for Peace" fluttered above the crowds.

As president of the sophomore class, Willie had made her mark on the political life of Berkeley. Though she had been one of only two women running for a post in student government, she'd been elected by a sizable margin. Leadership came naturally to her in the liberal atmosphere of Berkeley. Her outspokenness, her missionary zeal, her passion for reform and change – these qualities were pluses here, gaining her a following in student activist circles. The women's liberation movement had hardly begun to gather steam, but its aims coincided with Willie's and inspired her to transmit them to other young women.

She had chosen Berkeley in spite of Neal's money and connections, rejecting his offer to ease her way into one of the prestigious eastern colleges. She preferred to stay in California, close enough to make the short flight or the long drive to Palm Springs – close enough to keep an eye on Mama. Willie couldn't ignore an intuition that Mama might suddenly need her help.

But so far the marriage seemed to be all right. At least Mama said it was, and Willie couldn't see anything specific to worry about. When she was home, Neal seemed to be the soul of generosity and consideration. Maybe this time,

Willie finally conceded, Mama did know what she was doing. It was a relief to find, for the first time in her life, that she didn't have to feel so totally responsible for her mother's welfare.

Suddenly the president of Students for Peace spoke Willie's name, introducing her as "the voice of Berkeley's conscience." She rose from her seat, clutching the notes she'd labored over for long hours – and prayed she'd be able to communicate what she so deeply felt: that where there was wrong, there were remedies, if only people cared enough to do more than sit passively by.

She stood in front of the microphone and began speaking in a strong, clear voice. "I love my country," she said, "and loving America means saying 'no' to a war that tarnishes all we stand for. I say we must make our voices as powerful and loud as those of the vested interests that took us into Vietnam." Here and there, a flashbulb went off, and near the makeshift platform, Willie saw a television crew from a local station. She spoke of actions that Berkeley students could take: gather petitions, conduct voter registration drives, organize boycotts.

But there had to be more, something she could say that would move her classmates to take a step beyond all the serious, responsible actions that so many had already tried – and with so little effect on a government determined to wage war. Glancing at her notes, she cited historical precedents for refusing to fight unjust wars, yearning to reach those students who still hadn't seen the folly of this one. While Berkeley was a liberal school, its large student body still included many young men who blindly supported the doctrine of "my country right or wrong" without examining the issues. Some had already enlisted, interrupting their plans to be doctors or lawyers or teachers. And all too often, word had reached campus that some promising ex-student had been killed or maimed on a battlefield in Vietnam.

"End the bloody waste of our best and finest," Willie pleaded passionately. "This country belongs to us – to the young – as much as to anyone else. We are not cannon

144

fodder to be used at the whim of politicians, and if they need to be reminded of that, let us do it. Let us fight for what is right, instead of being dragged along into what is wrong."

Abruptly, she aimed an accusing finger at the crowd. "You, out there, if you say nothing in the face of wrong, then you are wrong's accomplice. You men, say No to military duty, if that duty is wrongfully demanded. Refuse to fight, and the fighting stops!"

She extended her hand toward a group of women. "And sisters, you can do better than cry into your handkerchiefs and watch your loved ones going off to war. Remember the example set by the ancient Greeks – recorded in the classic play *Lysistrata*. Remember how the women demonstrated their power, how they protested against the love their men had for war? They closed the doors of their bedrooms and withheld the pleasure of love from those who preferred the plunder of war . . . " Willie paused dramatically. "Why should we do less for the men we want to save from pain or death? If they can't see the folly of this rush to die, give them an object lesson. If they love making war more than making love, then close your doors, close your arms. Just tell them 'No more wham-bam for 'Nam, Sam!'"

There was a moment of shocked silence, and then laughter began to roll through the crowd, followed by cheers and applause. Suddenly a chant rose up, gathering the voices of the assembled thousands in waves, until they were all shouting the slogan in unison: "No more wham-bam for 'Nam, Sam!"

Willie took it all in, almost intoxicated with the heady taste of victory. She had made them listen, and she had made them hear. She raised her arm in a clenched fist salute, just as the television crews moved in for a close-up.

It was nearly midnight when she got back to her dormitory room. Students had crowded round her after the rally, shaking her hand and asking when she would speak again. Reporters had pushed through, with questions about her politics and her ambitions, which she answered, and

145

inquiries about her love life, which she brushed off. She reveled in the attention, promising one and all that they hadn't heard the last of Willie Dellahaye, not by a long shot.

Too keyed up to sleep, Willie curled up on her narrow bed and tried to concentrate on an English lit assignment. The telephone rang. It was Ginny, her voice excited and happy. "Where were you, baby? I've been trying to get you for *hours*." Without waiting for a reply, she continued. "Remember when we were talking about a shop for me? Well, Neal's persuaded me to set up the business. He's gonna give me all kinds of help, Willie. He's got a property on Palm Canyon Drive that he says would be just right, and I can have the lease free. Isn't that nice of him?"

"Yes," Willie agreed, remembering the day Ginny's cherished fantasy of designing clothes had been buried by derision and laughter. Ginny had put her dolls away, saying she was too old for that kind of thing – and Willie had felt her heartbreak as if it were her own. "I'm happy for you, Mama," she said softly. "I hope the shop is everything you want it to be . . . "

"It's gonna be," Ginny said. "Neal's gonna take care of everything . . . How about you, honey? Are things going good at school?"

"Everything's fine, Mama. I made a speech about the war tonight . . . I think I got people to listen, really listen."

"That's nice, Willie . . . I'm really proud of you. I'm gonna hang up now, so you can get your rest."

As Willie was drifting off to sleep, she recalled that it had been Neal who had first tried to revive Mama's dream. Willie had been home on holiday when she'd heard him say to Ginny, "I understand you have a flair for design, my dear."

Willie had jumped right into the conversation. For once, she'd talked to her stepfather with enthusiasm and animation, describing Ginny's ability to capture the glamour of old Hollywood in the clothes she made.

"Well, then," Neal had said, "there we have it, Virginia

. . . the solution to all your free time. How about a boutique filled with all your designs?"

Willie had done everything she could to boost the idea, but Ginny had remained reticent. Willie understood that she feared another humiliation. The memory of scornful laughter seemed to be stronger than the power of her oldest fantasy. But Willie kept trying to reawaken her mother's enthusiasm, and now it seemed the dream was about to come true.

For a moment, Willie's customary cynicism about her stepfather surfaced, and she wondered if the boutique wasn't simply Neal's way of gilding Ginny's public image, of erasing the record of her years as a pool girl at the club. Yet she felt his motives didn't matter; the important thing was for Ginny to have something of her own, something other than her marriage to Neal. And now Willie had to admit – with an odd reluctance – that she and Neal had been effective partners in getting Mama to reach for her dream.

The celebrity that had begun with the peace rally built throughout the following day. Pictures of Willie were on the front pages of two local newspapers, and teachers as well as students made a point of congratulating her on the speech. The presidents of two student groups invited her to speak at future meetings, and the manager of a local television station asked her to moderate a panel discussion on "Who Speaks for America Today?" She accepted all invitations, first wondering how she'd find time, then resolving she'd make the time.

Willie liked the feeling of being overscheduled and in demand; it left her no time to dwell on what was missing in her life.

Though she was a campus leader, Willie often felt she didn't really fit in. She studied a lot, though studying was considered "square." She didn't date much, though dates were there for the taking. She wasn't sleeping with anyone, though everyone around her was sleeping with everyone else. They called it a sexual revolution – they called it "making a statement" – but Willie couldn't see exactly what

147

the statement was. There was plenty wrong with the way men and women behaved with each other, but she didn't believe that free-for-all sex was the cure. She didn't think for a minute that her virginity was old-fashioned, and she was quick to slap down any boy who tried to insinuate that it was. Sleeping around, she thought, was just as pointless and extreme as the old-fashioned morality that said it was allowed only after you were married. And anyway, she wasn't here to build a social life. She was here to move as brilliantly and effectively as she could toward her goal – her mission.

After her last class, Willie waved to a group of students who called out congratulations and got into the Thunderbird convertible she had received from Neal as a high school graduation gift. She felt uncomfortable taking so much from Neal, but she feared that declining the gesture would ruffle the smooth surface of his relationship with Ginny. And in truth, she enjoyed the freedom and mobility the car gave, just as she enjoyed the luxury of Neal's monthly checks. She had finally admitted there was nothing noble about being poor, nothing wrong with luxury, and a lot to be said for the choices that money provided.

She drove quickly to the dormitory, where she roomed alone. Upperclassmen were allowed to live in off-campus apartments, but that wasn't an option that Willie wanted – too many distractions, too many interruptions. She parked the Thunderbird and let herself into the modern red brick dormitory. Her private cubicle was as spare and functional as a nun's. A single small poster hung on the wall, a picture of John F. Kennedy with one ringing line from his inaugural address: "Ask not what your country can do for you, ask what you can do for your country." Lines she believed in, though they seemed so ironic in this time when so many students were at odds with the policies of their government.

Her clothes hung neatly in the closet. Her wardrobe consisted mainly of comfortable sport clothes – another little way she thought she was different from Mama. Ginny cared too much about clothes and appearances; Willie liked to believe she didn't care. Her cosmetics were few, no flashy unnatural colors, nothing to suggest she was just another pretty face. Sometimes Willie reproved herself for making such an effort to be different from Ginny, for the criticism of Mama those efforts implied. Yet it was hard not to be critical. Willie felt that her mother almost invited people to belittle her, or at least not to take her seriously, and that was not what Willie wanted for herself.

Willie was straightening up her room when the call came. It was Ginny again, the happiness of last night replaced by panic. "Oh, honey," she said, "I've been trying to get you all day. It's terrible, Willie, terrible. I don't know what to do . . . "

"What's happened?" she asked, her triumph suddenly shadowed by the panic in Ginny's voice. Neal . . . it must be something Neal had done.

"It was on television this morning . . . in the paper, too. How could you, baby? Don't you know what could happen? What if your father sees it? He'd know where you were – and then he could find me . . . "

Now Willie understood what Ginny was talking about. Her first reaction was anger. How long were they going to look over their shoulders, thinking like fugitives, waiting for the past to catch up with them?

"Mama," she said impatiently, "it's been years. Papa probably doesn't even remember what I look like. And besides, they don't care about this stuff in Belle Fourche."

But Ginny wasn't listening. "He'd send me to jail, baby. Don't you understand? Neal will leave me" – her voice rose – "you'll never get to law school. We'll be ruined, oh, God, we'll be ruined. Please, Willie, promise me you won't do anything like that again. Promise me . . . "

Willie wanted to argue, to reason, but Ginny's panic had escalated into hysteria. *You're asking too much,* Willie wanted to say, but she felt like an ingrate for even thinking it. Didn't Ginny have a right to ask for sacrifice after those she'd made?

"All right, Mama," Willie agreed wearily. "I'll be careful. I promise."

*   *   *

Making the promise was hard, but Willie found keeping it even harder. It meant backing out of commitments, doing everything possible to avoid attracting attention, pulling out of student activities without real explanations, pleading too much work and family responsibilities. The excuses didn't sound convincing, even to her. "Chickenshit move" and "Can't take the heat" were the first accusations she heard when she let it be known that her days of public protest were behind her. All too quickly the cheers and applause she had earned turned to disappointment and recriminations. Her supporters dropped away, and her credibility as a campus leader was lost.

Soon she was alone again – now more than ever.

2

Willie picked up her suitcase, efficiently packed the night before, collected her notes for a paper on constitutional government, and headed toward the coast highway for the trip south. The weather was chilly and cloudy, but she drove with the top down, enjoying the throaty response of the powerful engine as she floored the accelerator. Willie liked driving fast. She liked the feel of the cold wind that stung her face and whipped her hair into a golden froth, the feeling of rushing through space, separate from everything around her.

The drive to Palm Springs was one she made with mixed emotions. It didn't really feel like going home. In fact, ever since she and Ginny had left their cottage, it was hard to think of any place as "home."

True, Neal had provided her with a spacious bedroom and bath in a separate wing. She had her own telephone and her own entertainment center – a big-screen color television set and the latest in stereo equipment. But somehow the luxurious surroundings did not keep her from feeling like a temporary guest, just as she'd been as a child, living in her uncle's home. Or Ben's ranch. Or Laura's bungalow.

To Willie it seemed that Mama's marriage, and not merely the geographic distance between them, had diminished the closeness they'd once shared. She was doing what she had to do – college and then law school was more a mission than a career. But there had been other changes that Willie regretted. Webb was gone, so now they no longer saw Laura. And Cheryl? Willie missed her, too. Her friend had chosen to go to the state university campus in Westwood, to study film, no doubt as a last-ditch attempt to get close to Malcolm, or at least to gain his approval.

The years were certainly proving that Cheryl was right. One way or another the people you cared for did go away. What remained, sometimes forever, were the hollow spaces they left inside you. Thinking of the people she missed, Willie felt a deep sense of loss. But if she were to grow away from Mama, that would be worse than emptiness and a longing for what had been lost. For too long they had been a team, managing to make their way through a hostile world because they had each other. Strong as Willie knew she was, she wondered if she could survive if anything were to come between her and Mama.

As she took the turn off the coast highway and drove toward the desert, the cool air turned dry, and the hovering clouds gave way to the sun. As her skin warmed, memories of Jedd – the warmth he had once made her feel – rose, unbidden, into her mind.

And the hurt. It was still there, the wounding recollection of her meeting with Sam, the way Jedd had walked away from her. Ginny was always reminding her that she was as good as anyone else, now that she was Neal Corcoran's stepdaughter. But none of that mattered to Willie. It had been a long time since she'd been impressed by the Fontana money and position. Jedd was arrogant and spoiled. Never mind that for a little while she'd believed something else.

What's more the Fontana clan no longer seemed as

151

lustrous as they once had. As Neal's stepdaughter she could move through Palm Springs's inner circles, close enough to hear the whispers and rumors that surrounded the family. Like the story of how one of Sam's bodyguards had been driving drunk one night and run over a young boy riding a bicycle – and how the charges had been mysteriously dropped.

Willie had done a little digging on her own and filled in the rest of the picture herself. Apparently Sam ran his business and a good part of his home state of Montana with the same iron will he used to keep his family in line – in the patriarchal style of his ancestors.

The roots of Jedd's family, she'd learned, went back to the Spanish settlers who migrated from Mexico to the American Southwest during the time of Maximilian. More adventurous and more daring than most, Sam's father Diego had married outside of the tight community of Spanish settlers in New Mexico. His choice was a young Irish-Italian woman, just sixteen years old, reputed to be as clever and strong as she was beautiful. Diego had taken his bride and moved north looking for opportunity. He found it in Montana. At a time when the price of land was reckoned in pennies, Diego bought large tracts, on which he raised cattle. As he prospered, he bought more land, and yet more, building a vast empire of grazing land, timber forests, and mountains rich in minerals. By the time his son was born, Diego was the largest single landholder in the state. By all accounts, Sam Fontana surpassed his father in his acquisitiveness and his hunger for wealth and power.

What Willie found most sickening were the stories she'd heard about how Sam dealt with his enemies. Efficiently, ruthlessly, he broke businesses and destroyed careers as easily as making moves on a board game. As for the law, he used it when it supported his purposes and bent or ignored it otherwise. There were rumors – and some carefully written magazine items Willie had found in the library went so far as to report them – that Sam owned the governor and enough of the legislature to do exactly what he pleased.

152

According to the Fontana legends, Diego had been something of a paradox, a scholar of Spanish history, an elegant man whose quiet demeanor belied the ruthlessness underneath. In Sam, Willie saw the ruthlessness, but no trace of a scholar – just expensive suits and haberdashery covering tempered steel. Her single encounter with Sam had left a sour aftertaste. She had no wish to meet him again unless the tables were turned, unless she could reject him – because he didn't measure up to her standards of morality and decency.

"Congratulations on your latest success, Willa, dear." Neal raised his wineglass to his stepdaughter. "Being president of your class should go a long way toward impressing the admissions committee of any law school. Don't you agree, Virginia?"

"What? Oh, sure . . . congratulations, honey. I'm really proud of you."

Willie sipped her champagne and looked across the dinner table at her mother. Ginny's beauty now had a certain luster and sheen, a sleekness that came of regular visits to her hairdresser Armand, and to the Spa Hotel for herbal wraps and massages and expensive facials by her favorite esthetician. But something was off. A tightness around the mouth and eyes. A distracted preoccupation, as if she were someplace else.

Willie had tried to draw her mother out, to find out how her life was going. But all she got for her efforts were a clipped "fine" or some nervous small talk.

Maybe Mama was still worried about those newspaper stories, even though Willie had assured her there wouldn't be any more. Or maybe she was worried about the new business. Maybe she was afraid that Palm Springs society would laugh at her dresses, just the way those saleswomen had years ago.

"I passed the new shop coming in," Willie ventured. "I peeked in the window . . . "

"There's nothing to see yet," Ginny said nervously. "The

153

windows aren't done, and we're supposed to be having an opening-night party in two days . . . "

"Virginia, dear," Neal began in that ever-patient way of his, "I hired you a fine window dresser. She tells me you dismissed her over . . . 'artistic differences.'" Willie noticed the edge Neal gave to the phrase, as though he didn't allow that Ginny might know the first thing about artistry.

Ginny had stiffened in her chair. "It wasn't like that," she said, turning to Willie in a plea for understanding. "That woman – she acted all, you know, superior. She was supposed to be working for me, but she kept throwing her weight around and acting like I was too dumb to know what she was talking about. She . . . "

"Now, Willa," Neal interrupted, speaking to his stepdaughter as if Ginny were too simple to comprehend, "you know how sensitive your mother can be. I'm certain no offense was intended. But I'm more than willing to hire another window dresser, someone who can do the job tomorrow morning, if that's what Virginia wants."

Willie looked at her mother, who had shrunk down into her chair, like a child waiting for the grownups to decide what was best. "Why don't you do the windows yourself, Mama? I'll help, and that way you can make them look just the way you want." She looked back at her stepfather, who simply shrugged and smiled.

"I bow to your superior numbers," he chuckled. "And what a delightful way to be outnumbered and outflanked. Mother and daughter. Two lovely women instead of one."

Neal's words made Willie squirm. There was something unwholesome and clammy about the man. It was hard to ascribe any specific negative intent to Neal, sitting there so pleasant and innocent and accommodating, but Willie's instincts told her there was more to him than met the eye.

"Well," he said smoothly, "now that Virginia's settled for the time being, what about you, Willa? When will you let me help you realize your potential?"

Willie had heard this before, and she reacted automatically, as she usually did when he offered assistance. "I'm

154

fine, Neal . . . thank you. Berkeley is a good school, and I don't see any reason to transfer."

"Of course, it's a good school," he said agreeably, never appearing to disagree with anything she said. "Academically. However, and this is a significant parenthesis, Willa, the law is a conservative profession, one which naturally prefers to recruit its practitioners from the more, shall we say, conservative schools. I need hardly point out," he continued, "that in conservative circles, the very name of Berkeley conjures up a certain radical, even revolutionary image. And you, my dear," he added tartly, "have made certain contributions to that image. May I suggest that colorful headlines may be useful later in your career, but now—"

"Yeah, Willie," Ginny chimed in. "Neal's right. For your own good, you want to stay out of the papers, if you get my meaning . . . "

Willie nodded stiffly. Neal might be right, but she still resented the reminder that she was in no position to take risks, even if she wanted to. When would it end, this bondage to the past?

After dinner, when she was alone with Willie, Ginny resumed her argument. "Neal's got a good point, honey. For your sake" – she pressed on eagerly – "I mean, what with your wanting to go to law school. Some reporter called the house five or six times . . . I finally took the phone off the hook. You know, honey, if you'd let Neal adopt you the way he wants to, at least you'd have a different name . . . "

"No." Neal's offer had repelled Willie. She preferred living a lie over pretending that she and Neal were really "family."

"Well . . . just be careful. I mean I hate to cramp your style and all, but Neal did say it wasn't good for you to get your name in the papers."

"I already told you I'd be careful," Willie said impatiently. "Please, let's not talk about it anymore. Tell me about you . . . have you picked a name for the shop yet?"

"Well . . ." Ginny said shyly, "maybe it's kinda silly, but

I called it Silver Screen, you know, like the magazines I used to read . . . "

"It's perfect," Willie said, "it's you. Silver Screen . . . Now when do we tackle that window?"

"Tomorrow morning, if that's okay with you . . . "

Silver Screen was located on Palm Canyon Drive, between a jewelry shop and one of Palm Springs's better hairdressers. The property belonged to Neal, and he had leased it to Ginny for a token sum. As his accountant had explained, the arrangement would be profitable even if the boutique wasn't.

"Promise you won't say it's okay just to make me feel good," Ginny said as she unlocked the door and switched on the theatrical pink spots that lit the interior of the shop and bathed the mirrors with a rosy glow that would flatter any woman's complexion. "The electricians left a mess, and I didn't get a chance to dress all the mannequins or—"

"Don't worry, Mama." Willie put in, anxious to reassure her mother. Now that Ginny's dream had started to take shape, she seemed to be afraid she couldn't see it through.

Willie didn't have much interest in either clothes or decorating, but when she looked around the shop, she could see that the place and her mother's designs had a certain innocent charm. Ginny had somehow managed to translate her vision of Hollywood glamour into reality, with a turquoise-and-pink color scheme, blond wood furnishings, and soft pink lighting. There were none of the usual racks. The stock was artfully arranged as if in a private dressing room, inviting customers to look and touch, yet in such a way that items would be missed if someone actually bought them. A black strapless sequined gown was draped dramatically over a zebra upholstered loveseat, and a white fox scarf had been flung casually over a white wool suit with padded shoulders and a daringly slit pencil-thin skirt.

"It's perfect," Willie said, "just like the name. I mean it. This place is just like the stories you used to tell me. I'm proud of you, Mama."

"Really?" Ginny smiled shyly. "I was scared, you know, that it was kinda . . . well, corny."

"It isn't corny. It's your fantasy, and it's just right. Now what about the window?"

Heartened by Willie's approval, Ginny spoke with more verve and certainty. "I had this idea of dressing one of the mannequins – Lola, I call her – in this chiffon nightgown with the marabou negligee. I thought I'd put her on this chaise with a black cigarette holder in her hand . . . and maybe there could be a champagne glass on this little mirrored nightstand."

"That sounds terrific, Mama. Why didn't you do it?"

Ginny sighed. "It was that woman Neal hired. She kept saying it wasn't 'tasteful,' whatever that means."

Willie smiled affectionately. Ginny's taste had always been original, and that was part of her charm. "It means you were right to fire her. Let's get to work."

For the next two hours, while they worked together, it almost felt like old times. They played the musical tapes Ginny had collected, to soothe and inspire her customers as they shopped – songs like "Stardust" and "Smoke Gets in Your Eyes." Once again Willie was impressed with how much thought Ginny had given to the atmosphere of her boutique. She had collected studio stills and mounted them in graceful art deco frames. Fabled leading ladies like Garbo and Shearer and Dietrich, and dashing leading men like Gable and Bogart and Flynn. They, too, would be part of the stage setting for Ginny's designs.

Together they cleaned up the debris left by departing workmen. They arranged stock in the drawers of the blond deco armoire, on graceful curved Plexiglas hooks in the mirrored alcoves Ginny'd had built. Then Ginny looked at her watch and frowned. "Oh, gosh," she said, "there's still a lot to do, but we're gonna have to quit and go home now. Neal made reservations at the Chi Chi Club tonight . . . Frank Sinatra's gonna be there, and Neal's got a couple of ringside tables for us and some of his friends." She surveyed the still undressed window and said worriedly, "I wish we had a little more time . . . I'd feel a lot better knowing the place was ready."

"I'll finish it, Mama," Willie volunteered, glad for the chance to help Ginny, to do something that Neal's money couldn't buy. "I'm not really in the mood to go out anyway."

"Oh, honey, that's really nice," Ginny said, relief showing in her face. But after a moment, she reconsidered. "I can't let you do that. You're supposed to be on vacation. How can I leave you here all by yourself?"

"I'll be fine," Willie insisted. "I want to do this – let's call it my grand opening gift to Silver Screen. Besides, this kind of work is a vacation from what I usually do. I'll phone a cab when I'm finished. Go on, Mama. Have a good time."

"Well . . . if that's what you want. Don't stay too late now."

Willie rolled up her sleeves and tackled the tricky business of dressing the mannequin in Ginny's chiffon and marabou confection without tearing the delicate fabric. This *was* different from the kind of work she did every day, and she found the change curiously relaxing.

Next she dragged the peach satin chaise into the window. She laid the mannequin on the chaise, but the figure looked stiff and unnatural. When she tried to move its limbs for a more relaxed pose, the gown slipped and slid. Hands on hips, Willie stood in the window, surveying the problem and frowning.

There was a tap on the window, then another. She peered through the darkness. Jedd Fontana stood outside, waving and gesturing for her to open the door.

She stared. The nerve of him, she thought, smiling and acting like they were the best of friends. She gave him what she hoped was a scowl and turned her back, concentrating on the mannequin and her chiffon dress.

The tapping continued. She turned to scowl again at Jedd, who was now waving a white handkerchief. He wasn't going to leave, she could see that.

She stepped out of the window and opened the door.

"Hi!" he said, grinning in that sure-of-himself way that could quicken her pulse – or ignite her temper.

She stared back coldly. "What do you want?"

"Ah, Willie, come on – whatever happened to 'Hello, Jedd'?"

"I don't have time for small talk. I'm busy."

"So I noticed. Why are you attacking some poor dummy in a store window?"

"I was 'dressing' the window – before you interrupted me."

"Going into a new line of work?"

"I'm helping my mother. This is her new boutique."

"Hey, it looks great. Can I give you a hand . . . ?" His expression was open, eager, as ingenuous as a child asking for a treat.

"Why?" The single word emerged more sharply than she'd intended. But she couldn't hide her suspicion.

He shifted on his feet, his expression changing. "Because I've missed you, Willie. Let me come in – please?"

Close the door, the little voice in her head commanded, shut him out. Don't listen to another word – and don't look into those dark, treacherous eyes . . .

She stood aside so he could come in.

He joined right in with the work, lifting the mannequin and holding it, while she tried to drape the nightgown around its stiff, uncompromising contours.

"Wouldn't it be easier if you pinned this material?" he suggested. "I don't think there's any way a dummy's going to wear a dress the way a real woman would."

Of course, she agreed inwardly. Why didn't I figure that out? Once again she draped the filmy fabric, securing it this time with a row of straight pins. With Jedd's help, she arranged the mannequin's arms and legs into a semblance of a languid, reclining pose on the lounge.

"Not bad," she said, surveying the results. "How did you know about pinning the material?"

He grinned. "I have two sisters, remember? They like to shop, and I've done a lot of time as driver and package carrier. While I wait, I look around, inspect the dummies."

"I'll bet," Willie said drily.

"What's next, boss?"

159

"We need a bottle of champagne and a pretty glass. And a pack of cigarettes."

"Leave that to me." Jedd left the store and was back in a few minutes with the props she'd requested.

"Thanks for helping," she said. "I can manage the rest. I think you'd better go now."

He looked bewildered by her abrupt dismissal. "Really? Here I've just found you again. It's too soon to—"

She cut in. "Why did you find me again, Jedd? Because now I'm one of the rich kids, too? Because now I'm 'socially acceptable'?"

"Whoa, slow down! I never cared about that stuff, Willie," he protested. "I liked you just fine before you got to be a rich kid."

"But your father didn't." It was a statement, harsh and uncompromising.

"Listen to me, Willie," he said, taking her hand with such authority that she let it rest there without protest. "Pop's kind of old-fashioned. He has this idea that the only kind of woman for me is someone old-fashioned, too."

"And you always do what your father says." Again, it was a statement, not a question.

His response didn't come quickly. When he spoke, it wasn't with his usual smooth assurance. "I try, Willie. That's just the way things are in my family. We've got a tradition that goes way back . . . son taking over from father. And before that happens, I have to be taught, prepared. It's a big responsibility to be a Fontana. If I'm going to do it right, I have to follow my father's example. It isn't always easy, but . . . that's the way things are."

"And what if your father is wrong about some things, Jedd? What do you do then? Or don't you think he's ever wrong?"

Jedd frowned, looking more hurt than insulted. "He can be wrong, sure. But . . . I don't like to disappoint him. When he said it would be better if we didn't see each other, I tried. I thought about you, though . . . a lot. And then," he smiled mischievously, "then I saw you on television. 'No more wham-bam for 'Nam, Sam!' God, you were great!

You're an original, Willie. Just like I always knew you were. Maybe that's when I realized my father might be wrong about us . . . "

Willie had almost been moved by his words. Until he mentioned the rally. "So," she said accusingly, "you thought you'd like to add 'an original' to your collection."

He gripped her shoulders firmly. "Goddammit, why do you twist everything around? All I said was that I thought about you and I missed you. And when I drove by this store and saw you in this window, just as beautiful as ever, I had to stop. Can't we just start over, Willie? You owe me a chance, don't you . . . ?"

Owe him? There was that arrogance, the idea that he – that his family – were owed whatever they wanted. But she said nothing. She was afraid to trust Jedd, who spoke of a debt to tradition that also included ruthlessness. Yet Willie was feeling things she hadn't felt in a long, long time. A warm spring breeze was melting the ice around her heart, filling the empty space with a promise of summer. "I don't know," she murmured. "I just don't know."

He touched her cheek with his fingertips. "That's a hell of a good start," he smiled, "for someone who seems to know everything else. Now let's get back to work. Let me show you what a dedicated, industrious guy I can be."

They worked together, the hours slipping by like minutes. Jedd's companionship in the quiet intimate stillness of the shop felt familiar and strange all at the same time. It was as if they had always known each other, as if they were meant to be this way.

Willie found herself talking easily to Jedd, sharing her experiences at school, telling him how much an education and the chance to make a career in law meant to her. "I just wish I didn't have to take so much from my stepfather," she said. "I wish I could pay for law school on my own . . . "

Jedd nodded thoughtfully, as if he understood why she felt as she did, even though he'd never had a moment's worry about money or where it was coming from. "You never know," he said. "Maybe by the time you get to law school, you'll find a way to make it on your own."

When they discovered they were hungry, they made a pot of coffee on the hot plate in the back room and found a half-empty box of doughnuts to go with it. Contentedly, they shared the makeshift picnic on the fluffy mauve carpeting of Ginny's Hollywood fantasy shop, with only her mannequins – Lola and Marlene and Ginger, smiling benevolently in attitudes of repose – as chaperones.

At last, without a word, Jedd turned off the lights and circled Willie with his arms, drawing her close. He kissed her hair, her eyes, then found her mouth. His lips were warm and sweet, loving and undemanding. It's all right, his kisses seemed to say, I won't hurt you. His very gentleness roused the deep, burning need she'd banked for so long. It was she who pressed against his strong young body, twining her fingers possessively in his dark silky hair, willing him to fill the aching void inside her. Lips parted, she drew his tongue inside her mouth, tasting it hungrily, losing herself in the rush of passion that stilled all her little voices, leaving only a hot, demanding urgency.

"Willie . . . Willie," Jedd whispered hoarsely, as he pulled away slightly from the ferocity of her embrace. "Oh, God, I want you so much, but . . . "

Willie heard only "I want you," the echo of her own heart. She clung to Jedd, intoxicated by his nearness, giddy with the teasing promise of fulfilled desire. She kissed him again, slowly this time, her heart pounding as she felt him tense and harden against her. She touched the planes of his face, as if to imprint them on her own flesh. So often she'd dreamed him like this, close enough to stir her deepest longings.

Clothing fell onto the soft carpeting, was pushed away hurriedly. "Beautiful Willie," he murmured, his voice husky with passion, as she showed him what no man had seen before, her ripened body eager for love.

Beautiful, Willie thought, stroking with trembling fingers the arms that held her, the narrow indentation of his waist, the tight, hard muscles of his thighs. She moaned softly as he caressed her breasts, the nipples quickening with arousal. He parted her legs, probing the warm wetness

162

inside, and she felt the boundaries of her body dissolve in a rush of hot excitement. Hungrily she pressed against him, digging her nails into his back. "Now," she whispered, "now."

He entered her, pushing against the tender resistance of her virginity. There was a sudden sharp pain, and then it was gone, lost, as her flesh yielded, melting with his in an exquisite fusion. He moved inside her, her back arching to meet him, to catch the pulse at the center of her being as it rippled through her body, building stronger and stronger . . . and there . . . and there, she was there, her long legs wrapped around Jedd's back, crying out his name, rising, floating on the waves that engulfed her.

She clung to him as the waves subsided, as her heart stopped racing and her breathing slowed. "Willie, my Willie," he said tenderly, "I knew it would be like this with you. I knew it . . . "

Wrapped in the wonder of newness and discovery, she lay still and quiet in his arms, not ready to leave the feeling of being whole and complete, not ready to trust it to the daylight of the real world.

Jedd finally said, "It's almost morning, Willie . . . I'd better take you home."

They dressed quietly, suddenly shy with each other, slipping into their private thoughts, as they put on the clothes they'd shed so hastily. Just before they locked the door, he kissed her. "That's to remind you it was all real," he said, just as if he'd read her thoughts.

Jedd drove fast through the last remnants of night, through the deserted streets of the town, slowing down as he approached Willie's street. "I hate to say 'good night,'" he said huskily. "It's taken us so long to get past 'hello.'"

"I feel the same," Willie said wistfully. "I wish there was someplace we could go. Oh, Jedd, I want to make a thousand memories tonight . . . "

"There'll be other nights, too," he said, seeming to understand that she spoke of storing memories as if there would soon be nothing else left. "But I could stand one more good memory tonight . . ." He dropped a tender kiss

163

on her nose, then suddenly steered the car into a sharp U-turn and headed up the steep, winding mountain road. At the top, he pulled off the road onto a shoulder overlooking the city of Palm Springs. The flag of dawn was just being unfurled ahead of them, the first slender ribbons of pink and orange streaming across the deep purple desert sky. "Perfect," he said huskily, "you and me and a brand-new morning."

She sighed, and the sound of contentment seemed unfamiliar to her ears. She rested her head on his shoulder.

"You know," Jedd mused, "this place . . . it's like America. It's all about breaking frontiers, discovering new things. I've been coming here ever since I was a kid. I used to imagine what it was like fifty years ago, when all you could see was mountains and desert. A Jewish woman – Ellie Kaufman was her name – built a sanatorium . . . "

"I know," Willie said. "Webb used to tell me stories about the old days . . . before the 'rich folks' came. Bought up land dirt cheap . . . twenty or thirty dollars an acre . . . so they could build tennis courts and houses with swimming pools."

Jedd laughed. "You're doing it again, Willie. Don't you have any sense of humor at all? The 'rich folks' bought land nobody else wanted – until they made this place what it is. That's what life is about, opening up new horizons, new opportunities, making things happen . . . "

She sat up. She didn't want to argue with him, but she couldn't help herself when he said things like that. "You think like a grandee, Jedd. I wonder if you'd think the same way if you'd been born poor."

"But then I wouldn't be me," he said quietly. "I come from a long line of 'grandees.' I'm proud of what I am. I can look down into that valley, all the way to the horizon, and see more than just a pretty sunrise. I can see the challenge in what people like my family did before. It's going to be my turn soon, to find new opportunities, to make new things happen."

"That's funny," Willie said. "What you're saying, it doesn't sound so different from how I feel . . . except it is. I know

164

what I have to do, but I still have to find out how to do it."

There was a silence, then Jedd turned and looked into her eyes. "Well, whatever you do, Willie Dellahaye, and whenever you do it, just make sure it includes me . . . "

"And if the great Sam Fontana says 'no'?"

Jedd hesitated. "We all have to grow up sometime, Willie. Some decisions, I'll make for myself." And, as if to emphasize his sense of power and determination, he revved the engine to a roar and started back down the hill.

The night was over. Willie prayed that more than the memories would remain.

3

Willie yawned and stretched languidly, still wrapped in the warm afterglow of her spent passion. She had slept only a few hours, yet she felt refreshed by her strange new sense of contentment. Outside her window, the morning was sunny and clear, living up to the bright promise of dawn she had shared with Jedd. It would be a good day, Willie thought, a day for Mama to taste the reality of a dream come true. As for herself, she was certain that sooner or later, all dreams could become real, if you chose the right ones and wanted them badly enough.

She got out of bed and showered quickly. Refreshed and wide awake, she smelled the aroma of freshly made coffee and realized she was ravenously hungry. She slipped into a pair of shorts and a T-shirt and went out to the pool, hoping to enjoy a hearty breakfast with her mother.

But as she walked across the landscaped patio, she saw Neal sitting at the poolside table, his morning paper spread out before him. He was on the telephone. "The terms of our agreement were clear," he was saying in a voice that was polite but cold, "and if you find yourself unable to meet those terms, I suggest that's your problem entirely."

Willie didn't particularly want to breakfast alone with

Neal, but before she could turn around and return to the house, he saw her and waved. Reluctantly she sat down at the table and helped herself to some coffee and fruit. While Neal finished his conversation, his eyes appraised her skimpy outfit in a way that made her feel exposed and uncomfortable.

"We missed you last night, Willa," he said, after he'd hung up, with just the barest hint of reproach in his tone. "Sinatra was in rare voice. Your mother said you'd made other plans. Anyone we know?"

"Jedd Fontana," she blurted out – and instantly regretted her candor.

"Well, well." Neal stroked his mustache, a habit of his that always made Willie think of silent-movie villains. "I can understand that, though your mother may not approve. A young woman like you, a mature and desirable young woman with very special needs . . . "

Willie felt her ears turn pink. Neal managed to make her most uncomfortable when he was being friendly. She took some toast and made a project of buttering it.

Neal chuckled conspiratorially. "Perhaps you'd like to invite young Mr. Fontana to your mother's party tonight. I hear on the club grapevine that he has quite a way with women. Do you find him . . . satisfactory?"

Willie couldn't bear to answer. Neal's words, his suggestive insinuations threatened to tarnish the memory of last night. Feeling trapped in her stepfather's company, she looked for a way out. "Where's Mama?" she asked. "Did she have breakfast already?"

"Your mother's a trifle indisposed this morning—"

"What's wrong?" Willie said quickly, guessing that Neal might be downplaying some serious problem.

"Really, Willa, it's nothing to concern yourself about."

But it was, Willie felt. Mama had always been an early riser and she had never before been "indisposed." Willie finished her coffee and got up. "I think I'll look in on her and see if she wants anything."

Without waiting for a reply, she headed for the spacious modern kitchen, where the housekeeper was busy polishing the silver. "Will you fix me a tray, Elena? Some orange juice and coffee and toast. I want to take it to my mother."

The housekeeper did as she was asked, shaking her head as she worked. "The missus don't take no breakfast when the door's closed . . . maybe later, eleven, twelve o'clock."

This was the first Willie had heard of Ginny staying in bed till noon. Her mother had always said morning was the best part of the day. "She isn't sick, is she, Elena?"

The woman shook her head again. "Mrs. Corcoran didn't say nothing to me about being sick."

Willie took the tray and made her way to the master bedroom suite, which was located at the far end of the house. The door was indeed closed. She knocked once, twice, but there was no answer.

Slowly she turned the knob. The room was shrouded in darkness, in spite of the floor-to-ceiling windows. Blackout drapes, Willie concluded, and she wondered when Ginny had stopped enjoying the morning sun. The air in the room was stale and close, and Willie caught an unfamiliar sweet scent that wasn't incense or cologne.

As her eyes got used to the darkness, she made out Ginny's form, curled up on one side of the king-size bed. Suddenly she felt a little embarrassed. This wasn't the way it used to be in the old days. This was the bed Ginny shared with Neal, and Willie felt like an intruder. "Mama," she called softly, gently making her presence known. "Mama . . . it's me."

"Willie . . . ?" Ginny stirred and rolled over heavily.

"I brought you some coffee. Are you feeling all right?"

Now Ginny lifted herself on one elbow, her eyes puffy and squinting even in the darkness. "I'm fine, baby," she said hoarsely. "Just a little too much party last night, that's all." She glanced at the tray Willie had set on the night table. "Thanks, honey," she said. "I'll have some of that later. Why don't you go outside and have a nice swim while I catch a little more beauty sleep?"

Willie left the room. It was clear that Ginny wanted to be left alone. But why? Was her mother just a little hung over, or was she hiding something? Was she ill and keeping the truth to herself?

By 7.30, all was in readiness for the Silver Screen party. A huge striped tent had been set up behind the boutique, in what would be the parking lot. The caterers had arrived early with their tables and chairs, pink tablecloths and turquoise china, floral arrangements of calla lilies and camellias. The musicians, who would play nothing but old movie scores, were dressed in vintage evening clothes.

Neal was paying the bills, but the menu and arrangements were all Ginny's. Although it had been a long time since she'd wanted for any material things, she'd chosen a meal that included items she'd once only read about – caviar and champagne, Beef Wellington, Crepes Grand Marnier.

Ginny looked splendid, and Willie marveled at her recuperative powers. It was hard to believe her beautiful vivacious mother was the same woman who could hardly lift her head off the pillow this morning. She was wearing one of her own designs, a creation she called "Lightning Strikes Twice" – a long-sleeved column of turquoise jersey slit to the thigh and splashed across the middle with a lightning spray of black bugle beads. Her shoulder-length hair had been arranged Veronica Lake style, pulled to one side by the diamond and jet clip Neal had bought for her last birthday.

Tonight, in black tie, murmuring words of encouragement and support to his wife, Neal seemed different, too. In his evening clothes, he looked like Gilbert Roland. Willie had to give Neal credit for one thing: he appeared to take his marriage seriously. He and Mama were always together, and Neal rarely seemed less than doting or attentive.

"Are you sure it was such a good idea to invite those newspaper people?" Ginny asked nervously. "I mean, what if they hate my stuff? I'll be finished off before I open."

"Not to worry, my dear." Neal assured her. "I can

guarantee you'll read nothing but accolades in tomorrow's paper. The secret to good press is good liquor and good food, in that order. We have both, and," he chuckled, "the owner of the paper is a friend of mine. Your press reception is, as they say, in the bag."

"But Neal," she fretted, "what if your friends, all the people you've invited, what if they . . . "

"Not another word," he said. "My friends adore you, hence they will adore your designs. Here," he said, handing her a glass of champagne, "why don't you take one of those pills of yours so you can relax and enjoy the party."

"Pills?" Willie's attention snagged on the word. "When did you start taking pills, Mama? What's wrong? Tell me . . . "

"Nothing, honey, it's nothing." Ginny laughed nervously. "The pills are just to calm me down when I'm tense. Like now."

The answer didn't satisfy Willie, and when her mother went off to talk to the caterer, she repeated her question to Neal

"Willa, dear, I can assure you that your mother is in the best of health. Virginia can be . . . high-strung . . . especially in social situations. My physician . . . her physician, too, prescribed a mild tranquilizer. It's as simple as that."

Willie wasn't completely satisfied, but the guests had started to arrive. She knew how important this evening was to Ginny, so she trailed the first group of women as they walked through the boutique, champagne glasses in hand, picking up hangers, examining designs, touching fabrics.

"Different," one woman said, "don't you think?"

"Yes," another agreed doubtfully. "These things are certainly different."

"They're not to be taken seriously, of course . . . "

"Of course, that goes without saying."

"But charming . . . yes, charming. This black strapless might do very nicely for Millie Carmichael's birthday, don't you think?"

"Charming." "Different." "Unusual." Willie heard the

169

words often, and even when they were said in a slightly patronizing way, they seemed to add up to an endorsement of Ginny's new business. Guests were reserving one-of-a-kind items. Appointments were being made for special fittings. Willie even heard someone suggest a special Silver Screen party at the country club, featuring nothing but original designs by Virginia Corcoran. The shop, it appeared, would be a success. Mama's oldest dream was finally coming true.

But where was Jedd? He had accepted her invitation eagerly, saying he couldn't wait to see her again. In anticipation of the admiration she hoped to see glittering in his dark eyes, Willie had dressed with special care tonight. At Ginny's request, she was modeling "Lightning Strikes" in peach, her strawberry blond hair dramatically upswept, in the style of the forties. She felt as sensual and seductive as the dress she was wearing, and she wanted Jedd to see her this way, to know how their lovemaking had made her feel.

"You look strikingly lovely, Willa," said a male voice at her elbow. It was not the voice she wanted to hear.

"Thank you, Neal."

"I don't see your young man. Will he be joining us tonight?"

"I don't know," she answered.

"Pity," he said, "though I'm not surprised. The boy's known to have a brief attention span where the ladies are concerned. Perhaps," he said softly, gently touching her arm, "you should try a man who has a real appreciation for beauty . . . someone a little older and wiser, more experienced in the ways of love . . . "

The suggestion in Neal's words horrified Willie; his touch made her flesh crawl. She pulled her arm away. "I'm going to forget you said that, for Mama's sake . . . but don't ever speak to me like that again."

She caught the flicker of a cold, ugly expression on his face, and then he was all smiles and charm again. "Really, Willa," he said smoothly, "I don't know why you should be offended. Your naiveté can be adorable at times, but you

170

must learn to accept a compliment in a reasonably adult fashion." He walked away, leaving Willie to wonder if there was a chance that she had misunderstood, had let her clinging suspicion of Neal color something innocuous.

A moment later, she saw Neal at Ginny's side, his hand on her mother's arm in the same way he had touched her own. Maybe she *had* overreacted; maybe Neal's pass had been his idea of sophisticated party conversation. But the remark about Jedd stayed with Willie; she had seen him with a wide assortment of girls, but not too long or too often with any one of them. Had she been foolish – or as Neal said, "naive" – to believe that she was more than a conquest or a moment's pleasure?

Willie moved among the guests, showing off her "Silver Screen" design, gathering up compliments to share later with Ginny. She did not notice the arrival of yet another floral offering, a turquoise basket filled with one hundred peach roses. It was Neal who accepted the delivery, who appraised the striking perfection of the flowers – and compared them with his own tasteful, but smaller, bouquet. He debated with himself only an instant before reaching into the turquoise basket to remove two small white envelopes. One bore Willie's name. Neal pulled out the card and read: "Dearest Willie, Forgive me for missing the party. Family crisis came up suddenly and Pop needs me. Will call you soon. Keep Lola's champagne chilled . . . and the memories warm 'til we're together again. Much love, Jedd."

The second envelope was addressed to Ginny. Inside was a "good luck" message, signed "With all good wishes, Jedd Fontana."

With a slow smile, Neal pocketed the cards and returned to his guests.

Two hours later, Willie's anticipation had turned to hurt and anger. Guests had started to leave, and still Jedd wasn't here. How could he be so uncaring? After the whispered words of endearment, the fiery passion they'd shared . . .

She felt an arm on her shoulder. "What's the matter,

171

baby? You don't seem to be having a good time . . . "

Willie turned to face her mother. "I'm okay."

"No," Ginny said quietly, "you're not okay. I've seen you watching the door. Who are you waiting for, honey?"

Willie hesitated in the face of Ginny's concern. She wasn't used to this mothering. It had been the other way around for so long. "Jedd Fontana," she answered, her voice constricted with pain and embarrassment. "It looks like he's standing me up."

"Jedd?" Ginny was obviously surprised. "He doesn't seem like the type who'd stand up a lady. Don't you think there might be a good explanation?"

Willie shook her head, unable to speak the words that came to mind as she looked into the eyes of her mother, a woman wounded so much by her own need to believe in love.

I should have known better, Willie thought. Wanting so much to believe in Jedd, in his promises of love, she had overruled her own natural caution. But it wouldn't happen again, she vowed. She wouldn't let herself be like Mama, a victim of false hopes and desperate dreams. She would know better next time.

With Jedd . . . and with any man.

After a long and lonely night, Willie rose early, eager to flee the bed where she'd spent restless hours in painful rumination and dark, unsettling dreams. She drank a tall glass of orange juice to quench the thirst that had wakened her, dressed quickly, and left the house, not wanting to face either Mama's sympathy or Neal's smirking curiosity.

But as she walked outside, she saw to her dismay that Neal was sipping a cup of coffee at the poolside table, almost as if he were waiting for her. She was forced to greet him politely, but she didn't sit down.

"Up so early?" he asked pleasantly.

"I thought I'd go to the boutique," she improvised. "I'm sure the stock needs rearranging after the party . . . "

"How very considerate you are," he said in the same pleasant tone. "You know, Willa, I do admire and care for

172

you. I wish you would believe that I have only your best interests at heart . . . "

Willie found that hard to believe, but she nodded, and for Mama's sake, she said: "I appreciate all you've done for me, Neal."

He smiled broadly and made a deprecating gesture with his hand. "Don't even mention it, my dear. I want you to be as happy and fulfilled as your mother is now . . . "

Willie nodded again, looking for a chance to escape.

" . . . and that's why I must express my concern about your obvious attachment to young Fontana."

Willie froze. The last thing in the world she wanted to do was discuss Jedd with her stepfather – especially since there was now nothing to say. "You must be mistaken," she said. "I've seen Jedd a few times, but that's all there is to it."

But Neal would not let go. "I'm relieved to hear you say that, Willa. The Fontanas have money and a measure of social position, but they really aren't our sort of people."

Willie sat down without even realizing she'd done so. "What do you mean?" she asked.

Neal smiled again, confident that he had Willie's attention. "I thought perhaps your mother's friend, the cowboy – what was his name? – might have filled you in on the Fontana family."

"Webb?" she asked sharply. "What did Webb have to do with the Fontanas? What *are* you talking about, Neal?"

"Don't excite yourself, Willa," he said soothingly. "I thought you knew that Webb was employed to transport large sums of money in a way that was, shall we say, not quite approved by the Internal Revenue Service. And that his death, while tragic, was certainly fortunate and timely for the Fontanas. I have it on good authority that federal agents were about to impound Mr. Foley's plane and to question the man himself as to his activities on Sam Fontana's behalf."

Willie stared at her stepfather in horror, and when she spoke, her voice was barely a whisper. "Are you saying that Sam Fontana had something to do with Webb's death?"

Neal shrugged and assumed a grave expression. "I'm not

173

one to spread rumors, my dear. Certainly Sam Fontana has been known to arrange . . . accidents of various kinds, when they suit his purposes. But let's not dwell on such an unpleasant subject. Since you tell me you're not seriously interested in young Fontana, there's no need to concern yourself with his family's affairs."

Reeling with shock and horror, Willie excused herself and left Neal, who bade her good day with a benevolent smile. She got into her convertible and headed east on Palm Canyon Drive. Could those awful things be true? she asked herself over and over again. She didn't think much of Neal, but why would he lie about something so terrible?

Webb – their beloved friend and protector – had his death been a tragic accident, as she had believed? Or had he been . . . eliminated, for the convenience of Sam Fontana?

And if Sam was no better than a common murderer in spite of his wealth and power, what did that make Jedd, who was blindly devoted to all that Sam stood for?

Willie parked the car, then walked to the shop, key in hand, surveying the scene of Mama's success. In the bright morning light, the window of Silver Screen looked like a cheerful anachronism, a fancy dress costume in a crowd of pinstripe suits. People bustled along on their way to work, while, reclining on her satin chaise wearing chiffon and marabou, Lola looked down on them, a Pall Mall cigarette tucked in her ebony holder, a bottle of Dom Perignon at her side. Passers-by stopped, gathering in small clusters, glancing from Lola to the gold-lettered name on the door, evidently trying to figure out exactly what could be bought in this unusual-looking place.

In spite of her distress, Willie was impressed with Ginny's imagination. Most of the shops on this strip of prime real estate had windows that could be interchangeable, all displaying dresses or shoes or sportswear in a straightforward, cookie-cutter fashion. But Silver Screen stood out, with its evocation of a mood, a state of mind, and for a moment Willie forgot her distress, feeling a deeper understanding of her mother as a beautiful, ingenuous woman who had once enriched a drab, humdrum life with her naive notions of glamour.

She didn't notice the long black limousine that pulled up at the curb a few yards away – and she jumped like a startled fawn when a voice called out her name.

"Willie! What a lucky surprise!"

She whirled around to face Jedd. "You!" The word sounded like an epithet. "I didn't think you'd have the nerve to talk to me again," she said, her voice constricted with fresh anger and raw hurt.

Now it was Jedd's turn to look startled, but he recovered quickly. "I'm really sorry I couldn't make the party," he said softly, lowering his voice so curious passers-by wouldn't hear. "I wanted to, Willie, more than I can say—"

"Really?" she interrupted sarcastically. "Then what kept you away . . . not that I really care any more . . . "

Jedd frowned in puzzlement. "I thought I explained in my note . . . the one with the flowers."

"What note?" she demanded. "What flowers?"

Understanding dawned on Jedd's face. "Ah, Willie," he said, "no wonder you're mad at me. I was halfway out the door when Pop called me back. He'd just had an urgent call from Butte . . . an emergency at Fontana Construction. We had to sit up half the night figuring out what to do. I'm flying out this morning . . . in fact, I'm on my way to the airport right now. But I did send you flowers – and a note explaining what happened. There must have been a mix-up . . . "

She looked into the face that had bedeviled and enchanted her. Hearing Jedd's explanation suddenly reminded Willie of the day Sam had let her know – very clearly – that she was not good enough for his son. But now she knew that the Fontanas would never be good enough for her. "There *was* a mixup," she said, her voice jagged with hurt and disillusionment, "on my part. I don't want to see you again, Jedd, not today, not ever."

Her tone made Jedd flinch, but he put out his hand, brushing her face with his fingers. "Don't be like that," he pleaded, "I'll make it up to you, I promise."

"Can you bring back Webb Foley?" she demanded, pulling away from the touch that even now threatened her resolve.

"Webb Foley?" he echoed. "What are you talking about, Willie? What do I have to do with Foley?"

"That's exactly what I want to know," she lashed out. "Webb was my friend . . . and maybe he was wrong to do your father's dirty work, but he didn't deserve to die for it!"

Jedd shook his head. "I still don't know what you're talking about, Willie. What dirty work? Foley's death was an accident . . . everyone knows that."

"No," she said coldly, "everyone doesn't. Accidents can be arranged, and from what I hear, it was very convenient for Webb to die when he did: just when he was about to be questioned about the flights he made for your father."

Jedd seemed to be struggling for control, and when he spoke, his voice was strained. "You must be mistaken. I don't know who you've been talking to, but you're way off base. My father would never do anything like that. I have to go now, Willie, or I'll miss my plane, but please believe me: Pop would no more hurt anyone than I would."

"That's exactly what I thought," she said. And with that, she turned the key in the door of the boutique, let herself in, and slammed the door in Jedd's face.

4

Shaded from the scorching summer sun by a striped umbrella, Willie sipped a lemonade and watched Ginny, resplendent in a leopard-printed bathing suit and matching sarong—a Silver Screen ensemble—move from one table to another, smiling and exchanging greetings, as if the club were her private domain.

It was fun to watch Mama in her new role as designer and businesswoman, enjoying the kind of success and attention

176

she'd never imagined among Palm Springs's chic and well-dressed women. Even among those who had never worn anything that could be described as faddish, it had become *de rigueur* to own at least one Silver Screen original.

"The Silver Screen Look" had become a descriptive phrase that turned up regularly on the fashion pages of the *Desert Sun* and on the lips of women who set trends. One of Ginny's Fabulous Forties suits, a black gabardine with built-up shoulders and an accompanying silver fox scarf, had sold out five times, in spite of its $1200 price tag.

When she'd opened the shop, Ginny had planned to use a half-dozen local seamstresses to produce her designs. But before Silver Screen had reached its one-month birthday, she had been obliged to contract with a small factory in Los Angeles in order to keep up with the demand for her clothes.

All of this had Willie happy for Ginny's sake. For the first time her mother had a career, instead of just a job. And a husband who seemed to dote on her. Yet Willie felt more and more out of place in the life Mama had made for herself.

Less than a week into the summer vacation, Willie felt that coming home had been a mistake. She would have been better off signing up for summer school – or taking a study program in Europe. Now it was too late to make new plans without hurting Ginny's feelings. Mama had been so enthusiastic when she persuaded Willie to spend the holiday helping out in the boutique and relaxing at the club, "just us girls."

Ginny was indeed relaxed here, Willie thought, as Ginny stopped to chat with a waitress, on her way to the kitchen to pick up a midmorning snack. But though Willie made an effort to socialize for Mama's sake, she felt awkward and uncomfortable in this place where she had worked as waitress and locker girl – especially with Laura, who hadn't recovered from the shock of Webb's death. Laura had lost her perkiness and bounce, and around Ginny or Willie, she had become somehow distant and too polite. But there was no one else at the club that Willie cared about.

177

Sam had seen to it that Jedd was spending the summer working in Montana, far out of her reach. Jedd would always do what his father wanted, and even if she still wanted him – which she didn't – Sam's will would prevail. And she wasn't about to let Jedd – or Sam – hurt her again.

Last month, just as if she hadn't told him off, Jedd had written a short letter saying he'd be spending the summer "learning the family business from the bottom," working on a shopping center being built by the Fontana Construction Company. "Pop says this kind of experience will make my MBA (when I get it) worth something. He says I've been a playboy long enough." The letter ended: "Miss you terribly." She had torn it up and thrown it away.

As she pondered the prospect of a long, long vacation with no one her age to talk to, Willie heard her name on the club loudspeaker. "Telephone call for Miss Willie Della-haye . . . please pick up the courtesy phone at the bar."

Who could be calling her? she wondered, getting up from her lounge and striding quickly toward the bar, oblivious to the admiring glances her slender body commanded. She picked up the telephone. "Thank *heavens* I've located you," a familiar voice exclaimed dramatically. "I'd have been devastated if you weren't here, today of all days."

"Cheryl!" Willie laughed with delight. "Where are you?"

"At Malcolm's house . . . expecting you for lunch. And you must come, you simply must."

"Of course, I'll come . . . but why didn't you tell me you'd be in Palm Springs?"

"No questions now. All will be answered in due course, I promise. Adieu."

Willie was still smiling when she hung up. Hearing from Cheryl was like a tonic. They hadn't seen each other in ages, though they'd had some strange phone conversations. Toward the end of the school term, Cheryl had reported she'd been put on academic probation – and she'd done it with such obvious delight that Willie had been at a loss to reply.

"Does that mean summer school?" she'd asked.

"No, old buddy," Cheryl had said airily. "Nothing of the

178

kind. I intend to make *much* better use of my summer. Malcolm notwithstanding."

So what was she up to now? Willie wondered.

Willie parked her convertible in the sweeping circular driveway of Malcolm Vinnaver's Hollywood-style villa, remembering that it had never felt like a happy home. There was nothing in it to suggest that Malcolm had ever had a family. The cinema (Malcolm never used the word "movies") memorabilia he'd collected suggested only that he'd had a career and some measure of success. Against this background, Cheryl had seemed most unhappy, and Willie puzzled over why she'd been invited here, when in the past Cheryl had been glad of any excuse to spend her time elsewhere.

Willie rang the doorbell of the somewhat run down mansion, and was startled to hear Cheryl sing out cheerfully: "Coming . . . *subito, subito.*"

As the door opened, Cheryl hurled herself into Willie's arms and hugged away until they were both breathless. "Dear Willie, how good of you to come on such short notice," she said, in a style that was broad even for a Vinnaver.

"I've missed you," Willie said. When she stepped back, she could hardly believe her eyes. "Cheryl! You're thin! My God, but you're . . . a string bean!" For the first time Willie could see the resemblance to Cheryl's famous mother. "And," she said, her voice filling with genuine admiration, "you're beautiful." Cheryl's mousy brown hair had been transformed by a fashionable Sassoon blunt cut and shimmering golden highlights. Her fair complexion was clear and glowing, and her eyes were artfully smudged with taupe shadow and outlined dramatically with charcoal pencil. Her round-shouldered slump had given way to a proud, erect carriage. The self-professed ugly duckling had become a swan.

Cheryl pirouetted, obviously enjoying Willie's surprise. "My latest shrink, and . . . well, I'll tell you the rest later. Come in, come in. Can I fix you a drink before lunch? Some white wine?"

179

Willie hesitated. "Only if you're having something."

"Of course I'm having something. After all those years of deprivation . . . " She caught the look on Willie's face and laughed. "I know what you're thinking . . . all those cheeseburgers and milk shakes and candy bars. Consumed, but not enjoyed. Now I only eat to enjoy. What about you, old buddy? You were always thin, but are you happy? Enjoying a glorious love life? First in your class at college?"

Willie took a sip of her white wine. "Well . . . I don't know about 'happy,' but I'm doing well in school . . . "

Cheryl smiled serenely and squeezed Willie's hand. "You know," she said, "for the first time since we've known each other, I don't wish we could change places. For the first time, I think I even prefer my own life."

Willie was more mystified than ever, and she was sure Cheryl had planned it that way. She was also sure that Cheryl intended to direct this visit just as Malcolm directed his pictures. "What's for lunch?" she asked, trying to move things along.

"Poached salmon. I'm making good use of Malcolm's cook while I'm here. Rita does a salad dressing you'll die from. But before we eat, I want to show you something." She pulled Willie into her father's study and pointed to a bank of framed photographs: leading men and leading ladies, celebrated screen writers and well-known producers, all posed with Malcolm in various attitudes of congeniality. "Find the one that doesn't fit," Cheryl commanded.

Willie scanned the wall. The mystery picture was in the middle. It was the new, slender Cheryl dressed in a white mini dress and matching boots, holding a bouquet of orchids and being kissed by a young man who looked vaguely familiar.

"I don't get it," Willie said.

"Look underneath."

In another frame was a wedding license issued to Cheryl Louisa Vinnaver and Robert Allen Mason.

"Cheryl, you didn't!"

"Bet your sweet ass I did," Cheryl announced dramatically. "And this," she pointed to the document, "is the only

180

announcement Malcolm will get, when he next visits the shrine of his souvenirs. And if this gesture has a certain 'fuck you' quality, that is exactly what I intended."

"Where's the lucky groom?" Willie asked. "Do I get to congratulate him?"

"He's at his mother's . . . my *mother-in-law's* . . . picking up some things. Come back tonight, and you can be our first official guest. Mr. and Mrs. Mason entertain – ta ra!"

"What about Malcolm? Where is he?"

"Who knows?" Cheryl answered impatiently. "Who cares any more? I have Robbie now. *Wait* till I tell you how we met again. It was in Beverly Hills, and it was *so* romantic . . . "

"Wait a minute," Willie interrupted. "I'm happy for you, Cheryl, I really am. And I'd love to have dinner with you tonight. But what happened? You used to call Robbie all kinds of names."

"I did, didn't I?" She smiled mischievously. "I lied. My last shrink showed me how I didn't believe anyone worthwhile could love me. So, naturally, I made Robbie into a drip."

"You sound like you have everything figured out." Willie felt a twinge of envy. She didn't hold much with psychiatry, and she had no interest in marriage. But they certainly had done wonders for Cheryl.

In between mouthfuls of poached salmon, Cheryl chattered animatedly about how she and Robbie had rediscovered each other and found true love. But for Willie, the meal was a little sad. She didn't begrudge Cheryl the first happiness she'd known, but she kept thinking that yet another chapter in her life was coming to an end. Cheryl was finally getting the chance to leave someone behind.

After she'd said good-bye, Willie phoned the boutique and told Mama she wouldn't be coming in this afternoon. The visit with her old friend had only added to her restlessness, the feeling that she should be somewhere far from Palm Springs, doing new things.

She decided to return to the house, to work off her tensions with a vigorous solitary swim. Neal had announced an overnight trip to Sacramento, and she could have the place to herself. Dodging Neal without seeming rude was getting harder, for he insisted on "taking an interest," which meant asking personal questions, poking, probing, and insinuating.

She changed into the one-piece Speedo she used for serious swimming and dove into the clear turquoise water. Back and forth she went from one end of the pool to the other, slicing the water with long steady strokes. Ten laps, twenty; she swam on until she'd done fifty.

Leaving the pool at last, she took a cold, bracing shower that left her energized and refreshed. Looking around her bathroom for her hair dryer, she realized it was missing. Had she left it at the club . . . ? Never mind, she could borrow Mama's—

She hesitated, struck by a momentary reservation about "trespassing." The part of the house where Mama lived with Neal felt oddly off-limits to her, unlike the free and easy exchange they'd had when she and Mama had shared a home together.

But she told herself not to be silly. Mama certainly wouldn't mind if she borrowed something of hers.

Willie checked the pink marble master bathroom, but there was no dryer in sight. She went into the bedroom, looked first in Ginny's closet, then opened the night-table drawer. No sign of the dryer at first.

Suddenly, a black snakey thing caught her eye. She plucked it up, thinking it might be the cord of the dryer . . . but as it came further out of the drawer, she realized it was something else, an item that made Willie recoil even as she clung to it in curious fascination: a leather cat-o'-nine-tails, ugly and sinister and suggestive. For a moment after it was fully revealed, she stared at it hanging from her hand. Then, half in disgust and half in fury, she flung it away onto the bed.

Again she paused, horrified and yet riveted. In her thoughts, she went through the exercise of asking herself what this thing had been doing in Mama's drawer. But she knew the answer, knew it in spite of not wanting to know . . .

She ought to put the whip back and leave the room now, Willie knew. But now she couldn't stop herself from returning to the drawer, opening it wider to forage through its contents.

With growing horror, she dug out a leather harness, a choke collar and an ivory box ornately carved with erotic designs which held a half dozen reefers, several pills of various colors and a dozen ampules which Willie recognized as amyl nitrate – "poppers" – of the kind favored at school by drug-taking students who swore they produced unforgettable orgasms.

She shrunk back in disbelief, her imagination running wild, drawing obscene, disturbing pictures of what went on in this room between Mama and Neal. Dizzily, she leaned against the wall, then subsided onto the bed, trying to collect herself . . .

All right, she told herself. Suppose Neal and Mama went in for kinky sex, things she would find bizarre . . . so did a lot of kids she went to school with. Maybe she and Mama just weren't on the same wavelength. She had no right to be here, to pry like this. Mama was an adult, and what she did in her bedroom was her own private business.

Quickly, Willie gathered up the offending articles and returned them to the drawer. When she tried to replace them just as she'd found them, she saw a large manila envelope. She reached for it, pulled back, then reached again. There was no turning back now.

When she tore open the envelope, the images that were revealed hit her with the force of a clenched fist. Photographs, Polaroid candids. Unthinkable, unreal. Her mother spread-eagled on the bed, being fondled by two strangers, a man and a woman. Mama, wearing the leather harness and black stockings, posed on an upholstered chair, her legs draped obscenely over the arms, masturbating with a vibrator. There were more, dozens of poses, and Willie looked at them all, just as if someone were holding a gun to her head, forcing her to see every awful detail. Suddenly she felt her stomach lurch.

She ran into the bathroom, vomiting in a trail that led

from the marble floor to the toilet. She felt lost, discon- nected, as if the real Willie had gone somewhere else, leaving this shell who huddled against the cool porcelain of the sink, weak and shaking and confused.

Time passed, she didn't know how long, but finally she made herself get up and begin cleaning the mess. Still shaky, she moved mechanically, wiping the floor, spraying the bathroom with the air freshener.

She forced herself to go back into the bedroom, to gather up the evidence of just how corrupt and sordid the life into which Neal had led her mother had become, and to put it back where she'd found it.

Finished with the task, she ran to her own room at the other end of the house, shut the door, and slipped onto the bed, pressing her palms against her eyelids, feeling trapped in her own head, trapped in this house. Mama was allowing herself to be used like a common prostitute. And only Mama could answer the question Willie was compelled to ask, went on asking over and over in her mind: *Why? Oh, why, Mama, why . . . ?*

She lay there, immobilized, barely aware of the fading daylight, watching the hours go by on her clock radio. She listened, straining for the sound of movement, until she heard a door being slammed. Then she dragged herself out of bed and into the kitchen, where her mother was pouring herself a glass of lemonade.

Ginny looked up with a smile. "Hi, baby," she said. "You missed the nicest dinner at Helen Palmer's. I figured you had plans when you didn't come into the shop. Gosh, honey, you look awful . . . are you coming down with something?"

"Oh, Mama." Willie murmured, heavy with misery and torn between anger and pity. "I went into your bedroom to borrow a hair dryer. I didn't mean . . . but I found . . . everything. All the stuff you and Neal use . . . and those pictures . . . " She felt nauseous again, and clutched her hands over her stomach as though to keep herself from flying apart. "Mama, I don't understand . . . you've got to tell me . . . "

184

She waited expectantly, desperately wanting Ginny to say something that would make sense.

Ginny's expression darkened, and she looked down at the floor. She was silent for what felt like a very long time. When she spoke, her voice was low and quiet. "You've never been married, baby. You don't know how it is between a man and a woman."

"No!" Willie said sharply. "I can't believe that. Neal's making you do those things. Tell me the truth. We don't have to stay here . . . we can go away."

Ginny shook her head, and looked back to Willie, her topaz eyes clouded with pain. "It isn't that easy. Oh, honey," she sighed, "when are you gonna understand things aren't all black and white?" She braced herself against the counter. "It's not the way you think," she said harshly. "Maybe I like what Neal and I do . . . "

"No! Stop it! You don't mean that! You think we need him . . . but we don't, Mama. I know you married him so you could give me all the things we didn't have. But I don't need that, Mama. We can manage without Neal."

"No, Willie! I need a man. Oh God, baby, I do love you. I don't want you to think I'm . . . no good. But I can't be alone, see? And what Neal wants, well . . . " She shrugged, as though no more explanation were necessary or deserved.

Willie recoiled. She couldn't stay and listen to Mama minimizing what she'd done. She shrank back through the nearest doorway, then ran to her bedroom and slammed the door. Turning the air conditioner on "high," she crawled under the light blanket that covered her bed. She wanted so desperately to feel safe and secure, but she knew that wasn't going to happen.

Lying in her cocoon, she thought of the awful pictures – and of Ginny's suggestion that she might enjoy Neal's depraved sexual scenarios. Was Mama really like that? she wondered.

She recalled then her own wanton hunger for Jedd, her craving for the pleasures of his touch. Maybe, she thought, maybe I'm like that, too.

185

Willie sat in the law offices of Callendar, Hodge, Ringley and Waite – and waited to be interviewed for a summer internship. The place reminded her of a scene from Charles Dickens, perhaps *Great Expectations*. The mahogany and brass furnishings had a quaint old-fashioned look, as did the framed portrait of the partners, in their three-piece blue suits and plain, serviceable spectacles. Callendar and Waite had shuffled off this mortal coil decades ago, but their names were still memorialized in gold letters on the ornately paneled door. In the fusty wood-paneled suite of offices on Boston's State Street, it was as if time had stood still. The old-world atmosphere, so removed from the hectic pace of the Boston streets outside, accounted for the nickname by which the firm was known – more in affection than mockery – among the rest of the Boston legal fraternity: "Ring and Wait."

Venerable the firm was, even for Boston. Traditional it was, even for Boston. Different, certainly, from anything Willie had known.

And though the pay would be negligible and the hours long, Willie badly wanted to work here. A summer's employment at Callendar, Hodge, Ringley and Waite would look good on her application to Harvard Law. And, of course, the internship would keep her well away from Palm Springs.

After that awful day in Mama's bedroom, Willie had wanted desperately to transfer to an eastern school, to get as far away from California as she could. But she had known that getting accepted so late in the summer would be almost impossible – unless she asked for Neal's help.

Willie could hardly bear to look at her stepfather, and

she had thought long and hard before she made the request. Neal, on the other hand, seemed delighted that she had come around to his way of thinking. He had called a few of his friends in the East, mentioning Willie's superb academic record. Within a matter of days, she was given a place in the junior class at Radcliffe, the women's college of Harvard University.

The move had meant another new start for Willie, a blank page to be filled with new achievements. When she'd applied for the summer internship program, there was no real competition for the position she wanted at "Ring and Wait."

At a few minutes before four o'clock, the elderly receptionist led Willie down a long corridor to the desk of a middle-aged secretary, who in turn escorted Willie to the office of Bodleigh Hodge III, ranking senior partner. "Good afternoon, sir," she said, extending her hand as he rose from his chair. Hodge, a Harvard trustee, greeted Willie with a look of surprise, as if it had slipped his mind that he'd agreed, as an accommodation to one of the Radcliffe trustees – a formidable dowager and past president of the Colonial Dames – to participate in the summer internship program. A slightly built man with a scholarly, somewhat absentminded air, Hodge had a graying, crusty exterior that marked his age as somewhere between fifty and seventy.

Looking across his desk, Hodge blinked several times behind his gold-rimmed glasses, as if he had not actually expected a young woman to turn up, and a beautiful young woman at that. Then he cleared his throat and summoned his secretary to produce Willie's file, which he also scrutinized with an air of surprise.

"Well, Miss Dellahaye," he said finally, "everything here seems to be in order. Your scholastic record is satisfactory, yes, more than satisfactory. Your duties will consist of cataloging the law library and generally assisting our associates. You will be working with my son, who will also serve a summer internship with our firm. If you'll report to my secretary on the first day of June, she'll introduce you to the staff and get you settled."

Now it was Willie's turn to be surprised. The interview was obviously over, and she hadn't been called on to answer a single question. She stood up and hesitated for a moment, not knowing if anything further was expected. Hodge shook her hand cordially and said, "If at any time you have questions, don't hesitate to ask them. At Callendar, Hodge, Ringley and Waite, we favor honest, forthright ignorance over the careless variety."

On her first day of work, Hodge's secretary introduced Willie to every member of the firm, most of whom regarded her with the same mixture of surprise and reserved cordiality, as if they didn't quite understand what she was doing there, but were prepared to welcome her to the extent that breeding and good manners dictated. The single exception was her fellow intern, Bodleigh Hodge IV.

Like Willie, "Bud" Hodge was an undergraduate at Harvard. And like Willie, he was intelligent and ambitious. He was tall and fair, attractive in a dry, cheerless way.

After the introduction had been made, Willie extended her hand and said: "Hi, I'm Willie Dellahaye. I'm the new intern."

Ignoring the proffered hand, he replied, "So I see," his tone intimating that he knew exactly who she was – and was not impressed.

Sour grapes, Willie decided. Bud probably resented her presence on his ancestral territory, and though she couldn't admire his attitude, she tried at first to understand it.

She'd arrived already convinced she would encounter all kinds of "isms" – snobbism, old-moneyism, and of course, sexism. She knew very well that the law was a men's club; she'd heard the statement made often enough.

But by the end of her first week, Willie found the atmosphere at this old and distinguished firm – where no woman had ever been employed in other than a secretarial capacity – was not what she'd expected. The partners of the firm were, by virtue of birth and breeding, members of a far more elite club than The Law. They were part of Boston's old guard. Snug and secure in their rarefied elitism, they were capable of a certain noblesse oblige, a kind of magnanimous tolerance toward outsiders – providing, of course, that such people did not make the mistake of presuming beyond their "outsider" status.

By the end of her second week, Willie learned that her employer, contrary to his outward aspect, knew more about the inner workings of the firm than all the partners and associates combined, and, for that matter, more about the law than most of the other lawyers up and down State Street. She also learned that he was generous with his knowledge and scrupulously fair – unlike his son, Bud.

Willie couldn't say exactly who disliked whom first, but she and Bud seemed destined for mutual antipathy, which only ripened as the weeks passed.

The first time Bud "forgot" to give her a memo from one of the junior partners, with instructions for researching a brief, Willie gave him the benefit of the doubt. A careless but honest mistake, she told herself.

But again, a week later, she was called on the carpet by no less a personage than Hodge the Third. "Miss Della-haye," he said sternly, "I believe you were instructed to complete the research on the Harkavy matter by yesterday afternoon. May I ask where your research is?"

Willie stared at her employer. Had she simply forgotten something so important as a memo from a senior partner?

"Come, come, Miss Dellahaye," Hodge said impatiently, "my memo was very specific. I wrote it on Thursday, and Bud kindly offered to deliver it on the spot. That means you've had four work days to compile some rather simple material. Will you explain to me why it was not done?"

Comprehension came in a blaze. Bud had done it again, and this time she could be sure it was no accident.

Yet she knew it would be foolish to tell the elder Hodge that his son was a sneak. She tried to think quickly, to find an explanation that would not sound childish and unprofessional. But there was none. At last she answered lamely,

189

"I'm sorry, Mr. Hodge. I'll have the research on your desk tomorrow."

She left the senior partner's office seething with indignation. Even if she worked through the night, the assignment would still be two days late.

She marched straight into Bud's cubicle. "Where is it?" she demanded hotly.

"Where's what?" he said blithely, not even looking up.

"That goddamn memo I was supposed to get last week."

His expression didn't change as he lifted his eyes from his work. "If you look through that mess you call a desk," he said evenly, "I'm sure you'll find it somewhere."

Willie didn't have to look. Something in Bud's tone told her she would indeed find the missing memo right there – buried, concealed, but planted right there.

"Damn it, Bud," she said, "why are you doing these things? Why not fight fair? This is your territory, I know that. I'm not trying to take anything away. I'll be out of here in September. Why can't you just give me a break until then?"

He favored her with a tight-lipped smile and a candid answer. "Nothing personal, Miz Dellahaye. Call it protectionism. Call it . . . my contribution to social Darwinism. I'm looking after my own interests, and it's up to you to do the same. I don't see why I should make any effort to help you succeed in a field that's very competitive and very crowded."

"To be fair and decent, that's why," she sputtered, disarmed by the blatancy of his challenge. "How are you going to be a lawyer if you can't be fair?"

The thin smile almost became a grin. "Go into the law expecting it to be fair, Miz Dellahaye, and your clients are going to have Don Quixote for an advocate."

She swallowed her anger and indignation, just as she'd had to do so many times before. But she vowed inwardly as she left Bud Hodge's cubicle that one day she wouldn't have to be so careful of those who could stop her if she said what she thought. Some day she'd be free and strong enough to say exactly what was on her mind. What a glorious day that would be!

Meanwhile, she tried to keep out of Bud's way, which wasn't easy, since they occupied adjoining cubicles in a far corner of the firm's suite of offices. But she never stopped being astounded that, even when he was virtually assured of acceptance into Harvard Law, with three sanctified generations of alumni before him, Bud felt it necessary to stoop to such petty acts of sabotage.

Determined to succeed in spite of him, Willie gave Callendar, Hodge, Ringley and Waite nothing less than her best. Most of her work was simple and mechanical: cataloging the library, filing, copying, elementary research. But as she showed herself to be hardworking and eager for more, the junior partners occasionally instructed their secretaries to give her freshly typed contracts and briefs for preliminary proofing and checking.

It was while she was performing that function, reading through a complex sixty-page merger contract, that Willie happened to spot a mistake, one that had gone unnoticed by both an associate and a junior partner. It was only a tiny error, an ambiguity in language – but one which, if uncorrected, could have compromised the client's right to exercise a stock option worth hundreds of thousands of dollars. Willie called the mistake to the attention of the client's staff attorney, and the error was promptly corrected.

Her diligence was rewarded with an accolade from no less than Mr. Hodge himself. "Miss Dellahaye," he said, stopping her as they passed in the corridor one evening when Willie had stayed late, "allow me to remark that although you are the first female we have ever employed outside of our secretarial staff, you have been a real asset. You show great initiative, and an aptitude that is remarkable in one yet untrained in the basic elements of law."

Caught between amusement and amazement at his testimonial, delivered in such a formal manner beside the water cooler, Willie barely had a chance to stammer out a thank-you before he went on:

"My partners and I would be most pleased if you were to return next summer."

Arriving the next morning for work, Willie could tell by the glowering look Bud gave her from his desk ten feet away that he must have heard about the encounter, probably directly from his father at dinner last night. Willie couldn't resist returning a smile redolent with triumph before chirping an overly cheerful, "Good morning, Mr. Hodge."

In return, Bud's expression darkened, as if to say he hadn't finished with her, not by a long shot.

For the remainder of the summer, Willie kept a sharp eye out for Bud's little tricks. But none were forthcoming, at least none she knew about.

When Mr. Hodge called her into his office just before the Labor Day weekend, she had a momentary flicker of apprehension. Had Bud set her up for a dressing-down by his father? Would the offer for next summer be withdrawn? Willie's concern grew when she saw Hodge the Third's solemn expression.

"Miss Dellahaye," he said, "before you return to your academic pursuits, I wish to speak to you about the single blemish on your tenure here. Please sit down . . ."

Willie sank into the seat facing her employer, her worst fears confirmed.

"I could not help but notice," he said, "that you have had a less than cordial relationship with your fellow intern – my son, Bud . . ."

Willie sat silently, unable to deny the charge.

"For an attorney, Miss Dellahaye, the ability to get along with one's fellow man, particularly one's peers – or at the very least, to maintain the *appearance* of getting along – can be a valuable professional tool."

Still Willie remained silent. The man was, after all, Bud's father.

"Silence can be eloquent," Hodge persisted, "but I am asking you now to explain the situation I have described."

It burst from her. "All right," she said. "You're right. I don't get along with Bud. I was willing and ready to work

192

with him, but he made it very clear that he wanted no part of that. All he's done since is undercut my work and try to make me look bad."

"And why would he do that?" Hodge's expression behind the gold-rimmed glasses was impassive.

"I don't know," she answered truthfully. "I suppose he resents my being here on his ancestral territory. Or perhaps he doesn't like seeing a woman invading the profession he's staked out for himself . . ."

Hodge stared at her, as if he were assessing her credibility as a witness. Abruptly, he dismissed her. "Thank you, Miss Dellahaye. I appreciate your candor."

Was that all? The interview had ended without any more cross-examination, any attempt to get beneath the surface to her complaint. But what could she say that would win Hodge's sympathy when the opponent was really his son? In Boston, blood was thicker than cement. Willie got up to leave.

But she had taken only a step before she decided there was nothing to lose by speaking on her own behalf. "Mr. Hodge," she said, turning back and walking to the edge of his desk. "I have never wanted to be anything other than a lawyer. I believe I will be a good one. I intend to apply to Harvard Law next year, and I had intended to ask you for a recommendation. I'm sure you know how much weight that would carry . . ."

Hodge eyed her impassively again. "Once again, Miss Dellahaye," he said quietly, "I thank you for speaking frankly. Good day."

Hodge's response to her appeal came with her final pay-check. In an envelope marked "Personal & Confidential" was a photostat of his letter of recommendation to the Dean of Admissions at Harvard Law, a glowing one which noted her fine record with his firm, as well as the "initiative" and "ability" he'd spoken of. No mention was made of the "single blemish" on her record that he'd discussed with her.

Accompanying the recommendation was a brief note,

193

handwritten in script as flowery and flowing as his verbal style:

My Dear Willa,
  Upon seeking the counsel of my heart, I must plead guilty to having done a better job of representing the interests of my clients than raising my only son. I hope you will not judge the tree by its branch, and I wish you well in all your endeavors.
  I should, however, add a word of warning: if Harvard Law is fortunate enough to claim you as one of its own, you may expect to encounter my son, on whom I am obliged to bestow a recommendation almost as fulsome as yours. You might turn the experience of dealing with an unwelcome adversary to advantage, as an opportunity to gain some valuable extracurricular training in the hitherto described tools of the trade.
    With all kind regards,
      Bodleigh Hodge III

6

The day before the first day of classes at Harvard Law, Willie arrived at the third-floor apartment on Hancock Street she'd leased after she finished her senior year at Radcliffe, to live while she worked at "Ring and Wait" over the summer, and to keep for her years at Harvard Law. Thanks to Hodge the Third's recommendation, she'd had no problem being accepted. Just as she pushed her key into the lock, the door was opened by a tall, stunning young woman. Lean as a whippet. A thoroughbred, vivid and high-strung, with wavy russet hair flying loose and dark brown eyes shaded with copper lights. She was dressed in emerald green pants and a matching oversize mohair sweater. This would be Willie's new roommate, picked

194

sight unseen from a pool of female first-year students –
exactly three in number – supplied by the dean of housing.

"Suzy Parker!" Willie blurted out.

"The name's Parkman, Suzanne," the young woman
said, "and only my father calls me Suzy – I hate it."

"Sorry. It's just that you look like her, Suzy Parker – you
know, the model . . .?"

Suzanne laughed, a rich throaty sound. "In that case,
you're forgiven . . . Willa. Come on in and let's get
acquainted."

"You can start by calling me Willie . . ."

"Willie, eh?" Suzanne Parkman paused to give her a
bemused look, as though perceiving that there was something a bit daring about the use of this nickname that might
as easily belong to a man. "Well, make yourself at home,
Willie."

The apartment was ablaze with color and detail. In the
few days she'd been there, Suzanne had hung a veritable
gallery of posters, filled vases with Mexican paper flowers,
covered every surface that wasn't in use with Spanish
shawls and hand-loomed pillows of a vaguely Mediterranean
character.

"I enjoy nesting," Suzanne said, watching her new
roommate's face as she took in the apartment.

"I can see that," said Willie, who had done very little
nesting in any of the temporary quarters she'd occupied
during her school years.

"You don't like my decorating?" Suzanne asked
anxiously, lighting up a cigarette, though one was already
burning in a giant Venetian glass ashtray.

"It's lovely," Willie assured her. In the way Suzanne held
her cigarette, in the tight set of her shoulders, Willie caught
a sense of something fragile in this vivid young woman,
something eager to please that roused her protective
instincts. As she watched Suzanne make a pot of tea, Willie
kept seeing Suzy Parker in *The Best of Everything*.
Although she thought of herself as immune to easy
sentimentality, Willie had been moved by that character,
by the story of her tragic love affair and descent into

195

madness. All the more so because she felt herself above that kind of thing.

Suzanne served the tea, along with a bottle of Jack Daniels. When Willie declined the bourbon, Suzanne poured a shot into her own teacup. "Don't be alarmed," she said. "It's for medicinal purposes. To loosen my tongue, so we can get personal histories out of the way. Suppose I start . . ."

She took a sip from her cup, pulled her legs up under her on the couch and went on. "I was brought up with four brothers. For the longest time, I tried to be just like them. When I was little, my father fooled me: he let me believe I could. As long as I was out there, playing touch football and tearing my jeans up, he never gave me all that sugar and spice stuff. Then tragedy struck." She paused for dramatic effect. "The Day I Became a Woman. My mother must have told him. And he must have said something to my brothers. That was the end of it. No more football. No more roughhousing. I felt like they'd hung a leper bell around my neck."

Willie listened with fascination. Suzanne was beautiful, and obviously well off. Yet she didn't seem any more comfortable in her femaleness than Willie was. A kindred spirit.

"Is that why you're going to law school?" Willie asked. "To fight against discrimination?"

"Hell, no!" Suzanne jabbed out her cigarette with long nicotine-stained fingers. "I just want to show them I'm as good – no, *better* than any boy. Even if I was born without a cock – excuse my French. Only one of my brothers has any brains worth mentioning, and he's going into marine biology. The old man was fit to be tied. 'Where's the profit in that, son?'" Suzanne harrumphed and dropped her husky voice a few octaves. "'Ivory towerism, my boy.' My brother did it anyway. He did me a favor. I figured out the world wouldn't come to an end if you didn't do what the old man said. I wasn't sure it would work for me – after all, I was only a girl.

"When I said I was going to law school, the old man acted

196

like I'd brought home a Jewish son-in-law or something he'd consider equally diabolical. I'll give him this – he put it right on the line. 'Nonsense,' he called it. 'Stuff and nonsense.'"

"What about your mother?" Willie asked.

"She couldn't figure out why I'd want a life any different from hers. A good house and good charge accounts. Marry good stock and breed good children. Do good volunteer work."

Willie thought of Ginny's ambitions for her. They weren't so different from the ones Suzanne had described. "Maybe that's part of the problem," she said. "Mothers wanting that kind of thing for daughters."

Suzanne lit a cigarette and took a gulp of her medicinal tea. "I can't think about what she wants now. First I have to do what nobody wants for me. I have to get that law degree and then . . ."

"Then – what?" Willie prodded.

Suzanne looked away through the window that faced out onto the street of trees and old wood-frame houses. "Then . . . I don't know," she confessed. "Then, if I'm lucky, I'll feel free to do something else." She turned back to Willie and smiled ruefully. "To do whatever I damn please."

Willie understood only vaguely. For most of her life, she'd had a goal, too, and proving herself over and over was a way to reach that goal. But she didn't yet see exactly why Suzanne Parkman had made law school her own personal battlefield. In time, though, Willie felt she would find out. "Why do you smoke so much?" she asked as Suzanne lit another cigarette.

Suzanne laughed. "I don't know . . . maybe because it's manly. I used to do Camels, unfiltered, but I finally got disgusted with tobacco on my tongue. So I switched to Marlboros – all those macho types sold me. My brother Jack says they're all fags, but Jack" – she rolled her eyes – "I'll let you make up your own mind about him. Now my brother Tony . . ."

Willie listened with fascination as Suzanne chattered on about her family, the little sagas of life with the Parkmans, even though another of her theories had been debunked. Suzanne had two parents, a nice home, a platoon of brothers. The family lived in Connecticut, summered in Maine and wintered in Palm Beach. Suzanne had enjoyed privileges, but not to excess. Yet she seemed to have the same restless hunger, the same displaced, dispossessed quality that Willie felt. Meeting Suzanne added to her growing store of evidence that simply having a home and a family was not a formula for happiness. But she had no idea what was.

The first year of law school left little time for thinking – or for philosophical musings about happiness. The work wasn't as difficult as Willie had been led to believe, but it was abundant and demanding. It filled up her life and gave her an excuse to avoid going home.

She had managed to sever her financial dependence on Neal in a way that seemed nothing short of an answered prayer. A few weeks into her first semester, she had been called into the office of the dean of students and informed that she had been chosen to receive a new scholarship, designed to aid aspiring female lawyers. She had accepted it gratefully, and wrote a brief note to Mama explaining that she would no longer need Neal's tuition checks.

Just before Christmas, she jumped on Suzanne's casual remark that it would be nice if they could spend the holidays together, and got herself invited to spend two weeks in Palm Beach. To Ginny, she offered explanations that sounded lame even to her own ears, steeling herself against the hurt in her mother's voice. The truth was that Willie meant to spend as much time away from Ginny and Neal as she could, until she graduated from law school and moved away for good.

When spring break came around, she told Ginny she needed the time to finish an overdue paper. And that summer, she accepted the invitation tendered by Bodleigh Hodge III to work once again in the offices of "Ring and Wait."

She missed Mama terribly, and she felt guilty about

leaving her to Neal's manipulations. But she couldn't think of another way to deal with the revulsion she felt toward the place she had never really been able to call home.

Willie shaded her eyes against the white glare of sunbeams bouncing off the Charles River and refracting into a million splintered shards of light. The April day was cold, but the intrepid crew of the Harvard Crimson was out there, skimming the glacial waters of the river with strong, smooth, even strokes.

Snuggling into her down vest, Willie uttered a spiritless "Rah, team," and blew on her chilled fingers.

Suzanne, her roommate and now best friend after almost two years together in law school, responded by lighting her thirtieth cigarette of the day. "Rah, yourself," she said, her husky voice laced with irony. "I think there's something seriously, genetically wrong with the male fetish for strain and pain. Give me a double Jack Daniels and an unfiltered cigarette, and I'll show you what manliness is all about."

Willie laughed, as Suzanne had intended. Throughout the months together, Suzanne had been a godsend, a breath of fresh air, a blessing in disguise all rolled into one. "Think they'll win this week?" Willie asked idly, inclining her head toward the swiftly moving sculls.

"Who the hell cares?" Suzanne replied. "That rah-rah stuff is bullshit. Those guys wouldn't lose any sleep if we never made it past this semester. Why should we care if they win some stupid race? Do they care if we make *Law Review*?" Her voice rose, mocking the declaratory court-room style. "Or if old Ferguson in 'Torts' grades like the Marquis de Sade? Would any of those jocks shed a single tear over the plight of two beleaguered female law students? No, your honor, I submit they would not."

Willie smiled. She loved to hear Suzanne carry on. It was almost the way it used to be with Cheryl. She had learned what to take seriously and what to season with a grain of salt.

She and Suzanne were a different breed of oddball. Together they made a striking combination that turned many a male head. Willie's reddish blond beauty, set off by Suzanne's rich earthy coloring. But they were both different from most of the other young women to be seen in Harvard Square, the 'Cliffies and the weekend dates brought in from Wellesley and Holyoke and the other "seven sister" colleges, and they wore that difference like a badge of honor.

"My mother's plane gets in at seven o'clock," Willie said abruptly.

"I can't wait to meet her. It's been a long time since you've seen her, hasn't it?"

"Yes." Though Suzanne wasn't one to pry, Willie knew her roommate wondered why she never visited the mother she talked about so often.

When Ginny had called to say she'd be in New York looking at a new line of accessories, then hinting that she'd like to make a side trip to Boston, Willie had grabbed at the chance to see her mother alone.

Now she was feeling a little nervous about that meeting. "Want to have dinner with us?" she asked Suzanne.

Suzanne favored her with a lifted eyebrow. "If that's what you want. Your mother sounds like a dynamite lady. But don't you need some time alone? To catch up . . . or something?"

"You're right. Let's go."

They drove back to the apartment in the dark blue Chrysler sedan that had been George Parkman's college graduation gift to his daughter. The car had been a bitter disappointment to Suzanne, who had hinted for something flashy and sporty like the Ferraris and Jaguars he'd bestowed upon her brothers. She vented her disappointment by abusing the Chrysler in every way she could think of muttering "take that, you sensible sonofabitch" every time she peeled out or brought the vehicle to a screeching stop.

Ginny was waiting in the rear of the Hampshire House. Surrounded by the walnut paneling, the clubby leather-upholstered furniture that reeked of tradition, she was as

200

conspicuous as a camellia in December. She was wearing a white ermine-trimmed gabardine pantsuit, a Silver Screen creation that might have been borrowed from a *femme fatale* played by Joan Crawford in her heyday.

Willie smiled almost in spite of herself. Mama certainly knew how to brighten a room. Willie reckoned there was more candlepower in Ginny's closet than a factory full of neon bulbs. "Mama," she said affectionately. Falling into a hug, Willie noticed instantly that her mother felt slighter than she had before.

"Let me look at you, honey," Ginny said. "Gosh, if you didn't have your head set on being a lawyer, honest to goodness, you could be a model or a movie star."

A man in a club chair nearby, his attention drawn by Ginny's loud compliment and his tongue loosened by a couple of drinks, looked over at Willie, raised his glass, and muttered, "You can say that again."

Embarrassed, Willie pulled her mother down into her chair and sat beside her, her back to the drunken admirer.

They ordered drinks. "Are you happy, honey? Are you okay? I think about you so much." Ginny's expression was so anxious, so sincere, that Willie felt a pang of remorse.

"I'm fine. How have you been? How are things with Neal? I worry about you, too, Mama . . ."

Ginny covered Willie's hand with her own. "Let's not talk about that now. Tell me what you've been doing. How's that roommate of yours working out? Is she nice?"

"Suzanne's great. You'll like her. We could all have dinner at our place tomorrow night . . ."

"That would be real nice," Ginny said shyly. After a moment she blurted impulsively: "I can't stand it when things aren't so good between us, Willie. I mean, I can see you're grown up and all, but you'll always be my baby . . ."

The love in Ginny's voice added to the guilt Willie felt at having cut her off, right along with Neal. Damn it, she thought, why did men always have to mess things up? "I've missed you too," Willie said, "but I still don't understand how you can . . . live that way." She waited expectantly. She could see that Ginny didn't want to discuss the issue

201

that had separated them so cruelly. But unlike her mother, Willie didn't believe in pretending, not when that meant ignoring problems that were real.

Ginny answered reluctantly, carefully. "Things are different now, baby, honest they are. Neal's not so . . . you know . . . not anymore."

Willie shot her mother a skeptical look. The older she got, the harder it was to accept Ginny's version of reality. "But you don't love him, Mama, do you? So why do you stay? Is it just the money . . .?"

"Oh, honey, why do you always have to be asking so many hard questions? I don't know . . . Neal and me, we're married. A woman like me needs to be married." She laughed nervously, almost apologetically. "Besides, it's good to have the money. Isn't it? Isn't that what makes it possible for you and me to do what—"

Willie jumped in. "I could get a summer job, a real one that pays. I can get a student loan to help with expenses. You have your designs . . . even if you left Neal, you could still live off that."

Ginny shook her head. "I don't know . . . please, honey, can't we just let it go for now? Let's just . . . have a nice reunion. Let me tell you about New York . . . "

Willie surrendered. She never would understand why Mama spoke of needing Neal. But she had a choice: try to change her mother – save her – or build her own life. And as long as Mama didn't want to be saved, wasn't the choice clear?

Dinner at the small apartment on Hancock Street was a great success. Suzanne created a spring centerpiece of daffodils and gladiolas and prepared a delicious meal of curried chicken and rice pilaf.

Ginny oohed and aahed over Suzanne's cooking and her decorating of the apartment. And Suzanne in turn exclaimed over Ginny's outfit – a black, jet-trimmed challis suit with a peplum.

Conversation was smooth and easy, and Willie listened with amusement and pride as her roommate, who had a way with a story, regaled her mother with anecdotes about growing up in the rarefied, clubby confines of Darien, Connecticut.

No one brought up Neal's name, and Suzanne for once had little to say about her father.

When it was time to say good night, Ginny kissed her daughter and whispered, "Your friend is really swell."

After the door closed behind her, Suzanne echoed her sentiments. "I can see where you get those gorgeous looks. And talent. If I had a mother like that, I'd go home more often."

"Things at home aren't that simple," Willie said, then added as an afterthought, "She likes you, too."

"Does that mean you'll be spending another summer at 'Ring and Wait'?"

"They've asked me back," Willie said slowly. "But that's coolie labor. I need to find a paying job this year."

"Are you having money problems?" Suzanne asked. "Because if you are, I can lend you—"

"Thanks, Suze," Willie broke in. "I appreciate the offer. But I've got to earn my way." She said it so fiercely – thinking of how money might liberate her mother from Neal – that Suzanne seemed to detect that it was a kind of vow. Putting her hand to her chin in an attitude of deep thought, she stepped back to appraise Willie.

"Just how far are you willing to go to earn some money?" she asked after a moment.

"What did you have in mind?" Willie asked warily.

"Something that would probably lead to getting you a good wage-earning job for the summer."

"Sounds good so far."

"But I warn you, Willie, the very first step will bring you face-to-face with one of the most fearsome creatures in captivity, a beast wildly dangerous to any independent woman. Do you still want to proceed?"

Willie detected the glint of mischief that was sparkling in Suzanne's eyes. "Tell me – what do I have to do?"

"Come home with me . . . and meet my old man."

203

Willie laughed. "Lead on!" she said, throwing an arm around her friend's shoulder. "Together we can handle anything."

7

"One more time," Suzanne laughed, gunning the engine of the Chrysler for emphasis and then taking off in a burst of speed.

"One more time," Willie agreed, and then she began singing: "No more pencils, no more books, no more teachers' dirty looks . . ."

"Rangely, Maine, here we come!" Suzanne shouted, pressing the accelerator even harder.

"Slow down, slow down, Suze, I'm too young to die. I haven't even met your father, and I don't have a summer job."

"You will," Suzanne promised. "There are dozens of summer jobs in Rangely, and a word from the old man is the only reference you'll need. Just don't tell George you need the money. The old man doesn't believe in helping anyone who really needs it. We'll tell him you want to work because it builds character. He'll go for that."

"Anything else I should know?" Willie asked.

"If I told you, you'd turn around. Be prepared to hear at least twice the story of how old George discovered Rangely."

"How *did* old George discover Rangely?" Willie laughed.

Suzanne cleared her throat, and in ponderous, stentorian tones told the tale of how young George Parkman, a sophomore at Yale, had been invited with a group of hand-picked economics majors to a four-day retreat by the chairman of the department, Dr. Henry Franklin.

Dr. Franklin, Suzanne said, had been her father's hero and mentor, the author of a textbook on the natural and

204

moral superiority of capitalism as an economic system, a classic in its field. In the comfort of his log cabin in Rangely, Maine – then a small resort village on the western border of the state – Dr. Franklin had lectured to his protégés on the value of creative relaxation to the man of commerce. "Clear thinking," Suzanne echoed in a deep voice, "is the primary tool of the successful man. And clear thinking is often best accomplished away from the marketplace, closer, as it were, to the Creator.

"Young George took this teaching to heart," Suzanne continued, "and as soon as he had joined his father in the family brokerage firm on Wall Street, he sought out a piece of lakefront property on which to build a retreat of his own. In quick succession, he sought out a wife and began producing sons of his own. When his daughter Suzanne was born, after three sons, he took that as a sign to cease production."

Willie did not laugh, hearing as she did a hint of real pain in the conclusion to Suzanne's tale.

The Parkman lodge turned out to be a reflection of its owner. It was a huge log-and-stone house set on ten lakefront acres, solidly built and somewhat lacking in imagination. Parkman's wife, Grace – Suzanne's mother – similarly built and equipped, had decorated and furnished the house with rugged and well-chosen American country antiques that could only appreciate in value – and withstand the wear and tear imposed by a family of men.

When Willie was introduced to George Parkman, she saw at once that Suzanne's broad parodies, her mocking descriptions of her father as an old-fashioned stuffed shirt, were not far off the mark. If Willie's sense of humor had progressed to a sense of the absurd, she might have found his pomposity, his prejudices, and his posturings amusing. As it was, she found him a living example of too many male attitudes that had too long worked against women.

However, she followed Suzanne's instructions and omitted

any mention of actual need when she told George she was looking for summer employment. And as Suzanne had promised, he agreed to help.

After a fair amount of harrumphing and pontificating, Parkman phoned Lester Rollins, proprietor of the posh Blue Bass Inn, on Willie's behalf. As Suzanne had also promised, her father's recommendation was all the persuasion Rollins needed to hire Willie for the summer.

Willie liked the Blue Bass Inn at once. It was a charming white clapboard Victorian structure, built around the turn of the century to house the sportsmen who came to hunt and fish in the area. It was surrounded by acres of virgin forest and granite mountains that evoked childhood memories of South Dakota.

She also liked the proprietor, a wiry, bespectacled little man who appeared to be of the same vintage as his inn.

"The pay's $125 a week – that's high for these parts – plus whatever tips you make, and room and board if you need it," Rollins explained.

Willie thought that sounded just fine. Especially the room and board part. Fond as she was of Suzanne, she liked the idea of having somewhere else to stay, especially on weekends when all the Parkman males were generally in residence. Suzanne's brother Tony seemed to have taken a more than brotherly interest in her, and George was definitely easier to tolerate in very small doses.

"What is it I'll be doing?" Willie asked Rollins.

"We-ell," the innkeeper drawled, "let's just say you'll be my assistant, a jack-of-all-trades. You'll work for the money, all right – manage the front desk when I'm busy, help the housekeeper when one of her girls is out, fill in when we're short a waitress in the dining room or a cook in the kitchen. When you're not doing those things, you'll guide our tenderfoot guests who want to go riding or hiking or fishing. Can you handle that?"

Willie thought quickly. Thanks to Ben Cattow, she knew how to ride. She knew what poison ivy and poison oak looked like. The rest she could pick up as she went along. "Yes," she said. "When do I start?"

206

"I'm short of help as it is. Let's say tomorrow at nine o'clock."

Willie reported the results of her interview and dutifully thanked George Parkman for his recommendation.

"Glad to be of help, Willa. It's admirable that you wish to prove yourself by gainful employment. But I confess I don't understand young women today. You're a fine-looking gal, just like my own daughter Suzy. Why the two of you don't find some outstanding young men and settle down is beyond me. All this law school nonsense. I don't mind telling you that I was against it. Wouldn't pay Suzy's tuition myself, no sir. But if she wants to squander her grandfather's trust on this crazy idea of a career . . . well, there's nothing I can do. I've told her, time and time again . . ."

Before George could expand his views on what "fine-looking young gals" ought to be doing, Willie pleaded fatigue and went to bed.

"Piece of cake" was Willie's reaction after one day of work at the Blue Bass Inn. She'd waited tables for breakfast and lunch and then spent the afternoon on the bridle path with a couple of twelve-year-olds. The hardest thing she'd had to do was push away from the dinner table before she exploded with the delicious hearty fare the inn served up to satisfy man-sized appetites.

The second day was something else. She seemed to be needed everywhere at once, and before she fell into an exhausted sleep, Lester informed her that she could expect to start taking fishermen out by the end of the week.

Willie knew next to nothing about fishing, or "angling" as the real sportsmen called it. Furthermore, her experience with fishing gear had been limited to the simple homemade kind: a line and hook attached to a hickory pole, fashioned by her father when she was a little girl.

But she did know how to do research. The following day, she visited the local bait and tackle shop on her lunch hour, armed with a new notebook and a ball-point pen. When she began to quiz the shopkeeper about the gear he sold,

207

several customers gathered around, amused by the beautiful young woman who seemed to think she could learn about fishing by writing things down in a book.

"Can you tell me which rod to buy?" she asked.

"That depends," the storekeeper drawled. "What're you angling for?"

Willie didn't know what she was after. "What kind of fish are there around here?"

"Come on, Charlie," one of the customers put in, "sell the young lady an eight-foot rod and some number six line. That'll do just fine, Miss," the man said to Willie. "If you're just starting out, brook trout are your best bet . . . speckled backs, red spots, and pink fins. They're little fellows, mostly under a pound. They make mighty good eating, but they won't test your strength . . ."

"Thank you," she said, writing down what the man said. "I'll take an eight-foot rod," she told the storekeeper.

"What kind? Fiberglass or bamboo?"

Willie looked questioningly at the man who had just advised her.

"I like fiberglass – it's lighter," he said.

"But fiberglass has no soul." The deep, resonant voice came from behind her. Willie turned around to see a tall, slender man with an outdoorsman's body, wearing a khaki vest with a dozen pockets stuffed with fishing paraphernalia and a battered old hat encrusted with trout flies. Under the hat, an unruly wave of silver hair fell across his forehead. His face was deeply tanned and ruggedly handsome in spite of the rakish bump that marred the bridge of his nose, as though it had been broken in some long-forgotten brawl; his clear gray eyes seemed to sparkle with secret laughter. "Choose a bamboo rod," he said. "It's friendlier and more forgiving."

Willie was charmed. "Thank you," she said. "I will. Can you tell me what else to buy?"

"My pleasure," he smiled. "Rods and reels are the body of tackle, but flies are its poetic essence. Here," he said, guiding her toward a glass display case. "These are the so-called dry flies. Our local trout seem to favor the Royal

Coachman, the Brown Bivisible and the Adams Blue Dunn. Try them," he said, "and add a few streamers and bucktails – those, over there, the winged ones made of silver or gold tinsel . . . I think the Green Ghost, the Mickey Finn, and the Dark Tiger."

Again, Willie wrote everything down. "This is more complicated than I'd thought, Mr. . . . ."

"Call me Matt," the stranger said.

She guessed he might be a local guide, he sounded so well informed about local fishing. "I'm Willie Dellahaye," she responded, "and I certainly appreciate your help. But there seems to be so much to learn. Is there a book you could recommend?"

Matt nodded. "Charley has a few dusty paperbacks that have been here for as long as I can remember. Any one of them can teach you the rudiments of fishing. But if you want more than mechanics, go to the library and get a copy of Izaak Walton's *The Compleat Angler*. That was written in 1754, and I'd say nobody's added a hell of a lot you'd need to know since then."

As she listened to Matt speak, Willie thought she might actually come to enjoy this part of her new job. "There's just one more thing . . . "

"Ask away, Willie."

"I was wondering if you could also recommend a good spot to fish . . . somewhere not too far from the Blue Bass Inn?"

Matt thought for a few moments. "Try the Three Widows," he said. "That's about a mile from the Inn, due south and just past Wesley's Corner. You'll know you've reached it when you spot three granite boulders in a triangle formation."

Willie thanked him again and carried her purchases to the counter in the front of the store. As the owner tallied up her bill, she saw Matt leave with a jaunty wave in her direction. She felt oddly disappointed that their acquaintance had been so brief.

Two days later, Lester Rollins caught Willie while she was

cleaning ashes out of the big stone fireplace in the inn's dining room and told her she'd be taking out one of his clients on a "fishing expedition" the next morning.

She had done as much homework as her busy schedule would allow, but she still felt woefully unprepared. That night she set her alarm for five o'clock, and went to sleep praying that her charge would catch something, anything, so her own lack of experience wouldn't show.

The next morning, dressed in worn jeans and a plaid shirt, Willie felt she looked like a seasoned outdoorswoman as she and the inn's paying guest, a stolid humorless corporate executive from New Jersey, made their way southward through the woods to the clear, swiftly moving waters of a nearby stream.

In a wicker basket, Willie carried some excellent sandwiches and a large Thermos of coffee, which she hoped would be some consolation if the fish weren't biting. She also hoped that the client's equipment, which looked new, expensive, and more complicated than her own, had been demonstrated by whoever had sold it.

"What do you think, Miss?" the man asked, when they reached a spot where the stream narrowed, just before it spilled over some rocks. "This looks like a good spot, doesn't it?"

They hadn't yet reached the place Matt had recommended, but Willie agreed to stop, since her client seemed eager to try his luck.

Fortunately the man seemed to know what to do with his equipment, requiring nothing more from her than an occasional comment about the beauty of the landscape and the clear, clean crispness of the air. Willie watched him cast, thinking she might pick up a few pointers.

The man fished patiently for two hours, and when he caught nothing, Willie suggested an early lunch, followed by a change of location. "This spot's a little tricky," she improvised. "Sometimes the fish practically jump into your basket – I mean creel – and sometimes it's like today: quiet."

She tried to draw the lunch out, but the man bolted his

210

sandwiches in his eagerness to try again. "Well," she said brightly, "let's head further south – I know a terrific spot, The Three Widows. It can be a little tricky, too, but I have a feeling . . ."

"The Three Widows, eh?" said her customer, evidently impressed with her apparent knowledge of local geography. "Sounds like just the spot for me . . ."

Willie smiled to herself.

They walked about a mile along the winding stream before they came to the formation of three granite stones that had been described to Willie at the tackle shop. Nearby, Willie spotted a lone man reeling in a fish. "Here we are," she said. "I see someone's beat us to it, but I'm sure there are fish enough for two."

While the businessman from New Jersey cast his line, Willie ambled toward the other fisherman. As she came closer, she recognized the battered hat and the khaki vest. It was the guide from the bait and tackle shop, Matt.

"Hello, again," she ventured, hoping he wasn't one of those fanatics who thought talking while fishing was sacrilegious.

He turned and favored Willie with a smile that lit up his gray eyes. "Good day to you," he said, and she noticed again how clear and strong his voice was. "I see you managed to find this place—"

"Thanks to your directions."

"You won't be disappointed. It's one of my favorites."

"Had much luck today?" she asked.

He smiled again. "Ah," he said, "there's much more to fishing than luck. It takes patience and skill and intuition and timing, just like anything worthwhile."

When Willie didn't reply, he said: "You're welcome to join me here if you like."

"I'm not fishing. I'm supposed to be the guide," she said. "I work at the Blue Bass."

"I see." Matt's gray eyes sparkled with amusement.

Willie flushed with embarrassment and lowered her voice so it wouldn't carry downstream to her charge. "It's only part of my job, and it's the only part I don't know how to do . . . but I'm trying to learn."

"Then allow me to help. Both you and your gentleman whose line seems to be tangled in the rocks."

Willie turned back to where she'd left her charge. "Oh, dear. I would appreciate your help . . . but, well, you see, he thinks I know what I'm doing. I'd better get over there myself . . ."

"I understand," Matt said solemnly. "Your secret's safe with me. Here . . ." He extracted a spool of new line from one of his many pockets and held it out. "The man seems to be using silk line, Willie. It's much too temperamental for a novice. Have him try this nylon one."

"Gosh, thanks, Matt . . ." She started away.

"And once his line is loose," Matt added in a hush, "tell him to move downstream about ten yards, to where that oak tree stands."

"Are the fish biting there?" Willie asked.

"I have no idea," Matt laughed. "But it'll be easier for me to keep an eye on him."

For the next few days Willie followed the same routine, bringing the guests from the inn to the spot she and Matt designated. He'd be close by, feeding her instructions and suggestions: "Wear darker, duller colors – khaki's best. You don't want the light to reflect off your clothes. And be careful not to cast a shadow on the water." He also shared odd bits of local lore that would enhance her credibility as a guide.

Willie felt more relaxed than she'd been in a long time. The sunshine and fresh air were wonderful after long months spent in classrooms and libraries. And her new friend Matt had piqued her curiosity. She had first imagined he might be a local sportsman or a guide. But now she wondered. He certainly knew a lot about fishing, but his manner hinted at a kind of refinement and worldliness that suggested more than a life spent outdoors.

"How did you get into . . . fishing?" she asked him once: "Are you a professional?"

"No, Willie," he replied with a lilt, as if enjoying some private joke, "though I can think of any number of people who wish I were."

She wanted to know more about this man, who was rugged and smooth at the same time, and completely at home in the outdoors. But she felt that to ask more would be prying.

She was surprised, at the end of the sixth day they had spent together by the stream, when he invited her to spend her day off with him. But then she realized it was exactly what she wanted, a chance to know him better, and she accepted at once.

Willie wasn't sure whether it was a "date" or a friendly day out, yet when she woke up and started to dress, she found herself taking a little extra care with her hair and makeup and choosing a new shirt to wear with her jeans. It was foolish, she told herself at moments. Matt certainly had some of the ageless attractiveness of, say, Cary Grant. But he had to be in his fifties. Why did she feel as if she was dressing to impress him? No, more: to show herself off.

After breakfast, she waited for Matt on the big wrap-around porch of the inn. A few minutes past nine, a 1947 Cadillac convertible, as shiny and immaculate as the day it had rolled off the assembly line, pulled up in front of the inn. Matt parked the car, took the stairs two at a time and presented himself with a courtly bow. "Ready?"

She noticed that people were whispering as they left. She supposed it did look scandalous, going off with him in his convertible. Did people think they were a couple? Or were they whispering about him – some scandalous rumor she should have taken the trouble to research?

"What's your pleasure today?" he asked. "Fishing . . . hiking . . . exploring the world around us?"

"How about a little of each?" Willie ventured. "I really don't know the countryside very well." And although Matt didn't ask, she found herself telling him how she'd come to spend the summer with the Parkmans, and that it was George who'd arranged for the job with the Blue Bass Inn.

"So you were old George's houseguest?" Matt's deep

213

chuckle seemed to hint that he knew everything there was to know about George Parkman.

He drove the convertible to a small clearing near "their" fishing spot and parked it. "I want to show you my lake," he said, "but it's a quiet place, and there are precious few of those left in the world today. So you've got to promise not to escort too many of the inn's population there . . ."

"Scout's honor," Willie said.

"Good enough."

Matt led the way through the forest with a long, brisk stride that had Willie almost running to keep up with him.

"Slow down," she finally pleaded, "or I'll be completely out of breath before we get there."

"Sorry," he apologized, moderating his pace. "We don't want you out of breath, or you won't be able to tell me about yourself. What is it you do when you're not working at the inn?"

"I'm in law school. Harvard."

He stopped for a moment to look at her. "I'm impressed. You must be very, very good."

"It's nice of you to say so."

Matt stared at her again. "Not nice . . . just accurate. The law has always been a competitive field. For women, it's been virtually off-limits. That's changing, but the trailblazers always have to be better and stronger and more tenacious than anyone else. I suspect you fill the bill, Willie. Tenacity is written in the set of your jaw."

Willie didn't usually take teasing well, but somehow she didn't mind it now because it seemed to say that Matt liked her.

"May I ask why you chose the law?"

Once again, Willie found herself speaking freely, telling Matt more than she usually told strangers. "My mother and father's marriage ended badly," she said. "It made me see how unfairly women are treated in the courts. I suppose it's because of what you said . . . lawyers and judges being men. I thought if I became a lawyer, I could help women like my mother. I'm sure it would have made a difference if there was someone like me around then. I believe there are

214

women all over the country who need that kind of help now."

"A noble reason, Willie," Matt said, and she could see he wasn't teasing. "But let me remind you of something Oliver Wendell Holmes once told a youthful critic. Justice Holmes said: 'This is a court of law, young man, not a court of justice.' It shouldn't be so, perhaps, but the distinction exists. You'll serve your clients best if you're aware of that distinction – and making your best efforts in spite of it."

"You seem to know an awful lot about the law," Willie observed. "Are you an attorney?"

"I was once," Matt replied cryptically. "But I don't practice any more. I miss that particular challenge at times, but . . ."

Willie waited for Matt to go on, but he seemed suddenly intent on examining the base of a tree trunk. "Look," he said, pointing to the column of ants. "They're telling us we're going to have an electrical storm."

"What do you mean?"

"The ants . . . they're one of Nature's barometers. When they march in a straight line like that, you can be sure there's a storm ahead."

Willie was more intrigued than ever by this man. Why didn't he practice law anymore? Striding on through the woods, he looked too vital and fit to be retired. Could he have been disbarred? No, she'd only known Matt for a week, but she'd take an oath that he wasn't capable of anything shady or dishonest. Then what *was* his story? She wondered. There had to be more than a law practice that no longer existed and days spent fishing and hiking.

"There," he said, as they broke through the woods and came to a clearing. Beyond it was Matt's lake, pristine and beautiful, its clear blue waters the color of sapphires. "One of Nature's treasures, undisturbed by man, unpolluted by his carelessness."

The air was fragrant with pine and honeysuckle and cool, rich earth. She felt inexplicably safe and peaceful, yet drawn by the powerful magnetism of this attractive man who seemed to know about so many things. Usually more

215

than ready to argue and debate and test, Willie was content now to let Matt lead and instruct her.

Sitting on two large rocks on the shore, they skimmed pebbles into the water, watching the ripples grow, watching the schools of minnows and sunfish that swam near the surface. They talked easily in the way of old friends, and the hours slipped by.

Matt said little about his life, revealing only that he'd been born into a comfortable middle-class family in St. Louis, and that his interest in the great outdoors went back to his youth, when he had escaped from the strictures of working in a law office by going hiking and mountain climbing and spelunking, which he explained is the exploration of caves. "Trying to find my way through the dark tunnels made by Nature seemed to be good practice for the law – which is only dark tunnels made by man."

Willie let him talk but remained too shy to pry. She didn't rein herself in, though. She told Matt more about herself than she'd ever told anyone.

But not all. Even in the serenity of this sylvan setting, she was too guarded for that.

As the sun moved close to the noonday mark, Matt suggested they return to the car for lunch. "Unless I miss my guess," he said, "Kate has packed food enough for an army. And I'm hungry enough to do it justice," he laughed, again as if at some private joke.

Kate? A wife? Willie wondered. Or merely a sister? And why did she feel disappointed at this mention of a woman who'd prepared Matt's food – and too timid to ask exactly who Kate was?

The lunch was a surprise. Willie had expected only sandwiches, but inside the picnic hamper were an assortment of cheeses, a tin of paté, some fruit, two loaves of French bread, several bottles of wine, as well as a checkered tablecloth and matching napkins. Willie ate heartily, her appetite whetted by the fresh air, the walking, and Matt's company.

When they finished, he carefully cleaned up the remnants of their picnic, burying the scraps of food in the ground. "A

216

courtesy to Mother Nature," he said, though Willie had already come to understand that Matt had a respect bordering on reverence for Nature's preserve.

"Now," he said, "maybe it's time for a casting lesson. You do want to live up to your credentials. You can fake a performance now and then, Willie, but you can't fake it for yourself. And that's what matters in the long run."

Matt had packed fishing gear for two in the convertible's trunk. He offered Willie his favorite, a deep mahogany brown rod with dark blue fittings and golden windings with brown tips. "This, Willie, is a Hawes rod," he explained as they walked toward the water. "A magnificent instrument, made about 1925. With a number four line, it will pick up a rhythm that can pace your heart, a rhythm that's palpably erotic."

Though Matt wasn't even looking at her while he described the equipment, Willie felt a seductive intimacy in his words. The feeling grew as he placed the rod in her right hand and loosely wrapped his arms around her, guiding her fingers to the cork grip. Keenly aware of the strong, solid feeling of his arms, she half turned to look at his face. A lovely face, she thought. She couldn't think of him as old anymore, couldn't remember what had ever made her decide that he was.

"Here," he said, "rest your thumb on top . . . that's it. Strip some line off the reel with your left hand. Wave the line forward and backward to let it slip through the guides. Now you're ready for an overhead cast . . . pick the line up and let it fly above and behind you . . . straight up . . . "

Eager to please him, Willie followed his instructions and sent the line sailing into the air in a graceful arc that ended in the water.

"Bravo," Matt exclaimed. "You're a natural, Willie. Try it again, but with a little more snap in the wrist and forearm . . . "

Though Willie had thought of fishing as standing around doing nothing, she found that she was completely absorbed in her casting lesson. After a dozen or so practice runs, Matt said she was ready for the real thing. He walked her to a spot where a running stream entered the lake. "Be careful," he said. "Don't bump the rocks and don't make any noise."

For an hour they fished side by side in companionable silence. Matt caught two small trout in quick succession and smiled encouragingly at Willie, as if to say "patience."

Ten minutes later, she felt a tug on her line. "I have one!" she called out excitedly, forgetting to be quiet, as the tip of the rod danced and she wound her reel furiously. "I have a fish! Help me, Matt – I don't know what to do . . . "

He laughed, enjoying her triumph, as she brought the fish all the way in and he showed her how to take it off the hook. "That's a beauty," he said admiringly. "Your first catch . . . I envy you, Willie. There's nothing as exciting as a 'first.' "

They fished awhile longer, and though she caught nothing else, Willie was content. Now she felt she knew something she could share with the guests from the inn. After Matt pulled in three more trout, he said, "That'll do it for us. The sun's about to set, and there's no need to take more than we can use. Now pay attention while I transform these succulent beauties into dinner. You may want to do this for your guests at the inn."

Matt settled in a clearing under a tree and started a campfire in the center of a safety wall of stones. With quick, expert movements, he cleaned the fish, keeping the one Willie had caught separate from the rest, then placed the trout neatly on metal skewers. From the convertible he took two kerosene lanterns and lit them. "For atmosphere," he said, "and to help me see when our dinner has reached the exact moment of done-ness."

Willie leaned back against a tree, closed her eyes, and savored the clean, piney smell of the forest mingled with the warm, sweet aroma of cooking trout.

"Bon appetit," Matt said as he served Willie her fish on a crunchy piece of French bread, with a glass of wine. It tasted like a feast, and she said so.

"I agree, but listen now, Willie . . . to the sound of night."

She listened. In the cool darkness, the quiet seemed

218

richer and softer, punctuated only by the chirping of crickets, the croaking of bullfrogs, the whispering rush of the stream.

"Did you ever go to camp?" Matt asked.

"No . . . never." She said this matter-of-factly, without a trace of self-pity.

Matt nodded, and in the flickering light from the lanterns, she could see that his face was thoughtful. And strong. "It's never too late to flesh out an education. Every campfire needs a ghost story."

Willie was delighted. "Do you know a lot of ghost stories?"

"Dozens," he said with mock solemnity. "The ghost story is a serious art form here in Maine. *But* we only allow ghosts who are certified natives of the state. With a pedigree that goes back at least three generations."

She laughed as gleefully as a child.

"I'm serious," Matt protested, though she could see that he was smiling. "The ghost I've selected for your entertainment is one Hiram Charles Hale. A scoundrel, by all accounts, at least for the first thirty years of his life. Then Hiram met Sarah Lee Winters, and he was redeemed, as scoundrels sometimes are, by the love of a good woman. Love, however, wasn't simple for Hiram and Sarah . . . "

While the campfire burned down to its last glowing embers Willie listened, enthralled as much by the strong rhythms of Matt's voice as by the tale he spun. For her it was the perfect ending for a glorious day.

There was a single awkward moment, after Matt drove her back to the inn. Filled with contentment, she turned to him. "Thank you," she said. "Thank you for one of the best days of my life." The words surprised her, though she knew after she'd said them that the sentiment was true.

"We can try for another. I'll be away for a few days . . . "

"Where are you going?" she asked – and was immediately embarrassed by her curiosity.

"Let's just say I have to cast my line in murkier waters. But when I get back . . . we can do this again. Your next day off?"

It was more than a simple question, Willie felt, but she had a ready answer. "Yes," she said. "I'd like that."

That night, lulled by a feeling of contentment and pleasure more complete than she had ever known, she fell quickly asleep. Her last conscious thought was that she didn't even know Matt's last name.

8

Over the following days, Willie found herself wondering where Matt was, what he was doing – and whether he was alone. On the third morning, she was folding the copies of the *New York Times*, which were delivered regularly to the inn, when her eye was caught by the front-page headline: "Supreme Court Upholds Government's Ban on CIA Book." She read on. The story told how the Supreme Court of the United States, meeting in special session, had ruled by a majority of five to four to uphold an injunction prohibiting a former CIA agent from publishing his memoirs. According to the article, the manuscript included a number of sensitive chapters, such as those describing the agency's recruiting practices on college campuses and its use of students and faculty members to spy on various radical groups. The Court ruled that the publication of such material would constitute a breach of national security, and that this consideration superseded the ex-agent's first-amendment right to free speech.

Opinion for the dissent, the story concluded, had been written by Justice Harding. The text was printed in a sidebar, accompanied by a photograph of the dissenting justice, wearing the long black robes of the highest court in the land. The face that looked up at her from the picture was Matt's.

"Why didn't you tell me?" she demanded without preamble,

waving the paper in his face when he came to pick her up at the inn.

He laughed, as if he were pleased with her response to his little deception. "Forgive me, Willie," he said. "No harm intended. I love my work, but it was more fun getting to know you as plain old Matt."

"There's nothing plain or old about you," she countered, knowing as she said the words that they were true. Whether he was wearing battered outdoor clothes or the powerful mantle of the country's highest court, Justice Matthew Harding was undoubtedly the most charismatic, sophisticated, and complex man she had ever met.

He had come prepared to repeat their first day together, and they did, but this time Willie gave her curiosity full rein. All day long, as they walked in the woods and fished together at the lake, she badgered him with questions about cases the Court had heard. Cases that had been part of her education now seemed exciting and alive because Matt had been a part of it, shaping and interpreting the very laws she had only read about. To her, Justice Harding was even more interesting than "plain old Matt," and certainly more fascinating. To Willie, who'd had little interest in Ginny's movie-star fantasies, Matt was the real thing. And when he brought her back to the inn that evening, Willie didn't wait for another invitation. "Same time next week?" she asked.

"I wouldn't miss it for the world," he answered.

In the weeks that followed, Tuesday became "their day." No two days were exactly the same, even when they went to the same places and walked the same paths. With Matt, Willie found there was always something new to learn, something new to discover. They would walk through the woods, Matt identifying the birds that nested in the trees, the animals that inhabited the forests. At night, he'd point out the stars that glittered against the dark, velvety sky. And as she walked beside him, Willie felt a growing urge to get closer.

When Suzanne called to ask why she hadn't come to the house in so long, Willie pleaded an exhausting work schedule.

"Tony's been asking about you," Suzanne said pointedly.

"Oh . . . " Willie answered, with evident indifference.

Suzanne laughed. "I can't say I blame you. I'd love to have you in the family, Willie. But wishing any of my brothers on you – I couldn't do that to a friend. I'm sorry those slavedrivers at the Blue Bass are working you so hard. I could ask the old man to talk to Lester, get him to give you at least one day off—"

"No, don't do that," Willie said hurriedly. "I don't mind, really I don't. I do get a day off, but I'm supposed to be a guide of sorts, so I'm using the time to scout the area."

"Ugh. Sounds tiresome. I'd rather lie on the dock or sail on the lake. It would be more fun if you were here . . . "

"We'll do that sometime, I promise."

To Willie, the other days of the week became prosaic and boring compared with the time she spent with Matt. She waited for his convertible like a child waits for Christmas.

Yet she didn't want to think of herself as a child. Where she had often been upset by the looks and passes her beauty had evoked, now she wondered why Matt didn't seem to notice. He liked her, she knew that. He was older, but from the day they'd first met, the years between them had been . . . irrelevant and immaterial. Their time together was always personal and very special, yet the setting and context were always the same as the day they met: the outdoors.

One day late in August, when Matt drove her back to the inn, Willie asked the question. "Summer's almost over," she said. "I've never seen the place where you live. Don't you want me to?"

He was quiet for a moment. "Yes," he said. "I want you to . . . very much. Will you have dinner with me next Tuesday evening? I'll pick you up at seven."

*   *   *

222

Dinner felt like a date, like being taken seriously. Willie looked through her summer wardrobe twice before she decided on a strapless black linen sundress and a matching challis shawl. She swept her hair back into a French twist and wore the diamond ear studs Neal and Mama had given her for her twenty-first birthday. The outfit was a shade too formal for the Maine woods, but Willie felt it gave her a look of sophistication.

When Matt arrived at the inn, she noticed that he, too, had dressed up for the occasion, exchanging his battered and worn daytime clothes for slacks and a sport shirt. "You look lovely, Willie," he said.

"Thank you." Ordinary as it was, Willie was deeply pleased by the compliment. It was the kind of thing a man said to a woman, not to a child.

His cabin was located at the far end of "his" lake, "their" lake now. From the outside, it was similar in design to the Parkman lodge, yet the feeling of the place was different. Matt had opened up the interior with an enormous skylight, which seemed to bring the surrounding trees and the heavens above into the cabin. Some of the furnishings were old, but Willie was sure these hadn't been picked at random from some antique store. She felt that everything Matt surrounded himself with had meaning and purpose.

He introduced her to his housekeeper, Kate Johansen, an attractive woman of about fifty. Willie smiled inwardly at this revelation of the "Kate" mystery. Kate in turn greeted Willie with a pleasant "hello" and cool appraising glance.

"Dinner smells wonderful," Willie said. "I'll bet it's as delicious as all your wonderful lunches." She wanted the housekeeper to know that she had shared those lunches with Matt.

"Pot roast and noodles," Kate said, "one of the judge's favorites."

"Come outside and see the garden," Matt said, "before we lose the light." In the back of the property was an English-style flower garden, an unstudied and unaffected profusion of impatiens and zinnias, lilies and geraniums,

223

now in full bloom. Willie stopped at the bank of marigolds. "The color's so lovely," she said. "I've never seen any quite like these."

"The Rangely Marigold . . . I developed them last summer. What you see is the first year of blooms."

Willie shook her head in disbelief. "Gardening, too? When do you find time to do so much?"

"There's always time for things you care about, isn't there?"

"You seem to care about so many things," she mused. And then she asked the question that had been on her mind since she arrived. "Has Miss Johansen been your house-keeper for long?"

"Almost nineteen years," he answered, with a smile that made Willie wonder if he'd guessed her question was more than mere curiosity. "Kate came to work for me the year my wife died. But she's more than a housekeeper. Kate's a friend. A good friend. She tells me the truth when few people would."

Willie wasn't sure how she felt about *that* answer. What had Kate said about "the judge" keeping company with a much younger woman?

"Come and see my pride and joy," Matt commanded, pulling her toward a patch of tomato plants, all carefully staked and tended, some still bearing fruit. "Here . . . " He picked one that was perfectly ripened and brought it into the spotlessly clean and efficient kitchen. "Let's have this in the salad, Kate," he said.

Kate's pot roast was sumptuously flavorful and juicy, served over homemade buttered noodles and accompanied by a mixed salad and a robust Beaujolais. Though Kate retreated discreetly to her room after she served the meal, Willie continued to feel her presence, and wondered if Matt did, too.

Her feelings for him were different from anything she'd experienced before. Not like the raw physical pull that drew her to Jedd, the treacherous current she had to fight against. With Matt, she was challenged, stimulated. A little starstruck. But more than that, she was attracted without being afraid. She imagined if he held her in his arms, there would be pleasure without doubt and pain.

She was pleased when he offered her brandy after dinner, when he lit a fire in the stone fireplace that covered an entire wall of the cabin, and put a recording of Vivaldi's "Four Seasons" on the stereo.

Tucking her long legs under her, Willie sank into a cushion in front of the fireplace, waiting for Matt to join her. Instead, he chose a leather club chair, leaned back, and closed his eyes, listening to the music. It had been a pleasant evening, yet more formal and less intimate than the days they'd spent outdoors.

When the record came to an end, Matt looked at his watch. "Maybe we should get you back to the inn."

Willie made no move to get up. "I don't have to be at work till nine o'clock . . ." she said quietly, looking down to hide the blush she could feel stealing over her cheeks.

Matt knelt beside her and kissed the top of her head lightly. "Thank you, Willie . . . for saying that."

Her blush deepened, her embarrassment compounded by the sting of rejection, however gently it had been delivered. But she looked up, not hiding anything now. "Thank you?" she repeated. "I didn't just pass you the pot roast, Matt – I was talking about something else. I don't do that kind of thing, you know."

"I'm sure you don't," he said gently, stroking her hair. "That's why I want to take you back. Summer's an enchanted season, Willie. Nature casts a powerful spell when everything's green and ripe and perfumed, and full of promise. It's easy to love then. Too easy. We forget the fading and dying of summer, the going away, the distances, the other lives we have to live . . ."

Willie understood that Matt was saying no, but she couldn't quite understand the reasons. Was he saying she was too young? That she could argue against. Or was he telling her, ever so kindly, something more hurtful – that their stations in life were too different? He was a powerful, accomplished man, and she, for all her hope and promise, was after all, still just a student.

225

"But what's wrong with having summer?" she pressed. "If it doesn't last, I could understand . . . "

"Dear, lovely Willie," he sighed. "You've misread my brief. I'm the one who's breakable. I don't know how to love 'just for now,' and I don't think I could stand to love you and then lose you."

His words startled Willie. Matt did want her. But he wanted something else, something she didn't believe she was ready to give anyone.

She stood up and let him lay her shawl over her shoulders. Together they walked out to the car.

"This is more than good night," he said, when they arrived at the inn. "I'm going back to Washington the day after tomorrow. But I want you to know how precious our friendship is to me. I don't want to lose touch, Willie. Can we agree on that?"

He took her in his arms and held her against his chest. She closed her eyes and listened to the even, steady beating of his heart. It felt just the way she'd imagined. Strong and powerful and safe, as if nothing could ever hurt her again.

But she knew the feeling would go away with Matt, and tomorrow she'd be on her own again.

9

In the last days of summer, the woods were still green and fragrant, the lake cool and crystal clear . . . but the best part had gone with Matt.

The Tuesday after his departure was an empty space, wanting to be filled. Willie revisited the woods and "their" lake. It was restorative to be there, yet the forest was somehow less wondrous and welcoming without Matt to show her its secret treasures.

Willie made no excuses when Suzanne insisted she spend Labor Day with the Parkmans. She was grateful for the noise and the activity, though she could have done without Tony's aggressive brand of charm.

Tony was the brother whose looks most resembled Suzanne's, but the physical similarity seemed coincidental when you compared their personalities. Tony had been born the right sex. And when Willie politely deflected his overtures, he didn't for a minute think she wasn't interested – only that she didn't recognize a golden opportunity when she saw one.

"I was just beginning to think you'd met some guy," Suzanne said, as she and Willie sunned themselves on the dock.

"When?"

"When you dropped out of sight this summer. I pictured you with some gorgeous creature making whoopee under the stars."

"No," Willie said, "there wasn't any whoopee going on this summer."

"Too bad. I met someone last week . . . one of Jack's buddies from Yale, and believe it or not, he's really nice – Uh-oh!"

"What's wrong?"

"Boredom approaching at twelve o'clock . . . every man for himself!"

With one quick movement, Suzanne got to her feet and dove into the lake, leaving Willie to fend off George Parkman's ponderous pronouncements on her own.

"I trust your job at the inn was satisfactory, Willa?" he said.

"Yes, very. Thanks again for the recommendation."

"No thanks necessary. I just hope you'll remember what I said about settling down. You gals can't afford to drag your feet the way a young fella can."

Willie was in no mood to hide her annoyance. "Are you saying I'll be over the hill soon?" she replied.

George gave her an uncomfortable laugh. "Now, there you go, talking like my Suzy. No, I'm not saying anything of the kind. There are certain laws of Nature, however . . . "

He inclined his head toward his son Tony. "That boy has a fine future on the Street, Willa. A gal could do a lot worse—"

"I'm sure," Willie said, as she stood and stretched. "Excuse me now, Mr. Parkman," she added tartly, "but this 'gal' better get into the water and cool off."

Returning to school was a relief. It gave Willie back her sense of purpose, the opportunity to work at what she loved best. Matt had called on her last day at the inn, to wish her well and to repeat his promise to keep in touch. The call only served to remind her of the "distances" and "other lives" he had spoken of on their last night together. He was in Washington, making decisions that would affect the life of every citizen in the land. The only decisions before her had to do with the academic year.

Law One had been taken up with basic courses: Contracts, Torts, Property. The only subject that had really interested her was constitutional law.

The second year she had tackled the intricacies of federal and corporate tax, trust and estates – and family law, the one she had waited for, the one she wanted so much to learn. Now, as a third year student, she could hone and sharpen her knowledge with specialized courses.

But most important, she had her chance to shine at law school's two plum extracurricular activities. As one of the top ten students in her class, she was eligible to join the staff of the prestigious *Harvard Law Review*. She was also eligible for Moot Court, which served as a showcase for law students to brief and argue hypothetical problems. Most of the outstanding students chose one or the other. Rarely, if ever, did anyone – no matter how gifted – take on the consuming demands of both. But, of course, that was precisely what Willie felt she must do. Her summer in Rangely, the time she'd spent in Matt's company, had fed her ambition. In the sheltered and structured academic environment, she felt there were no limits to what she could accomplish.

Her optimistic mood sustained her until she made her

first appearance in the offices of the *Review*. Trouble appeared immediately in the shape and form of Bud Hodge. Dressed as usual in the same conservative style favored by his father, he sat laughing and joking with the editor, as if he had staked out the territory for himself.

When Bud saw Willie, his smile broadened. "Missed you at 'Ring and Wait' this summer," he said.

She was in no mood for banter with Bud. "The only thing you missed me with, Hodge, were your darts and arrows."

"What are you doing here?" The smile was gone, as she and Bud stared each other down like a pair of oldtime gunfighters at high noon.

"I belong here," she said coldly. "As of yesterday, I'm on the staff. I'm here to pick up my first assignment."

Bud scowled. "I heard you were going out for Moot Court."

"That, too," Willie said evenly, taking pleasure in his displeasure. Obviously Bud had believed he'd have a free hand here. With no competition from her, he would have a good chance to make editor. But Willie had other plans for the editorship.

"Isn't that a bit much even for you, Wonder Woman?" he said sarcastically, his bulging eyes angry. "The Greeks had a word for the sin of overweening pride: hubris. And they had a warning for anyone who—"

Willie cut in. "Yes, it was hubris that brought down the high and mighty kings – men who tried to do too much. I'd worry about that, too, if I were you. But I don't remember the Greeks saying the queens had much of a problem . . . "

Bud stared at her coldly for a moment, then abruptly turned on his heel and left.

She had a momentary thrill of triumph as she watched him go. Same old Bud, she thought. Trying to intimidate me. Afraid I'll show him up. But then she wondered: was she reaching too high, trying too hard . . . ?

Willie knew that as an alumna of Harvard Law, she could expect to be interviewed by the most prestigious firms in the country. With both the *Review* and Moot Court on her

229

list of accomplishments, she would be courted and sought after the way few beginning lawyers – and even fewer women – were. She wanted the chance to practice law, not to be buried in dusty research libraries, and to get that chance she would have to work harder and shine brighter than anyone else. And that was what she would do, no matter what Bud Hodge said.

But Bud wasn't the only one who remarked on Willie's ambitious plan to do the *Review* and Moot Court at the same time.

"You're crazy," Suzanne said bluntly.

"Not you too!" Willie dumped her pile of textbooks on their kitchen table with an emphatic thump. "I expected support from my roommate. Maybe even a little applause."

"Applause goeth before a fall," Suzanne quipped.

"That's pride."

"Exactly."

Willie wasn't amused. "Are you saying I'm only doing this to show off? You, of all people?"

"Aren't you?" Suzanne's expression was serious. "God knows I understand about the need to prove yourself, Willie. I've been trying to do that all my life. But I've been doing a lot of thinking lately about how I've missed out on a lot of good things just because I've been so busy fighting my family. Maybe you've been too busy fighting, too . . . "

Willie almost said "you sound like your father," but held it back. She was disappointed that Suzanne wasn't as supportive as she used to be. Once she might have said "Right on, Willie – show the bastards what a woman can do." Now she was acting as if none of that mattered.

But Willie couldn't stop striving. Never. Even if there weren't new battles to win, there would always be the old ones.

That night she wrote a short note to Matt, telling him what she had done. Surely he'd be impressed, commend her for striving and reaching. Hadn't he once quoted the line from Browning that said: "A man's reach should exceed his grasp/Or what's a heaven for?"

As she was putting the note in an envelope, it suddenly

occurred to her that impressing Matt was probably at the heart of her reasons for taking on so much. She wanted him to see her not simply as a promising young student, but as someone outstanding. She thought twice then about mailing the letter, and kept it propped against the mirror of her dresser for two days. She thought of rewriting it, but mailed it anyway. What the hell, she thought, I do want to impress him. Why shouldn't I . . . ?

Though they had implicitly agreed to remain friends, Willie still felt drawn to him, and she reacted with disappointment and even a surge of jealousy when she saw magazine pictures of Matt escorting beautiful and accomplished women – like the newly appointed Secretary of Commerce and the publisher of a leading magazine – to Washington parties, and read captions describing him as "the city's most eligible bachelor."

When his response to her letter came, it was brief, much less fulsome and more distant than she'd expected. "You've set yourself a challenge," he wrote, "but don't forget to stop and smell the wildflowers on the side of the road." The letter went on to wish her "a richness of experience" during the coming term.

Disappointed, she crumpled the letter and threw it in a corner.

But later, when she had trouble sleeping, she got up, smoothed out the letter, and read it again. He was moving away from her, she felt. But perhaps that was the way it had to be.

The challenge she'd set herself proved to be brutally demanding, even for Willie. The course work wasn't significantly harder than it had been the year before, but the editors of the *Review* were worse slavedrivers than all her professors put together. For the first issue, she was assigned what felt like a mountain of "tech checks" – the tedious and painstaking job of checking the legal references and precedents cited in articles, to make certain the references were accurate and the precedents relevant.

Meanwhile, in her initial Moot Court appearance, she

would be coming up against a student from the law school at Boston University. When the faculty adviser handed Willie her assignment, she read it through with horror and disbelief. The case involved the hypothetical Clara Barton School in the hypothetical town of Holister. The school's educational philosophy was based on teaching through the accomplishments of women. The school had failed to receive accreditation from the State Board and, believing the decision to be prejudiced, had filed suit. The suit had been lost, and now the case was before an appellate court. Willie's assignment was to argue *against* the Clara Barton School's appeal.

Her first reaction was that it was an impossible assignment. How could she muster her best arguments against a cause in which she believed? She stared at the offending document in her hand – and then at her faculty adviser, Lowell B. Sharp, a fussy, spinsterish man who had written textbooks, but never practiced law.

"Is there a problem, Miss Dellahaye?" he asked, not without malice. "Perhaps you need some assistance . . . "

Willie knew exactly what he meant. She hadn't the slightest doubt that Sharp had hand-picked the assignment for her. If she challenged or refused it, she wouldn't be given another. The adviser was simply doing what her professors had done, making special rules for her because she was a woman, putting the burden of proof on her, challenging her pride, insisting that she demonstrate her worthiness of a law degree in ways that weren't demanded of the male students.

"No problem," she declared, retreating from Sharp's office, from the smirk that told her he'd be waiting to see how she'd handle herself in her first simulated courtroom appearance.

Willie felt she couldn't complain, not even to Suzanne, who seemed preoccupied and distracted anyway. Suzanne would never say "I told you so." The problem was in Willie herself. She couldn't admit, not even to herself, that she had probably taken on too much.

She kept up a brave front, though, telling herself it was

232

going to be all right. She had commitment and ability. This work was her life. It was all that mattered, she told herself, and one way or another, she would get it done. Better than anyone else could do it.

And then she got a phone call from Matt.

"Are you going home for Christmas?" he asked.

"I don't think so . . ." Willie's mind was almost made up. Staying in Cambridge for the holidays would provide free time to help reduce her work load to less mountainous proportions.

"Then I have an invitation for you. A couple of days here in Washington . . . and then Christmas in Georgia . . ."

The invitation startled Willie, and pleased her enormously. To be in Washington . . . to see the Supreme Court through his eyes . . . it was an exciting prospect.

But she felt a certain awkwardness about being with Matt himself, cloaked in the power of his office, so different from the man she'd known in Maine.

"Hello? Have we lost our connection?" he teased.

She heard the double meaning. "No . . . it's just that I have an awful lot of work to do . . ."

"Bring the work – we'll make time for it. Come, Willie, please." After a pause, he added: "I've missed you terribly."

His last words made all the difference.

Matt's chauffeur met Willie at the airport, a reminder that she was visiting a Justice of the Supreme Court, and not an ordinary mortal. When she saw that the limousine was empty, she felt a moment of pique. Was Matt being "discreet" – not the way he'd been in Maine, when they'd been partners in a little conspiracy – because it would be embarrassing to be seen with her in so public a place as the airport? The question bothered her during the entire ride to Matt's house in Georgetown.

It was a beautiful red brick Georgian mansion with white shutters and clean graceful lines. Off to one side and set back a ways was a spacious garage that sheltered Matt's collection of vintage automobiles – a yellow Packard touring

233

car, a silver Bentley, a rare maroon Hispano-Suiza and the gleaming black Cadillac convertible he'd driven in Maine.

From the outside, the house and grounds had a stately elegance. Inside the impression was of richness and warmth. Like Matt himself. The wood of the antique furniture was burnished with a rich patina. The brasses were polished, the colors of the oriental carpets deep and vibrant.

Let into the entrance hall by the chauffeur, Willie had only a moment to savor the aroma of cinnamon before Kate Johansen came bustling out from another room.

"Matt sends his apologies," she said, taking Willie's coat. "The Court is meeting late on some thorny matter . . . "

"Thank you, Miss Johansen." Willie had not yet been able to bring herself to call the housekeeper by her first name. Not while she felt that she was being constantly judged by this handsome woman whom Matt regarded as his right hand.

Kate showed Willie to a lovely second-floor guest room with white walls and a mahogany canopy bed covered with a wedding-ring quilt. "After you've freshened up," she said, "you might like to come downstairs for some Viennese coffee. Matt always enjoys it on cold evenings."

Willie unpacked the few cold-weather clothes she'd brought, took a leisurely shower and dressed in a pair of velvet slacks and a soft matching angora sweater. She pulled her hair back with a velvet ribbon and added a pair of gold earrings.

When she descended the thickly carpeted stairs, she saw that Matt had arrived. He was sitting with Kate in front of a crackling fire, laughing and sharing coffee. She had a moment to regard them, looking very comfortable and at home together, before Matt noticed her in the doorway. He got up at once, and came forward to meet her.

"Dear Willie," he said as he gave her a hearty hug. "Come and have some of Kate's inimitable coffee."

"You have a beautiful, characterful house," she said.

"Like me, eh? Or so the press likes to say. I'm sorry I

wasn't able to meet you personally, Willie. I hope we can make that up to you at dinner."

She looked at Matt in this new setting. He was quite distinguished in his navy blazer, crisp white shirt and maroon tie, though his manner was the same. Yet in these formal, traditional surroundings, he struck her as being more powerful and less accessible than he had in the Maine woods. She yearned to be back there with him, standing knee-deep in a trout stream. There – perhaps only there – they were in a Shangri-La where age and station made no difference.

Dinner was served in the mahogany-paneled dining room, furnished with a Queen Anne table and matching chairs. Soft light filtered through the prisms of the crystal chandelier, casting a glow on the serving pieces of antique Georgian silver. Kate had prepared a superb rack of lamb surrounded by baby asparagus and tiny parsleyed potatoes, accompanied by an endive salad.

For dessert and coffee, Matt and Willie moved into his study, which was lit by a glowing fire. Kate brought a tray of fruit and cheese and left the room.

Willie settled herself in front of the fire, ready to enjoy a juicy pear. The gentle strains of Handel's "Water Music" that issued from the record player relaxed her, and the anecdotes Matt freely told about his colleagues on the court – all prefaced with a warning that "if you repeat this, the other brethren will have me skinned" – made him seem less formal and intimidating.

"Tell me about this place in Georgia," she asked finally. "What's it like?"

"A small island off the coast . . . pastoral, unspoiled. Some friends have offered their house for our holiday. We can fish, hunt ducks—"

"Hunt ducks?" she asked, her forehead creased with disappointment. "How can you do that, after all your talk about Nature?"

Matt laughed and took her hand. "Is hunting ducks less natural than catching fish?"

Willie was unconvinced. "I still think it's wrong. Hunting for sport."

"Defer judgment for now," he said. "Let me show you. And if I can't convince you, then let me remind you I'm human and fallible." He registered the look on her face. "I know. You want me to be as grand and exalted as the office I hold. I'm sorry to disappoint you, Willie, but I was a man before I was an office."

"I'll try," she said reluctantly, sounding very much like an eight-year-old denied the illusion of the Easter bunny or the Tooth Fairy.

"Does that mean you'll suspend disapproval until all the evidence is in?"

"Petition granted."

"Good. Then tomorrow, I promise we'll engage only in the higher pursuits. We'll visit the court in the morning – and I'll take you to lunch in the Senate cafeteria."

Willie felt pacified. The treat Matt had promised was enticing enough to make her smile in anticipation.

It was Matt who decided when the evening was over, kissing her cheek and leaving her with an unsatisfying "sleep well."

As she slipped under the puffy quilt, she found herself trying to imagine what it would be like if Matt were beside her, holding her close, warming her with a different kind of kiss. She fell asleep holding the image, and wishing for it like a child wishing on a star.

10

Walking through the marble halls of the Supreme Court Building, Willie felt as awestruck as any tourist. More so, for with Matt at her side, she, too, became part of the deference and recognition he evoked – from building staff, from passing clerks, even from actual tourists. She could almost smell the power that emanated from this place, sense the urgency of purpose in the people who moved through it, even during this holiday season.

When Matt showed her his office, she could see the man she'd come to know in Maine and in the Currier & Ives prints, the paintings by Winslow Homer and Edward Hopper, the collection of intricately carved wooden duck decoys. As he introduced her to his secretary, she caught the same speculative looks his housekeeper Kate had given her. Matt certainly seemed to have a lot of women looking out for him, Willie thought, disconcerted by this discovery.

"The rest of the staff has gone home for the holidays," he said. "Maybe you'll meet them another time."

The promise of that statement pleased Willie, as did the prospect of lunch in the Senate cafeteria. "The food's passable," he said, "though the surroundings are rather institutional."

Willie didn't agree. She scarcely noticed the simple furnishings or the meal set before her, so intent was she on scanning the faces of the people around her. Here and there she saw an occasional woman. But most of the diners were men. Men of power and influence. Legislators. Lobbyists, some of them as well known as the men whose favor they curried. Like Matt, these men were in a position to affect the lives of thousands, even millions, of people.

"Your lunch is getting cold," Matt said.

Willie nodded, still distracted by the traffic that buzzed around them. "I'm sorry," she said. "I guess I was being rude, just staring like that."

Matt laughed. "I'm glad you're enjoying lunch, even if you've barely tasted the food."

"I'm sorry," she repeated. "There are so many things I wanted to talk to you about. I—" She stopped, her mouth open but unable to form the next word, as her roaming eyes caught sight of a familiar face, seated across the room at a table with another man. Jedd Fontana, as handsome and confident as ever, was leaning across a table, talking animatedly to Harrison Fairgate, the Republican senator from Montana.

Seeing him made her flush with confusion and anger. She

237

remembered the hunger and passion of that long night she'd spent in his arms – and the hurt and disillusionment that followed. Just like Jedd to show up now, she thought, when the very sight of him could spoil her anticipated holiday. What was he up to?

But after a moment, she found the answer to her own question. Senator Fairgate was the leader of the opposition to a major conservation bill before the Senate, a bill that would no doubt affect Sam Fontana's sprawling empire and interfere with his absolute rule over that land. He would fight the bill with all the means at his disposal.

So here was Jedd, looking every bit the Fontana crown prince, the arrogant rich boy she'd always known he was, bringing Sam's message – his *orders* conceivably – to a United States senator. The scene filled Willie with disgust.

She turned to face the handsome, charismatic man at her own table. Matt, who was everything the Fontanas were not. Honest. Decent. Ethical. In his hands, power was a positive force, used constructively and with integrity, to support the values he believed in – not a self-serving tool wielded for private gain.

Now she attacked her lunch with vigor, eager to finish and leave. The last thing she wanted was for Matt and Jedd to meet. She didn't want to face the questions that would surely appear in Jedd's eyes, questions that would include Matt and the nature of their relationship. It's none of his damn business, she thought defiantly.

"Would you like more coffee?" Matt asked.

"No, I'm fine. I'm eager to see your law library again . . . "

At that moment she noticed Senator Fairgate rise, shake Jedd's hand, and move to join some colleagues on the other side of the room. She ducked her head, hoping that Jedd would pass their table and leave the cafeteria without seeing her—

"Willie! What a wonderful surprise!"

She lifted her face up with what she hoped was a cool, unwelcoming expression. "Hello, Jedd," she said, making no move to introduce him to Matt.

And being Jedd, he ignored the slight, extending his

238

hand to Matt. "I'm Jedd Fontana," he said, "a friend of Willie's from Palm Springs. It's an honor to meet you, Justice Harding."

"I'm glad to meet any friend of Willie's," Matt responded graciously. "Won't you join us?"

No, Willie prayed silently, please go, leave me alone.

But Jedd sat down. "I can't tell you what a privilege this is," he said boyishly. "I've admired so many of your opinions, sir . . . on the war issues and segregation and . . . "

"And conservation?" Willie cut in sharply, angered that Jedd would pay lip service to the values Matt cared so deeply about even while he was here doing Sam's dirty work. "The Justice cares about conservation, too. Do you admire his position on that?"

Jedd remained unruffled by her assault. "I admire a man who stands by his opinions, whether or not they agree with mine." He looked at Matt. "There is a place for dissent, Justice Harding, isn't there?"

"Dissent is what I do best," Matt agreed with a smile. "I've never been a stranger to unpopular opinions."

"Is that why you're here?" Willie demanded accusingly. "To dissent – or to *prevent?* To make sure that nothing gets in the way of your family interests, not even the law?"

There was a moment of embarrassed silence. Matt looked long and hard at Willie, her flushed cheeks and angry eyes. And then he looked at Jedd, who appeared almost composed under Willie's attack – except for the tense set of his jaw and shoulders. Matt glanced across the room, waved, then stood up. "Excuse me for a moment," he said. "Court business . . . "

Willie glared at Jedd. "I wish you'd stay out of my life. Now you've ruined my lunch—"

"Why?" he protested. "I didn't pick a fight."

"Is that what you think I did?" she said indignantly. "I just expressed my opinion at what you've become."

Jedd's composure cracked, his face flushing under his tan. "And what is that?" he asked, his voice hard.

She answered quickly. "Someone who only cares about

239

himself, his own interests, a manipulator, a wheeler-dealer, a . . . a *grandee*, just like your father."

Willie's answer made him smile, in the easy way that always got under her skin. "Is that really so terrible? 'Grandees,' as you call them, built this country. America has always needed them, needed *us*, if you want to put me in that company. We get things done."

"At any cost. Even if you have to break the law," she said heatedly.

Jedd smiled again. "I don't see any lawbreakers at this table. Better go back to the books if you think you do."

Willie looked past Jedd and caught Matt's inquiring glance from across the cafeteria. She stood up. "I think Justice Harding is ready to leave. He's promised to show me his law library, so I'd better not waste any time getting to those books you think I need."

"Willie, wait." He gripped her hand. "Don't go like this," he said, his smile gone, dark eyes serious. "Not when I've just found you again. I need to see you . . . alone, where we can talk."

"No," she answered quickly. "We don't have anything to talk about." The prospect of being alone with Jedd again brought Willie to the point of trembling. She could handle arguing with him, using the powerful emotions that drew her to him to fuel her anger. But she couldn't risk anything more, not when her life was so much easier without him.

"I won't let you do this," he said stubbornly, the set of his jaw matching Willie's. "I'm not going to leave until you agree to see me. Have dinner with me."

"I have plans for dinner."

Jedd peered deeply into Willie's aquamarine eyes, then turned to glance across the room, to where Matt stood chatting with a group of men. His jaw set even tighter. "Fine. Drinks, then. Six o'clock at my hotel, the Mayflower. I'll be waiting for you."

Till hell freezes over, she wanted to say.

But the words wouldn't come. She could only stare at him without replying until she broke away toward Matt's welcoming smile.

While Matt introduced her to two members of the House of Representatives, she watched Jedd leave. Against her will, she studied the easy grace of his walk, remembered the lean, hard muscles of his body. She shook her head, a barely perceptible "no" in the movement – and found Matt's clear gray eyes studying her.

"I'm sorry our lunch was interrupted," she said.

At five-thirty Willie looked at her watch. She was still sitting in Matt's law library, feeling deceitful and angry with herself – and with Jedd, for intruding into her holiday with Matt. An hour ago, she had urged Matt to return to his house without her, saying she wanted some time to study his vast collection of law books. A half-truth at best, when here she was, drumming her fingers against the dark, polished surface of the library table, watching the minutes tick by and wondering if she would go to meet Jedd in spite of her resolve. What good could come of it? she asked herself. Seeing him alone, away from the protection of Matt's strength, could only lay open her old vulnerability, expose her once again to Jedd's easy and unscrupulous charm. It would be too risky, too foolish . . .

But at five-forty-five Willie was in the street, hailing a taxi, telling the driver to take her to the Mayflower Hotel. Just this once, she said to herself. Wasn't it better to see Jedd and confront her feelings, instead of struggling alone with them?

He was waiting at a corner table in the cocktail lounge. He stood when he saw Willie, smiling as he held a chair for her.

"I can only stay for fifteen minutes," she said shortly, wanting to erase the confident look from the arrogant, aristocratic face that bedeviled her so.

He nodded and summoned a passing waiter with an easy lift of his hand. "White wine?" he asked Willie.

"I don't care . . . I told you, I have to leave in a little while."

"A bottle of Pouilly-Fuisse," Jedd ordered. "Look, Willie," he began as soon as the waiter left, "what I have to

241

say won't take long. I don't know why you're so mad at me. If it's because I had to leave Palm Springs after we'd been . . . together, I thought I explained that. We had a crisis at home, and Pop needed me to take care of it. If you still have some crazy idea that my family had *anything* to do with Webb Foley's accident, I can swear to you that it isn't true. After you let loose at me, I even asked Pop about the kind of work Foley did for him. He told me, Willie – just the way I told you – there was never anything wrong going on. Webb just made deliveries from time to time . . . machine parts, stuff like that. Why won't you understand?"

"I understand more than you know," she said. "That night we spent together was a mistake, Jedd. I'm glad you gave me the chance to find that out."

"No, dammit!" he said, ignoring the waiter who proffered a bottle of wine for his approval. "That was no mistake! That was right . . . I felt it, and you did, too, Willie. If only you could stop fighting me and give in to your feelings, you'd discover what I already know. We're good together, Willie. We belong together . . . "

Willie felt the heat of his intensity across the few short feet that separated them. She fought it now, as the power of his dark eyes, the sensual lift to the corner of his mouth, threatened to draw her in once more.

"There's more to a relationship than feelings, Jedd," she said, as much to herself as to him. "You and I are from two different worlds. I'm not just talking about money. We don't agree on anything important . . . we'd only destroy each other. I know," she said, her voice barely above a whisper. "I've seen people do that to each other . . . "

He tried to reach for her hand, but she drew it away abruptly, almost knocking over her wineglass.

"I should go now," she said, her eyes downcast, her body poised for flight.

Jedd studied her for a long moment and then a flicker of comprehension crossed his face. "Are you . . . involved with *him* . . . with Harding?" he asked, his voice edged with a bitterness that was barely controlled. "Is that why you won't listen to me?"

242

The mention of Matt's name sparked Willie's anger, giving her the weapon she needed to rescue herself from the physical magnetism of Jedd's presence. "My personal life is none of your business," she said. "You've made your choices – I saw that today when I saw you with Fairgate – and I've got to make mine. We're on opposite sides, Jedd . . . you couldn't possibly understand a man like Matt Harding. Or a woman like me." She stood up to leave. "It was wrong of me to come. I'm sorry . . ."

Jedd's control broke as she started to walk away. "Go on," he called after her, "run like you always do, run from what you feel. But this isn't good-bye, Willie, not on your life. You belong with me, and sooner or later, you're going to see that!"

Willie hurried out of the hotel, taking the echo of Jedd's words with her. No, she said to herself, he's wrong. I'm free of him, free . . .

As long as I don't look back.

When she arrived at Matt's house, she could see that he had been waiting for her. She murmured a vague apology for losing track of the time. Matt was rather quiet as they shared a pre-dinner sherry, and afterward, when they moved into the mahogany-paneled dining room for another of Kate's superbly prepared meals. At first, Willie didn't seem to notice the change, for she was still tense from her confrontation with Jedd. But as she sipped the fine Montrachet, as she began to taste the delicate and succulent veal in lemon sauce, the tensions dissipated, and she relaxed into the warmth of her surroundings.

Though she had been in Matt's home for only a day, already she felt sheltered by its solid strength, the gracious hospitality that was enhanced by Kate's expert ministrations.

When the meal was finished, she and Matt once again sought the glowing fire, the classical music that awaited them in the study. Kate appeared with a Baccarat decanter filled with brandy and two crystal balloons. She set these on an inlaid table facing the fireplace.

243

"That was a lovely dinner," Willie said. "Thank you . . . Kate."

"You're welcome, Miss Dellahaye." The housekeeper started to leave the room, then paused a moment in the doorway. "I hope you and Matt have a pleasant holiday in Georgia," she added before she went out.

Matt looked after Kate for a moment, obviously noting the implicit approval of Willie she had expressed, but saying nothing about it. He poured some of the fifty-year-old Napoleon brandy into the glasses, handed one to Willie, then sat in his favorite chair facing the fire. For a long time he watched the flames crackle and dance.

"You seem preoccupied," Willie said. "Court business?"

Matt smiled, but his eyes were serious. It was a while before he spoke. "I had a remarkable experience today, Willie. Strangely exhilarating . . . and, at the same time, disconcerting." He looked away, as though reluctant to meet her eyes.

She waited for him to continue.

"Jealousy," he sighed. "For the first time in years, I've been feeling jealous as hell. I thought I'd outgrown jealousy. I don't want to feel it, but there it is." He turned to her at last, his face youthful in its perplexity.

He got up from his chair and sat beside her. "Tell me, Willie, do I have reason to be jealous? Is that handsome young man I met today someone you could love?"

Willie threw her arms around Matt and hugged him fiercely. His revelation awed and delighted her. This brilliant, distinguished man was saying he cared for her as a man cares for a woman. Not for a minute would she lie to him – though his question didn't have a simple answer. She couldn't tell him how her body never failed to respond to Jedd's presence, even while her mind rejected everything he stood for.

She responded truthfully: "No, a man like you has no reason in the world to be jealous of Jedd Fontana. There was something . . . once . . . but it's over."

"He's young," Matt persisted. "I've never before wished

244

to be young again . . . but, let's face it, Willie I *am* old enough to be—"

"A mere technicality, your honor," she cut in lightly. "I don't think of you as any age. You're just too special to be measured in ordinary ways. And being with you, knowing you . . ." She paused, searching for words. "Matt, you're the only man who has ever made me feel good, made me believe that what happens between a man and a woman doesn't have to be a world of danger and pitfalls. You've helped me believe in all kinds of things . . . "

His eyes welled up, and when he spoke, his voice was vibrant with emotion. "That's a beautiful gift, Willie. You've made me believe, too . . . in richer possibilities." He touched her hand, and looked into the fire again. Softly, Matt recited:

> "Sweet is the scene where genial friendship plays
> The pleasing game of interchanging praise.

"That's from a poem by the father of Supreme Court Justice Oliver Wendell Holmes, Willie," he said. "A verse appropriately called 'After-Dinner Poem'."

Willie noted the word "friendship." What was Matt trying to say now? Was he stepping back again?

Her answer came when he finished his brandy. "I think I'll say good night now. We have an early flight in the morning."

Once again, he left her with a kiss and a fond "sleep well."

11

The cattail tickled Willie's nose and she sneezed.

"Hush!" Matt admonished quickly. "And bless you."

"I'm tired and cold and cramped," she said, giving vent to a childish wish to complain.

They had been sitting for what felt like hours in the duck blind nested in the long swamp grass. At first she had enjoyed the brilliant colors of early morning, the briny tang of sea air, the luxurious intimacy of feeling as if she and Matt were the only two people in the world. This holiday island was more than Matt had promised. It was like a fairyland, created by Nature, made luxurious by the expenditure of enormous sums of money. The owner, heir to a fabled timber fortune, had bought the island some twenty years before and made it a private fiefdom, complete with a small landing strip, a deep-water dock, staff cottages, and a comfortable but unpretentious house that blended harmoniously with the rolling sandy hills and verdant pine forests.

Matt had surprised her with a Christmas tree – a beautiful blue spruce outside their door – and trimmed it while she was still asleep, with tinsel and tiny antique ornaments. He had wakened her with a sprig of mistletoe, a kiss, and a gift that brought tears to her eyes – a leather-bound first edition of Holmes's *The Autocrat of the Breakfast Table*.

"This is the best Christmas I've had in a long time," she whispered. "Thank you."

"Thank you," he said, "for making me happy."

They had spent the day walking hand in hand on the beach, talking until sunset. It was almost the way it had been in Maine; better, now that they were no longer strangers. Away from the power and the responsibility of the court, in his pullover sweater and rolled-up khaki pants, Matt looked like a silver-haired boy, his ruggedly handsome face tanned by the sun, his gray eyes brimming with enjoyment. More than anyone Willie had ever known, Matt seemed to be at ease with himself and the world around him. He took pleasure from his surroundings and in every moment; in his presence, Willie, too, felt renewed, and the pressures of law school seemed once again challenging, rather than oppressive.

Now, huddled against the reassuring warmth of his windbreaker, she fidgeted restlessly, wishing they were somewhere else. She still had reservations about being Matt's accomplice in this duck blind.

When the flutter of wings announced the arrival of a flock of the feathered creatures, she watched apprehensively as he cocked his rifle, took aim, and fired three quick blasts in succession. The formation of birds quickly scattered, as one of their number plummeted to the ground.

"I hate this!" she erupted vehemently. "And you should, too. You call yourself a naturalist, but you just blasted that poor thing out of the sky."

He answered her seriously. "I am a naturalist," he said, "in the truest historical sense. Hunters – like fishermen – have always been a part of Nature's thinning process. Cavemen, Indians, the natives of the rain forests. All part of Darwin's equation."

Willie pouted silently, unable to muster anything but a purely emotional argument against Matt's solid rationality.

"This isn't so different from what's been happening to your class at law school," Matt resumed. "I'm sure most of your classmates are good people. But some of them will fall by the wayside in the winnowing process . . . blasted out of the sky, as it were . . . leaving the strongest and most resourceful to carry on the practice of law. As a woman, you'll need to be especially strong and resourceful, because it's up to you to show the old reactionaries that the female of the species is no less worthy of the Juris Doctor degree – perhaps even more – than her male counterpart."

247

Still Willie said nothing. She understood Matt's point, even accepted his reasoning as sound. But she just couldn't bring herself to endorse the scene she had just witnessed.

"Truce," he offered at last with a smile. "Let's agree to disagree on this issue. No more duck hunting this week."

"You are perfect," she said, her eyes glowing. "You can't convince me you aren't. But . . . you did come here to hunt . . ."

He touched her cheek lightly with his fingers. "I came here to play and explore. We have this whole island as a playground. I promise you won't be bored."

"I'm never bored with you," she said truthfully. Wherever they were, whatever they did, Willie marveled at how he was able to make her see what she had never noticed before.

In deference to her feelings, Matt gathered up his single bird, wrapped it in an oilcloth sack, and promised to prepare the best Duck à l'Orange in the western hemisphere. "Unless that would offend you?" he asked, half teasingly.

She shook her head. At least they would be utilizing what had been killed.

They walked back to the house, a low chaletlike structure perched on a rolling hill overlooking the sea. It was a spacious home, with two separate bedroom wings, and an open living area in the middle: a modern cooking island, birch Swedish-style dining furniture and white down-filled modular couches. A white brick fireplace dominated one wall.

The enormous stainless steel refrigerator-freezer had been stocked with food. In a temperature- and humidity-controlled cabinet was a selection of vintage wines.

Willie whipped up an omelette, while Matt prepared a salad. They lunched on the glassed-in front deck, watching the surf.

Later they walked barefoot on the beach. The breeze was salty and cool, too cool for swimming, whipping Willie's golden hair around her face. Matt set the pace, striding briskly, ramrod straight even in relaxation, his arm draped protectively around her shoulder.

248

"Tell me about the semester's work," he said. "You sounded overwhelmed the last time we talked about it."

"The work's not hard, not really," she explained, "but there's so much of it. I've done my tech checks for the *Law Review*, but I haven't even started my first article."

"Aim high, Willie," he said, "and shoot straight and fast. Timing and luck are important here. If you choose a case that's going to be heard on appeal, and make your presentation well, that article will have impact. It may even be quoted by the judge who hears the case."

Willie already knew what Matt was telling her. The *Law Review* could become a showcase for her skills. The kind of circumstances he described were rare, but possible. If she could produce at least one outstanding article, if she could keep her grade-point average up, then she could be a leading contender for the editorship she coveted.

"There's something else," she said, "something I've wanted to talk to you about . . . "

"Anything."

"My Moot Court brief, Matt. I'm not asking you to do my 'homework,'" she added hastily, "but I'm having problems with the assignment. You see, I've been assigned to argue against something I believe in."

She went on to explain the case of the fictional Clara Barton School, and her assignment to uphold the position of a state board that had denied accreditation. "How can I do that?" she asked. "If there were such a school, I'd fight heart and soul for accreditation. How can I argue even a hypothetical case against it?"

Matt stopped walking and put his hands on her shoulders. "Sit," he said, "and listen." She settled herself on the soft, cool sand.

His face was serious as he spoke. "I know you have passion and dedication and integrity, Willie. Those are fine qualities, but they aren't enough. It's important – no, it's vital that you be able to see the merit of an opposing view."

"But what if there is no merit?" she argued. "What if I think the opposite side is dead wrong?"

He gripped her hands tightly, as though to force her to

hear. "Willie, in all my years on the bench, I've never met such a creature as 'dead wrong' – nor its counterpart 'dead right.' If you can't concede merit, at least concede that there's some reason behind a point of view that's different from yours."

Willie sat in the damp sand, a picture of puzzlement and dejection. She hadn't expected this stern lecture from Matt. In fact, she had expected him to support what she saw as integrity. "Why should I?" she asked. "After I graduate, I don't ever intend to take a case I don't believe in. If I start defending what the other side thinks, I'm halfway to losing."

Disappointment clouded Matt's eyes. "You're wrong, Willie. Not 'dead wrong,' but I hope you'll believe me when I say that this assignment is the best you could have been given. You may win case after case, but you'll defeat yourself if your vision is so narrow, so limited, that you can't see beyond your own point of view. 'Dead right' may win cases, Willie, but the price . . ." he trailed off, his eyes focused on some distant point in the horizon.

Willie walked the rest of the way back to the house in silence. Having come to expect Matt's support, she was stung by his obvious disappointment in her. She found it as hard to accept his disapproval as to believe what he was saying.

The poker game was Willie's idea. She wanted to see Matt smile again, she wanted the mood of intimate camaraderie to return. "I learned from a real cowboy," she warned him, "so be prepared to lose."

"And I," he answered with a wink, "have played with a real riverboat gambler, so the stakes had better be interesting."

They found a rack of poker chips and assigned them extravagant dollar values – $10,000 for white, $50,000 for red, $100,000 for blue. Playing as Ben had taught her so long ago, Willie took the first three hands. "You owe me half a million dollars, Justice Harding." She leaned across the table. "But I'll settle for a dollar if you'll stop being mad at me."

250

"Mad at you?" For a moment Matt looked genuinely puzzled. Understanding followed. And a smile so loving it melted Willie's anxiety. He got up from the table and put his arms around her. "Darling Willie," he said tenderly. "I was never mad at you. Forgive me . . . I want so much to teach you lessons you'll need . . . but a teacher has no right to judge. You'll learn in your own time, not mine."

He ruffled her hair affectionately and went back to his chair. "Now deal those cards, kid. I'm ready to break this losing streak."

Relieved that Matt's displeasure had passed, Willie dealt the cards. The gleam in his eyes told her that she'd dealt him a good hand. So much for his poker face, she thought indulgently, enjoying the fact that there was *something* she could do better than Matt did.

She bet recklessly, watching his smile broaden after he drew a single card.

"Aha!" He threw his hand down triumphantly. "Straight flush – what do you say to that?"

"I say that beats my two pairs. Double or nothing?"

They played another hand, and once again Matt won. For a little while, Willie felt their usual roles were reversed. She watched his handsome face light up with excitement and felt a stirring of desire. She had meant to follow the rules he'd set, but it was hard to ignore the fact that they were alone on this fairytale island and that she felt so close to Matt in every way but one.

"This seems to be my lucky day," he said exuberantly, scooping up his chips. "I think I've been missing something."

"I think you have," she said. "Maybe you should raise the ante."

"Fine," he laughed. "I'm already ahead a couple of million."

She hesitated, then pushed her chips aside and reached across the table to take his hand. "I was talking about something else. About taking a risk with me." She could feel his fingers stiffen, but she held on tightly, pulling his hand closer. "I love you, Matt, and I think you love me, too . . ."

251

He gazed at her intently for a long moment. "From the first moment I saw you, Willie. Who wouldn't? But, you know—"

"No, darling," she cut him off, placing her fingertips gently to his lips. "Not now – no opinions for the dissent. I do want you so much . . . "

He released her fingers, then stood up abruptly. With a suddenness that took her breath away, Matt swept Willie from her chair and carried her into the bedroom, showing what he had held back before, his passion and his need. They undressed each other and lay down side by side. And as he kissed her golden skin, caressing the curves of shoulders and breasts, her body responded with a freedom and trust she had never known.

Matt was a skilled and experienced lover, yet as he explored her body with his fingers, his mouth, orchestrating a symphony of delicious sensations, she felt as if his touch was intensely personal, as if no one before had really mattered. Making love with Matt was like a love poem, rich with meaning and discovery. A touching of hearts, as well as a joining of bodies, that told Willie she was cherished and loved, that allowed her to open like a flower, to unfold slowly with each kiss and caress. To taste and savor the treasury of delights that had been locked within her, without fear of losing herself.

"So different," she whispered, holding Matt in a lover's embrace, arms and legs intertwined. And it was, different from the wild, consuming passion that had left her feeling hurt and used.

"For me, too, Willie. If I'd known it could be like this, I couldn't have stood the waiting . . . "

"What *did* take you so long?" she teased.

"Love," he said, with a boyish grin. "It makes me feel unselfish and noble. I've been asking myself what's best for you, and I couldn't be sure it was me."

"Oh, Matt. I love you for caring, but I'm a big girl, Matt, no matter what you might think . . . and I know there isn't anything better than this."

She curled up contentedly in his arms, thinking how good

and right it felt to be there – and fell asleep easily, knowing that Matt would light the dark corners and keep the shadows at bay.

They went through the next days enjoying each other's company as lovers and friends. In the kind of blissful harmony Willie had not believed possible between a man and woman. And finding it at last made her want to hold on, without knowing how. Matt's work – his life – was in Washington, and soon, all too soon, she would have to go back to school.

When New Year's Eve came, Willie insisted on making it her project. Matt was sent to explore the other side of the island while she made her preparations. "When you get back, it's black tie," she instructed him. "And stay in your room until I call you."

She selected a tender filet of beef from the freezer and some mushrooms and artichokes from the well-stocked refrigerator. To accompany dinner, she chose a bottle of vintage Chateau Lafitte Rothschild and carefully decanted it, so the sediment would settle. For their celebration of the New Year, she chilled a bottle of Dom Perignon.

She had packed but a single dress for this holiday, a floor-length white cashmere with a soft, luxurious cowl neck. She belted it with a circlet of white suede studded with turquoise stones. As a finishing touch, she put a Debussy recording on the stereo – and then she summoned Matt to join her.

When Matt appeared, more handsome and vital than she had ever seen him, in his starched white shirt and black tuxedo, his eyes told her more eloquently than words could that she looked lovely.

"You *have* been busy," he said appreciatively, taking in the lit candles, the flowers on the table, the soft strains of music and the tantalizing aroma of sizzling steak intermingled with Bearnaise sauce.

Bathed in the soft glow of candlelight, Willie felt the enchantment of the moment and wondered if it could possibly last. The old year was slipping away and another was about to begin. With Matt in her life, everything would be different – but was it possible to have him without giving up the dream that had been born before she believed in love?

"My compliments to the chef," Matt said, raising his wineglass. "It appears you have hidden talents . . . "

"Not hidden," she said pointedly, "Just undiscovered. You see, you can make discoveries, too, Matt, no matter what you think. Now I'm going to make you an offer . . . call it a plea bargain."

He laughed. "I'm a judge, Willie, not a district attorney."

"Don't be so technical," she said airily. "I'll promise you that I'll remember everything you said when I do my Moot Court brief . . . "

"Excellent."

"*If* you promise to tell the whole truth and nothing but the truth tonight . . . "

Matt smiled, obviously amused by Willie's game. "That's a deal," he said.

Once she had established her role as "leader," Willie held on to it. And when they had finished dinner, Matt got up to help clear the dishes. "Leave it," she commanded. "That can wait till tomorrow." She opened the bottle of champagne and offered him a glass. "To us," she said.

"To us." He sipped the champagne and remarked, "A good vintage . . . "

"Every vintage has its good points," she said, with a determined lift of her chin. She went to the record player and put on an album she'd selected earlier in the day. Not the usual classical music they listened to, but a collection of vintage band arrangements. As the first sweet notes of "Stardust" filled the room, she came toward Matt and held out her hand.

"Ah, Willie, it's been a while."

"I don't believe that," she said stubbornly. "I remember seeing pictures of you at Washington parties in the newspapers. If you say 'no', I'm going to think you just don't want to . . . "

He gave a bemused sigh, as he rose and quoted with

mock seriousness. " 'Man has his will . . . but woman has her way.' "

"Sounds like Holmes again," Willie observed.

"Holmes again," he admitted, as he held out his arms and she moved into them for the dance.

She moved in close, resting her head against his chest, inhaling the pine woods fragrance of his aftershave, and listening to the strong, steady beating of his heart.

Suddenly they heard a ringing sound, shrill and tinny and insistent.

"What the hell?" Matt jumped.

"It's the alarm clock," Willie laughed. "Happy New Year, Matt." She reached up and drew his head down for a long, passionate kiss.

"Have I told you how much I love you today?" he asked, his voice husky with desire.

"Show me," she whispered, taking his hand and leading him into her bedroom. She pulled off the soft white cashmere dress and let it drop to the floor. She stood before him, her blue eyes dark with invitation – and then it was Matt who led, circling her waist with a powerful grip that left Willie breathless. He covered her with kisses, murmuring endearments that warmed her heart, as his touch warmed her flesh. She tugged at his clothes, impatient to feel the hard maleness of his body against her. They sank onto the bed, her arms wrapped around his neck as if she'd never let him go. He entered her quickly and held her still, caressing her breasts until she began to tremble. Slowly he began to move inside her, bringing her to the brink of orgasm, then stopping and starting again until her breath was coming in short ragged gasps. Her back arched and she moaned his name. He stroked faster and harder, as her inner muscles began to contract, tightening around him, and they came together in a hot rush of release.

Willie snuggled into Matt's body, as if she were seeking more than the physical love they had just shared.

"Happy New Year, my love," he said adoringly.

She hesitated before answering. "I want it to be," she

said haltingly, "but in a couple of days, we'll have to leave
. . I don't want this to be over, Matt . . . I want us to be
together . . . "

"Is that what's bothering you? Darling Willie, you don't
think a few hundred miles will change what we have, do
you? I told you – love makes me noble. I want you to be
everything you want to be, but I will find a way for us to be
together . . . I promise."

And for the first time Willie tasted the richness of a
happiness she could trust.

Willie tiptoed through the darkness, stumbling over a chair
as she made her way into the kitchen. Still drowsy, she
poured herself a cold drink from the refrigerator.

Her sleepy eyes tried to focus. Moonlight filtered
through the window, giving an eerie glow to the shapes
around her. Against the rhythmic rustle of the surf, she
heard a muffled thump. It must be an animal, she thought.
A rabbit or a raccoon.

The sound came again, louder and more ominous. She
wanted to run, back to the safety of Matt's arms. But an icy
frisson of fear rooted her to the floor. The shapes around
her became darker, seemed to be closing her in . . .

If only she could get back into the bedroom. She began to
perspire, though the air was cool. The distance between her
and Matt seemed like a moat, filled with shadows born of
dreams and fragmented memories.

His voice, calling her name, broke the spell. "Willie . . .
are you all right?" She ran to him, throwing the shadows
behind, hurling herself into his arms. "What is it, Willie?
Did you have a nightmare?"

She huddled closer, burrowing against the warmth of his
body. He stroked her hair, crooning sounds of assurance.

Finally she spoke, her voice was barely audible. "It goes
back to my first nightmare. Only this one wasn't a dream. I
was eight years old. I woke up . . . it was very dark, and I
heard noises, terrible sounds of shouting and . . . and a
beating . . . coming from my parents' room."

Slowly, haltingly, as if the words and the memories were

256

being pulled through the jagged edges of a broken heart, Willie told Matt what she had never told anyone, the story of the night her family had died – and orphaned her in ways she still couldn't understand.

When she finished, he took her hand and led her outside, onto the covered deck. "Come and see," he said. "There's nothing to be afraid of here, I promise you." He wrapped her in a blanket, settling her comfortably on the old wicker couch. They sat together, looking at the night sky. Softly he murmured: " 'Day hath put on his jacket and around his burning bosom buttoned it with stars . . . ' "

Nestled against his chest, Willie smiled in recognition. "Holmes . . ." she murmured.

"From his poem *'Evening'*."

The fear was gone, and she wanted to stay with him forever. As long as she was with him, she felt, the night would hold no terrors; it could only be the inspiration for an unspoken poem they would write together.

12

Willie returned to school with a secret, the memory of a treasured holiday she planned to share with no one, not even Suzanne.

But when Willie left the apartment for her first morning class, there still hadn't been any sign of Suzanne. No phone calls, no messages. It wasn't like her to be so completely out of touch. Willie remembered that her roommate had gone home for the holidays with a bad case of bronchitis. Maybe she was still sick, Willie thought. She would call the Parkman home tonight.

After her last class, Willie picked up a roasted chicken, a loaf of Italian bread, and a quart of milk from a little deli near Harvard Square. As she walked up the stairs to the apartment, she heard the unmistakable sound of Suzanne's favorite rock-and-roll station.

257

When she let herself into the apartment, Suzanne was lying on the couch smoking a cigarette, her overnight bag still unopened, on the floor.

"Welcome back," Willie said. "I was starting to worry about you. Too much celebrating? Are you okay?"

"I'm fine," Suzanne replied. "Except for one thing: having to say what I have to say to you."

"That sounds serious." Willie put her packages down and waited.

"It is." Suzanne got up and walked to the liquor cabinet, poured herself a double from her private bottle of Jack Daniels, and lit a fresh cigarette. She marched back to where Willie sat and stood in front of her. "Okay," she said, "there's no easy way, might as well give it to you cold turkey. I'm not coming back to school. I'm just here now to see you and get my things. I'll pay my share of the term's rent," she added hastily. "I want to be fair—"

"I don't care about the damn rent," Willie interrupted. Her friend's announcement made no sense at all. Suzanne's grades weren't brilliant, but they were better than passing. "This is crazy!" Willie vented her feelings aloud.

"I knew you'd feel that way," Suzanne said, and sat down on the couch beside Willie. She inhaled deeply, then released a puff of smoke. "But I can't stay in law school just so you don't think less of me."

Willie stared even harder. "What has this got to do with *me?*" she asked incredulously. "You wanted to be here. You've wanted it for a long time . . . "

"True. But all that's changed for me, Willie. It started to matter less last summer, and when I went home for the holidays, it was all settled."

"What . . . what was settled?"

"I'm getting married." Suzanne ground out her cigarette and covered her ears.

But Willie didn't explode. She simply stared, her mouth open, her eyes blank.

"Close your mouth," Suzanne said. "People get married every day. Come on, Willie, I didn't take holy orders when

258

I came to Harvard. I want to do all the, you know, normal things . . . a home, a family . . . "

Willie shook her head vigorously. All of this seemed to be coming out of nowhere. Had she been asleep while Suzanne was hatching all these . . . these George Parkman notions? "But you never seemed—" she began to protest.

"Maybe I've changed," Suzanne broke in. "Remember when I told you about meeting Jack's friend last summer? I put Jim off at first because he was so perfect – good looks, good family, good future in banking . . . everything the old man wanted for me. But one thing led to another, and then it didn't seem to make sense to fight it. Just because that's old George's idea of happiness for me doesn't mean it can't be mine."

Willie couldn't hide her disappointment. In the newness of her love for Matt, she could almost understand giving up one dream for another. But Matt didn't demand sacrifices to love; he had urged Willie to fulfill herself – and she wanted that for Suzanne, too.

"All right," Suzanne said, lighting another Marlboro, her eyes squinting against a puff of smoke. "Here's how it really is. For the first time, since I was a little girl, I'm back in the family again. The old man likes Jim, my brothers like him, my mother likes him Willie," she was almost pleading now, "I don't have to prove anything anymore. Say you understand . . . "

Willie nodded. Perhaps it was unfair but it felt like she had lost more than a friend; she had lost an ally in a battle. Yet whatever her feelings, however Suzanne's defection clashed with her own dreams, Willie was careful to say nothing that would hurt. Suzanne already looked as vulnerable and fragile as she did the day they'd met.

"Are you leaving right away?" Willie asked.

Suzanne began to cry. "Oh, Willie . . . I hate to be leaving like this . . . "

"Then don't," Willie urged. "Finish law school. It's only half a year. You can still marry Jim, but do this first. Stay. Do it for you."

Suzanne shook her head.

"Jim won't let you," Willie ventured.

"It isn't Jim. It's me. A half year is a long time. I could lose him. I have to do this the right way, the way my mother did."

Willie wanted to argue, to say there was no right way, no guarantees where marriage was concerned, but Suzanne seemed so tightly wound, so desperate to convince.

"I'll be here till tomorrow," she said. "The old man's sending his driver to pack my things. Can you beat that?" she laughed nervously. "I finally did something right." She brushed the tears from her face with her fingers and forced a smile. "Be my maid of honor, Willie . . . please?"

"Sure," Willie said, and gave Suzanne a hug. "I'm going to miss you terribly."

"We'll stay in touch," Suzanne declared passionately. "Just because I'm getting married doesn't mean we can't be friends . . . "

Willie released her friend and gave her a smile. She wished the words were true, but she knew in her heart that staying in touch wasn't the same as being friends.

For the next few weeks Willie found herself in a foul mood. Her days had taken on a grinding, unrelenting sameness. Even with her prodigious appetite for challenge and work, she had started to feel like an eating, breathing robot, with no reality outside the classroom and the library.

As much as she had expected to miss her roommate, she could not have predicted the vacuum that seemed to exist in the wake of her departure. Willie had become accustomed to Suzanne's wit, her throaty laughter, even the familiar odor of cigarette smoke and the overflowing ashtrays. Without the warmth of her presence, her persuasive urging to take a walk or share a companionable cup of coffee, Willie became almost reclusive.

Only Matt's weekly phone calls broke through the rigid discipline of her routine. She shared her work with him, but as the weeks slipped by, the time they'd had in Georgia slipped further away, too. His voice on the telephone seemed less immediate, less intimate than when he'd held her close, driving her night fears away with promises of love. The closest, most intimate relationship she had was with her work. She woke up with it and took it to bed at night.

During his last call, Matt had said he missed her. He had expressed the hope he'd see her soon, but all Willie could manage was a vague, murmured response. She loved Matt dearly, but he was in Washington and she was here; living alone like a nun and trying to cram a month's worth of accomplishment into every precious week. Yesterday, she'd almost nodded off in class. And last night, she'd been up until five in the morning working on her Moot Court brief.

Now, as she slammed into the *Law Review* office to drop off her latest batch of "tech checks," she heard the irritating sound of Bud Hodge's laughter.

"Hey, Willie," he called out, "have you heard the latest Cliffie joke?"

Gritting her teeth, she ignored him. In the two years she'd spent at Radcliffe, she'd heard dozens of puerile, tasteless, and disgusting "Cliffie" jokes.

Bud refused to be ignored, playing to the appreciative chortles of his audience of third-year students. "What's the difference between a toilet bowl and a Cliffie? Give up? The toilet bowl doesn't have sagging tits."

Snickering and guffawing, the male staff members turned toward Willie, waiting for her reaction. Pigs, she thought. Adolescent sexist pigs. She gritted her teeth harder, throwing her briefcase down on one of the desks. She went to the files, searching through the back issues for a reference she needed. Working silently, she pretended to be alone in the room. And when she was finished, she noticed that only Bud was still there. Still ignoring him, she marched to the door.

"Leaving, Wonder Woman?" Bud called after her. "Parting is such sweet sorrow . . . "

It wasn't until much later in the afternoon, in the quiet of the law library, that Willie opened her briefcase. She rummaged through the stacks of papers she always carried, looking for her Moot Court brief. It wasn't there.

But it *had* to be. The brief was vital – weeks of meticulous research, references, documentation. She turned her case upside down, dumping its contents out, foraging frantically though the mess . . . until there was no doubt. The brief was gone.

In less than a week, she would have to face her opponent from Boston University. Not to mention Professor Sharp's smirk. There was no way on earth she could reconstruct her brief from memory. Without it, she would utterly fail Moot Court.

Frantically she retraced her footsteps, going from classroom to classroom, searching under desks, in wastebaskets. Nothing.

Where could it be? she asked herself over and over again. She went back to the *Law Review* office and searched there.

And then it struck her. Bud! She had left the briefcase unattended. For Bud to see. To invite another of his rotten, dirty tricks.

She went through every drawer, every desk, every wastebasket. He wouldn't have left any evidence, but she didn't know what else to do.

Like a madwoman, she raced around the campus, asking if anyone had seen Bud Hodge. She finally ran him down in the Hayes-Bickford cafeteria in Harvard Square.

"You!" She spat the word in his face, ignoring the staring faces of students at surrounding tables. "You're a contemptible lowlife," she raved, "but this time you've gone too far."

Startled by her attack, Bud laughed nervously. "I know you're crazy about me, Willie – but what the hell are you talking about?"

"You know damn well!" she raged, full of righteous indignation. "You took my Moot Court brief – probably burned it by now! But I'll get you for it . . . I promise I'll get you, Bud."

He bolted up from his chair, seized her arm, and pulled her into a corner. "Now just hold on a minute – hold it one damn minute. I declared war on you fair and square. I never pretended to be your friend. I told you what was what on day one. That's how it is in law – and those are the limits I set myself. I'll use your weaknesses against you, I'll find ways to make you look bad. And if you've lost your brief, I may not be the first to say I'm sorry. But I didn't steal it, Willie! That's not my style." He turned on his heel and went back to his table.

She slunk out of the "Hayes-Bick." Bud was lying, of course. No one else would have sabotaged her so mercilessly. But why should she have expected him to confess? There wouldn't be courts of law if everyone told the truth.

Disconsolate and exhausted, Willie returned to her apartment. Without Suzanne's little decorating touches, her careful attention to detail, and her regular tidying up, the place had fallen into a dismal state. Under the crushing pressure of her overambitious schedule, Willie had all but given up trying to keep order. Now, dizzy with exhaustion, she surveyed the accumulated litter of weeks of neglect. She knew she had reached her limits.

She fell into her unmade bed, fully clothed. For sixteen hours she slept.

The following morning, groggy, hungry, and unrefreshed, she dragged herself out of bed. The apartment looked even worse. She would have to find her notes, make some attempt to reconstruct her case as best she could. After a hasty shower and two cups of coffee, Willie reluctantly attacked the disorder – the piles of paper and books, the unwashed dishes, the discarded clothing.

She was busy sweeping dust balls and crumpled notes from under the bed when she caught sight of the folder. The pages of her missing brief protruded from under a pair of shoes. Relief and confusion hit Willie all at once. She had been so sure the folder had been tucked safely in her briefcase. How could she have been so wrong?

She flushed with embarrassment as she remembered the scene with Bud, her angry accusations. He had been telling the truth. It had been her own fatigue, her own carelessness that had misplaced her precious brief.

She was far from ready to apologize to Bud. But maybe there was something to what he said about the law being all-out war. Within the limits of the law.

Willie stood before the Moot Court, her notes clutched in her hand. Her opponent, a third-year – male – student from Boston University, had just finished arguing the appeal for the Clara Barton School. He had claimed that the state board's failure to accredit the school had been a flagrant instance of gender discrimination. Willie found his argument flat and unconvincing. Maybe that was because he didn't know the first thing about discrimination, she thought. She could have done a better job, she knew it. Just as she knew she was going to beat him.

"Your honor," she began, "we have just heard that the Clara Barton School has been the victim of gender discrimination, which is prohibited by law. On behalf of the state board, I maintain that there has been no such discrimination. The board denied accreditation on the grounds that the philosophy of the school, the teaching of a curriculum based on the accomplishments of women, is educationally unsound. In so doing, the board has not interfered with the school's right to teach. There is nothing in the statute book of the state which requires accreditation. Therefore, the school is free to operate, and its pupils are free to attend.

"Your honor, I respectfully submit that the court is expert in the principles of law, not in the principles of education. I submit that the court should therefore defer to the expertise of the state board and not override its decision . . . "

The appellate judge in the hypothetical court was Ken Harper, a young lawyer who had gained a national reputation as a champion of liberal causes. He had defended student radicals and draft resisters, and Willie had enormous respect for his skill and integrity. As she was making her argument, she thought she saw Harper smile, almost imperceptibly. And from the corner of her eye, she had noticed Professor Sharp, minus the smirk, nodding his head as she spoke.

In his role as Judge, Harper returned a decision in Willie's favor. The moment she heard it, she thought of Matt. She had done exactly what he'd told her she must do. She had taken an issue that went against what she believed. She had built a solid case and she had presented it well. She had hated every minute – and she had won.

But now she made herself a promise. When she graduated, when she became a practicing attorney, she would never again argue against what she believed.

13

It was almost midnight when Willie walked into the vestibule of the Hancock Street apartment. She dropped her bulging briefcase on the cracked tile floor and turned her key in the lock of the old-fashioned metal mailbox. The light in the hallway was dim, but amidst the bills and advertising circulars, she caught a glimpse of a white parchment envelope bearing the return address of a U.S. Supreme Court Justice. Strange, she thought – Matt had never written to her on official stationery before.

But when she examined the letter, she saw that it was not from Matt, but rather from "The Chambers of Justice John Martin Gibbs." It had been written by one of Gibbs's clerks, and it notified Willie that she had "been brought to the Justice's attention" as an outstanding student of the law. She was invited to come to Washington, to be interviewed for the position of law clerk.

The invitation soothed Willie's bruised ego as nothing else could have. In spite of all her hard work, all her punishing efforts, she had been passed over for the editorship of *Law Review*.

To make matters worse, the position had gone to Bud,

who smugly implied that she had lost out by spreading herself too thin. Willie had a different opinion. She was absolutely certain that Bud had been chosen because he was a man.

On paper, they had both been outstanding candidates. Their *Law Review* articles, though different in style, had been noteworthy. Bud's grade-point average had been a shade higher – Willie conceded that her extracurricular activities had cost something. And he had spent more time in the *Review* office, politicking and "romancing" the advisers. But she felt that her superb showing on the Moot Court circuit gave her the legitimate edge. She'd been bitterly disappointed by the sexism that put her in the second slot instead of the first.

The opportunity to clerk for a Supreme Court Justice softened Willie's disappointment. For all his machinations, Bud would have nothing like that in his résumé.

And then her balloon burst. Of course: Only Matt could have brought her name to his colleague's attention. It had nothing to do with her distinguished record.

She telephoned Matt, told him about the letter – and demanded to know if he was responsible.

"Yes," he admitted readily. "I did give your name to John. But I wouldn't have – no matter how much I love you – if I didn't think you're damn good, and deserve the job. I'm just betting that once another good judge has met you, he'll see the qualities I've seen . . . "

"Not *everything* you've seen, sir," Willie joked.

Matt laughed. "No, not everything." He paused. "I said I'd find a way for us to be together, remember? Nothing means more to me. You will come for the interview, won't you?"

"Of course I will," she said. "And thank you."

"You're welcome. But, Willie . . . don't believe for a minute that you're a shoo-in. Gibbs is a friend, as well as a colleague. We see eye to eye occasionally. But John Gibbs is also a fierce, independent old goat. Possibly even more tough-minded than I am. He'll put you through the wringer

266

at your interview. And he'll decide for himself, *by* himself, if you can do the job. Have I put your doubts to rest?"

Willie sighed. "You certainly have. I'm not doubtful any more. Now I'm *terrified*."

Matt laughed. "You'll knock his socks off, my love. Just believe in yourself. Believe you deserve the chance. Women in this country are going to need a great advocate . . . and soon. You just might be that person."

She was touched by his words and his confidence. But she knew how Matt felt about her. "Matt," she said. "I need your advice. There's no one else whose opinion I value more. So please be objective . . . don't put me on a pedestal because . . . "

"Because I'm blinded by love? Don't worry, Willie. The only woman I keep on a pedestal is Justice herself. She's also the only one wearing a blindfold. I see your talents and abilities very clearly, Willie. In fact . . . " He hesitated. "I would have liked you to be *my* clerk . . . "

"I know."

He dropped his voice, taking on the familiar conspiratorial tone: "Only the truth is . . . Johnny Gibbs needs a good clerk a hell of a lot more than I do. Good luck, Willie."

It was cherry-blossom time in Washington when Willie arrived for her meeting with John Martin Gibbs. The extensive studying she'd done of opinions rendered by Justice Gibbs might have prepared her in mind for the test of meeting him, but it had done little to diminish her trepidation about being interviewed by the oldest and – many said – most opinionated member of the court ("His problem," Matt had explained, "is not so much hardening of the arteries as hardening of the heart.") However, there was no denying that Gibbs was a brilliant jurist, a man who could teach Willie a great deal. If she could survive the interview.

Although Matt had urged Willie to be herself, she felt she should be "more so" for Gibbs, who was as conservative as Matt was liberal. She had chosen a dark gray suit for her interview, and was wearing her hair pulled back into a bun. She almost wished she had bought herself a pair of clear-glass spectacles to mask her face. Although she had applied no makeup this morning, she still worried that Gibbs might hold the old-fashioned prejudice against "just another pretty face."

As she walked through the cavernous marble halls of the Court building, hearing the echo of her clicking heels, feeling the nervous thumping of her heart, she wondered how much Justice Gibbs knew about her and exactly what Matt had said when he'd recommended her.

It was fifteen minutes before the hour when Willie presented herself to Gibbs's secretary – and ten o'clock precisely when the secretary ushered Willie into the great man's presence.

At age seventy-eight, Gibbs was more imposing in person than in pictures. With shaggy gray hair and mustache, wearing a vest with a gold watch chain draped across it, he resembled an unsmiling, humorless Mark Twain. Like each of the other eight justices, Gibbs had his own private suite of offices. Willie had imagined him in a traditional setting much like the one she'd known at "Ring and Wait." But the elderly justice's office was a veritable museum, decorated with fragments of cultures far older than America's. On one wall hung an antique Scottish tartan; on another, a framed copy of the Magna Carta. His desk was a massive English refectory table, and behind it was a glass case containing what seemed to be fragments of Etruscan pottery.

Willie anticipated a moment or two of amenities, the opportunity to take a personal reading of the man. But Gibbs said no more than a perfunctory "good morning," while inviting her to sit in a carved straight-back chair that might have come from an English manor house. Then, staring at her through dark, piercing eyes, he began at once to fire off a barrage of legal questions.

She answered them easily, with just enough deference to avoid offending the justice, and began to feel her nervous-ness fading.

Unsmiling, and without a hint of either approval or disapproval in his expression, Gibbs nodded his head and then launched into a statement of his conservative philosophy. Willie tensed as he predicted "the twilight of this misguided liberalism." She disagreed, respectfully, and with an uncharacteristic attempt at diplomacy, she refrained from arguing.

A moment of silence followed, and Willie thought the interview might be over. Then abruptly, and without a change of expression, Gibbs said, "I've rarely had a colleague express such an interest in a young student as Justice Harding has in recommending you to me. Can you tell me why he's so willing to help you, Miss Dellahaye?"

The suddenness of the question almost took her breath away. "Justice Harding is a friend," she answered carefully, hoping Gibbs would drop this line of questioning.

But he didn't. "There is, in that status, a large potential for what we call in the law 'a gray area.' Can you define it a bit more precisely, Miss Dellahaye?"

Her first reaction was indignation. And confusion. How much did she dare say to a colleague of Matt's? "There are no *gray* areas in our friendship," she replied quietly. "Everything is *green* – growing and blooming. I met Justice Harding on the banks of a stream in Maine. He gave me a lesson in trout fishing, and he's been teaching me something new ever since. That's the nature of our friendship."

"Then if he wants this job for you . . . it's only so you can continue to learn?" Gibbs asked shrewdly.

"He has said that was his reason for recommending me."

Gibbs gave a small nod as he paused to scrutinize Willie again, his eyes raking over her in a way that indicated he was studying not just the whole, but all its parts. Before he had seen her as an applicant for a job; now he seemed to be looking at her as a woman.

"A simple friendship between you and Justice Harding strikes me as rather extraordinary," he said at last. "From my venerable position, Matthew often seems a mere boy, but compared to an attractive young woman like you, one might call him old. Would you agree, Miss Dellahaye?"

Willie paused. Gibbs was bearing down. And how could she deny that there was likely to be more than met the eye? Once she agreed, the way would be open to more and more questions.

Then suddenly a way to defuse Gibbs's interrogation occurred to her – suggested unwittingly by Matt, in one book he'd given her by his favorite poet. She began to recite:

> "Call him not old, whose visionary brain
> Holds o'er the past its undivided reign.
> For him in vain the envious seasons roll
> Who bears eternal summer in his soul."

Gibbs favored her with a thin smile. "A sentiment I can heartily endorse," he said, and abruptly stood. "Thank you for coming, Miss Dellahaye. That will be all."

The interview was over. Again, there were no amenities, no clues as to what the Justice thought of her candidacy, no promise to let her know. Willie got up to leave. But just as she reached the door, he said: "By the way . . . that quotation, where did you get it?"

"It's from 'The Old Player' – by Oliver Wendell Holmes."

Gibbs looked at her steadily for a moment, then a slight smile crept over his lips. "Ah yes, of course," he said with a wry edge. "Holmes."

Two weeks later, Willie received the letter – a few handwritten lines from Gibbs himself, saying he looked forward to having her join his staff and to report at the end of June.

14

Graduation was anticlimactic. From the moment Justice Gibbs's letter arrived, Willie had already moved, emotionally and mentally, to Washington.

Ginny and Neal came to Cambridge to see her receive the long-awaited Juris Doctor degree. And for this one day, Willie was able to accept Neal's presence and his congratulations with a measure of surface politeness and grace. She had only two other guests at the graduation: Suzanne and her husband, Jim St. Clair, who had driven up to Boston from their home in Westport, Connecticut, to witness Willie's rite of passage into the legal profession. As she listened to the ceremonial speeches, Willie couldn't help wondering what Suzanne must be feeling today and whether she had any regrets about the choice she'd made.

Later, as they all celebrated over champagne and lobster at the Ritz-Carlton Hotel, Suzanne presented Willie with an elegant morocco briefcase.

"I'm so proud of you," she said. "Do it for both of us," she added in a whisper, hugging Willie hard.

When Suzanne heard about Willie's clerkship with Justice Gibbs, she immediately called her brother Jack, who worked at the Securities and Exchange Commission in Washington and lived with his wife in a spacious townhouse in Georgetown. She returned from the telephone with the news that Willie would be welcome in Jack's home for as long as she was in Washington.

With his usual flourish, Neal announced that his graduation gift would be a two-week European holiday for "mother and daughter." In spite of her negative feelings about her stepfather, Willie was touched by the thoughtfulness of his

271

gesture. It would be nice to get away with Mama for a little while, before she started her job with Justice Gibbs.

But in the midst of dinner, Ginny excused herself to go to the ladies' room, asking Willie to accompany her. As soon as they were away from the table, Ginny said urgently, "We can't take that trip, honey. I'm real sorry, but we just can't. You'd have to get a passport, and if anybody took notice of your name, that would mean trouble . . . "

"What kind of trouble?" Willie asked, forgetting for just a moment the secret that had become a permanent part of their lives. Then she frowned, remembering.

"You understand, don't you baby? You're all set now, and Neal and me, well, we don't need any more trouble . . . "

"Trouble?" Willie had believed until now her mother's vague assurances that things at home were all right. Now Ginny was acting worried and nervous. "Has Neal been giving you problems?"

"Not exactly. He just . . . well, he just . . . I don't know, he just doesn't seem so interested anymore. He's been taking a lot of business trips, and . . . " She shrugged. "But it's nothing for you to worry about, honey. Just do me a favor and tell him 'no' about Europe . . . please?"

Once again, Willie gave in to Ginny's fears of the past. Neal raised a bushy eyebrow but then smoothly promised a large check instead, "to help get you settled in Washington."

When Willie arrived in Washington, there was still one important question to settle: Matt. Though they spent a happy evening celebrating her new position with Justice Gibbs, it had raised a certain awkwardness between them. What would they do about their relationship? How would they see one another without compromising either of them?

Matt might be a liberal, ideologically. On the surface, he might even be one of Washington's men about town. But in matters of the heart, he was, as he had once told her, serious and traditional. In the fishbowl that was Washington society, he had reservations about a public liaison with a beautiful and very young woman, one who had been employed, following his recommendation, by a fellow Supreme Court justice. "I don't give a damn what people say about me, Willie – but I won't have you tarnished by cheap gossip," he said.

Willie was touched and disappointed at the same time. The clerkship with Justice Gibbs was a precious opportunity, one she didn't want to compromise in any way – and yet she was impatient to "have it all," the fullness of Matt's love and the career she'd always wanted. "So what do we do?" she asked quietly. "We can't lose each other . . . "

"We won't," he promised. Matt's solution was a traditional, conservative one. They would see each other in circumstances that were "correct" – at an occasional lunch, or at large parties at Matt's home.

At first the arrangement was workable. Willie had work enough to fill her days and nights. At the home of Jack and Tilly Parkman, she had more than a lovely third-floor room and bath. She had a surrogate family whenever she needed one, and a ready-made social life that made no great demands on her, with the attractive, ambitious young people who gathered regularly at the Parkmans' spacious home.

What troubled Willie most was how Matt seemed to be spending his time. More and more often, he was lunching with "her" justice, playing golf or bridge. It seemed to Willie that for the first time since she'd known him, Matt was "acting his age," putting aside, along with her, all the vital, young qualities that made him special – and different from his Court colleagues.

But after she settled into her new life, she missed him. The affection, the laughter, the private time. All the reasons why they should be apart wore thin. She wanted more.

One evening, at the end of a work day that had stretched past eight o'clock, she bumped into Matt on the steps of the Court building. After a moment or two of correct small talk, Willie said bluntly: "This is silly, Matt. I want to be with you, the way we were."

Relief showed plainly on Matt's face. "I've missed you,

273

too," he said. "And right now, I can't seem to remember all the good reasons why we haven't been together."

"Then let's go," Willie said, linking her arm in his and propelling him toward the waiting black limousine.

They shared a late supper in a small Italian restaurant and returned to Matt's home. Kate greeted them in her housecoat and slippers, smiling a warm welcome that told Willie she had been missed.

Matt's lovemaking told her more. In the quiet of his oak-paneled bedroom he murmured words of love, kissing her tenderly, passionately. In the strong, encircling shelter of his arms, she rediscovered what it was like to feel cherished and adored and unafraid of a man's love.

In the morning, a breakfast tray, deposited outside the bedroom door, bade them a discreet "good morning."

"Isn't this better?" Willie asked contentedly, between mouthfuls of fresh strawberries and croissant. "Admit it." She gave Matt a playful poke in the ribs. "Even the great Justice Harding is allowed to have a personal life. This isn't the dark ages, Matt. Tell me I'm right . . . "

He kissed her shoulder affectionately. "Loving you could be nothing but right. It's the consequences that worry me . . . "

The first consequence came about a half hour later, as she was getting ready to leave. Kate stepped out of the kitchen and approached Willie nervously. "There's something I've wanted to say for a long time . . . "

"Yes?" Willie prompted, wondering if Kate, too, might have a word of warning about the recklessness that had brought her and Matt together again last night.

"I just want you to know how happy I am that Matthew has someone to love again . . . "

"Thank you, Kate," Willie said warmly. "I can't tell you how much that means to me. You know," she said hesitantly, "I wasn't sure for a long time if you . . . approved of me. I even thought . . ."

"That I might be a little possessive where Matthew was concerned," Kate finished with a knowing smile. "I'd be lying if I said I didn't care for him. But when I came to work in this house, Matthew's wife had just died. And by the time he was ready to love again, we were . . . just friends."

Now Willie could see a trace of sadness in Kate's eyes, and she was touched by the woman's generosity.

". . . when Matthew had his heart attack he became so withdrawn, I worried he might never come out of himself . . . and then he met you, in Maine . . . "

"Heart attack?" Willie echoed, full of concern. "He never told me . . . "

Kate smiled again and squeezed Willie's arm. "That's because it wasn't your sympathy Matthew wanted. The attack was a mild one, and the doctor assured us he was in no real danger. Matthew Harding's as strong as an ox, but he's vulnerable, too, Willie . . . I guess you know that."

Willie nodded. Though Matthew had tried to show her only his strength, she had seen him in moments of boyish vulnerability – but having Kate remind her made Willie love him all the more.

The next consequence came in the shape of a photograph that appeared in the society section of the *Washington Post*. The picture showed Matt handing Willie into his limousine and was captioned: "A Secret Romance?" The item below read: "One of Washington's most elusive bachelors, Supreme Court Justice Matthew Harding has been even 'more so' lately – until this reporter spied him in an affectionate tête-à-tête with Willa Dellahaye, a clerk in the chambers of a fellow justice. Could it be that this outspoken advocate of 'full and open disclosure' has something to hide? Might there be a secret romance between the perennial bachelor and the beautiful law clerk young enough to be his daughter?"

Willie tucked the paper under her arm and marched into Matt's office. She set the newspaper on his desk. "There," she said, "that's not so terrible, is it?"

He smiled, though his eyes were serious. "I don't suppose you'd think so . . . but maybe that's because you're the 'May' in this romance, while I'm the 'December' . . . "

"I thought we'd settled the age business a long time ago."

She sat on his desk, brushing the stray lock of silver hair that fell boyishly over his forehead. "What will it take to put it to rest?"

"That business," he said, taking her hand and kissing it, "is a fact of our lives. But if we're going to be together, I won't let the press or anyone else cheapen what I feel for you. I want to go on record with my honorable intentions. This isn't a very romantic setting for what I want to say, but Willie . . . will you marry me?"

The proposal took her breath away. She loved Matt with all her heart and soul – and even now she could hardly believe that he wanted only her. Yet something in her pulled back from the word "marry."

"That's an ominous silence," Matt observed gently.

She had never felt so stuck for words. "Oh, Matt . . . I do . . . uh . . . I love you for asking, Matt. But . . . umm . . . does it have to be right now?"

Matt forced a smile as he recited quietly:

> "And when you stick on conversation's
> burrs
> Don't strew your pathway with those
> dreadful *urs*."

"Oh, for heaven's sake, don't give me Holmes *now*!" she snapped. "You're always so damn . . . wise. Being married to you would be wonderful. Any woman in her right mind would jump at the chance to be your wife. But why do we have to rush into marriage because of one picture in a newspaper? We know what we're all about. Isn't that what truly matters?"

Matt didn't attempt to hide his disappointment. "I'll abstain from that vote, counselor. At my age – and forgive me for bringing 'that business' up again – I don't think you can fault me for 'rushing things'. Just as I understand that at your age, you can see a world of time ahead."

Willie threw her arms around Matt and kissed him, wanting to erase the look of disappointment from his face. How could she make him understand what she herself

276

couldn't explain – that while she felt a forever kind of love for him, she couldn't, wouldn't cheat him with anything less than a wholehearted "yes." "Just give me a little more time," she pleaded.

"Time isn't really mine to give," Matt said. "But take as long as you need."

Willie's excitement was like a fever. The case of Loretta Barker versus the School Board of Fernhill, Illinois, was all she could think about.

For the first time since she came to work for Justice Gibbs, she had a Cause in one of the hundreds of cases presented to the Supreme Court seeking a hearing. In her first six months as a clerk, she'd gained a reputation, well-deserved, as Gibbs's number one workhorse. And now the case of Loretta Barker claimed her attention, driving her into even longer hours of painstaking and meticulous research.

Mrs. Barker was a teacher who had filed for divorce. Her husband had filed a countersuit, alleging various incidents of sexual misconduct. While none of these allegations had been substantiated at the divorce hearing, Mrs. Barker was dismissed from her job, the school board taking the position that "where there's smoke, there's fire."

Willie was certain her efforts would convince "her" justice to vote "yes" on hearing Mrs. Barker's position. She was prepared to argue, to debate, to present the merit and relevance of "her" case. The only contingency she hadn't prepared for was lack of interest. Maddening, frustrating, flat-out indifference. Yet that seemed to be Justice Gibbs's attitude as he brushed aside the Barker petition – and persuaded enough of his colleagues to do so as well.

"I can't believe it," she complained furiously to Matt, pacing back and forth in front of the fireplace while he sipped his after-dinner brandy. "The Court is ignoring the most important issue to come along in months. No one even seems to recognize how important it is."

Matt waited until Willie wound down. "No," he said, "the most important case at hand involves the Pentagon

277

Papers. This case of yours . . . it's a local matter. I can understand your personal passion here . . . and maybe one day, similar issues will warrant our intervention. But that time isn't now. Give it up, Willie."

Silently she considered his words. Her heart, her passion didn't want to give it up. Mrs. Barker had been wronged. By her husband and by a school board made up of men. It didn't seem right that the highest court of the land did not feel this was issue enough. But Gibbs and now Matt were saying Mrs. Barker would have to wait. And so would Willie.

It was cherry blossom time again. Willie had made up her mind that Matt would not wait for her any longer. Her year with Gibbs was almost up, and soon it would be time for her to strike out on her own, to take her bar exams and choose from among the many law firms that wanted her.

It would be time to move her belongings from the third-floor bedroom of Jack Parkman's home and find a home of her own. But when she thought about that prospect, she found that she had little enthusiasm for choosing yet another temporary lodging. Over the past year, it had been Matt and Kate who had made Washington a gracious and comfortable place to live. Matt had been her mentor, her lover, her best friend. He had supported her hopes and ambitions as no one else ever had, and she loved him freely and without fear. As the end of her employment with Gibbs drew closer, there seemed to be no good reason why she shouldn't accept Matt's proposal and have what she hadn't been able to imagine before she met him – a home and a complete life.

With Kate's help she prepared a picnic, reminiscent of those they'd shared in Maine. This time, they planned to spread their tablecloth on the bank of the Potomac and talk of their future.

"I hope you're still willing to make an honest woman of me," she said as they sipped May wine by the river. "Because if you're not, I'll file a breach of promise suit tomorrow."

278

"Willie . . . are you sure?" he asked, his clear gray eyes studying her face. "What about all those things you wanted to do?"

"Of course, I'm sure. I wouldn't trifle with a Supreme Court Justice! I've had several offers from law firms here in Washington. There's no reason why I can't have a career and make you happy, too."

We'll have a good life, she thought dreamily, resting in the strong shelter of Matt's arms, inhaling the dewy freshness of the newly cut grass around them, imagining herself as Willa Dellahaye, Esquire, champion of just causes by day – and Mrs. Justice Harding, Matt's beloved Willie by night. It would be a good life, she was certain of it. Better than anything she might have hoped for if she'd followed the wild, wanton desires that had drawn her to Jedd.

Curiously enough it was Ginny she was thinking of when the telephone rang. Willie had gone back to her room at the Parkman house after promising to come to Matt's for Sunday brunch. She planned to call her mother, to give her the news of her coming marriage. She looked forward to Mama's reaction. A good marriage was all that Mama had ever wanted for her. Though Matt was older, Willie was sure he would be "star" enough for Mama. Washington wasn't Hollywood, but even Ginny would agree it was, in its own way, glamorous.

And then the telephone rang. "I've been meaning to call you, Mama," Willie said apologetically when she heard her mother's voice. "I've been so busy, and now . . . "

But Ginny wasn't listening. In a voice that was so shaky, so strangled, that Willie could barely make out what she was saying, Ginny kept repeating, "It's happened, Willie, it's finally happened. The thing I was always afraid of. I warned you, oh God, it's all over . . . "

"What's all over? Mama, for heaven's sake, tell me . . . "

"Your father . . . he's called. He saw that picture of you and the judge. And he found out about us, about me and

Neal. He wants a lot of money, or else he's going to the law. I don't know what to do . . . Willie, what's going to happen to me?"

"Money . . . ?" In the shock of the moment, Willie grasped at the straw, reaching for a way to protect herself, all that she'd worked for, the marriage she'd just begun to plan. Even as she said the word "money," she hated herself for it. But if Perry were to expose Mama now, how could Willie possibly marry a justice of the Supreme Court? "How much money?" she asked.

"A hundred thousand dollars . . . "

Willie thought for a moment. It was blackmail, plain and simple – though of course Mama had also broken the law. Regardless of what was fair and right, with all that was at stake, perhaps it was better not to fight. After all, Mama's husband – one of her husbands – was a rich man.

Willie hesitated, finding it difficult to suggest simple surrender. "If you could give him the money, Mama, maybe that would be easiest . . . "

"I don't have near that much," Ginny sobbed. "Neal's accountant handles the boutique's books . . . I couldn't get more than twenty or thirty, tops, and then I'd have to show him I was using it for merchandise . . . "

"But how about Neal? It's not that much for him."

"Oh, baby, he wouldn't give it to me, even if I could tell him what it's for. There's only one hope, honey . . . maybe if you go to Belle Fourche and talk to your father, maybe you can get him to change his mind . . . "

"Me?" The very thought of confronting Perry put a knot in Willie's stomach and made her mouth go dry with fear. "Why would he listen to me? Wouldn't it be better if the two of you tried to settle your differences? I could be there . . . "

Ginny's response was a pitiful moan. "He hates me, Willie. He . . . he doesn't want to settle anything . . . he just wants to hurt me. But you being a lawyer . . . and his daughter . . . please, honey, please try, it's our only chance . . . "

Willie saw she had no choice but to do as Ginny asked.

280

"All right, Mama, I'll go to see him tomorrow. Then I'll come out to Palm Springs." With a strength and confidence she didn't feel, she added: "Don't worry – we'll get through this together, the way we always have."

The words seemed to satisfy Ginny. "Thanks, honey. I feel a little better . . ."

After they hung up, Willie knew she would not sleep. The long dark hours of night would be spent going around in circles, trying to build hope on the slenderest of possibilities. Trying to imagine the look on Matt's face when she told him what had happened. When she told him she'd be flying out of Washington instead of planning their wedding. And why that wedding was now impossible.

All night long, she drifted between despair and anger. How *dare* Perry do this, after all the misery he had already caused, after all those years he'd hounded them – turned them into fugitives? How dare he now add blackmail to his list of crimes?

For the first time in her life, Willie understood the meaning of murderous rage. If she had been facing Perry at this moment, hearing him demand money as the ransom for her happiness, Willie couldn't answer for what she'd do.

15

She would have understood if Matt had withdrawn from her when she brought the news to him. How could he ally himself with a young woman whose mother was a bigamist? – a crime that Perry's vindictiveness was likely to make public any day.

But there was no shrinking away, no attempt to evade or postpone the commitment he had offered. Yet it did not surprise her. His steadfastness was what made Matt the rock she leaned on, the one constant in a world that always seemed to be shifting dangerously around her.

As they stood before the mantel in his library, he held

her in his arms, and all she saw in the rugged contours of his familiar yet remarkable face was compassion and concern for her.

"How can I help?" was his first question.

Although Willie had no clear plan of action, nothing more than shadowy possibilities in mind, she was clear on one point. Matt was not to be involved. Her father's anger, her mother's past, her own complicity – none of this would touch the finest, most decent man she had ever known.

"This is my problem, Matt. It was my problem before we ever met. I can't run away from it anymore, and I won't let it ruin what we have."

Speaking with a strength and conviction she didn't really feel, she told him that she would be resigning her clerkship and returning to Palm Springs, to be with Ginny and to face what finally must be faced. Marriage would have to wait.

Matt argued with the same eloquence that had made his opinions legend. Willie was right, he said, to stand by her mother. But there was no need to punish herself for what her parents had done. "Marry me today," he urged. "I can arrange that. Take my love and my commitment with you."

Willie was adamant. Matt's position as arbiter and interpreter of the nation's laws was more important than either of them. This was a time when the country was facing a moral crisis that reached all the way to the Oval Office. There was a collective sense of revulsion toward the callous disregard of law shown by the country's elected leaders. If, now, a Justice of the Supreme Court were to marry a woman who came from a background of broken laws – and particularly the sacred laws of marriage – the office itself would be tarnished and weakened. Matt would undoubtedly be forced from office, his liberal voice fatally compromised at a time when his humanitarian principles, his unblemished integrity were most needed.

Willie closed her argument with a promise. "When this is all settled, I'll come flying back to you. We'll be married the minute I return. I promise . . . no more delays."

Matt tried to smile, to send her away unburdened by his

disappointment. "You'd just better do that," he said, "or this time, I'll be the one who sues you for breach of promise."

Willie parked her rented car on the shoulder of the unpaved mountain road. She got out and stood for a long moment, shivering in the cold night air. Her body felt leaden as she pushed herself forward, walking a long, weed-choked path that led to a small log cabin.

As she reached the rough-hewn oak door, she heard the sound of a television set from inside. She knocked and waited. A few moments later, she knocked again, but still no one came. She turned the knob and walked in.

The mingled smells of rancid cooking fat and cheap alcohol hit her. Then she saw him, shadowed under the light of a single small lamp with a cracked shade that burned in a corner of the room. He lay on a torn plaid sofa, a grizzled giant, worn down by a lifetime of hard, grinding work, clad in frayed dungarees and a stained shirt. He turned rheumy eyes in her direction.

"Who're you?" The voice was hoarse, serrated by years of heavy drinking.

"Hello, Papa."

Perry raised himself on one elbow and squinted into the gloom, as though suspecting an apparition. "Willie?" His voice fell to a hush as he repeated her name. "Willie?"

"Yes, Papa," she said, the familiar term sounding – feeling – so strange on her lips.

He was silent for a moment, then suddenly became animated, overly hearty, as if she were hardly more than a drinking buddy he had last seen only yesterday – belittling all the years and the heartbreak that lay between them.

"Well, now . . . my little Willie. Come on . . . " He made a wan gesture. "Sit down. Over here by me. I want a good look at ya."

She moved forward, her eyes sweeping over the shadowy room as she sat down. This wasn't what she had expected. The log cabin Perry had constructed with such pride when

283

his dreams were fresh and young was a shabby ruin, uncared for and unloved. The man who had been her father was in poor repair, too, reeking of alcohol and disappointment. Though Willie had come in anger, to argue and plead Ginny's case, her assault was blunted when she saw that life had not been good to her father, that it had repaid his unkindnesses many times over.

"Mama called me last night," she said at last.

He nodded, as if he had expected this overture. But he didn't respond to her directly. "My God," he said, his eyes wide as he stared at her. "You grew up real pretty. But you was always a pretty thing . . . a real little princess with red-gold hair . . . "

His words echoed in her mind: a pretty thing. Just a thing that he had thrown away. The memories raised her ire again. "She tells me you went after her for money . . . a hundred thousand dollars."

He sat up ramrod straight, his face setting in a combative frown. "That's right," he declared. "And there ain't nobody can say I got a penny less comin' to me. I been to see a lawyer over in Pierre. He told me I got rights. You bein' a lawyer, you oughta know that . . . "

"There are all kinds of rights," she said evenly. "If you want a divorce, there are ways to arrange that without Mama getting hurt . . . " She paused, her emotions threatening to break through, an appeal forming on her lips: *Please, Papa. She's been hurt so much . . . "

But he cut her off explosively. "It ain't a divorce I care about! It's gettin' what's due to me. That woman ruined my life, I tell ya, and now she's got to pay!"

The burst anger pushed Willie far back into another time. For an instant she felt like a frightened little girl, powerless to fight the giant's wrath. She struggled to keep calm as she explained that Ginny didn't have the kind of money he'd demanded. "I can get a few thousand together," she offered, "and I can send you something every month . . . "

"No – goddammit! I ain't lookin' for no charity handout. And this ain't all about money neither. Worked hard all my life, nothin' to show for it . . . no family, just . . . nothin'. *She* did it to me . . . took the heart and soul outta me. Ruined my life. Didn't even feel like a man when she got through with me. Ruined my life. But did it matter to her? Found someone rich to take care of her, didn't she? Lives on easy street and calls herself his wife, and there's no way you can call that right. She's *my* wife, dammit! *Mine*."

Willie's heart sank as she listened to Perry's litany of grievances. His claim of ownership was at the heart of what had destroyed the marriage so long ago. He had given Mama no room to be anything but his possession. And even now, so long after she had tried to claim possession of her right to be an individual, he still couldn't bring himself to forgive her. His anger was so strong, so demanding. Could it be satisfied with anything but Ginny's destruction?

"Papa," Willie appealed fervently, "Mama's suffered, too. She's worked hard, too, just as you have, and she didn't have any kind of home for a long time . . ."

Perry seemed to be listening. Encouraged by his attention, Willie went on, arguing eloquently that the past had already claimed a full measure of pain from all the Dellahayes.

But when he spoke, her fragile hopes evaporated. "Don't you talk to me about suffering, girl," he said bitterly. "That woman deserves everything bad that happened to her. It ain't enough. Not nearly enough . . . somebody's got to pay . . . I got my rights . . . " His voice trailed off, thickening with tears.

In spite of her resolve, Willie felt a twinge of pity. She knew it wasn't Mama who had ruined Perry's life. Yet a life had been ruined all the same. He had driven his family away, and now he was alone and destitute. But hardship had done nothing to soften his anger or wear down his will.

He had listened to her arguments with deaf and unhearing ears, invoking his misguided ideas of "rights" and "the law" as he had done so long ago – as if his bitterness had rediscovered a champion, one that would stand up against both reason and compassion.

285

She had only one plea left. "What about me, Papa?" she asked quietly. "Do I have to pay, too?"

Perry frowned and stared at Willie, as if he had never thought about how she might be affected by his war with Ginny. "That ain't fair," he said finally. "Don't you put yourself in the middle of this thing, Willie. It's between her and me."

"Oh, Papa," she cried out passionately, all her professional restraint shattered as she was hurled back into the full pain of her childhood. "Don't you know I've been in the middle all my life? I could never be anywhere else. Every time you hurt Mama, you hurt me."

"Whose fault is that?" he demanded stubbornly. "Honest to God, Willie, I loved that woman. All I wanted was a good wife. Was that too much to ask?"

At last, Willie thought, he's talking to me, really talking. "Maybe it wasn't anybody's fault," she replied. "All Mama wanted was a chance to do something of her own, something different from keeping house for you and me. That didn't make her a bad wife, Papa. A woman has the right to make some choices, even after she gets married . . . "

He gave a short, mirthless laugh. "God, Willie, you sound just like her, you know that? Looks like you turned out to be one of the chest-poundin' female libbers . . . Answer me this, if you're so smart – what kinda choices did I get after I married your Mama? I'll tell ya – I got the choice of goin' down into those mines every backbreakin' day or seein' my family go hungry."

Now it was Willie's turn to be silent, to feel the sadness and waste that lived here, in this house where her parents had once loved each other.

The sound of the television set filled the silence – a football game, she realized now, where teams pounded at each other, trying to achieve their separate goals. A microcosm of all contests, all battles of will. But in a football game, there could be a winner. In the battle between her parents, there had been goals, but the fight to attain them had only made losers of them both.

She reached across the couch and touched his hand. It

was rough and calloused. "I'm asking you for me, not her," she said. "Let it go. Please, Papa . . . " This time, finally, the word felt right.

His hand closed over hers for a moment. She felt something warm rain down on the skin of her wrist. "I never meant to hurt you, Willie, honest to God. Her, neither. I mean, the way it started, I was just . . . " His voice broke and he looked away.

She waited for him to continue, but he sat for a long time without moving or speaking, and she gave him the silence, a chance to find forgiveness for himself, absolution for all of them.

But he stood abruptly and went to a battered pine cupboard to pour himself a drink. "I'll think on it," he muttered.

Relief flooded over Willie. After so many years of anger and bitterness, there was a chance for peace. "Does that mean 'yes'?" she asked eagerly.

"It means I'll *think* on it," he said gruffly, his back still to her. "I'll let you know. Now go on, git!"

For an awkward moment Willie lingered, wondering if she should press her father for more – or if she should cross the chasm between them, to try building a more permanent bridge. He seemed so alone, holding his glass and staring out the dirty windowpane.

"Good night, Papa," she said softly, as she let herself out of the cabin.

She gave a last look back before she stepped into her rented car, searching for the childhood home she had left behind so long ago.

But it had vanished, and she left, wondering if it had ever really been there.

When she arrived in Palm Springs, Willie saw each and every one of those fears mirrored in her mother's drawn and haggard face.

"What happened?" Ginny asked anxiously. "Did you see your father? What did he say?"

"He said he'd think about it and let us know." Willie

287

longed to say something that would ease her mother's distress, but she didn't want to hold out false assurances.

"That's all?" Ginny asked, her voice tight with fear. "Is that all we can do – just sit and wait?"

Willie had been asking herself the same question all during the flight from South Dakota. She had come up with only one answer. "Where's Neal?"

"He's away on business for a couple of days. What's he got to do with it?"

"Tell him yourself," Willie urged her mother. "Make him understand how it was. If Papa goes ahead with his threat, Neal can help you fight this thing. If he backs you, Mama, it'll make all the difference."

"I can't risk it," Ginny responded brokenly. "He won't understand, and he won't care. I told you, baby, things haven't been so good. If he finds out we're not really married, he'll . . . he'll dump me. Oh, Willie, what am I gonna do?"

Once again, Willie felt the familiar sense of guilt that she had somehow let her mother down. She hadn't given much thought to the state of Ginny's marriage. If anything, she'd harbored the idea that Mama would be better off without Neal. Now here they were, looking at a chapter of history that seemed to be repeating itself. She and Mama were better fed, better housed, and better clothed, all that was different. Yet here was Ginny, still afraid that yet another man would abandon her . . .

The difference lay in Willie. No longer the angry child she once had been, she was determined to succeed in protecting her mother this time. If she couldn't use her skills and her education to do that, then all the years of work would have been for nothing. If Neal indeed tried to "dump" Ginny – as Perry had – he'd have to go through Willie first.

Tired and spent, Willie fell into bed, her mind still working, unwilling to rest until she had wrestled all the worst possibilities into manageable problems. Sleep came just before dawn, a restless sleep ridden with a kaleidoscope of dreams.

She and Jedd were on horseback, riding side by side along the mountain trails that surrounded the Fontana property in Palm Springs. They were smiling and happy. Jedd held out his hand, as if to draw her close.

Suddenly the terrain changed, and she was alone, on the Badlands, surrounded by dark, looming buttes and spires, riding fast and hard, as if her life depended on it. She looked over her shoulder and saw him, the masked man on a black horse, galloping toward her, closing the distance betwen them. Her terror grew because she knew that no matter how fast she rode, he would catch her.

She heard a clap of thunder, felt her arm gripped in a hold of iron, felt her body being lifted from her horse. A flash of lightning illuminated her attacker's face. It was Papa.

She pounded on his chest with all her might, gaining strength from her fear and anger. The attacker fell to the ground, and lay there quiet and still. But he wasn't Perry any more. He was Matt.

The waiting and not knowing were the hardest part. Willie blamed herself for backing off when Perry had ended their conversation. She should have questioned him further, found out exactly what cards he held.

She was certain the statute of limitations had run out on whatever charges had been filed against Ginny in South Dakota. The crime of bigamy had been committed in California. Would Perry, or his attorney, try to persuade the local authorities to bring charges against Ginny? Or would they contact Neal and try to extract money from him?

She wondered what kind of attorney would encourage her father in this cruel and ugly scheme. A cynical voice in her head supplied the answer: an attorney who smelled money somewhere down the line – and who was willing to pervert the law, on the possibility of collecting a fee.

Willie steeled herself for *something* – a phone call, a telegram announcing Perry's decision. He had promised to "think on it" and let her know.

When his answer came it struck with the shock power of a sneak attack. A banner headline in the morning paper hit Willie with the impact of a clenched fist: "Socialite Designer Is Bigamist!" Stunned and disbelieving, she looked at a picture of her mother at the opening of Silver Screen. Alongside that was a photograph of Perry, looking every bit as beaten and impoverished as he was, bearing the caption "Abandoned Childhood Sweetheart."

Sickened by the lurid sensationalism, Willie forced herself to read on, to take in the story that bore little resemblance to the truth as she had known it. Ginny was portrayed as a spoiled malcontent, a woman who ran out on a simple but good life, in pursuit of wealth and luxury. A woman who deprived her husband of his only child, of everything that had made his life worth living.

Willie filtered the story through her legal experience, searching for something she might use in a court of law. But while the account was distorted, it couldn't be judged slanderous. It was merely Perry's version of his own experience, twisted by his need to win, once and for all, over the wife who still eluded him.

Willie swore she'd never forgive Perry for doing this. He had held out a slender hope of peace and then betrayed her by dashing it in the cruelest possible way.

To make matters worse, the story carried a wire service dateline. That meant it would be carried in newspapers all over the country. A Pandora's box of ugly possibilities had been opened, and Willie couldn't begin to guess how much damage would be done before it was closed again.

Her first instinct was to hide the paper, to keep it from Ginny, who had taken to her bed last night, with a stiff drink and a "nerve pill." But there was no point. Not now, not when everyone in Palm Springs would know what she had struggled so long to hide.

Willie made a pot of strong black coffee and brought it

into Ginny's bedroom. She poured a cup and handed it to her mother, along with the newspaper.

Still groggy, Ginny stared at the realization of all her nightmares, come alive in vivid black and white, for all the world to see. Her eyes clouded over, her face went slack, her body fell back on the pillows. But she didn't cry. It was as if she had always known this moment would come, as if everything else had been a postponement.

Alarmed by Ginny's posture of defeat, Willie reverted to the way things had been with them so many times before, playing the part of parent, soothing, assuring, promising that things would be all right. "Drink this coffee, Mama . . . the worst is over now, don't you see? Now everyone knows, and there's no more running and hiding. Now it's our turn, we haven't even started."

Yes, they were finished with running, Willie thought to herself. But she didn't believe for a minute that the worst was over.

She unplugged the telephone and told the housekeeper to admit no one, and to see that Mrs. Corcoran was not disturbed. She left Ginny with a promise to return in half an hour.

Willie wanted to make a sweep of the newsstands, to collect everything that had been written so far. She hadn't the slightest doubt that the story would be picked up by the local radio and television stations – and that life for the immediate future would resemble some nightmarish circus.

As Willie drove away from the house, she silently prayed that Mama would be strong enough to survive the days and weeks ahead. As an afterthought, she added the hope that she would not run into anyone she knew.

When she returned with a stack of newspapers, Willie realized that the nightmare was about to escalate. Neal's car was in the driveway.

She ran into the house. Mama was in no condition to face Neal alone. Then she heard the sound of Neal's voice raised in anger. "I knew you were a cheap little waitress . . . I knew that, but I married you anyway. *Married!* You've

291

made me into a joke! I walked into a meeting this morning and everybody was in on the joke but me!"

Willie burst into the bedroom, where Ginny still lay beneath the covers, cowering under the onslaught of Neal's words. The sight roused Willie's fury.

"That's enough!" she commanded. "Can't you see she isn't well?"

"Oh, I see well enough," Neal sneered, moderating his tone. "Your mother is indisposed – again. Very convenient, no doubt. And since you're here, Willa, I suggest you help your mother pack. As another man's wife, she has no right whatever to be in my home. I want both of you out of here before nightfall. Take anything other than clothing and personal effects, and you can expect a visit from the local police."

Not again, Willie vowed inwardly. No, not again. A long time ago, she and Mama had been thrown out of their home by the man who was supposed to love them. And now, this man who had professed to care for Mama was trying to do the same thing.

"Not so fast, Neal," Willie said coldly, hands on hips in an attitude of defiance. "We'll go – neither of us wants to stay under the same roof with a man like you. But don't think for a minute that this is the end of it. Mama has rights, and I mean to see that she gets them."

Neal glowered at Willie, then gave a peculiar half-smile, as though the irony of the situation had just struck him. His stepdaughter, trained in the law through an expensive education he'd encouraged, was now turning what she had learned on him. The smile disappeared and he left the room.

Willie sat on the bed and tried to mobilize Ginny, to rouse her from an almost trancelike stupor. I'll let her rest, she finally decided. There would be time enough for reality later.

She pulled her mother's matched luggage out of the closet and began to fill the cases with clothes. Not for a minute did Willie intend to let Neal dump Mama with nothing more than her personal things.

Legal or not, Ginny had been Neal's wife. And Willie knew all too well what Mama's wifely duties had included. No, by God! Neal wasn't going to use her and then walk away.

16

After the ugly confrontation with Neal, Willie moved her mother into a rented house. The rent was low during the off-season summer months, and that was important. Technically Ginny was still the proprietor of Silver Screen, but the boutique's finances were intertwined with Neal's in ways that gave him the power to disrupt or reduce the income from the business.

That would change, Willie promised herself. But she didn't underestimate what lay ahead. The newspaper stories had done Perry's dirty work for him. By making the bigamy a public scandal, he had forced the Palm Springs district attorney to issue a warrant for Ginny's arrest. Willie had promptly arranged for bail, promising all the while that everything would be all right.

Willie found herself constantly thinking in terms of "last time" – and reminding herself that everything would be different now. It was important that Ginny be well defended and well represented. Willie couldn't do the job herself – she hadn't yet taken her bar exams – but she would be there, every step of the way, looking out for Ginny's interests.

She thought long and hard about who would handle Mama's case. It would have to be someone decent, someone principled. If Matt were a practicing attorney, he would have been Willie's first choice. A close second was Ken Harper, who in her eyes, was one of the profession's real heroes. Harper was a fighter who worked for causes, rather than for fees, and that was the kind of man to whom she would entrust Mama's future.

Willie drove from Palm Springs to Harper's storefront office in downtown Los Angeles. It was a far cry from any legal office she had ever seen – casual and cluttered, informally furnished with odds and ends that might have been salvaged from street corners, its walls covered with framed newspaper pages chronicling Harper's controversial cases, many bearing close-up photographs of the renegade lawyer, his brown hair grown to shoulder length, sometimes worn in a pony-tail. There was no receptionist, only an assortment of young volunteers, who were busy answering telephones, typing, and filing. When Willie asked for Harper, she was waved toward a smaller back room. She found the young, slightly built attorney in his shirtsleeves, intently sailing paper airplanes into a wastebasket.

Noticing Willie at the door, he smiled sheepishly. "This helps me concentrate," he explained. "What can I do for you?"

Willie introduced herself, reminding him of the time she had argued her Moot Court case before him.

Harper's eyes narrowed thoughtfully. "The Clara Burton School . . ." he recalled.

"That's right!" It pleased her to be remembered.

"Hell of a good presentation," Harper said. "What can I do for you?"

She brought out the newspaper story detailing Ginny's arrest, and passed it across to him. "We need a good lawyer, Mr. Harper—"

"Ken," he put in.

"Ken," she said with a smile. "My mother never should have been arrested, and this case never should have come to trial. Can you take the case?"

Harper studied the clipping, running his fingers through his long hair. "I'm fighting to help migrant labor, unwed mothers, minority discrimination, that kinda thing. Palm Springs and matrimonial problems isn't really my bag . . ."

"This isn't about marriage," Willie said forcefully. "It's about how women like my mother have been treated by the courts. If she'd been treated fairly, she would have gotten a

294

divorce in South Dakota. What happened to her was a form of discrimination, and it's as real as any of the cases you've taken into your court. Please . . . Ken. At least, come to Palm Springs and meet my mother. I think that'll convince you . . . "

Harper picked up a piece of paper, folded it nimbly and sailed another paper plane neatly into his wastebasket. Then he stood up. "When do we leave?" he said.

The State of California, City of Palm Springs in Riverside County, brought the matter of Virginia Dellahaye, also known as Virginia Corcoran, to trial in record time. It was an embarrassment to the district attorney, and an embarrassment to the community.

Certainly the state had more pressing matters to try. But the attendant publicity, the finger-pointing by the press, convinced the state to move quickly, to squelch any suggestion that the rich or well-connected could disregard the laws of the land, especially the sacred laws of matrimony, with impunity.

On the face of it, the case of Virginia Dellahaye seemed open and shut. The woman had entered into a bigamous marriage, deceiving one man as to her legal status, while she was lawfully wedded to another. She had been cited for contempt of court by the state of South Dakota. The district attorney assured the press he had not the slightest doubt of a speedy conviction.

As to the sentence, that would be the judge's problem. Perhaps if Virginia Dellahaye had turned up sick and destitute, leniency would have been called for, even applauded, by the press. But it was her abandoned husband who was in that condition. While here she was, still youthful, still beautiful, the owner of a glamorous business – profiting enormously, it would seem, from the deception she had perpetrated.

Disgusted by the sensational headlines, Willie had instructed her mother to talk to no one, to issue no statements and make no comments to the reporters who besieged her, looking for fresh material to keep their stories going. It was a decision that cost Ginny any hope of generating public sympathy.

Faced by Ginny's silence, the reporters manufactured their own material, using her good looks, her affluent lifestyle, to paint her scarlet. In this, they were aided and abetted by Perry's willingness to talk, to say anything and everything that would punish the woman who had eluded his anger for so long.

Surrounded by his few remaining cronies, in the ramshackle cabin he had built, Perry basked in the spotlight of public attention, discoursing tirelessly about the high-school sweetheart who had ruined his life.

In a more subtle and dignified fashion, Neal jumped into the fray. Willie had expected to battle Neal, but she had no way of anticipating his opening volley. He had retained the legendary and notorious Francis Aloysius Harrigan, the "Silver Fox," an attorney whose clientele ran the gamut from a former president of the United States to a reigning Mafia chieftain. Flanked by Harrigan, Neal called a press conference – and made his own contribution to Ginny's public biography. He stated that the subject of his marriage was "extremely painful," but that he would make a single statement to the "ladies and gentlemen of the press."

The statement was brief but lethal. It pained him, he said, to find himself in the company of men who had been transformed into fools by the power of a pretty face. Yes, he had fallen in love with Virginia Dellahaye – and had been moved to generously provide, for her and her daughter, all manner of comforts and luxuries. Implying that even this did not satisfy Ginny, Neal went on to say that he had gone so far as to furnish her with a business, so that she might not be bored with her pampered idleness.

With Harrigan at his side, Neal presented a convincing portrayal of a man who has been taken in by a scheming, avaricious gold-digger.

When Neal's statement appeared, Willie felt the faint stirrings of doubt. She rarely doubted herself or her decisions, but now she reconsidered. Perhaps she had made a mistake, a costly one, by persuading Ginny to maintain a public silence. Now it was too late to speak on her own behalf. All she could offer were vehement denials of half-truths and innuendoes. Even in her inexperience, Willie could see what a weak and indefensible position that would be.

Willie had scorned the notion of displaying her mother in the press. And because of her advice, a dreadful, distorted caricature of Mama had been held up instead, for all the world to see.

If it had been anyone else but Mama, Willie would say she didn't care, that principle was more important than cheap show-business tactics. But for all of Willie's unswerving, uncompromising sense of right, she couldn't help wondering if someone like Harrigan might not have created a more favorable climate for Ginny's defense than Ken Harper.

The doubts multiplied during their first day in court. It did not go well for Ginny – or for her attorney. Willie felt like she'd lived it before. In Belle Fourche, her mother had been frightened, poor, and unknowing – easy prey for a cheap lawyer who did slipshod work. Now both she and Mama knew better and they had a good lawyer, an ethical lawyer. Yet the deck still seemed stacked against them

Willie and Ken had decided that Ginny should waive a jury trial. After the characterizations in the press, Willie felt her mother's future would be better entrusted to a judge. She knew that under the right circumstances, a judge would have the power to render a "not guilty" verdict even if the state proved – as it certainly could – that Ginny had willfully committed bigamy.

But Ken Harper wasn't off to a good start. The district attorney, a popular "local boy," stepped all over him, making him look like an upstart carpetbagger, come to Palm Springs to gain more of the kind of publicity that had attended his defense of liberal and radical causes.

The judge had a reputation for fairness, but even he seemed to have a brusque and sarcastic attitude toward Ginny's attorney. Ken's opening move was to call a few character witnesses, people like Laura and members of the country-club staff who had known Ginny before she'd married Corcoran. But the district attorney managed, through objections sustained by the judge, to block testimony that he called pointless.

"Your honor. We don't need to waste the court's time with a parade of people talking about how good this woman was as a country-club waitress. That's irrelevant to the charges . . . "

So there was no chance to establish that Ginny was not a gold-digger but simply a hardworking woman and a good mother who'd been lucky – or unlucky – enough to receive a proposal of marriage from a rich club member.

Later Willie took Ken aside and asked: "Do you think we'll have enough to ask for a new trial? It seems to me that you aren't being given the chance to defend your client . . . "

He shook his head. "I don't know, Willie. Maybe you want to find another lawyer. Judges don't miss a chance to nail me. It's like they're looking for an opening to get even for all the times I've beaten the establishment. I feel like my hands are being tied here. I don't want your mother to get a bad deal . . . but let's face it, she did commit bigamy. And unless we come up with a dynamite defense, it'll be all I can do to keep her out of jail."

Willie understood all too well what Ken was saying. Once again, Mama was fighting against bad odds. The outcome of her case was important. Keeping her out of jail was the first priority, of course. But it was also critical that she come out of the courtroom not as a scarlet woman, but as a woman who had been wronged and unjustly accused. Willie needed that and more to wrest a settlement from Neal.

She had to find a way to make the judge see Ginny's life as it had really been. As Willie had seen it, and not the way Perry had painted it. She needed to show the court some tangible evidence – and there was only one place she could find it.

"Do the best you can," she instructed Ken. "I'm taking

the next plane to South Dakota. There has to be *something* there we can use."

Willie spent two precious hours in the county courthouse, one of them in prying loose a copy of the transcript of Ginny's aborted divorce trial from an officious clerk. She went directly to the airport and spent the next five hours studying the document while she waited for a flight to Los Angeles.

Her anger built with every turn of a page, as she imagined how Mama must have felt on those awful days. In her mind's eye, she drew a picture of her mother, young, naive, and frightened. Speaking the truth and seeing her very words twisted and used against her. Denied justice in a court of law. That was the picture Ken would have to bring to life.

When Willie returned to the rented house, she found that Francis Aloysius Harrigan had made a visit in her absence. He had offered Ginny a new lease on Silver Screen – as Harrigan put it, "out of the goodness of Mr. Corcoran's heart, because he isn't a vindictive man." The new lease called for five times the present rent. "A fair market value," Harrigan said.

Scared and bewildered, Ginny handed the paper to Willie, saying she didn't understand why Neal was sending it in the middle of all this trouble, when her present lease still had six months to run.

Willie understood all too well. Neal was attempting to establish the fact that he had every right to treat Ginny like a stranger, that he had no obligation whatever to her, no legal involvement other than that of landlord. The quin-tupling of rent served notice that Ginny's landlord was not the same man who had, until recently, called himself her husband.

"I'll take care of the lease," Willie promised. "Right now, I have some work to do for Ken."

She sat up all night, summoning all the passion and

eloquence she'd carried inside her all these years, composing a plea for justice too long denied.

She handed the brief to Ken in the corridor of the courthouse, only half an hour before the trial was set to reconvene. Ken scanned it quickly, and gave Willie an approving nod. "If only it were Moot Court," he said, "I'd give you another decision . . . "

"You can still get it for me, Ken."

"I'll try, Willie." With that, he retreated into a conference room, to memorize the words Willie had given him.

He delivered them as dramatically as if they were his own. After detailing the history of Ginny's long futile battle to gain her independence from Perry in Belle Fourche, Ken reached the summation. "Your honor, we do not deny the charge of bigamy. Yes, my client formalized a relationship with Neal Corcoran in a manner prohibited by law. But as the court has heard, my client – a young woman then without the resources to secure adequate representation – my client endeavored for six years, six long, painful years, to gain her freedom from the man who had abandoned her and their child. Your honor, we submit that this is a period of time which defies the honorable concept of due process. Under constitutional guarantees, even hardened criminals are assured due process, the disposition of justice in a timely fashion. We maintain, your honor, that the woman who stands before the court is not a criminal, but a victim of a system that failed her. It was the failure of our system of justice that allowed Perry Dellahaye to abdicate the responsibilities of husband and father – and at the same time to pervert the intent of the law, to misuse its power to prevent this young woman from making a life for herself and her child. We maintain, your honor, that it was the law itself which failed to protect Virginia Dellahaye's rights and that this failure caused her untold pain and suffering. We ask that the court now remedy this suffering by finding Virginia Dellahaye not guilty. The defense rests."

The judge retreated to his chambers and returned in less

than an hour. When he pronounced his verdict, Ginny turned and blinked incredulously at Willie, as though unable to believe that the fear and the hiding were finally over. Then Willie rushed to her and embraced her.

"You're free now, Mama," Willie said and added quietly, "We're both free."

With the court victory she had engineered behind her, Willie decided to face Harrigan herself. Even without credentials, she could represent Ginny as an interested party. Ken could do the paperwork, but Willie wasn't about to trust Mama's future to anyone else.

She buried herself in the law library of a local attorney, searching for something she could use as a bargaining tool. She reckoned that Neal, with his fastidious tastes and his overblown dignity, would not be anxious for a court action. The newspapers would have another field day, and while Ginny had little to lose, Neal would care very much about what was left of his public image and his social standing. He had proved that by hiring a heavyweight like F. A. Harrigan, Esquire.

Willie searched through the vast reservoir of family law cases decided in the state of California, but found nothing that would support Ginny's claim to any part of Neal's estate. Still, she refused to be discouraged. She would simply have to expand her research. All she needed was one case, just one, anywhere in the United States. She meant to find that case, no matter how long it took.

For five days she had worked, with little food and almost no sleep. Now, as she dressed for her meeting with Harrigan, Willie was still keyed up, energized rather than depleted by the intensity of her efforts. She had heard the amusement in Harrigan's voice when she called, suggesting they meet on "a matter of mutual interest." The fact that he hadn't summoned her to his hotel suite, that he'd graciously offered to come to Ginny's house, told Willie something important. Harrigan believed he was dealing from a position of strength – no, invincibility – and he was leaving

301

her room to accept defeat at his hands with a shred of dignity.

When she opened the door to admit him, his broad smile, his patronizing manner – even the rakish angle of the carnation in his buttonhole – confirmed Willie's suspicion.

He seated himself in a comfortable chair and placed his alligator briefcase on a coffee table. "My client naturally would like to see an end to this unfortunate publicity—"

"I'll bet," Willie interrupted. "Now that it hasn't done him any good."

"Miss Dellahaye," Harrigan said quietly, standing up and straightening his vest, "I am prepared to leave your home at this moment. You will then have no choice but to begin litigation – which will, I promise, be costly and extended. My condition for continuing this conversation is a few moments of your undivided – and silent – attention. Are we agreed?"

Willie nodded. Something in his attitude, his stance, made her not want to cross F. A. Harrigan, Esquire. Not fear. More like a grudging respect.

"Now then, young woman, let me say that you may well be a clever and resourceful fledgling attorney . . . my client assures me you are. Else I would not be here this fine morning. But there is more to this business of ours than what we take from textbooks. We are, first and foremost, colleagues. We may be opponents, as you and I are now. But cases come and go, and we remain, to face one another in yet another arena. If we are to serve our clients, then we learn respect for one another. We practice civility, courtesy. Do we understand each other, Miss Dellahaye?"

Willie nodded again, her ears burning. She felt like a schoolgirl being taught something very basic. She had heard this particular lesson before. Bodleigh Hodge III had tried to teach it. "I'm sorry," she said. "I was rude. Please go on."

"Apology accepted. Now let me tell you what my client is prepared to offer, not out of weakness, you understand, but as a means of avoiding litigation." The Harrigan charm returned in full bloom, as he outlined a settlement which would give Ginny "Silver Screen" rent-free for ten years, her personal property, including such gifts as had been left behind at the Corcoran estate, and a cash payment of $10,000. In return Ginny would sign a document releasing Neal and his estate forever from claims of any kind. "Under the circumstances, I feel that's a very generous offer."

Willie would have liked to laugh in Harrigan's face. But she had quickly learned his rules. "On the face of it, yes, it's a respectable offer. And like your client, we're certainly open to an agreement that would avert litigation. Certainly we're aware that he would be embarrassed and humiliated if certain of his . . . personal habits were made public."

Willie saw Harrigan shift in his chair. She didn't like what she had just done. She had no intention whatever of exposing Neal's sordid sexual predilections, not when that meant tarring Mama with the same brush.

But she needed to let this arrogant man know that his client had more to lose than money if no settlement was reached. Now she unveiled her ammunition. "I'm sure you're also aware of the matter of Reynolds vs. Dobson, which was upheld on appeal by the State Superior Court of New Jersey."

With slow, deliberate movements, Willie placed a folder on the coffee table, next to Harrigan's briefcase. It contained the gold she had mined after exhaustive hours of digging: the case of Linda Dobson, a minor who had run away from her parents in Ohio and falsified her age in order to marry Stanley Reynolds, a wealthy manufacturer. After eight years, the marriage had faltered. In preparing a divorce action, Reynolds's attorney had uncovered the deception. And while the court set aside the marriage as invalid, it upheld Linda Dobson's claim to a generous portion of Reynolds's property, on the grounds that they had cohabited as man and wife for an extended period of time.

Harrigan glanced at the folder but did not pick it up. Willie saw the flicker of recognition – and surprise – in his eyes. Knowing Neal as she did, she also knew that he would not want to go to trial, and was probably prepared to tie

Harrigan's very able hands. She guessed that Harrigan would shift his position – now that there was a strong probability that Virginia would win.

Solemnly Francis Aloysius Harrigan stood up and removed his jacket, his vest, and his tie. "You'll excuse me, Miss Dellahaye, but I think we have a rather long morning ahead of us. Would you be so kind as to offer me breakfast . . . "

"Breakfast?" Willie said, nonplussed. She had stood being patronized for the sake of diplomacy, but did he really think she was going to cook for him?

But before she could explode, Harrigan explained: "A working breakfast – in my case, a whiskey if you've got it, please." He smiled, and now Willie saw clearly the flash of Irish charm that went along with knife-edge shrewdness in making Harrigan the winner he usually was. "Considering the opposition," he added, "I hope you won't mind making that a double . . . "

Together they sat for the next six hours, arguing, debating, negotiating. Harrigan's glass was refilled several times. And when they were finished, he got up – still steady as a rock – put on his tie again, his vest, and his jacket. "I will have the documents drawn up. Shall I send them here?"

"Mama's lawyer will have to see them," Willie said. "I'm merely acting as an interested party here."

Amusement glinted in Harrigan's eyes. "And a hell of a party it was, too," he said. "Good day to you, Miss Dellahaye. We'll meet again, I'm certain of that."

The settlement gave Ginny the boutique with a thirty-year lease at one dollar per year, as well as the business inventory and goodwill – in short, Silver Screen, lock, stock, and barrel. She would keep all the gifts Neal had given during the years they'd been together, including the Cadillac convertible, the jewels, and the furs. Finally, and most important, Neal would pay a cash settlement of $750,000 – in three installments, to ease the tax bite.

Willie was satisfied that justice had been served, that

now at last, she and her mother were free to live in the present. No more secrets, and no more hiding.

But when the news was conveyed to Ginny, she seemed strangely subdued for a woman who had not only come into a small fortune, but had been freed of a man with whom, by her own admission, she had not been happy.

"What's the matter?" Willie asked. "I thought you'd be thrilled. It's all over now. Nobody can hurt you anymore."

Ginny sighed. "I don't know, baby. This is Neal's town. I don't know how people are gonna feel about me, no matter what the judge said—"

"For goodness' sake," Willie said impatiently. "Neal doesn't own the town. Make your own friends. You don't need that crowd of Neal's, can't you see that? Even now?"

What on earth would it take to get Mama on her feet? Willie wondered in exasperation. But seeing Ginny's face, now close to tears, made her next words more gentle. "Mama, listen to me . . . I thought you'd be happy now. You have money, you have a business. You can do anything you want . . . "

Ginny sighed again. "I know, baby, and I sure don't want to burden you anymore. Problem is, I can't think of anything I want to do . . . "

For a moment, Willie felt almost stifled by her mother's need. What else could she do that she hadn't done? She couldn't tell Ginny what to want, what to dream – could she?

A lifetime of habit gave her a familiar answer. She would try. "Mama," she said, "if you want to get away from Palm Springs for a while, you could come back to Washington with me. I didn't want to say anything before . . . I'm planning to get married."

"Oh, baby, that's wonderful!" Ginny's face was transformed. As if Willie had said she'd won the Nobel Prize. As if she had finally done what Ginny had dreamed about for both of them. "Who is it, honey? Tell me all about it . . . how could you keep so quiet all this time? Gosh, I would have busted with it if I'd had that kind of news . . . "

"It's Matt Harding, Mama. The judge . . . the one in the newspaper picture."

Ginny's radiance dimmed slightly. "But honey, he's . . . I mean . . . " she stumbled, not knowing how to say what was on her mind.

"He's older than I am," Willie intervened. "That doesn't matter. He's the finest man I've ever known. And we love each other."

Ginny brightened again. "Well, gosh, I guess that's all that matters, isn't it? You have a good head on your shoulders, Willie – not like me. I only want the best for you, honey. You know that . . . "

"I know. I have the best. You'll like Matt. Come back with me and meet him."

"I'll come, baby." Ginny agreed. "But I need a week or two to take care of things here. Then I'll meet your . . . fiancé. I wouldn't miss it for the world!"

"Congratulations, counselor," Harrigan said, smiling broadly, as he stood in the living room of Neal's house and handed Willie a sheaf of documents, including the lease to Silver Screen and a cashier's check for $250,000. Now that there were no more battles to fight, his charm was even more pronounced. Another day, another case, his attitude seemed to say.

"Meeting you," he remarked – after their formalities were completed and Willie had put a "breakfast" in his hand – "has put me in mind of a Biblical tale, the story of David and Goliath. In following your mother's case, I suspected that her attorney was not the architect of that very able defense. The words were not the usual style of our firebrand Mr. Harper. But I must admit that your youth, your beauty, and most particularly your feminine gender . . . these led me to overlook the possibility that you might be carrying a loaded slingshot aimed in my direction. Hence," he sighed theatrically, "the recent debacle."

"I don't know that I'd call it a debacle, Mr. Harrigan—"

"Call me Francis. I insist—"

"All right . . . Francis. I'd say we reached an equitable settlement. In spite of your best efforts in another direction."

"Indeed, Willa – I hope I may call you Willa – my best

306

efforts, indeed. But as to equitable, I define that very specifically by my client's needs."

"I see." Just as she'd figured.

"I want you to come and work for me. I don't want a mind like yours helping any of the competition."

The offer startled Willie, as did Harrigan himself. She knew what he was all about, she was certain of that. But with all his chameleon changes, the man could be unsettling.

"I have taken the liberty of finding out a thing or two about you, Willa. I like what I see. You're smart and you'll be worth every penny of the $40,000 per annum you'll start with. Unless I miss my guess – and I don't often, in spite of what has happened here – you can expect significantly more in the near future. And, of course, there will be advancement. You'll start in the corporate law department, and—"

"That's a generous offer," she broke in, "but that's not the kind of law I want to practice. I'm not interested in helping big corporations get bigger and richer. They can hire any one of a dozen good lawyers in any big city – or all of them at the same time. In fact, I'm not so sure I want to work with a big firm at all. I want to help people who really need help, even if they can't afford to pay—"

"Ah, yes, counselor," Harrigan interrupted smoothly, "it's a favorite dream these days, isn't it? Find yourself a nice storefront location, hang out a shingle made with colored crayons, and set to work saving mankind. That's very noble, to be sure," he said patronizingly, as if he were talking to a child who wanted to be a fireman.

"But if you don't mind my saying so," he continued, "you might not be doing any immediate service to the weak and disadvantaged. You'll spend a few years learning the ropes – and believe me, Willa, you have a great deal to learn – and fighting harder to pay your bills than to sway your juries. Before you can get the training you need, there's every chance you'll lose your office for nonpayment of rent and see it turned into a fast-food franchise. Now that would be a shame. You have a fine mind. But as I've said – as I've seen – you have a lot to learn. Paying dues, I believe you young people call it. Whatever your noble dreams, you could do with the kind of seasoning you'd get in my corporate department. Think of it as postgraduate education, Willa –the kind you won't find in any classroom, I promise you that. And I don't mind telling you that half your bright young classmates from Harvard would kill for this opportunity . . . "

In spite of herself, Willie listened to what Harrigan was saying. And in spite of the way she had managed to pull Mama's irons out of the fire, she knew there was some truth in Harrigan's words. There *were* things she had to learn if she was going to be as effective as she wanted to be. But she could learn in Washington – after she and Matt were married.

"Thank you," she said. "You've given me something to think about. But I still have to take the bar exams. And I have some personal business to take care of before I join any firm."

"Do that. And think quickly, counselor," Harrigan said, smiling to soften his words. "I don't mind telling you that Francis Aloysius Harrigan doesn't ask twice. Not even someone as eminently desirable as you." He headed for the door.

She was wondering if his choice of words could possibly imply a personal interest, when he turned back, as though reading her thoughts. "From the legal standpoint, that is, counselor. Beautiful as y'are, it's your mind I'm after."

Wily bastard, Willie thought as she watched Harrigan go. There was nothing he could have said that was more likely to bend her to his will.

17

A few more minutes and they'd be together. Willie felt like a victorious warrior, spent with combat and hungry for the warmth of a lover's embrace. She hadn't called Matt to announce her arrival, and she smiled now in anticipation of the surprise on his face.

It had been too long, Willie thought as she pulled into the driveway of the stately Georgian mansion. Too much making do with letters and phone calls in place of Matt's love. Thank heavens that was all behind them now.

Worries and pressures had vaporized during her six-hour flight, making room for excitement and anticipation – everything a bride-to-be should be feeling. She scooped up the bouquet of asters and the bottle of Napoleon brandy she'd bought at the airport and ran to the door. Impatiently she gave the brass knocker three sharp raps.

Kate opened the door and stared for a moment, as if Willie's presence were not only surprising but somehow strange. But her greeting was warm: "Miss Dellahaye . . . how good to see you again . . . we've missed you."

"I've missed you, too," Willie said, "but now I'm here to stay. Where's Matt?"

Kate hesitated. "I . . . he's in the garden, catching some afternoon sun."

Willie ran along the flagstone path bordered with privet hedges to the garden in back of the house. Surrounded by banks of gold and white chrysanthemums, and under a striped awning, Matt was stretched out on a wrought-iron chaise, his eyes closed.

"Surprise!" she called out, flinging herself into his arms. "Oh, darling, it's so good to be back!"

His arms circled Willie without holding her. And when he sat up, she noticed that his face was thinner, the gray eyes more serious than welcoming. Lovingly she brushed the familiar wave of silver hair that fell stubbornly across his forehead.

"I'm proud of you, Willie," he said softly. "I followed you every step of the way. Your name wasn't in the papers, but I could see you there, fighting like the champ you are . . ."

"Now it's over," she sighed, snuggling closer in search of the warmth she'd missed for so long, "and I'm ready to plan

309

that wedding. I feel so free," she exulted. "You don't know what that's like, Matt . . . no more dark secrets. Now there's nothing to stop us . . . "

"Wait . . . Willie . . . wait." There was pain in Matt's eyes as he spoke. "The wedding . . . we can't plan it, not now . . . "

"Not now?" As she echoed the words, she felt first a stab of disappointment and then the chill of fear. What was he saying? And why did he look so unhappy? "Then when?" she pleaded, a cold knot forming in her stomach.

He shook his head – a silent "never."

"But . . . I don't understand . . . " She shook her head, refusing to accept the truth. "I thought this was what we both wanted, and I'm ready, really ready . . . "

"Time, Willie," he said angrily. "Time, that silent son-of-a-bitch . . . he's stolen our moment."

"What are you talking about?" she pleaded. "Matt, you're scaring me."

"I had another heart attack while you were away. My doctor managed to keep it from the press—"

"But what about me?" she demanded. "Why didn't you let me know? I would have—"

"Would have what?" he cut in, his voice harsh. "Sat by my bed? Held my hand? That's not what I had in mind for us, Willie. You were needed where you were and I . . . apparently needed a reminder that Justice Matthew Harding isn't immortal. And that the next attack could kill me."

The words cut through Willie like surgical steel, but she fought against them. "You don't know that. You don't even know that there will be a next attack, not if you're careful. What did your doctor say? I'll bet he said you could live for years . . . "

He smiled, and for a moment she felt again the spark of love that matched her own. It flickered and faded with his next words. "Strictly speaking, that's true – but not good enough. Being careful's not my style – and the odds here . . . they're mine. I won't share them, not even with you, sweet Willie."

"What do I care about odds?" she argued heatedly. "We

310

agreed, Matthew . . . we agreed to take what we have now. Your precious Holmes said it: 'A moment's insight is sometimes worth a lifetime's experience.' What about a moment's true love? Isn't that precious, too?"

" 'The Professor at the Breakfast Table,' " Matt mused. "One of his weaker pieces. Dearest Willie, don't try to out-lawyer me. I was writing closing arguments before you were born. Just listen. I love you – don't ever doubt that. We've had a glorious time together. I've been everything with you that I could ever hope to be. But now . . . time's catching up, and I'm too damn selfish to let you watch me grow old. I won't let those images fill up your memory and crowd out the rest. *That* would be worse than the dying, and I can't do it . . . not even for you."

He took her hand in the way that had defined his limits before they'd ever made love. Willie's heart was bursting with pain. "Go now," he said. "Please. Let the man in your memory stay young forever – because that's how long I'll remember your love."

With another man she might have argued. But she knew Matt's strength. There was no changing his mind, softening his will – not on a matter of principle.

Blinded with tears, she ran from the graceful Georgian house into a burst of gray, drizzling rain.

She leaned against the cherry tree, bare of blossoms now – the spot where she and Matt had promised to marry. She stared with swollen, tearful eyes over the murky waters of the Potomac, oblivious to the cold, wet clothes that chilled her body, letting the rain soak her face.

Abandoned, forlorn, saddened almost beyond endurance, Willie remembered another time long ago. The day Perry had gone, taking away his love and protection, leaving her with the awful realization that there was no one in the world she could count on, no one who would kiss her tears away when she was sad or promise to chase the shadows away.

Now Matt had done it, too, leaving an awful ache where there had been hope and joy. And the worst thing of all was that none of it made any sense. Perry had gone in anger and

311

ignorance; Matt had deserted her with sadness, in the name of love. The pain was still the same. What good were noble ideals and principles if they caused the same kind of pain as unthinking stupidity?

She was alone again, cast adrift. And all the plans she'd made here, all the fragile illusions that Matthew had awakened on a lovely spring day, had died stillborn on a cold and cruel autumn night.

It was very late when Willie checked into the Shoreham Hotel. She was like a stranger again in this city, with nowhere else to go. She couldn't face the Parkmans. She had no strength or energy to explain what she herself couldn't understand.

More than anything, she wanted to run and hide, yet she couldn't bear to be alone with her pain. Willie knew only one remedy, one resource: to keep busy, to not think, to not feel.

She waited out the long, lonely hours of night, pacing restlessly in the gray anonymity of her room, unable to sleep. When the first pale rays of morning appeared, she showered and changed and went downstairs to the coffee shop.

It wasn't food or refreshment she was after, it was distraction – the hum of conversation, the clanking of silverware and dishes – anything that would help pass the few more hours she needed to wait. Willie had made a single decision during the dark and sleepless night.

When her watch showed that business hours had begun in California, Willie dialed the number on the business card she'd tucked away in her wallet. She gave her name to the woman who answered and asked to speak to Francis Aloysius Harrigan. As soon as she heard the theatrical baritone, she said tersely: "I'd like to accept your offer."

"A sound decision," Harrigan said, matching her brevity.

"I still have to take the bar exams," she said, "but I can fly out to Los Angeles—"

"You can take the bar exams on my time, Miss Dellahaye. But Los Angeles wasn't what I had in mind. I want you in my New York office, and I want you there as soon as possible."

"New York . . . " she repeated. Even in her exhaustion, Willie's first thought was of Mama. Going to Washington as a bride had been fine with Ginny, but to move clear across the country for a job? Her second thought was that New York was clean of memories, innocent of associations.

"Is there a problem?" Harrigan asked.

"No problem," she said.

None, she assured herself again after she had completed the call to Harrigan. Her future was taken care of now. There would be no problem at all, as long as she didn't dare again to surrender her heart.

Book IV

Convictions

Prologue

The cold, black eyes of Seif al-Rahman held Willie in a fixed gaze as he stared at her across her desk. "It will do you no good to hide my wife, Miss Dellahaye," he said. "She is mine and nothing you do can change that."

Willie bristled at his use of the word "mine." "Women may be property in your country, sir, but let me remind you that Sofia is an American citizen, and I mean to protect all her constitutional rights. My client no longer wishes to be 'yours,' Mr. al-Rahman, and her wishes are my only concern. In fact—"

"Please." With an imperious lift of his hand, Seif al-Rahman halted Willie's sentence in midair. "I have not come here to discuss your constitution or your concerns . . . or, for that matter, my wife's wishes. I'm here to inform you that Sofia is mine for as long as I want her. And it can be very dangerous to interfere with what I want. If you're wise, Miss Dellahaye, you will not provoke me into demonstrating just how dangerous . . . "

Enraged by Seif's blatant malevolence, Willie bolted from her chair and walked around her desk to confront him where he sat. She looked directly down into the face of the man she meant to defeat at any cost. "Save your threats. You'll never touch Sofia again. You'll pay for what you've done to her — and that's a promise."

Seif al-Rahman rose slowly from his chair, a thin smile on his lips, as if Willie's speech meant nothing at all. "There's an old Arab saying," he intoned softly. " 'A friend of my friend's is my friend as well. But a friend of my enemy becomes my enemy.' " He moved to the door. "I always have the last word, Miss Dellahaye, and today you have made yourself a powerful enemy."

Al-Rahman pulled open the door, but Willie stopped him in his tracks with a voice as icy as her blue eyes. "I've made enemies like you before, Mr. al-Rahman. As we Americans say, 'It comes with the territory.' No matter what you say or do, being a friend to my clients is all that matters to me. I'll see you in court."

Willie caught a flicker of pure hatred in the cold black eyes, portending a battle unlike any she had ever fought in the restrained and civilized atmosphere of a western court-room – a war fueled by savage passions, with no mercy shown the loser. But the Arab nodded as cordially as if he had just enjoyed a polite tea, and left.

Seif al-Rahman's presence lingered long after his departure. Willie leaned back in her soft leather chair and closed her eyes, pressing her fingers against her throbbing temples. Anger – that ferocious, righteous anger that burned every day in her, fueled afresh by each battle she had to fight for her clients – had given her the courage to face Sofia's husband. Yet there was a price to pay for the diet of bitterness and recrimination that nourished her unending search for justice.

In the ten years since she'd become one of America's leading divorce attorneys, Willie had represented hundreds of women, many with husbands as angry and vindictive as Seif al-Rahman. Whenever she heard a story that touched the deep recesses of her own heart, a story that stirred her memory of a simple woman denied justice because no one but her own child had cared, Willie responded with all the fire and passion of a dedicated crusader. Once she made a case her own, there was no thought of losing – and because her commitment was to win, she almost invariably found the way to do so.

Yet with each victory, the thrill of winning became somehow less satisfying, the trophies of success less lustrous.

In the quiet retreat of a moment between appointments, or in the dark solitude of her bedroom, Willie was nagged by a question that came into her mind with ever-increasing frequency.

Why, with every new triumph on another woman's behalf, why did she feel her own womanhood diminished?

318

1

From the jets that circled its airspace New York looked like a sophisticated board game. By day it was played in corporate offices in towers of concrete and glass, at choice tables at "21" and Le Cirque. By night the winners celebrated their victories in the trendy playgrounds of SoHo and the upper East Side and in sybaritic apartments overlooking rivers and parks.

For Willa Dellahaye, Esquire, New York was more than a playing field. It was a fresh start. A place to forget. A chance to rediscover meaning and purpose in the one thing that had rarely failed her: hard work.

She found a comfortable brownstone apartment in Greenwich Village, two blocks from Washington Square Park. The previous tenant, a jazz musician, had been evicted for nonpayment of rent, and the landlady offered the apartment "as is", for $300 a month, a bargain Willie could well appreciate after looking at places half the size for two and three times the price. Having no real interest in making a nest of this retreat, Willie kept the musician's furnishings, which had a rakishly Bohemian quality that reminded her of Suzanne and the cozy Cambridge walkup they'd shared.

The apartment had a small, well-equipped kitchen that Willie rarely used and a lovely old woodburning fireplace she used almost every night. The front window overlooked a charming tree-lined street; the back faced a row of tiny gardens, priceless little oases of greenery and flowers in a city dominated by concrete and steel.

Nearby were the pungently fragrant Italian shops on Bleecker Street, where Willie discovered the pleasures of

319

crusty, chewy breads, spicy sausages, and sun-dried tomatoes. At the sidewalk tables of the Figaro and the Reggio, she sampled foamy cappuccino, served up with a view of neighborhood street life.

On weekends she strolled through Washington Square Park and watched old men playing checkers amidst the serenade of street musicians and the frenetic patter of drug peddlers. She browsed the arcane treasures of the Strand bookstore and the tiny antique shops.

Once a week, sometimes twice, Mama would call. Willie would talk of new places she'd seen and how hard she was working, and Ginny would inevitably become wistful about the three thousand miles that separated them. Each time Mama hinted that she'd like her to come back to California for a visit, Willie felt the pull of Ginny's need, tearing at the new life she was trying to make. She knew she couldn't live both Mama's life and her own, yet a plaintive sigh from Ginny was enough to feed the kind of guilt that defied reason. Though Willie could never quite put the guilt aside, neither could she go back to being a child again, to a time when she had no need or purpose other than to help her mother.

Her place was in New York – a labyrinth of treasures and secret corners waiting to catch her eye and capture her attention. The city pulsed with a tough, raw energy that challenged Willie and often left her feeling there couldn't be hours enough in a single day. She welcomed that feeling and the chance to lose herself without being lonely.

It wasn't the kind of life Willie had dreamed of lying in the shelter of Matt's arms, but she knew all too well how treacherously fragile dreams could be. Much better to banish dreams and trust only her own strengths and talents.

Willie's day began with a hasty breakfast and a taxi ride to work – the buses and subways promised more adventure and combat than she cared to handle at such an early hour – watching the city change face as she left behind the relative tranquility of the Village and moved slowly past the historic buildings of Chelsea, toward the jagged monoliths and canyons of midtown New York.

The firm of Harrigan and Peale was almost as regressive as "Ring and Wait" had been. A men's club, but without the history and tradition, without the good manners and breeding that had given "Ring and Wait" a leavening air of gentility. In place of century-old wood paneling and brass, the offices of Harrigan and Peale surrounded Willie with chrome and glass and steel.

In Boston, Willie had regarded the partners of "Ring and Wait" as quaint but decent old dinosaurs. Here she felt surrounded by sharks, greedy, ambitious, and hungry. Here it was every man for himself, with very little pretense – just as Bud had told her it would be. The backstabbing went on in many ways, subtle and direct. Associates vied to outmaneuver one another in the push for junior partnerships. Junior partners did the same in the push for senior partnerships, everyone up and down the ladder of seniority jockeying nervously for position.

In Boston, the senior lawyers had regarded Willie with a certain polite bewilderment. In New York she was treated like an expensive, overqualified secretary or like an attractive work machine, to be loaded with the tiresome, tedious donkey work of research and kept hidden away in her tiny office, with no client contact and no credit for billable hours.

Though compromise and acceptance were the hardest of all lessons for Willie, she tried, at Harrigan and Peale, to see her working conditions as "paying dues." She was learning, under the Harrigan umbrella, more about how the law really worked than any textbooks in the world could teach her. She watched Harrigan build cases out of nothing but his own brassy confidence and his repertoire of legal parlor tricks – and win. She saw justice prevail and justice falter, as questions of right and wrong were decided on the basis of Harrigan's superior showmanship.

And while she learned, Willie wondered how long her apprenticeship would last, how long it would be until she'd be recognized as a "real" attorney, like the rest of them.

*　　*　　*

On a cold March morning she saw an article in the *New York Times*, an interview with several women lawyers, including two who were partners. The women all described the kind of atmosphere Willie had experienced. Tokenism, they called it. Condescension, exploitation – everything, in short, but equal treatment.

The article made Willie angry. And then it made her think. The young lawyers said they accepted unsatisfying conditions knowing there were plenty of other women who would gladly replace them. To Willie that kind of thinking was self-defeating. Whether it was for her brainpower or as protection against a gender discrimination suit, Harrigan and Peale wasn't the only firm who'd have her.

Willie took her anger into the office of her department supervisor, Jacob Korn, the only Jewish senior partner, a man who was middle-aged and unfailingly blunt. Without preamble, she launched her assault: "When I was hired, Francis promised me advancement and meaningful work. Where is it, Jack?"

Korn seemed unsurprised by Willie's gauntlet. "Be specific," he said. "What do you call 'meaningful'?"

Willie named a symptom of her dissatisfaction. "I don't want to spend the next couple of years in the back rooms of this firm because the front says 'Men Only.' "

"Ah. What if I tell you, just between us, that's how it's got to be?"

Willie shook her head vigorously. "Not good enough, Jack. You didn't get where you are by accepting 'Keep Out' rules," she said bluntly. "I see what the score is, and I'm looking to change the size of the playing field. If I can't do it here, I'll go elsewhere. Today. You can give the news to Harrigan."

Korn was silent, not only impressed with Willie's forthright approach, but concerned at how the chairman of the firm might feel at losing this bright young attorney he had personally brought to the staff. "All right, Willie. Would you settle for having some more client contact . . . ?"

"Depends on the client. No ambulance chasing, Jack.

This firm has a lot of heavyweight clients. I want to get in the ring with one of them . . . "

"How about Judson Madden?" he said. "Will he do? If you want something more cosmic, take it up with His Eminence himself." Korn looked back to his papers, brusquely signaling that the meeting had been brought to a close.

Judson Madden had the well-fed, self-satisfied air of a successful grocer, which was exactly what his father had been. Madden had amassed his personal fortune over the space of two decades by virtue of shrewd planning and hard work. The firm was handling his acquisition of the *Village Crier*, a faltering tabloid that had been founded by a group of liberal writers and editors, and was known for its support of liberal causes.

At first glance, Madden reminded Willie of Clayton Handy, the richest and most unpopular man in Belle Fourche. No one had ever accused Clayton of wrongdoing, but it was generally agreed that he was woefully short on loving his neighbor and other Christian virtues.

At their first meeting, Madden handed Willie a copy of the *Crier* with an article by Nick Rossiter outlined in red. Rossiter was a columnist who had made his reputation writing about an eclectic combination of boxing and football . . . and public issues. He was also known as a rakish, hard-drinking man-about-town who had escorted movie stars to film premieres and the widow of a well-known senator to museum benefits.

Rossiter's article described Judson Madden as a soulless merchant who traded in newspapers as Wall Streeters trade in paper. "To run the *Crier* for profit is to destroy its identity," it concluded.

"I've run into this kind of attack before," Madden explained. "It doesn't mean a damn thing when I'm buying and someone else is selling. The *Crier* is small potatoes, but I can use it to build a base of operations in the New York area. I don't much care what people like Rossiter say, but bad press could get in my way when it's time to ask the city for favors and tax breaks. I want the public to see it's a good thing that I'm protecting jobs and making new ones."

Willie nodded, waiting for Madden to explain exactly what he expected of her.

"Jack tells me you understand these liberal types," he said. "Should I talk to the *Crier* people and tell 'em to stop biting the hand that's gonna feed their families? Should I get rid of the troublemakers and replace them with people who know what side their bread's buttered on? What's your opinion, counselor?"

Willie found it hard to muster passion for a public relations exercise, but she couldn't very well go back to Jack and refuse the assignment. "I'm against intimidation on principle," she said. "And I can give you a practical reason as well. Rossiter's in no position to do any real harm. He's part of what gives the paper its particular identity. If you get rid of him or frighten off the staff, you'll lose that character and the *Crier* will turn into a carbon copy of all the other neighborhood papers."

Madden smiled, as if he'd anticipated this answer. "We have another option. We can let the staff know their jobs are safe. Maybe we can give them a raise, just to show them that working for me is better than working for a publisher who's going under . . . "

"No," Willie cut in. "With all due respect, your idea's a good one, but the timing is wrong. The *Crier* people are professional anti-establishmenters. They're geared up to be angry. Any money offer now would be wasted. They'd take it as an attempt to buy their integrity. Wait until the deal's concluded and the dust settles. We can send out a memo letting the staff know that anyone who wants to work is welcome to stay. Later, you can call a general meeting and talk about salary increases on the basis of performance."

Madden stuck out his hand. "I like your thinking, counselor. Let me take you to lunch."

In the weeks that followed, Judson Madden came to be

seen among the city's press corps as a provincial William Randolph Hearst, a press baron of the old style who ran his newspapers like personal fiefdoms. As Madden's legal representative and occasional companion about town, Willie began to get public exposure. Pictures of the two of them began to show up in the gossip columns, accompanied by speculations on Madden's business dealings – and his relationship with his beautiful counsel.

Although publicity of any kind was like food and drink to her employer, Francis A. Harrigan, Willie was no more satisfied than she had been before. She began muttering to herself, a practice she found unattractive but necessary, since no one else seemed overly interested in her frustrations.

These frustrations came to a head on a Monday morning. As Willie logged her billable hours for the previous month, she saw that most of them had been spent not on the practice of law, but on Madden's image work, smoothing over her client's rough edges, helping prepare publicity handouts that made him sound like a savior of ailing newspapers.

As Willie simmered in her dissatisfaction, her secretary handed her a memo signed by Harrigan himself. It informed Willie she was expected to arrange a cocktail party for a group of third-year law students the firm was courting. That does it, she muttered. Now I'm supposed to be a stewardess, for God's sake.

She threw the memo into the wastebasket, squared her shoulders and stalked into His Eminence's office. "We need to talk," she said.

"Careful, Willa," Harrigan said. "I see that fire in your eye. Am I to be the target of your righteous wrath once again? We're on the same team, my dear . . . "

Willie bit back the "hah" that so often came to her lips in the face of Harrigan's rhetoric. Instead she smiled and said: "You're right, coach. What I want to say is: Play me or trade me."

Harrigan smiled back. Willie didn't quite like that. She mistrusted his good humor more than anything else.

"Very good," he said approvingly. "You're thinking on

325

your feet. I thought we were providing ample room for your talents to take root and grow, but perhaps your point is well taken. As it happens" – the smile broadened – "I can show you how much we respect and appreciate those talents. Clear your calendar for the next week or so. And be in my office this afternoon at three. Sharp."

This better be good, Willie said to herself, as she marched back in to her own office. Before she could begin wondering what Harrigan had on his mind, her secretary announced that a Mr. Nick Rossiter was calling – the same Nick Rossiter who had written thousands of words condemning Willie's client, now his employer. She grabbed the telephone.

"Do you know who I am?" a deep, smooth voice inquired.

"Of course I know who you are. You're the man who helped make my client a household word – and not an especially nice one."

Rossiter's laughter was rich and appreciative. "I'm flattered you take my humble talents so seriously – especially since your client got exactly what he was after. I can be a good loser," the voice said, softer now, more subdued. "Can you be a good winner and give me an interview?"

"I don't have the time, Mr. Rossiter," Willie answered quickly, on principle.

"I'll camp on your doorstep," Nick coaxed. "I'll take whatever crumbs you can spare . . . ten minutes when you're smoking a cigarette, five minutes while you're combing your hair . . . "

Willie was engaged in spite of herself by Nick's easy banter. "I don't smoke, Mr. Rossiter, and I comb my hair in private, but what is it you want to talk about?"

"Cabbages and kings?" he answered. " 'Lady Lawyers in the Corporate Jungle'? My pen will be yours to command . . . "

Willie flipped open her appointment book. If she accepted Rossiter's invitation, she could stop muttering to herself long enough to speak out in print. She wouldn't mind having a chance to air exactly what "lady lawyers" were up against. *And* what she thought they could do about it.

"All right," Willie relented. "As the guilty say when they're ready to confess . . . I'll talk. But it will have to be tomorrow – or not for a couple of weeks."

"I'll take confession at your convenience," Rossiter said smoothly. "I hope this means there are no hard feelings . . . "

Willie smiled to herself. "It means I'll talk," she said. "My feelings are my business."

Nick didn't seem to take offense. "Tomorrow, then, lunch at the Lion's Head?" he suggested. "That's located on—"

"I know where it is," she interrupted. "I'll see you there at 12.30." Of course, she thought, Rossiter would choose a place like the Lion's Head. He'd be in his element at the legendary Village haunt favored and celebrated by writers and newsmen.

Willie sat in one of the leather Fames chairs of Harrigan's office and appraised the man who could be her next corporate client. Harvey Silverstein seemed to be about Harrigan's age, but there the resemblance ended. Silverstein's flashy Italian suit said something about his taste and style, just as Harrigan's dark wool Paul Stuart reflected his.

Their disagreement aside, Willie preferred Harrigan's look and his style, but as he so often reminded her, "If we only handled clients we liked, we'd soon all be out on the street."

She listened to Harrigan explain that Silverstein was president of Marco Enterprises, a major distributor of wines, both domestic and European. "I've been assisting Harvey in negotiations for an Italian vineyard," he said. "The deal closes in two days, and I've been telling him that you're the best person to handle the closing . . . "

Willie looked over at Harvey, who didn't seem overly pleased by her presence. Francis probably has bigger fish to fry, she thought, and he's trying to make this guy think he's doing him a favor by sending me.

Sure enough, a moment later, Harvey asked, "What

kind of clients have you worked for, Miss?" – just as if he were asking a salesgirl to show him her wares.

Willie flashed a glance at Harrigan. Was she being interrogated about her qualifications? "Big clients, Mr. Silverstein," she answered with a blandness that undercut her intent, "as big as you are."

Silverstein grunted and turned to Harrigan. "This is a fifty-million-dollar deal, pal. This lady better be as good as you say."

"Not to worry," Francis said genially. "When it comes to the law, our Willie thinks like a man. In a dark courtroom – a very dark courtroom – she could even pass for one," he laughed.

Willie flushed with repressed anger. Harrigan's pandering praise was as devaluing as Harvey's prejudice. Pride made her want to get up and leave the room, but she knew that running away wasn't the answer. The law was a bastion of male chauvinism, and the only way to feminize it was to be as good, or better, than *they* were.

" . . . and you'll be flying to Rome tomorrow night," Harrigan was saying.

The words snapped Willie to attention. She'd never been to Italy; for that matter, she'd never been anywhere outside the United States. She caught the twinkle in Harrigan's eye as he dangled the carrot. Okay, she thought, maybe this is his way of saying "Welcome to the club." And as she glanced once again at Harvey Silverstein, she had no doubt whatever that she'd be earning her initiation the hard way.

Willie had already made up her mind about Nick Rossiter. He'd be like one of those Peter Pan boy-men the magazines liked to warn women about. Slightly long in the tooth and short on development. Frequently photographed with an assortment of desirable women, his private reputation was as a man-about-town, while the column he wrote in his decidedly macho style had brought him public regard as a man of the people.

Armed with her prejudices, Willie arrived at the Lion's

Head promptly at 12.30. She walked down the stairs and into the low-ceilinged, dimly lit, dark-paneled room.

John Lennon's "Whatever Gets You Thru The Night" was playing on the jukebox. At the mahogany bar, a group of men were having a heated discussion about a recent scandal involving a well-known city councilman. In the middle of it was Nick Rossiter. He was in his mid-forties, of medium build, with curly sandy hair lightly streaked with gray, and beard to match, the kind of short beard that suggested he had just spent a week or two somewhere out of touch with civilization. He was wearing chino pants, a gray cotton knit pullover, and a tan English raincoat slung over his shoulder. "Abe Beame's a stand-up guy," he said, slapping a bill on the bar, "and I've got ten bucks that says he gets the D.A. to indict before the week's up."

The bartender covered the bet. Nick turned to Willie. "C'mon counselor. There's a table for two waiting in the corner just for us."

When they were seated, he stuck out his hand and favored Willie with an easy boyish smile. "Miz Dellahaye – at last we meet."

She appraised Rossiter coolly, prepared to be unimpressed with whatever he was selling. "Why did you want to talk to me?"

"Do I need a reason to talk to a beautiful woman – who's also a hotshot lawyer?" he asked rhetorically with another lazy smile. "Hell, Miz Dellahaye, I never know exactly what I'm after when I start an interview. In your case it was something about women and the law. But we don't have to pin it down. I get the best stuff when I just let people talk. They always give me *something* I can use . . . "

"I know how to watch my words."

"Oh, I'll bet you do," Nick said suggestively. "Hey, Mickey," he called out to a passing waiter. "Bring me a Bud." Turning to Willie, he said, "White wine for you, right?"

"Wrong," Willie said, though in fact a white wine was exactly what she would have ordered. "I'll have a . . . Miller's."

Nick grinned knowingly at Willie and ordered "a Miller's for the lady." "So," he said casually, "what's our Mr. Madden up to these days? I got it from a very good source that he's got his eye on *Metro* magazine—"

"Mr. Rossiter," Willie interrupted, "you should know better than to ask me about a client's business, and if *that's* what this interview is really about, I ought to leave now—"

"Hey, wait a minute." He put a hand on Willie's arm, then took out a white handkerchief and waved it. "No offense, counselor, but if I only asked the questions I was supposed to ask, I'd never get a decent story. Doesn't a lawyer have to step out of line sometimes to do his – her job well?"

Willie conceded the point. In spite of her prejudices, she was beginning to enjoy Nick's brash, cocky manner.

"I just don't like what Madden's doing to the *Crier*," Nick explained. "I can understand that a client is a client for a young lawyer like you, even a client like my new boss. But just between us, what do you really think of our Mr. Madden?"

Willie debated the merits of candor for a moment. "Is this off the record?"

Nick smiled. "Sounds interesting already . . . "

"I'm asking if I can trust you," Willie persisted.

The smile became a full-bodied laugh. "I'll tell you one thing for the record, Miz Dellahaye: I can *never* be trusted."

"I see." Willie nodded in mock seriousness, enjoying the game – and Nick Rossiter, too. "Can I rely on that?"

"Trust me."

"In that case," she said, "all I'll say about 'our Mr. Madden' is that he's a businessman. He's no worse or better than anyone else who's interested only in improving his own bottom line."

"You haven't run into any good guys in your line of work?" Nick probed. "No white knights?"

"Gray knights," she said, "some in lighter shades than others."

"Okay," Nick agreed cheerfully. "Now tell me more

about you. What's it like working in Harrigan's office . . . being the first girl on the team?"

Willie had a ready answer to this question. "Working with Harrigan probably isn't much different from working in any big law firm. The boys make you fight harder for every inch, and when you win it, they try to make you feel like it's a gift."

Willie described for Nick the discrimination and the patronizing attitudes she'd encountered since the day she'd told her high-school guidance counselor she wanted to study law. Without naming Matt, she talked of the help she'd received from "an authentic liberal with rare vision."

"That sounds almost like a white knight," Nick observed when Willie paused for breath.

She shook her head and looked directly into Nick's brown eyes. "I told you – there aren't any."

Nick looked back. "You won't find one here, Miz Dellahaye, but I think you should go out with me anyway. Preferably tonight."

She laughed at his brashness. "No, I have to go to Italy tonight," she began, prepared to make her usual excuses. But then she thought: Why not? He's bright and attractive and easy to talk to – and I haven't had a real date in months. "Tell you what," she said, "I'll call you as soon as I get back."

Willie climbed the four flights of stairs to her apartment, "the garret" as she thought of it on mellow days. The day had been long and exhausting, and she sighed wearily as she bent down to pick up the mail propped against the door – a handful of bills and advertising circulars and a huge manila envelope.

Once inside, she kicked off her shoes and poured herself a glass of white wine. The wine made her hungry, but she was too tired to salvage a meal from the contents of her refrigerator.

She leafed through her mail, then tore open the manila envelope. Inside was a poster-size blowup of a newspaper photograph – of Willie and Judson Madden. Sketched in over Madden's suit was a period Spanish costume, and a note was inked across the bottom margin: "You seem to like this grandee well enough." It was signed "Jedd."

Willie giggled. The sound was startling to her own ears. And then she started to laugh, the tensions of the day dissolving in giddy waves of release. Ah, Jedd, she thought, you always say I have no sense of humor – and when I find it, you're not here to see.

She propped the poster against a brass coffee table and stretched out on her Mexican couch. Looking up through the dusty skylight at the stars twinkling against a navy blue sky, she thought of how much she ought to be doing to prepare for the Italian trip. Packing. Studying the pounds of legal documents Harrigan had handed over. More important things than the thinking about Jedd that overtook her now – the insistent wondering that came back to haunt her on so many lonely nights . . .

Why, when there was no one else who affected her as he did, why couldn't he have a little less charm and a lot more character?

And why, since she couldn't let herself love him, couldn't she forget him either?

2

From the moment she stepped off the plane, Willie felt Italy was more than a place, it was also a state of mind. The first pleasing symptom was the waves of appreciation she experienced from the Italian men. She was accustomed to admiring glances, but here there was something more. It was as if the same celebration of beauty in art was directed at the proud tilt of her cheekbones, the curve of her mouth, the lift of her brow, the clarity of her aquamarine eyes. "*Que bella visione*," crooned the customs inspector as he passed her bag without so much as a perfunctory peek.

"C'mon, Jack, hurry up," Harvey said peevishly when

his own bag was opened and thoroughly checked. "I got a car outside."

"*Bellissima,*" murmured the driver of the waiting limousine, handing Willie inside as if she were royalty.

The limousine sped along the airport road and slowed as it reached the city limits. As they drove through the streets of Rome, Harvey simultaneously ordered the chauffeur to "step on it" and pointed out sights with a quick flick of his finger – "the Trevi Fountain . . . the Colosseum . . . Via Veneto" – as though he were merely window shopping.

He spent more time, however, talking about the business deal he was here to conclude. As if assuming Willie was incapable of retaining information, he reminded her three times that $50 million was tied up in the acquisition of the Celestine Vineyards.

"But it's more than the bucks," Harvey said. "When I took over Marco Enterprises, it was just a chickenshit company. I busted balls and made it a big operation. Now I'm getting outta jug wines and going world class. I need these Wops to give Marco glamour and class. Mark my words, counselor, Americans are gonna be drinking wine just like the Frogs do. And yours truly is gonna be ready . . . bottles with fancy crests and the whole nine yards."

Willie tried, without success, to staunch Harvey's narrative flow by taking the contracts out of her briefcase.

Harrigan's pep talk notwithstanding, Silverstein seemed to be having second thoughts about accepting Willie, an apparent second stringer, when he'd wanted the captain of the team. Pointedly he reminded Willie that he was a man who traveled "first cabin all the way," that his suits "never cost less than a thousand bucks," and that his hairstylist barbered not only movie stars, but also a former president of the United States, at "a hundred bucks a pop."

The recital ended when they pulled up in front of the Hassler Hotel. "I need a steam and a massage, pronto," Harvey announced. "But what say we have some dinner later?" he asked, his tone suggesting that a female lawyer might be of some value after all.

Willie politely declined the invitation. "This *is* an

important deal," she said pointedly. "I want to review the papers again tonight and turn in early."

After being Harvey's captive audience, she welcomed the smiles and attentions of the doorman who opened the limousine door and the bellman who carried her bag with a care that bordered on tenderness and handed over her key as if it were a gift from the heart. Gratefully, she took refuge in the peaceful room. After showering quickly and reviewing her notes, she went to sleep, alone in the city called "Eternal."

The boy who brought her breakfast flirted outrageously, plucking the rose from the tray and handing it to her with a gallant flourish, just as if he'd been a Borgia or a Medici duke.

Willie feasted on the warm, crusty bread covered with rich, creamy butter and raspberry preserve and the strong black coffee laced with hot milk; certain that no breakfast had ever tasted so good before.

Though she had little use for Harvey Silverstein, she felt some zest for the work ahead today – playing a role in consummating the deal in which Marco Enterprises would take over the ducal vineyards of the Celestines. The Italian name had a romantic ring to it, conjured up dreamy images of graceful, ornate palazzos peopled with decadent nobility exchanging languid glances, of lazy, sun-drenched afternoons spent in the pursuit of sensual pleasures, of rich, soul-satisfying foods and robust yet enervating wines. A fairyland time and place, a vineyard producing ambrosial grapes, a title and property stripped of wealth – that was what Harvey Silverstein intended to acquire, with Willie's expert assistance. By the close of the business day, Harvey would have purchased what he himself never would be: the product of centuries of class and breeding.

The cavalcade of three limousines carrying attorneys, clerks, and bank personnel left for the Tuscany countryside at noon. It had been made very clear that the Duke di Celestine could not, simply would not, execute the sale of his ancestral legacy in a lawyer's office or a banker's conference room. And so it was necessary to come to him, hopefully without interrupting his afternoon siesta.

In the golden spring sunshine the countryside was bathed in a warm light that would gladden a painter's heart: mountains smudged with burnt umber, rich, green fertile valleys, pine forests touched with sienna.

The tape deck in Willie's car played a Neapolitan air sung by Pavarotti. No one spoke, and even Harvey Silverstein for the moment subdued his peculiar brand of charm, perhaps in deference to the occasion.

Carlo Martinelli, the twenty-seventh Duke of Celestine, was sixty-seven years old, a man who had outlived two wives and buried his only son. During the last two decades of his life, Martinelli had seen his patrimony dwindle, though the Celestine grapes still produced the finest Brunello wines. Yet as his personal fortune declined, forcing him today to sell the heritage that had been in his family for centuries, Martinelli was no less an aristocrat. His wavy silver hair, his beard, and his mustache were trimmed by his housekeeper, and his dark suit was of a vaguely 1940s cut, yet he was still that one thing money couldn't buy: a gentleman.

"Welcome to my house," Martinelli said with a somber irony, bowing stiffly from the waist, as he stood in the soaring marble foyer of his palazzo. He greeted the cortege from Rome as if it were a funeral party, come to pay its final respects to the last Duke of Celestine as he departed his ancestral home, to live out the remainder of his days with his housekeeper Angelica in a whitewashed cottage near Porto Ercole.

Shaking hands with Signor Silverstein, the Duke frowned, as if he could take in with a glance the character of the man who would soon own his palazzo, his beloved vineyards, and the right to use his family name.

But when the old duke saw Willie, his eyebrows lifted in welcome, his manner warmed with a genuine cordiality. He took her hand as if it were a precious flower, brushed it

335

lightly with his lips, then extended his arm to escort her formally across the marble floor and into the library, where the housekeeper had laid out light refreshments.

The library represented the shrunken dimensions of Martinelli's world. Out of the palazzo's forty-two rooms, only this one had not been despoiled or cannibalized in any way. The silk damask that covered the chairs was thread-bare but clean, and the oriental carpet unsullied by rips or stains. The bookshelves were crowded with well-used works of history and literature in rich leather bindings. As his wealth had diminished, his family treasures sold piece-meal at discreet Rome auctions, Carlo Martinelli had held on in this single room.

It was here that he had chosen to transact this sad and final piece of business, to surrender the legacy that had been in his family for 400 years. But like the aristocrat he was, Martinelli introduced no talk of money and instead offered his guests several bottles of Celestine wine from his private store and a silver tray laden with antipasti – thinly sliced Parma ham and salami, green olives from Sicily, pickled mushrooms, red peppers, and a platter of assorted cheeses, tomatoes, and onions.

"First class," Harvey declared, smacking his lips appreciatively as he sampled the first bottle of wine. "Hearty, robust, but not overpowering, if you know what I mean."

Martinelli smiled politely, inclining his head toward Willie. "Signorina . . . Signorina Dottore," he said, adding the respectful title reserved for men of learning. "How do you find the wine?"

"It's lovely," Willie said, feeling strangely saddened that Silverstein's money could take away what Martinelli had treasured – and that to Harvey it would mean something very different from what it had meant to this proud old man. She wondered if Harvey really believed that pride and tradition could be bought and sold like pieces of furniture. Class was something Harvey could only buy, and even then it might not wear very well.

"Perhaps you would like to see the palazzo and the grounds," Martinelli suggested, as if Willie were a weekend guest rather than part of a group who would require some sort of inspection before documents were signed and moneys delivered.

"Thank you," Willie said. "I'd like that very much, Your Excellency."

"Call me Carlo," the duke said. "Please. I would be honored." Taking Willie by the hand, he walked her first through the vineyards, the others trailing behind like attendants after royalty. She inhaled the sweet fragrance of the grapes, touched the veiny leaves as the old duke explained that at harvest time, his family traditionally held a feast for all the workers, and how any child born during the harvest would be given a silver cup bearing the Celestine crest.

"Not even war could destroy the Celestine vines," he said proudly. "The bombing took my wife, Laura, and my son, Pietro. For two years the harvest was meager, but the stock was strong, and after the war, the grapes were richer and sweeter, Signorina. It was as if Bacchus himself blessed our sacrifice . . . " The old man's voice trailed off and his eyes wandered to some distant horizon, where his precious memories rested, protected from the intrusion of time and man.

He brought Willie back to the house and escorted her up the marble staircase and into the grand ballroom, which was now pitiably bare, except for an enormous grand piano, a golden harp, and a fading fresco on its walls. "In the old days," the duke reminisced in a voice as dry as a whisper, "this room was very beautiful. When I was a boy, I would stand in the doorway and count the candles that lit the parties on the saints' days . . . the feast of the Epiphany . . . " Bereft of family and besieged by debt, the old man seemed to have an intense need to share with someone all that his name and his home had meant to him, to plant in someone else's memory a tiny piece of the history that would have no caretaker once he was gone.

"This must be very hard for you," Willie said gently, hoping the old man didn't know that Silverstein planned to make this place a corporate retreat, complete with electronic equipment and steam rooms and Jacuzzis.

Carlo's eyes clouded, but he recovered quickly. "We Martinellis have a sense of history. Things must change, Signorina."

Yes, Willie thought, but how sad that a boor like Harvey should be the instrument of change.

The duke took Willie's arm again, and as they strolled along a spacious gallery, she stopped to admire a group of family portraits. She pointed to one of a handsome young man with blond hair and hazel eyes dressed in riding habit, then looked at her host. "What a wonderful picture of you," she said.

A look of pain crossed the duke's face, as he shook his head. "That is not me," he said, his hand on Willie's arm. "It is my twin brother, Bruno."

"He died?" Willie asked softly.

"Alas, yes . . . but worse, he was not right." Martinelli tapped his head lightly. "We had many doctors, specialists from Rome. He died in the hospital in Sienna."

Willie strained to hear every detail as Martinelli told the story in a near whisper, so the others would not hear.

As they walked on, the duke showed her splendid bedrooms with soaring ceilings and magnificent arched windows, all in the same state of bare desolation, but something nagged at Willie and she could barely listen.

As a lawyer, she felt the "something" was of inestimable value. But as a woman who had walked through a fragrant vineyard with a proud and lonely man, she could feel only a guilty sense of betrayal.

When they returned to the library for espresso, the lawyers from Rome exchanged glances, as if to say: It's time for the business at hand.

"Excuse me," Willie said to Harvey. "I wonder if I might speak to you privately for a few minutes."

Once outside the library, she said: "I think we'll have to hold on this closing."

"What do you mean 'hold'?" Silverstein asked impatiently.

"I've spent a bundle on legal fees already. Do you know . . . "

"Hear me out," she interrupted. "I've just learned that Martinelli's brother died insane. We don't know if he was of sound mind when he assigned his share of the vineyard. That makes for a muddy title, Harvey. If any of the brother's children file a claim in the future, you could be tied up in the courts for years."

Harvey's face went from disbelief to disappointment, as he pictured the Celestine grapes and all that went with them slipping from his grasp. And then he looked at Willie with admiration. "If you're wrong," he said, "I'll make sure that Harrigan takes it out of your hide. But if you're right, then you're better than he said you were."

Willie braced herself as she went back into the library. Though Harvey was her client, her sympathies were with the old aristocrat who must now be told that the wealthy American and his money would be leaving – all because he had told a beautiful young woman a story that might have been left untold.

Ignoring everyone else in the room, Willie took the duke's hand. "Signor Martinelli . . . Carlo," she said softly, "I'm so very sorry, but my client cannot buy the Celestine vineyards. There appears to be a legal problem . . . "

Martinelli's hazel eyes came alive with comprehension as Willie made her explanation. Yet there was no reproach in his expression. "Don't worry, Signorina," he said, squeezing her hand. "I understand that you must do your job. And I did enjoy our walk . . . "

All eyes were on Willie. And then the quiet erupted into a babel of protest, punctuated by broad gestures and dramatic waving of arms. The Roman lawyers protested that this was unheard of, after all this work, all this preparation. The bankers agreed. Only the duke said nothing, a half smile on his face, as if the money did not matter so much after all, since the vineyards of the Celestine would be his for yet another harvest.

Willie dreaded the ride back, the recriminations that

would surely follow from all these busy men. Yet once it became clear that there would be no business conducted today, they shrugged and smiled and began to flirt with her again, just as they had before.

"Listen," Harvey said when they were back in the limousine. "It's no secret how I felt about you. Like I said, I pay top dollar for the best, I expect to get it. I didn't figure on dealing with a woman. But I'm a broadminded guy," he said, chuckling at his witticism and squeezing Willie's knee. "If you'd been a man, that old geezer wouldn't have opened up to you like that. You turned out fine, Willie."

She fought back a sharp reply as she pulled her briefcase further onto her lap, knocking Harvey's hand away. "Martinelli wasn't the kind of man to hide anything," she said. "He was a great gentleman." Pointedly, she added, "We might all learn something from him . . . "

Harvey paused to assess her remark. "No offense," he continued then, "but I'm not ready to call this deal dead until I get a second opinion from your boss. And I'm going to take a look at another vineyard just in case. I want you to come with me to Venice until I see what's what."

Willie was quiet for a moment. Was Harvey getting ready to make a pass? she wondered. And how should she handle this request without insulting him?

As if he knew exactly what she was thinking, Harvey smiled broadly, showing capped teeth that were as slick and excessively perfect as his sharkskin suit. "Don't worry, counselor," he said. "My wife's flying in to meet us. I promised her a second honeymoon when this business was over."

If Harvey was telling the truth, then she'd be quite safe, Willie decided. But how would he explain her presence to a wife who expected a romantic holiday?

3

From the terraced rooftop restaurant of the Danieli Hotel, Willie watched the lavenders and pinks of the spring sunset play on the waters of the Grand Canal, drenching the bobbing gondolas below with picture-postcard color, bathing the rooftops of Venice in a romantic glow. A beautiful picture, but Willie felt outside the frame, a spectator set apart by her own rules and boundaries. Now she sat across a table from Harvey and Marion Silverstein, trying to reconcile the notion of a second honeymoon with what she saw. Harvey was holding forth in a loud voice on the money he had tied up in the stalled Celestino deal, as if he wanted all the neighboring diners to hear what an important man he was. Marion Silverstein sat stiffly in her chair like a reluctant bystander, a puzzled frown on her face as she listened to her husband's grumbling tirade.

Marion was a tall, slender woman whose delicate features were set off by fine platinum-gray hair swept smoothly back into a simple chignon. Her well-tailored burgundy silk suit and gracious soft-spoken manner bespoke breeding and understatement. Marion might have been beautiful once in a stately, almost regal way. But now her face had a pinched look that somehow reminded Willie of the poor women of Belle Fourche, who aged so quickly on their daily ration of worry and anxiety.

The Silversteins seemed an unfortunate couple to Willie. She had learned that Marion had been the only child of Marco Enterprises' founder, Nathan Rosen, and that Harvey had been one of Nathan's salesmen. Willie could see why Harvey would have wanted the boss's daughter – just as he'd wanted the Celestine vineyards – but she couldn't understand why a woman of taste and refinement who must have had other choices would pick a man who had the manners of a garment-district hustler.

Harvey paused in his recital as the waiter brought broiled chicken for him and Marion and langoustine accompanied by melted garlic butter for Willie. "You oughta go easy on the grease, counselor," he warned. "You're young now, but the cholesterol will destroy your arteries."

"Well, then," Willie said mischievously, soaking a chunk of prawn in the butter, "I'd better enjoy this right now, while my arteries are intact."

Marion Silverstein smiled discreetly as she picked up her knife and fork and applied herself to the grease-free chicken.

"Listen, ladies," Harvey said. "I hate to do this, but I have to go back to Tuscany tomorrow. My man in Rome says there's another vineyard near Florence that might be for sale. I might as well look at it, so this trip shouldn't be a total loss. But" – he smiled ingratiatingly – "that'll leave you free to shop your little hearts out."

"Aren't we going to have any time together?" Marion protested. "You promised we'd walk around the city and—"

"Sure, sure," Harvey agreed hastily. "Tonight . . . after I make a couple of phone calls, we'll walk around all you want."

"Speaking of calls," Willie said, "what did Harrigan advise when you called on the Celestine deal? Did he agree that you should withdraw the offer?"

"Everything's on hold," Harvey replied. "Harrigan's still talking to the Italian lawyers. That's why I want you standing by while I have a look at another deal."

"Why are you so set on Italy?" Marion finally asked. "I know you're anxious to expand Marco's premium wine division, but if you wanted a vineyard, there was Jack Sterling's property in California. The wine has an excellent reputation, the overheads are good, and you wouldn't have all the complications and problems you'll have here."

Willie thought the question was a good one, but Harvey brushed it off impatiently. "You don't understand, Marion. The business has changed since your father's day, okay?

342

I've done a damn good job of making Marco into a world-class outfit, so just leave the decisions to me."

Marion winced as if she'd been struck, and a rush of embarrassment overcame Willie. A moment later, Harvey was showing them both his gleaming, artificial smile. "Forget business, ladies. Just have a good time tomorrow, on me. Get some of that pretty glass they make here, Marion, it'll go good in the apartment . . . "

As Harvey expanded on all the ways in which they might "do Venice" and "spend some of my good American dollars," Marion seemed to shrink into herself. Willie felt even more awkward. Here was a woman who flew to Venice expecting a vacation with her husband, only to find herself stuck with his lawyer, a near stranger, instead. Willie felt as if somebody owed Mrs. Silverstein an apology, and if Harvey wasn't going to do it, perhaps she would.

When the waiter came for their dessert order, Harvey said: "I'll take some fruit . . . make sure it's fresh, you got that?" Turning to his wife, he asked, "Same for you, right?"

Marion nodded automatically, and Willie wondered how much nodding it took to sustain her marriage to Harvey. Though she was quite full, Willie felt compelled to order the specialty of the house, Coupe Danieli, an elaborate ice cream and spun sugar confection rife with cholesterol-laden calories.

But if she'd thought to provoke Harvey, she was wrong. No sooner had the desserts arrived than he called for the check and began drumming his manicured fingers impatiently on the table, as if he couldn't wait to be on his way.

Without thinking, Willie looked directly into Marion's eyes and saw something familiar – the same trapped, helpless look she'd seen so often in Mama's eyes, the same pain and need that had moved Willie to make a career in the law. It drew her now like a magnet, and though she was here to render legal services to Harvey, Willie couldn't help but care far more about the wrongs of his marriage, and the problems of his wife.

*　　　*　　　*

Willie strolled along the Riva degli Schiavone, toward the Piazza San Marco, following the trail of the music that floated on the balmy evening breeze. It was a night for lovers, and Willie watched them, arm in arm, locals and Americans and Europeans, all with one thing in common – unlike her, they were not alone.

The square was crowded with tourists. Some browsed the three-sided arcade shops, their brightly lit windows brimming with jewelry and ceramics and leather goods. Others clustered in front of the Basilica San Marco, snapping flash photos of the magnificent church whose marble and gold interior held such treasures as Titian's "Last Judgment" and a tenth-century altarpiece of gold and enamel studded with precious gems. On two sides of the piazza, orchestras serenaded those who had stopped for the refreshment of a fragrant espresso or creamy cappuccino.

The sense of yearning to be part of the romantic scene – a part of one of the couples who sat silhouetted at the little café tables lining the piazza – rose from her very center.

"*Guarda quisti – que carina*," she heard a deep masculine voice say, followed by several others echoing their agreement. Willie turned to see a group of teenage boys eyeing her boldly and smiling.

She smiled her appreciation at being described as adorable and cute and walked on, catching a reflected glimpse of herself in a shop window. A strong, shapely body in mocha-colored linen slacks and matching pullover, enormous blue-green eyes sparkling like gems over high cheekbones, framed by breeze-tossed reddish hair. The reflection affirmed the compliment and the admiring glances. But if it's true, Willie thought, then why am I alone?

She sat at one of the tiny round tables in front of the Quadri café, a small, luxurious gem of a restaurant once favored by such romantic poets as Keats and the Brownings. Sipping a *limonata*, she watched the romance around her quicken in intensity as the night grew shorter. Lovers dancing under a canopy of stars to violin-sweetened melodies, passing silent secrets with their eyes, savoring longings that – for them – would soon be satisfied.

Amidst this unfolding sensuality Willie craved relief from the growing hunger that pressed against the barriers with which she'd surrounded herself. The time with Matt was almost like a dream now. The moments with Jedd were always there, like a part of herself she'd learned to ignore. Both men had failed Willie, convinced her that being alone was the only condition she could trust, yet on nights like this it was hard to care about the reasons that made her a bystander in the game of love.

Above the golden Venetian lion that decorated the fifteenth-century clock tower, a single gong began signalling the hour. Willie looked up and saw the two bronze "Moors" move forward to strike their hammers against the ancient bell eleven more times.

She paid her bill and was about to return to the hotel when she spotted Marion Silverstein, also alone at one of the tiny tables. "Hello again," she said and looked around. "Where's Harvey?"

Marion seemed embarrassed by the question. "Still on the telephone," she said. "It's such a lovely night, and Venice has always been one of my favorite cities. I didn't want to miss everything . . . " Marion gestured toward the empty chair. "Won't you join me?"

Willie sat down. "Mrs. Silverstein . . . Marion, I'm sorry this business with the vineyard cut into your holiday. Believe me, I'll be out of your way as soon as—"

"You're not in my way," Marion interrupted. "I welcome the company." Her smile was gracious and a little wistful.

Although Willie had just met Marion, she was touched by her vulnerability and felt a need to be kind. "I'd like the company, too," she said. "I've never been to Venice . . . It might be fun if we did some exploring together."

"Harvey and I spent our honeymoon in Italy," Marion said. "My father gave us the trip as a wedding present. We were so young and innocent . . . we had such big dreams . . . "

Willie found it hard to imagine Harvey as "innocent," but she could see Marion as a young bride, dewy with hope and ripe for disillusionment. She remembered the fantasies that had brightened Mama's life for so long – but failed to bring more than fleeting happiness when they became real. "It's a funny thing about dreams," Willie said. "Either they never happen or you get what you dreamed of and it isn't what you thought it would be."

Marion looked long and hard at Willie. "You seem young to talk about such disillusionment. If I had a daughter . . . I'd want her to believe that anything was possible, because once you stop believing, there doesn't seem to be anything worth doing . . . "

Willie knew that Marion was talking about herself, but she could have been describing Ginny.

"Have you ever been in love?" Marion asked abruptly.

"Yes." The single word sounded sharp, more defensive than Willie had intended.

But Marion smiled sympathetically, as if she understood all too well the disappointment behind it. "Then you know how it feels to entrust your happiness to someone else, to make that person the cornerstone, the center of everything that matters . . . " She paused to sip her coffee, looking at the couples who drifted through the square.

"It's such an important investment for a woman," Marion continued, "and when it fails, we seem to lose something of ourselves . . . something irretrievable."

Willie nodded, feeling a flicker of recognition in the older woman's words. She had never been able to tell anyone why she was so deeply afraid to trust any man, but Marion seemed to understand just how dangerous and damaging that kind of trust could be.

"You're right," Willie said, "but what's the alternative? To be alone?"

"I've been asking myself the same question," Marion replied. "At my age, it's a hard one to ask. I don't know what it's like to be alone . . . " She hesitated, and then her face became more animated, her eyes brighter as she began to speak again. "I was Nathan Rosen's daughter and then I

346

was Harvey Silverstein's wife. I don't know what it's like to be anything else. I've stayed with a broken dream because I don't have anything else . . . "

Willie thought about her mother, who seemed to feel that life had no meaning without a man. And then she looked at Marion, who seemed to be diminished by living *with* a man. "But if you aren't happy now," she argued, "if you feel alone and lonely already—"

"I know what you're going to say," Marion interrupted, placing a slender hand on Willie's arm, "and you're very kind to care, but there's more than just a marriage involved. That may be a failure, but Marco Enterprises is a great success. Even if I could find the courage to leave Harvey, I couldn't wreck the company my father spent his whole life building . . . "

"I don't understand," Willie said. "Why would leaving Harvey destroy Marco Enterprises? How much of the outstanding stock is his?" As she asked the questions, Willie realized she might be treading on the edge of ethical impropriety: Harvey was her client, and she shouldn't be probing the situation with a state of mind that cared less about his interests than his wife's. But right now she couldn't stop herself from responding to the pull of another woman's need.

Marion shook her head. "It's not that simple," she sighed. "My father intended for Harvey and me to be partners in the business, he set it up that way. But as Marco got bigger, Harvey said a ship could have only one captain. He said he needed control of my shares . . . and now it seems Harvey *is* Marco Enterprises . . . "

"What kind of control?" Willie pressed. "Maybe it's possible to . . . assert yourself more."

"I don't know, Willie. I can't think in those terms yet. It would mean a fight with Harvey . . . and I can't think of what would happen then . . . " She shook her head and looked down.

Willie, too, was stymied. She had compromised her professional obligation enough without offering advice.

Marion looked up. "Thanks for listening. It helps just to

be able to talk to someone . . . Now what about tomorrow? Would you like to go sightseeing?"

As they entered the palatial luxury of the Danieli lobby, Willie was again struck by the beauty of the old wing of the hotel, where the magnificently decorated soaring ceiling and Juliet balconies evoked the splendor of a more elegant time. Though she had estranged herself from love and passion, and though she had just said good night to a woman who had been betrayed by love, Willie felt all the more susceptible to the subliminal suggestions of romance around her.

She took the old-fashioned elevator to her second-floor room and flipped the switch that illuminated the gold-and-white chandelier that hung over the delicately painted Venetian bed.

Too restless to sleep, she stripped off her clothes, dropped them in the terrazzo and marble bathroom, and stepped under a stinging shower. As she lathered her skin with jasmine-scented soap, her body responded with a stirring of desire.

Closing her eyes, Wilie cupped her breasts in her hands, fingering the rosy nipples until they grew firm and hard. Bracing herself against the cool tile wall, she unhooked the shower head and directed its pulsing stream against her inner thighs, then between them, straining for release as her clitoris began to tingle and throb under the steady rhythm of the water. Impatiently, she dropped the shower head and pushed hard with the palm of her hand until she came with a quick, shuddering orgasm that nearly buckled her knees.

Standing naked before the gilt-framed mirror, Willie saw a goddess with tawny golden skin, flushed with warmth and beaded with glistening drops of water. A body made for loving. And though the tensions had slipped away, the blue eyes that looked back at Willie were still filled with need.

It was almost two when she crawled into bed. She lay restlessly awake for a while, then impulsively picked up the telephone and gave the operator the number in New York of Harrigan's apartment, hoping he would be home. It would be nine p.m. in New York.

"Willa, darlin'." Harrigan's voice had a tinny transatlantic echo, but he sounded enthusiastic all the same. "I hear that compliments are in order, my dear."

"Is there any word from the Italian lawyers?" she asked.

"I don't understand," Francis said. "I've already told Harvey we couldn't plug the loopholes, and he instructed me to withdraw the offer. It's all settled – didn't you know?"

Realizing that her client had told at least one outright lie, Willie tried to cover her ignorance smoothly. "I've been taking care of another matter for Harvey . . . I just wanted to make sure everything was covered in New York."

She hung up feeling gratified that her instincts had been on the money where Harvey was concerned. But though it gave Willie some small pleasure to be right, she felt all the more that there was something wrong in using her time and energy in his service.

This wasn't what the years of study and hard work had been about. For Willie, they had been about a call she'd heard in a country courtroom a long time ago – a call that was growing louder in her head as it waited to be answered.

4

Willie woke early and breakfasted on coffee and rolls served in front of the tall, arched windows overlooking the water. She ate slowly, watching the city wake up under the morning sun that dappled the waters of the Grand Canal. The gondolas tossed restlessly, awaiting their first tourists, while the commuters boarded the ferries that would take them to shops and offices, and souvenir vendors set up their wares in the shadow of the Doge's palace.

An idyllic setting for a honeymoon, and Willie wondered whether Marion Silverstein had made her pilgrimage to

Venice out of a last slender hope that her marriage could revive here – or out of desperation. Had she registered more than a gentle protest when Harvey's promise of a holiday proved to be an empty one?

Willie looked forward to spending the day with Marion, but she bitterly resented the way Harvey had lied to both of them. Was he really inspecting a Tuscan vineyard today? For all she knew, Harvey might be off to a rendezvous with a foreign mistress. Willie finished the last of her coffee and went off to offer solace to Marion.

At Willie's knock, the door of the suite was opened almost immediately, as though Marion had been eagerly waiting. She was beautifully dressed in a pants outfit of gray silk, but her eyes looked red and puffy.

Willie wanted to ask why she had been crying, but was afraid the question might embarrass Marion. "Well, where should we start?" she said brightly, trying at once to work up Marion's enthusiasm for some sightseeing. "Shall we go to Murano first?"

"If you like." Marion gave Willie a warm smile, but after last night's shared confidences, she seemed quiet and subdued.

The boat ride to Murano relieved Willie of the need to make small talk. Their guide, a short, balding man in a jaunty red beret, took care of that. At the sight of two women, one distinguished, the other stunningly beautiful, he launched into a nonstop commentary, mingling his touristy descriptions with extravagant compliments in two languages, shouted at the top of his voice to be heard over the roar of the motor.

By the time they disembarked, the morning sun was high in the sky, warming the tiny island and its inhabitants with an anticipatory glow, as they welcomed the boats, hoping that the tourists scrambling ashore would dig deep into their purses and buy with abandon.

The guide, Franco, led Willie and Marion past dozens of tiny shops displaying glassware of every possible shape and size, from vases to candelabra, from overblown cherubs to emaciated saints. Marion dismissed most of these wares

350

with a well-bred lift of her eyebrow and deemed a very few "charming." And though Willie had never been much of a shopper, she admired the older woman's certainty of taste and wished that Ginny could have the same kind of confidence.

By checking his watch and sighing heavily, Franco directed the women away from the shops and toward the Fondamenta dei Vetrai, the street of the glass blowing factories.

"They are the true artists here," the guide explained proudly, as he walked them through a small barnlike building, where a cluster of tourists had already assembled for a demonstration of Murano's single and ancient art.

A slender young man with a Roman profile and jet black hair glistening with perspiration greeted the group with a bow and a rakish grin that stirred Willie's memory of another man's smile.

As the tourists pressed forward for a closer look at the bubbling vat of molten glass, Willie's eyes were drawn elsewhere – to a high forehead and a sharp, perfectly defined nose, a thin cotton shirt open to the waist, a pair of muscular arms gesturing gracefully. Suddenly the artisan turned and looked in her direction with a knowing smile that forced her eyes away in embarrassment. It's this place, she thought defensively, all those violins, all that *amore* in the air, that's what has me staring at a handsome stranger who just happens to look very much like Jedd Fontana.

The young man took a blob of lapis-colored molten glass and laid it on a wooden palette. With a pair of metal tongs, he quickly pulled the stuff as if it were taffy. A pair of legs took shape, then two more. A head followed and a body was formed. With the tongs, the craftsman crimped the neck to shape a mane, pressed on another tiny blob to form a tail. With a final flourish and a smile in Willie's direction, he pulled a tiny horn in the center of the creature's head, and the blob of glass had become a unicorn.

She joined the scattered applause. "*Prego, signorina*," the man said, bowing as he set the blue unicorn on a tiny stand and presented it to Willie, touching her hand a moment longer than was necessary. The glass was still warm, like his fingers. This is crazy, she thought, this isn't *Three Coins in the Fountain* or *Summertime*. If I stay in this place much longer, I'm likely to start picking up strangers.

The demonstration officially complete, Franco invited the "lovely ladies" to buy from the cornucopia of glass shapes that lined the factory walls. Willie declined, but Marion paused in front of a display of bottles. She seemed genuinely interested, as she examined the simple shapes in gemlike colors of ruby and emerald, onyx and amber. "I wonder . . . " she said, almost to herself.

"Very beautiful, good prices," Franco said encouragingly, hopeful of the commission he'd earn on any purchases made by "his" tourists.

"I'll take one of each color," Marion said, thereby earning the guide's gratitude and a fresh wave of flattery.

"They're very pretty," Willie said in a low voice, "but I think Franco's surprised you didn't bargain for them."

"I'm sure," Marion agreed, smiling conspiratorially. "But it hardly seems worthwhile to negotiate for a few small pieces. I was thinking of something on a larger scale," she explained, growing more animated. "Since Harvey's intent on distributing Italian wines, we should launch with something that will make ours unique. We could bottle a limited amount in Venetian glass souvenirs, for our retailers to give out as premiums. We could even send them to food and wine critics."

"What a good idea," Willie said, feeling an almost proprietary pleasure in Marion's enthusiasm. "I'm sure Harvey will think so, too," she added encouragingly.

But the mention of Harvey's name had the opposite effect, driving the smile from Marion's face. She seemed to be on the verge of speaking, then changed her mind and picked up her parcels. As they left the factory, she said: "You know, if we'd had a daughter, she'd be just about your age."

Willie wished that Marion did have a child to give some comfort for the lost years of her marriage. "I can't be your daughter," she said softly, "but I'd like to be your friend."

Tears welled in the older woman's eyes. She squeezed Willie's hand in a silent "thank you."

Marion was quiet during the return trip to Venice, but when they reached the dock, she seemed stronger and brighter, as if she'd resolved to have a pleasant day in spite of her problems. Promising Willie "the best tortellini in Venice," she led the way to a tiny trattoria near the fruit-and-vegetable market along the Ruga degli Orefici, at the foot of the Rialto Bridge.

The food was delicious, the wine relaxing, and Willie found herself talking about her childhood and the years she and Ginny had spent running away from Perry's anger. "That's all behind us now," she said, "but somehow it never seems to go away, not for Mama and not for me . . . "

"I understand," Marion said, looking into Willie's face as if she could see right through the clear blue eyes and beyond. "We all seem to carry those early lessons with us forever. I had a perfect childhood. My parents loved each other deeply and I never doubted they loved me. It never occurred to me that I wouldn't have the same kind of love and happiness in my marriage. I kept thinking 'this is a terrible mistake and one day I'll wake up and it will all be fixed.' "

"Your mother wasn't as fortunate as I was," Marion continued, "but maybe she waits for life to fix her problems for her, too. You're different from both of us, Willie. You learned early not to count on anyone but yourself. You've probably had that lesson more than once . . . "

"Yes," Willie said quietly, "that's exactly how it's been." Strange, she thought, that a woman who had been born to wealth and privilege should understand how she felt.

After lunch they strolled through the narrow street behind the Piazza San Marco. As they passed a tiny jewelry shop, Willie had a sudden impulse to buy Ginny a gift. "My mother would love one of those," she said, pointing to a group of coral necklaces displayed on black velvet. "Will you help me choose?"

"Your mother's a lucky woman," Marion murmured, as the shopkeeper presented a tray of beads for a closer look.

"This one," she said decisively, naming a price that made the merchant sputter with indignation. But when Marion smiled and explained in Italian that the young signorina could afford to pay no more, the man threw up his hands in mock surrender – and the sale was made.

"Thanks," Willie said as they left the shop, thinking how self-assured Marion seemed to be when Harvey wasn't around.

"You're welcome – that was fun. In fact, spending the day with you has been like a breath of fresh air," Marion said, as they walked companionably toward the Doge's Palace.

The day had been well spent for Willie, too. Though she'd offered her friendship as an act of kindness, she felt a growing bond with Marion Silverstein.

They climbed up the Staircase of the Giants that fronted the pink-and-white Palazzo Ducal, admiring the statues of Mars and Neptune sculpted by Sansovino and surveying the city from the very spot where the Doges of the Republic had been crowned.

Inside, they found enormous rooms decorated in gilded stucco, with glorious wall and ceiling paintings – mythical and historical scenes and religious masterpieces by Tintoretto and Veronese.

They finished their tour on a somber note, on the Bridge of Sighs, a baroque construction connecting the Ducal Palace with the Piombi Prison. Here, through the open latticework, condemned prisoners saw their last bit of freedom while they were being led to the dismal dungeons on the other side.

Willie and Marion paused to watch the warm colors of the setting sun reflected in the Rio di Palazzo below. "I suppose we should go," Willie suggested. "Harvey may be back from Tuscany."

Marion didn't move. When she did turn, the expression on her face might have been that of a prisoner, struggling against an unjust sentence. "I don't care," she said. "It doesn't matter if Harvey comes back tonight or tomorrow or the next day. He doesn't come home to me, not really.

Maybe it's time for me to stop hoping for miracles . . . "
Her voice choked off into a sob.

Willie put her arms around Marion and held her, just as
she'd held Ginny so many times. She held out a handkerchief, and as Marion wiped the tears from her face, her
expression became more peaceful.

"I didn't sleep much last night," she said. "I kept
thinking that perhaps I've been a coward . . . making the
business an excuse for staying married because I was afraid
to be alone. And today . . . today I felt less alone and less
afraid. If I were to file for divorce, Willie . . . would you
handle it for me?"

Willie was torn by a deep, wrenching conflict. More than
anything she wanted to say "yes" – but she felt paralyzed by
her professional code of ethics. "Marion," she said softly,
"I want to help you . . . I will help you in any way I can, as a
friend. But Harvey's my client – I can't take any legal action
against him. I could give you the names of other lawyers
. . . I'll make sure they're good people . . . "

"No . . . never mind." Marion brushed the suggestion
away as she struggled to collect herself. "I don't want
another lawyer . . . I'm sorry I put you on the spot," she
said, retreating behind a façade of quiet dignity. "Shall we
go back to the hotel?"

As Marion walked slowly away, Willie noticed that her
packages were still on the bridge. She picked up the parcels
and carried them to Marion. "You forgot your glass
bottles," she said gently.

Marion shook her head. "I didn't forget," she said. "I
just decided it didn't matter any more."

On her first day back at the office, Willie was treated like a
conquering hero. There was an extra bit of deference in the
receptionist's "good morning" and a new edge of respect in
the greetings from the other associates. It was as if
everyone knew she was Harrigan's current favorite, and
Willie took the attention for what it was – fickle and
fleeting, but pleasant while it lasted.

As she sorted through the backlog of correspondence on

her desk, her secretary buzzed the intercom. "There's a phone call from Harvard Law School, Miss Dellahaye. I think it's a fund-raising drive of some kind. Do you want to take the call – or should I take a message?"

"I'll take it," Willie answered without a moment's hesitation. If her law school was looking for contributions, she'd be happy to make one; it was the least she could do to repay the financial help that had been given to her.

The caller identified himself as a Jonathan Claridge, class of '57, and as he made his plea for the scholarship fund, Willie suddenly had an idea.

"Mr. Claridge," she broke in, "I will make a donation – but I'd like it earmarked for the particular scholarship that put me through school. If you'll let me know how to make out the check, I promise you'll have it before the week is up."

"I'll check the school records, Miss Dellahaye," he said, "and I'll get back to you within the hour."

But it wasn't until noon that Claridge called again.

"I have some bad news, Miss Dellahaye," he said. "The scholarship that funded your tuition no longer exists . . . I hope that doesn't mean we'll lose your contribution?"

"No," Willie said, disappointed that she couldn't make the symbolic gesture she'd planned. "You'll have my donation . . . but can you tell me why that particular scholarship was terminated? If it's a question of insufficient funding, I'd be willing to canvas other alumnae to revive it . . ."

There was a moment's hesitation before Claridge answered. "To tell you the truth, Miss Dellahaye, there doesn't seem to be a reason. According to the records, the scholarship was given only once – to you – and then withdrawn."

How strange, Willie thought. Had some large corporation decided to help female law students – and then changed its corporate mind? Or had she proved a disappointment in some way? "Mr. Claridge," she said, "could you tell me the source of the funds? Perhaps I can persuade whoever made the contribution to reconsider . . ."

There was another hesitation. "The scholarship was supposed to be given anonymously," Claridge said, "but I don't suppose there's any harm in telling you now, since you're so keen to help. The donor was listed as 'The Jedd Fontana Trust Fund,' and the address was The Merchants' Bank in Butte, Montana."

A barely stifled gasp was Willie's response to Claridge's revelation, and she hung up in shock, with a mumbled "thank you." For a long time she stared unseeing at the accumulation of work on her desk, as she digested the lie she'd accepted for so long.

All the time she'd been congratulating herself on getting free of Neal's tainted largesse, it had been Jedd's money – Sam's, really – that had financed her law school education.

How superior Jedd must have felt – and how smug – as he made Willie his private charity. Knowing what she knew about the Fontana fortune, she found the position of being in Jedd's debt unbearable.

How dare he, she thought, as she dialed the number of Fontana Enterprises in Montana, how dare he play God in her life! No doubt he inherited the tendency from his father, who seemed to believe that other people lived or died for his convenience.

When the receptionist answered, Willie asked for Jedd, and when the woman said he was out of town, Willie insisted on having a number where he could be reached, wishing she could confront him face-to-face, to tell him exactly what she thought of his charity.

"He's at the Plaza Hotel in New York City," the receptionist said, and Willie smiled grimly at having her wish granted. Impulsively she did something as imperious as Jedd would have done. She called the switchboard at the Plaza and left a message informing Jedd that she would meet him at the Palm Court at five o'clock.

Willie caught her reflection in the lobby mirror as she hurried out of the building that housed Harrigan and Peale. Her cheeks were flushed pink and her aquamarine eyes were shining brightly. She looked almost like a woman in

357

love, yet though she felt driven by a deep and powerful feeling, Willie would have called it anger, this force that drew her to Jedd, even while she could give chapter and verse to the reasons she wouldn't – couldn't – love him.

The Palm Court was a perfect rendezvous for lovers. Cocktails were served in an atmosphere of pastel colors, green plants, and subdued excitement, the piano playing a medley of romantic ballads. But romance was the last thing Willie had on her mind.

Jedd was waiting for her at a corner table, looking as dashing and at ease as if he owned the place. As Willie approached, she could see that a woman at a neighboring table was flirting outrageously and trying to pick him up. But as soon as he caught sight of Willie, Jedd had eyes only for her.

"I can't tell you how great it was to get your message," he said, standing up and leaning toward her, as if to give a friendly kiss.

Willie moved stiffly away. "This isn't a social call," she said, wanting to wipe the confident smile from his face.

"Oh?" he said, the smile still tugging at the corners of his mouth. "Is this a citizen's arrest, counselor? I always seem to be running afoul of your personal brand of justice, even when I think I'm minding my own business."

"But you don't mind your own business," she said, taking the chair he held for her. "How could you?" she demanded. "How could you interfere in my life without so much as a by-your-leave?"

"What are you talking about?" he asked, a look of puzzlement on his face. "Are you mad about that poster I sent? I thought it was kind of cute—"

"What you did wasn't cute at all, Jedd Fontana . . . setting yourself up like some kind of Medici duke, making me into your personal charity. If I'd known where the money for my tuition came from, I would have scrubbed floors before I accepted it."

Comprehension dawned on Jedd's face. And then hurt. "I didn't commit murder," he said softly. "I only wanted to help you, Willie . . . you said you hated taking money from your stepfather, and I thought—"

"Then why didn't you ask if I wanted your help?" she asked heatedly. "I'll tell you why – because you knew I wouldn't take it. Yet you went ahead and did it anyway – because you Fontanas do exactly as you please."

"That isn't true," Jedd protested. "I know how proud you are, Willie. I didn't want you to feel like you owed me anything. I—"

"I'll tell you how I feel right now, Jedd, just so there won't be any more misunderstanding. As far as I'm concerned, your money isn't any better than Neal's – and you'll have it back soon, every penny, with interest." She stood up to leave and added a parting shot. "Next time you decide to go into the charity business, try the Salvation Army – maybe they can help you clean up your act."

5

The executive offices of Marco Enterprises occupied the penthouse suite of a sleek new skyscraper that overlooked Fifth Avenue – a world away from the modest Union Square loft where Nathan Rosen had founded the business. The decor was slick and arrogantly upscale, produced by the latest, trendiest Italian decorator and the hottest young architect working hand-in-hand with Harvey's accountants to produce a setting that reflected his climb into the Fortune 500.

To celebrate Marco's acquisition of Barzani vineyards, Harvey had employed a team of chefs plucked from one of the city's finest hotels. The menu included light-as-a-feather hors d'oeuvres, delicate chicken paillards and thinly sliced fresh tuna, all reflecting the CEO's concern with cholesterol levels, not only his own but those of all his executives.

As soon as Willie returned from Italy, she'd kept her

promise to Nick, and had invited him to this cocktail party. She was glad she had. Without him, the party would have been another routine business function, spent listening to Harvey boast of how the Barzani property had turned out to be an even better deal than the Celestine vineyards.

Now she looked forward to an evening with a man who carried off "black tie" with a careless but appealing jauntiness and whose approving glances at her low-cut black linen sheath reminded Willie that she was a beautiful woman, not simply the work machine she'd been for months.

"This could be boring," she warned Nick, as they pushed their way through the crowd toward the bar that had been set up against a bank of windows overlooking a dazzlingly lit city panorama. "After I pay my respects to Harvey, I have to hang around long enough to satisfy what Francis calls 'the client's sense of proprietorship.' Harrigan believes that makes his bills easier to swallow."

"What about you?" Nick asked, smiling at her cynicism. "What do you believe?"

"I believe . . . " Willie paused, her crystal-blue eyes serious. "I believe that I may be wasting my time learning lessons that aren't for me." Just then she spotted Harvey in a far corner of the room, holding court with a group of Marco executives. "Excuse me," she said to Nick. "The sooner I show myself, the sooner we can get out of here."

He squeezed her arm reassuringly. "Do your stuff," he said. "I'll just nose around all this power and money and see what kind of grist I can pick up."

Willie presented herself at Harvey's shoulder with a dutiful smile. He turned quickly and introduced her to his inner circle of executives. "This young lady saved us plenty of money and headaches," he said emphatically, "and I'm going to see to it that she gets a nice piece of what we're paying Harrigan and Peale."

As Willie acknowledged the flurry of compliments and congratulations that followed Harvey's little speech, she glimpsed Marion a few feet away, looking quite lovely in a simple gown of forest-green silk, as she moved among the

360

guests murmuring greetings. Willie tried to attract her attention with a wave, but Marion's eyes had a distant, lost look that belied the gracious smile on her lips.

Since they'd returned from Italy, Willie had called twice to ask Marion how she was and if there was anything she could do. Their talks had been friendly and pleasant yet somehow distant, as if Marion had retreated into the unhappiness she'd known for so long.

When a lull in the conversation enabled Willie to politely slip away, she looked for Marion, who seemed to have disappeared. Willie stopped at the bar for another glass of white wine, scanning the crowd for Marion's face, half-listening to the cocktail chit-chat around her – until she heard her client's name.

"Another home run for Harvey, this Italian thing," one of the men at the bar was saying. "If he's right about wine sales taking off in the next five years, Marco will lead the pack."

"No doubt about it," his companion answered. "But what do you think the old man is really up to these days? He's taken Marco offshore in a big way. It could make sense tax-wise, but if I know Harvey, he's got something else up his sleeve. Do you think he's planning to sell piña colada mix to Fidel? Or Marco's near-beer to the Saudis?"

"I never second-guess Harvey. But when he gets himself chartered to do business in the Netherlands Antilles, you can be sure he's hiding something."

The words triggered a recent memory for Willie. Marion's plaintive question: "Why Italy?" Why, indeed, Willie wondered. Italian vineyards might be legitimate profit-making ventures, but why was Harvey Silverstein moving Marco Enterprises all over the globe? Was it merely to protect corporate profits from the Internal Revenue Service, or was he hiding something – and from whom?

Willie frowned as she recalled the moment when Marion had mentioned divorce and Marco Enterprises almost in the same breath. Did Harvey suspect that his control over his wife – and her father's company – might be slipping?

Suddenly Willie felt as if she couldn't stay at this party a moment longer, as if she had to get away from Harvey Silverstein and everything he represented.

Willie left the bar and searched the room until she found Nick. "I'm ready to leave," she said. "Just give me a minute to freshen up."

It was in the powder room that Willie saw Marion again. She was sitting in front of a mirrored vanity shelf, staring blankly at her own reflection. Willie put her hand on Marion's shoulder. "Are you all right?" she asked gently.

Marion's face came to life as she covered Willie's warm hand with icy fingers. "Willie," she said. "I've thought about calling you back so often . . ."

"What would you have said?" Willie asked softly.

Marion's eyes answered with twin teardrops that slid down her pale cheeks.

"What's wrong?" Willie asked.

"Everything," Marion whispered. "I can't go on like this . . . I'm going to leave Harvey. I'll need that list of names you mentioned, Willie . . ."

All the questions in Willie's mind came together in a single answer. She put her arm around Marion. "Wait a couple of days," she said. "I want to make sure you have the right person, someone who cares about you as more than a client. It's going to be all right, Marion – I promise."

When Willie rejoined Nick, he was exchanging pleasantries with Harvey. "I've been hearing great things about you," Nick said. "You have one satisfied client here."

"That's only the beginning." Harvey smiled expansively. "I want you to draw up a charter for a new subsidiary. It's a golden opportunity, counselor."

"I already have one," Willie said. "And you're the man who's given it to me. Good night, Mr. Silverstein."

Without waiting for a response, Willie took Nick's arm and steered him into a waiting elevator. Once inside, she began to tremble. "I can't believe I just did that," she said.

"You sure did," Nick said admiringly. "I don't know what or why, but it looks to me like you're about to burn some bridges."

362

"Maybe they needed burning," Willie said, with a determined lift of her chin.

"And maybe you need a friend tonight."

Nick lived in a small well-maintained limestone building a few steps west of Central Park. Willie noticed that there were two names on the bell for his apartment: Rossiter and McDowell. Was McDowell a roommate? she wondered idly, or – more likely – an ex-lover not yet completely erased.

Just as Nick hadn't been exactly what Willie expected, neither was his apartment. The rooms were spacious and well-proportioned, with high, ornately carved ceilings. The place was thoughtfully decorated, and much more personal than her own. A well-worn kilim rug defined a cozy seating area in front of the marble fireplace. Flourishing philodendrons hung from a bentwood coatrack. A collection of tin soldiers filled an old bowfront china closet.

"This is nice," Willie said, settling herself comfortably on a down-filled sofa.

"Be it ever so humble," Nick shrugged, but she could see that he took pride in his home. "What can I get you?" he asked, opening an antique English music case that served as a bar.

"A little brandy, please."

Nick opened a can of beer for himself, then splashed some Courvoisier into a crystal balloon, which he handed to Willie with a flourish. He put a tape of *La Bohème* on the stereo and sat on the sofa, draping his arm casually over Willie's shoulder.

"Aren't you afraid all this will leak out and spoil your image?" she teased.

"Nah," he said. "I'm a writer, not a politician. I'm allowed to be a little eccentric."

She nodded, but her thoughts were elsewhere as she warmed her glass between her palms, looked into the empty fireplace, and remembered the quiet evenings she'd shared with Matt. It hadn't been that long ago, yet it felt like forever. Her life had changed so much, and now it was about to change again. This time the choice was hers, but was she crazy to stake an entire career on a cry from the heart?

"What's on your mind?" Nick asked. "I get the feeling I'm sitting next to this gorgeous woman, but she's really somewhere else."

"Sorry." Willie badly wanted to talk about the conflict that had been building for months, about her need to help Marion Silverstein – and how it had all come together tonight. But she couldn't. "One way or another, men always seem to leave," she said instead, as if that were the subtitle to the story.

Nick looked startled – and then he smiled knowingly, sympathetically. "You've been hurt," he said, drawing Willie a little closer.

"It isn't just me," she said, more to herself than to him. "It seems to happen to every woman who cares . . . "

"Hey," Nick broke in, shaking Willie gently. "Women don't have a monopoly on getting hurt. Maybe they just expect too much. By women's standards, most of us are just no damn good. Maybe the answer is to lighten up and not take it all so seriously."

Nick's face was very close to hers. Willie could feel the roughness of his beard against her cheek, and it seemed natural to let him kiss her. She relaxed in his arms for a little while. There was a question in the air and she knew instinctively that Nick would not push it.

Willie picked up her drink and stood up, almost as if to leave. Instead she walked around the room, inspecting the furnishings and listening to the sweet, lilting Puccini melody, the song of a love that bloomed for a brief moment and then slipped away.

She stopped in front of the floor-to-ceiling bookcase and appraised Nick's books: Charles Dickens, Nathanael West, Mark Twain – and then a neat row of detective novels by Sean McDowell. McDowell . . . the name on the bell. Was there a roommate after all? Willie pulled out one of the books and turned to face Nick. "Do you live with this guy?"

"You're very observant," he said. "McDowell works here on weekends and late at night."

Willie looked around, trying to discern traces of another personality. "What's he like?" she asked.

Nick laughed. "You're looking at him. Nick Rossiter a.k.a. Sean McDowell. It pays the alimony – and it keeps me in a better class of trouble."

"At least this part fits," she laughed with him. "I was beginning to think you were Jekyll and Hyde."

"That's what my ex-wife called me," he said, still smiling, though the laughter had left his eyes. "But you have nothing to fear, beautiful lady. As long as you take my advice and never, ever take me – or any guy – too seriously."

Before she could answer, he crossed the room and circled her waist with his arms. He kissed her again, his mouth strong on her lips, yet still undemanding. He ran his hand up the small of her back, stopping where the shoulders knotted with tension. With the flat of his hand, he massaged deep firm circles across her shoulder blades and up her neck.

It had been such a long time since she'd been held close. She had done without, but her body hadn't forgotten how to waken to a man's touch.

I don't want to be alone tonight, Willie thought, her arms reaching around Nick's neck. Her lips parted, inviting a deeper kiss, as she pressed herself against the starched crispness of his tuxedo shirt.

With a quick movement, he scooped Willie up and carried her into his darkened bedroom. "Lights on or off?" he whispered against her ear.

"Off," she answered, choosing the velvety anonymity of darkness for making love to a man she hardly knew. Yet there was a certainty here, she felt, as she kicked off her shoes and peeled away her stockings. Nick Rossiter was easy and there was no chance that he could hurt her.

She unzipped the linen sheath, let it drop to the floor and moved into Nick's waiting arms. "Beautiful," he murmured, his fingers tracing the outline of her breasts, her waist, the curve of her hips. "Even in the dark, you're beautiful."

"Am I?" she asked, wanting the words, too.

"Magnificent," Nick obliged, easing her onto the bed, "but you need to relax, counselor." He picked up her right foot and began to massage it, beginning with her little toe. With his knuckle he pressed hard into her arch, sending what felt like an electric current up her leg.

"Ouch!" she protested. "What are you doing?"

"Mysterious tricks I learned in the Orient. Trust me – I'm good at this."

Willie lay back on a nest of pillows and let Nick work his oriental magic upon her legs, along her hands and arms and shoulders, alternating massage with little electrical shocks.

She could hear the music drifting softly from the living room, and soon her entire body felt as if it was relaxed and alert at the same time, as if she were floating on a cloud with every nerve ending tingling. "Nice," she said dreamily.

"I told you so."

When he covered her breasts with his hands, she sighed contentedly, feeling deliciously warm. As he traced her nipples, they rose rock-hard to meet his fingertips.

Now Willie wanted more. She turned to meet him, throwing her leg over his thigh, opening herself. He laughed softly. "Slow down, counselor. It's the oriental way."

With his erect penis he parted the soft down of her lower lips and touched the tip to her swollen clitoris. Eagerly she moved against it, abandoning herself to the warm, pulsing sensation that was growing stronger and more intense with every touch. The tension built until Willie's body desperately craved release. She had never been touched like this before.

Finally Nick pushed inside her with a deep-throated groan, cupping her buttocks, thrusting rhythmically until her back arched and her legs stiffened. A few quick, hard strokes and they came almost together, their voices mingled in sharp cries of pleasure.

*　　*　　*

"That was wonderful," Willie said later. "I can't tell you how good I feel."

"See," Nick said, "what some uncomplicated lovemaking with no emotional baggage can do . . . " He put his arms around her and a few minutes later they were both asleep.

About four or five Willie woke up and walked around the apartment, wondering if Marion had ever enjoyed a night like this with Harvey. *Something* about him must have drawn her into marriage and kept her there for so long.

Willie touched Nick's things, wanting to know more, yet half-believing that their lovemaking had been good because they were strangers.

She pulled a Sean McDowell book from the shelf, opened it in the middle, and read a line. "I pushed his back against the wall and shoved my gun against his chin." How puzzling that the man who wrote those words could be such a sensitive lover.

Nick Rossiter seemed to be a decent man, yet Willie believed what he'd said – that a woman who loved him was likely to find Mr. Hyde. She wasn't at risk here, but was the answer to love no one?

Too tired to ponder that question, Willie went back to bed and fell back to sleep nestled against the warmth of Nick's body. She dreamed of Marion, tearful and unhappy. She saw herself, trying to speak words of reassurance and comfort, and as her hand touched Marion's cheek, the face became Mama's.

Willie was wakened by the sunlight streaming through the floor-to-ceiling windows. Seeing Nick beside her was a shock. Sex with a wonderful stranger had been fine in the dark, but by daylight it seemed less important than the fact she didn't know him.

The clock on the nightstand said six. Not wanting to wake Nick, she slid gently out of bed, picked up her clothes, and tiptoed into the bathroom. Hastily Willie washed her face and brushed her hair. There was no time for dawdling today, she thought grimly. She'd have to rush home for a shower and a change of clothes and get herself to the office before Harvey called. She dreaded facing

367

Francis, but there was no turning back now. She put on her underwear and her rumpled dress, another embarrassing reminder that she'd spent the night in a near-stranger's bed.

Willie was tempted to scribble a hasty note and leave, but she decided that would be tacky. She tiptoed back into the bedroom and gently touched Nick's shoulder. He opened his eyes and smiled lazily. When he saw that Willie was dressed, he sat up.

"I'm sorry for waking you up," she apologized, "but I have to get to the office early."

"See," he said ruefully, "women leave, too."

"Touché," she said, then dropped the bantering tone. "Nick . . . thanks for coming to the party with me."

"Thanks for coming to *my* party . . . "

"Hey, be serious a second."

"Why? It's more fun not to be—"

"But I want you to know it made a real difference to me that you were there."

The laugh lines around his eyes smoothed out as he adopted the serious tone she'd asked for. "Does this mean we can be friends?"

"I'd like to be . . . "

He smiled again. "Even if you commit the decidedly unfriendly act of having your way with me, then sneaking out of my bed at the crack of dawn?"

Willie laughed, losing the awkwardness she'd felt a moment before. "Exactly," she said. "On those conditions, I think . . . for the present, Mr. McDowell-Rossiter . . . that I might have a beautiful friendship." She leaned over and gave him a quick kiss. "With both of you."

6

Willie hadn't realized that certainty could be as unsettling as doubt and confusion. She was sure that leaving Harrigan and Peale was right, but she knew that telling His Eminence she was about to defect would be an ordeal. Although Harrigan often infuriated her, she respected his skills and even felt a kind of adversarial affection for him. He was full of blarney, he was full of guile, but he had a peculiar kind of integrity. Harrigan presented himself as a showman. It was understood he would do parlor tricks and sleight-of-hand when necessary, and he never pretended to be more righteous than he was.

Shortly after a buzz from Harrigan's secretary alerted her to his arrival, Willie went straight to his office. "I have to talk to you," she said solemnly.

"Of course, Willa dear," he said expansively. "Sit right down."

Willie sat and mustered her nerve. "Francis—"

"No, let me speak first, Willa. Because I can no longer contain the pleasure of informing you of the ten-thousand-dollar bonus you are to receive, compliments of Marco Enterprises. And though my vanity is wounded, I'll admit you've replaced me in Harvey Silverstein's affections. However, I've just had a rather puzzling phone call from himself. He tells me you didn't exactly jump with joy when he mentioned your next assignment—"

"That's what I wanted to tell you," she interrupted. "I won't be handling any more assignments from Harvey Silverstein."

"You will if you want to stay in this office," Harrigan said without a change from his pleasant tone.

"That's right to the point, Francis. You've taught me a lot, but I want to go out and use it."

"Go out . . . " Harrigan echoed. Though he was an expert at feigning incredulity, his astonishment now seemed to be genuine. "What are you talking about, Willa dear? You couldn't be so foolish as to leave me." He lowered his voice as though sharing a confidence. "I shouldn't be telling you this so early in the game, but you'll be a partner here in a few short years. Do you know what that means? At least a hundred and fifty thousand per annum, not to mention the prestige and power of this office."

"I appreciate all of that," Willie said, her chin jutting out stubbornly, "but my mind's made up, I'm resigning. I'm going to practice the kind of law that means something to me." As she said the words, Willie knew she'd done the right thing.

Harrigan appraised his youngest associate for a quiet moment that made her uneasy. "You understand this is going to create problems with Silverstein for me, though I haven't the slightest doubt we'll keep his business in spite of your departure. That's the kind of . . . predicament I don't take kindly. Brings out my Irish, Willa, might even cause me to think of making your life equally difficult. I could, you know . . . "

"Oh, I know, Francis. Through your friends in high places I can imagine you've got a very long reach indeed – a reach probably exceeded only by the length of your memory."

Harrigan nodded pridefully.

"I also know there's not a damn thing I can say that will stop you if you decide to use your power against me." She edged forward on her chair. "But I'm hoping you won't, Francis. Because I want a chance to use all that you've taught me in a very different arena from the one where you work. And nothing you can say, no threat, not even the use of your most awesome weapon – that wily Irish charm of yours – can change my mind."

Harrigan spent another moment staring her down. Then,

suddenly, he was all broad smiles and effusive Gaelic goodwill. "Ah, well, what's the use of hard feelings? Enough of that in this cruel world we live in. Sad I am to lose you, but I wish you well, my dear." He paused for a moment. "May I ask if it's storefront law you'll be practicing after all my best efforts to the contrary?"

"No," she said, "you were probably right about that, Francis. But you might say I've found my calling. I can't tell you any more right now . . . client confidentiality. But thank you," she added, extending her hand, "thank you for being so gracious. Let's say I owe you one."

Harrigan took her hand and squeezed slightly harder than a gesture would require, as if to give Willie a farewell reminder that he was bigger and stronger than she was. "I'm glad you said that," he smiled. "It seems you have learned a thing or two after all."

As she left his office, Willie wondered how long the goodwill would last when he learned that her first client was Marion Silverstein and that she'd be representing her against her husband, one of Harrigan's biggest clients.

In Marion Silverstein's Park Avenue penthouse, Willie could see the story of her marriage to Harvey. The apartment was enormous and opulent, surrounded by a terraced garden, but it was less a home than a reflection of Harvey's constant striving for class and status. Marion's inherent good taste had been overwhelmed by the things Harvey could buy – hard-edged modern furnishings, paintings by trendy contemporary artists – just as her personality had been all but obliterated by his overbearing need for control.

The more Willie spoke to Marion, the more she reminded her of Mama. Yes, she was wealthy and well educated, but like Ginny she had invested herself completely in a man. Marion was intelligent enough to have taken an active part in Nathan Rosen's company, yet because Harvey hadn't wanted her there, she'd stepped aside. Now, as Ginny had done, Marion seemed to be teetering on the edge of emotional bankruptcy because her marriage had failed.

371

Sitting in Marion's living room sipping tea, Willie tried to focus the conversation on the documents that were spread out on the coffee table – tax returns, bank accounts, and year-end reports for Marco Enterprises. But Marion was caught up in recalling her marriage, retreating into the past and resisting Willie's gentle attempts to move her forward.

"It was different in the beginning," Marion was saying. "Harvey and I were very close then. He was very attentive then, always asking my advice about this or that, so eager to do the right thing . . . " Her voice trailed off in a wash of memories.

Willie waited patiently, understanding Marion's need to make peace with her past.

"I don't know when things changed," she continued. "After Papa died, Harvey seemed to need me even more. He was president of Marco then, but he cared so much about what people thought of him. He'd ask me to pick out his suits and ties, even the books he read. And then" – her voice broke – "he stopped asking."

Willie held Marion's hand. "That wasn't your fault," she said.

Marion's eyes were glazed with pain and self-doubt. "I can't be sure of that. My parents were so happy, so close. I tried to be the kind of wife my mother was, but maybe Harvey needed something else—"

"He could have asked," Willie cut in, wanting Marion to feel angry, to feel cheated – and more than anything, to fight. "He took everything you had to offer," she went on, making her voice hard, her words harsh. "Without you, he would have been just a hungry nobody. With bad teeth!" she finished, remembering the shiny caps that had probably been bought with Marion's money.

Marion smiled in spite of her pain. "Maybe you're right, Willie – but doesn't that make me a stupid fool for choosing him?"

"No! You made a wrong choice, and now we're going to fix that . . . "

" . . . and I'll live happily ever after? I think not."

Willie felt the same stubborn impatience that Mama

evoked. Why couldn't Marion see there *was* a life ahead, one she could shape as she chose? Why did it always have to revolve about a man?

"No matter what you say, I think you can be a winner, Marion. I know you're feeling bad . . . that's natural. Your marriage is over. You made that your whole life, but now you can do something different. You're smart and attractive and wealthy – use those resources, for heaven's sake!"

Marion smiled again. "Ah, Willie, when you talk like that, I can almost believe in—"

"Believe in yourself," Willie said passionately. "I do. I quit my job to get you the kind of divorce settlement you deserve. The chance for a fresh start. Take it, Marion, please take it." Willie pleaded desperately, as she'd pleaded so many times with her mother.

But unlike Ginny, Marion showed a glimmer of response. "I'll try," she said, picking up a sheaf of tax returns, "I promise I'll try. Now what do you need to know?"

For the next three hours, the two women pored over all the documents that Harvey's lawyer – Steven Jessup, the chief of Harrigan and Peale's matrimonial division – had provided at Willie's request, as well as all the records Marion had kept during the years of her marriage. The picture they provided was incomplete, and Willie knew that the missing parts were far more important than what she had in hand.

Willie was sure that Harvey had married for ambition and money and power – and that his intentions now were to get rid of Marion and to keep a very big piece of Marco Enterprises for himself.

Getting evidence that would support her certainty was another matter. Nathan Rosen had left fifty-one percent of his company to his daughter, the remainder to his son-in-law. Marion had made it all too easy for Harvey to deceive and cheat her when she'd given him voting control of her legacy.

As Willie looked over the company's last annual report, she said a silent "thank you" for the corporate experience she'd gained at Harrigan and Peale – which now made the names of several Marco subsidiaries leap up at her as if they'd been flagged in red. Regency Insurance, chartered in Bermuda; Conrad Consulting, in the Netherlands Antilles; Star Management, chartered in Gibraltar.

On more than one occasion, Willie had helped construct elaborate corporate webs that allowed clients to shelter money from U.S. taxes. She knew how such "creative structuring" could be made to disappear, become almost impossible to trace.

Backed only by Marion's substantial retainer and her own modest savings, Willie launched her private law practice. She combed the *New York Times* classified ads for "Space to Share" and found exactly what she needed at the office of Acme Insurance, in a modest art deco building on lower Fifth Avenue.

After a short meeting with Harold and Jake Jenner, who ran Acme, Willie struck a deal. For $300 a month, she got her name painted in gold letters on the door, underneath those of the brothers Jenner, a desk near a window, a telephone, and part-time help from Acme's secretary.

Best of all, Willie got an introduction to Acme's claims investigator, Larry Kusack, who'd been mustered out of the New York police force with a bullet-shattered knee and a disability pension. Kusack was a plain, soft-spoken man in his late forties, a tireless researcher with an information network built up during his years on the force, with pipelines into city and state bureaucracy as well as ties to people who sold information for money.

He had the kind of unremarkable, easy-to-forget face that made him excellent at surveillance, and an unerring eye for liars and phonies – all of which made him the kind of investigator lawyers dreamed of having.

At their first meeting, Willie learned that Kusack lived in Brooklyn's Park Slope and that he was the divorced father of two children. As if he sensed that Willie was ready to hold these facts against him, Kusack quietly added: "The divorce was my wife's idea, counselor, and I couldn't blame her. Being married to a cop isn't easy, but I still care about Sally and I love my kids. Divorce can be an ugly business, but when two nice people can't make it together, sometimes calling it quits is the only way they can make peace."

Kusack seemed sincere and genuine, but in spite of her cynicism about love and marriage, Willie rebelled against his point of view. "How can you love somebody and walk away?" she asked. "How can you turn love on and off like a faucet?"

Kusack sighed heavily, as if he'd wrestled with questions like this before. "You don't walk away, Miss Dellahaye, you just do the best you can. I live two blocks away from Sally and the kids. We see each other every Sunday and we still call each other when we're lonely or down in the dumps. It hurts that we're not a real family anymore, but like I said, you just do the best you can."

Though Kusack's answer didn't ease the questions that had nagged at Willie's heart for as long as she could remember, it seemed as honest as the man himself.

She wrote a check for a small retainer and handed it over. "It isn't much," she apologized, "but I hope to have more clients and more work for you soon."

"I believe you will," Kusack smiled. "You look like a winner to me, Miss Dellahaye, and I can always spot 'em. Now what about this first job – what do you need?"

"My client's suing for divorce – I think of it as a preemptive strike. Her husband's a sleazy guy and I think he's been planning to leave her for a long time . . . "

" . . . And?"

"And there's a major corporation and a lot of money at stake. I think there's breach of a fiduciary trust and fraud. What I have is circumstantial," she said, handing over a copy of Marco Enterprises' latest annual report. "A bunch of offshore charters that could be legitimate tax dodges, but my gut says Harvey Silverstein's used them to steal from his wife. I need hard facts that show how it's been done and numbers that show how much. Without those facts, all I can show is that the husband's not a nice person. Can you handle it?"

375

"I can handle it," Kusack said. "If there's evidence to find, I'll find it." Coming from this quiet, unprepossessing man, the words sounded solid and reassuring.

Willie shook hands with her new investigator, impressed that he used the word "evidence." She remembered a lecture F. Lee Bailey had given at Harvard Law. "There's a difference between information and evidence," Bailey had said emphatically, "and it can be the difference between winning and losing a case."

Willie intended to win. This was more than her first private case, and Marion was more than just a client. Whatever it took, she would deliver on every promise she'd made – and open justice's eyes to the kind of wrongs Willie had seen so vividly a long time ago.

And, she would earn enough money to settle her debt to Jedd Fontana.

7

It was a day of gains and losses. Larry Kusack had sniffed out Harvey's trail of petty infidelities and found a bigger one: a mistress ensconced in a Federal townhouse over-looking the Charles River in Boston. "I have it all on paper," he said. "The house is owned by Marco Enter-prises, the woman's bills are paid from corporate accounts, her telephone records—"

"Terrific," Willie said. "That'll get us a judgment of divorce. But what about the money, Larry? I need to show that Harvey's a crook, not just a philanderer."

"Patience, counselor. Our man may be a crook, but he's a smart one. Those dummy corporations fit together in a Chinese puzzle that would make Robert Vesco proud."

"Find the seams, Larry," Willie said urgently. "Go to Bermuda if you have to, but get me what I need."

"Relax, counselor," Kusack said quietly. "Even the

smartest ones make mistakes, and finding mistakes is what I'm good at."

Willie believed that Kusack would deliver on his promises.

But when she called to tell Marion an easy divorce was assured, her client seemed more stricken than triumphant. "A mistress?" she repeated. "My Harvey has a mistress?"

"I'm sorry," Willie said. "I know it hurts to hear these things, but that's all behind you now. We're going to win, Marion, and we're going to make Harvey pay for everything he's done . . . "

Willie talked for a long time, trying to bolster Marion's morale, to make her believe in her own future. But when she hung up, Marion was on the brink of tears.

Remembering Harvey's hand on her knee, Willie found it hard to believe that his wife had been so unsuspecting. Yet hadn't Ginny, too, refused to admit what kind of man Neal had been, even after he'd made her part of his shabby, perverted games?

That's never going to happen to me, Willie thought. If I can't find a man who's good and decent, I'd rather have no one at all.

When it was time to dress for a date she had made with Nick, Willie tried hard to get into a party mood. A date with Nick called for a certain etiquette, no emotional baggage being one of the cardinal rules. It wasn't that Nick was shallow or superficial or incapable of friendship. But while he was the sort of man who would gladly lend a hundred dollars, help a buddy find a job, or even put himself out to do a personal favor, he drew the line at the kind of emotional clutter that would tangle him in someone else's life.

Most of the time that suited Willie just fine. She wasn't in love with Nick, so she needed none of her usual defenses. She could relax and enjoy the pleasures of being occasionally and lightly coupled.

As she showered off the day's tensions, Willie tried to lose the frustration that lingered whenever she talked with Marion. She couldn't live Marion's life for her, yet she felt

377

like a doctor, knowing she could cure one symptom – and then have the patient insist on keeping the rest.

She wrapped herself in a thick white bath sheet and rubbed her skin until it tingled. She wiped her face with cold witch hazel – one of Mama's beauty tips – and applied her makeup, the bronze blusher, a smudge of gunmetal shadow that made her blue eyes look deep-set and mysterious, and two coats of mascara. In spite of all Willie's militant independence, she found that when there was a man in her life, she spent just a little more time in front of the mirror and cared a little more about the results.

She slipped into a silk jumpsuit of a cobalt blue that looked almost electric against her tawny skin and coppery hair. When she was satisfied she looked just right for the *Village Crier* anniversary party, she locked the door and ran downstairs to look for a cab. Going out with Nick Rossiter was pleasant enough, but Willie had quickly learned that it meant a tradeoff in certain niceties – like being picked up for a date.

The party was at Miranda's, one of the myriad new night-clubs springing up in SoHo. Once occupied by commercial buildings and artists' lofts, the neighborhood was taking on a new life and identity, as shabby old stores became chic galleries displaying the work of underground artists and trendy boutiques featuring the creations of bold new designers. Gossip columnists trekked nightly to SoHo, in search of tidbits from the rich and the celebrated – from ex-mayor John Lindsay to Andy Warhol – who rubbed elbows in the neighborhood's restaurants and clubs.

As her taxi turned into Greene Street, Willie could see the clusters of kids that hung around Miranda's, hoping to gain admittance or at least to catch a glimpse of a passing celebrity.

As Willie presented her invitation to a formidable-looking doorman, one of the teenagers called out; "Hey, are you anybody?"

"I try," she answered with a smile.

Lighting in the club was almost nonexistent, the decibel level of the music deafening, but ever since she'd returned from Italy, Willie had tried to be more open about new experiences.

The costumes she glimpsed made her smile. Marabou feathers worn with skintight jeans, black leather with lace, tie-dyed tuxedos and tennis shoes.

The sections of the club were strung together like a maze, and only by asking directions twice did Willie find the *Crier* party – in what looked like a pink-lit museum room, with photographs and pop culture displays set behind glass. Nick was enjoying the obvious adoration of a very young girl in a black ruffled prom dress, but when he saw Willie, he broke away and came to greet her.

"I'm not interrupting anything important?" she teased, confident because she didn't feel any kind of proprietorship where Nick was concerned.

"Nah – the kid's just a fan. We literary types have our groupies, too, you know. Dance?"

The tape was blasting the latest Supremes hit, and Nick danced with an easy sensuality, just the way he made love. Willie noticed that the young girl in the ruffled dress was watching with an envious wistfulness, and that several other female partygoers seemed to have more than a passing interest in Nick – and, by association, in her.

"How big is your fan club anyway?" Willie asked. "If looks could kill, I'd be flat out on this floor."

Obviously pleased, Nick executed a few fancy steps, then finished with an old-fashioned dip, acknowledging the scattered applause with a jaunty wave. "It's all part of my plan to show you what a popular guy I am," he said, leading Willie to the buffet table.

"I'm impressed. I can see you're a real heartbreaker," she said, helping herself to some cheese and crackers.

"Who's the gorgeous creature, Nick? Introduce us at once or you're off my party list." The voice belonged to a tall woman with an elfin face and a slender, muscular body.

"Hey, Betty, give me a break," Nick laughed. "Go find your own dates – Willie's with me."

"Fresh!" The woman playfully punched Nick's shoulder and smiled at Willie. "Pay no attention to him – I never

379

poach, not even from a rascal like Nick. I'm Betty Lockwood, and your face is familiar. Are you in show business?"

"I'm Willie Dellahaye, and no, I'm not in show business. I'm a lawyer."

"A lawyer?" Betty laughed with delight. "That's it – I saw your picture in the papers a while back. My astrologer was right – this is a lucky day. Nick, be a prince and go flutter a few hearts somewhere. Give me a minute with your lawyer friend, please?"

Seeing Nick's hesitation, Willie said: "It's okay – just be sure to come back."

"Thanks," Betty said when he'd left. "Nick's a good guy – as a friend, if you know what I mean."

Willie smiled. "I know exactly what you mean. What can I do for you?"

Betty Lockwood's expression became serious. "Listen," she said, "I know it's tacky to bother doctors and lawyers at parties, but I have a problem, and I've been trying to get my courage up for weeks to ask somebody about it."

Willie waited expectantly.

"How old do you think I am?" Betty asked.

Willie knew that people told their stories in their own way, so she studied the woman carefully. "Hard to tell," she answered truthfully, "but you're in great shape, whatever age you are."

"I'm a dancer, twenty-two years' worth. Mostly chorus, a few feature spots, a standby gig for Gwen Verdon, and a couple of commercials. I'm forty-three years old, Willie. The legs still look great, but every morning the body feels like it's been run over by a sixteen-wheeler."

Willie murmured sympathetically and waited for the rest.

Betty took a deep breath and exhaled it slowly. "I guess you picked up that I'm gay from what Nick said. The thing is . . . I've been living with Margo Hawkins for fifteen years . . . "

Willie recognized the name of Broadway's leading choreographer, a woman who'd had at least a dozen hit shows and won four Tony awards.

380

" . . . and last month she asked me to move out."

"I'm sorry," Willie said, "that must have been rough."

"You could say that." In sadness, Betty Lockwood's face suddenly showed all the years her dancer's body belied. "The thing is," she pressed on, "I feel like I deserve better than that. I was like a wife to Margo. I took care of everything she was too busy to do . . . the apartment, the bills, her correspondence. I even helped her block out routines for her shows. It doesn't seem right that I'm turned out into the street after all this time . . . "

"What happened?" Willie asked softly. "Did you have a quarrel?"

Tears welled up in Betty's eyes. "I wish that's all it was. No, it's the same old boring story. Margo met somebody younger, and you know the funniest thing of all?" Now Betty's tears were falling freely. "She looks enough like me to be my daughter."

Willie felt Betty Lockwood's heartbreak as if it were her own. And yet there was no man behind it – just a betrayal of love and another shattered dream. "How can I help?" Willie asked.

"I don't know . . . I read about gay guys getting married in San Francisco. It was just like that with Margo and me. She said we were partners. Then she picks up some new kid, and I'm left with a year, maybe two, tops, in my career. It doesn't seem fair . . . "

Willie thought for a moment. The courts had never recognized the rights of heterosexuals who lived together without marriage, let alone gays. Maybe it was time they did, she decided. "It isn't fair," she said. "Come to my office tomorrow. Bring your tax returns and all the cancelled checks you have and let's see what we can do." Willie gave Betty Lockwood her business card and set off to reclaim Nick from yet another female admirer.

"Thanks for inviting me," Willie said as they left the club. "I had fun – I may have a new client."

Nick looked puzzled for a moment. "You mean Betty? What does she want a lawyer for?"

"No you don't, Mr. Rossiter. You get a 'thank you' and that's it. The rest is between Betty and me. And you'd better remember that – or else."

"Okay, okay, I don't want you getting mad at me again. But if you ever have any journalistic tidbits 'on the record', I want them first. Promise . . . ?"

"Promise."

"Now that we understand each other, can I entice you to spend the night at Chez Nick?"

"I'd like to," Willie said, "but I have an eight o'clock appointment . . . "

"You could invite me to your place." This was more a reproach than a suggestion, for Willie had avoided taking Nick home, almost as if she'd made her apartment off limits, a measure of how unserious this affair was.

"Okay," she decided.

"Nice place," Nick said, surveying Willie's apartment. "Rent controlled?" He asked the New Yorker's typical question.

"Rent stabilized."

"Doesn't look much like you, though," he observed.

"You have a good reporter's eyes, Mr. Rossiter. Only the books and plants are mine. The rest was here when I moved in."

"Busy career woman, huh? No time for nest-making – or no interest?"

"Good questions," Willie answered, "but the answers are private. Remember – you're the one who doesn't believe in emotional baggage, and when you start poking around, you don't know what you'll find."

Nick didn't say anything more, and Willie wondered if she might have hurt his feelings. "Can I get you a drink?" she offered, trying to soften her last words. "I don't have any beer . . . "

"Brandy's okay."

She gave Nick a snifter of brandy and went to check her telephone answering machine. There were two messages, both from Ginny, both saying the same thing: "Please call me, honey, I really need to talk to you."

Immediately Willie dialed the Palm Springs number. Ginny had a funny blurry sound in her voice, and Willie couldn't tell if she'd been drinking or if she was just down, the way she'd been so often lately. "Where were you, baby?" she asked. "I needed to talk to you so bad, and I was worrying you might not call me back, and I didn't know what I'd do . . . "

Willie listened for a while and then asked, "What's wrong, Mama?"

Ginny sighed. "I don't know, honey . . . it's just that nothin' much is right."

"Why don't you come to New York for a few weeks?" Willie suggested. "You could do some buying for the boutique . . . I'll get tickets to a couple of shows . . . I bet you'd love 'Gypsy' . . . "

"I can't do that," Ginny said plaintively. "Who's gonna take care of the shop?"

"Are you doing a lot of business?" Willie asked, hoping to get her mother on a positive tack.

"It's a graveyard," Ginny answered bitterly. "Now that I'm not married to Neal anymore, all of his society friends are snubbing me and my boutique."

"Well, if you aren't doing much business, why don't you just close the place for a couple of weeks?"

There was no answer. Willie understood that Ginny wanted her to come to Palm Springs. "Listen, Mama," she said, "I'm in the middle of an important case right now, something that means a lot to me. But as soon as I'm finished, I'll fly out to be with you for Christmas. Just the two of us . . . like old times. We'll think of a way to make things right for you, I promise. Try to cheer up a little . . . please?"

"You're a good girl, Willie," Ginny said, sounding blurry again. "You were always so good to me . . . "

When Willie hung up, Nick was standing behind her.

He asked no questions and made no comments on the

conversation he'd overheard. He simply put his arms around Willie and began stroking her neck.

It was all she needed from him.

8

For weeks, Willie ate, drank and slept the Silverstein case. She allowed herself only the occasional dinner with Nick and frequent long phone calls to Ginny.

And while she prepared the legal documents that would free her client from a loveless and demoralizing marriage, she spoke to Marion almost every day, giving transfusions of hope – and assurances that divorce could be a beginning, as well as an end.

This is how it should be done, Willie thought, remembering how vulnerable and frightened Mama had been when her marriages had broken apart. Willie knew that other lawyers might disagree – or even say it was unprofessional to care more about the client than the case. But for her they were one and the same. She met several times with Harvey's lawyer, Steven Jessup, in an attempt to reach a settlement. But between what Willie thought was fair and what Jessup was willing to offer, there seemed to be a world of difference. For Willie, the most important issue was to regain for Marion control of her shares in Marco Enterprises, and for Jessup this issue appeared to be non-negotiable.

The battle of Silverstein vs. Silverstein began on a crisp autumn day. Jessup brushed past Willie on the steps of the Supreme Court in lower Manhattan. He stopped and smiled confidently. "Do yourself a favor, counselor," he said. "Spare your client a lot of grief . . . you know how ugly it gets when matrimonial linen gets washed in public. Get serious about a settlement."

"You get serious, Steve," Willie said grimly. "I haven't seen any fair settlement offers and you know it. Your client's the one with dirty linen . . . maybe he hasn't told you just how much there is . . . "

The flicker in Jessup's eye told Willie she had struck home. Jessup probably knew about Harvey's infidelities, but she doubted very much that Silverstein had admitted how he'd used Marion's corporate stock to enrich himself.

But Willie knew. Thanks to Kusack's painstaking investigation, she had enough documentation locked up in her office to wipe the confident smile off Jessup's face.

She went into the courtroom and presented an opening statement that was terse and crystal clear. Harvey Silverstein, she said, was a man who married for money, who used and exploited his wife, who was cruel and neglectful and who not only committed adultery, but used funds from the company founded by his father-in-law to finance his love nest and buy his mistress expensive gifts. Willie asked for a divorce on the grounds of adultery and mental cruelty, requesting the Park Avenue apartment, half of the remaining marital assets, and spousal support in the sum of $150,000 per year. She also asked for the return of custodianship of Marion's stock.

Willie watched the judge's face as Jessup made his opening remarks, painting Marion as a neurotic and unsatisfactory wife – the kind of wife, he implied, who drove her husband into the arms of other women. She heard a sharp intake of breath beside her when Jessup mentioned a history of psychiatric care. Quickly she turned to Marion with a silent question. The answer was in her client's stricken expression.

"Why didn't you tell me?" Willie asked during a brief recess.

"I . . . it was a long time ago," Marion answered, her face pale with worry. "Oh, Willie, I was so unhappy . . . I thought a psychiatrist might help. I begged Harvey to go, too, but he wouldn't. I never dreamed he'd bring it up now . . . "

"It's okay," Willie said reassuringly, "it's no crime to be unhappy when you're married to a man like Harvey. Jessup hasn't got anything . . . he's trying to appeal to the judge's male chauvinism, and I won't let him get away with it, Marion. That's a promise."

Jessup's smile dimmed when Willie put Larry Kusack on the stand. Contrasted with Willie's intensity and anger, Kusack's quiet demeanor was startlingly effective. Under questioning he revealed and documented, piece by piece, a story of Harvey's affairs, "first cabin" and paid for out of corporate funds. Strangely enough, it was Kusack's dry and factual recitation – unshakable throughout cross-examination – that made Harvey's infidelities seem all the more tawdry.

That impression lingered in the courtroom throughout Harvey's testimony. Even with Jessup's coaching, Harvey did not stand up well under questioning, and his complaints about Marion seemed whiny and self-serving.

When court adjourned for the day, Jessup approached Willie. "Half the marital assets and a hundred thousand a year alimony," he said tersely. "Is that an offer you can live with?"

"What about control of Mrs Silverstein's corporate stock?" she asked. "Is your client ready to sign that over?"

"No way," Jessup said emphatically. "Harvey Silverstein made that stock a winner, and he's not about to hand it over to a woman who knows beans about the business. These folks may be getting a divorce counselor, but as I see it, they're staying married in business."

"We'll just have to see," Willie said with a smile. "Meanwhile, I'll pass your offer on to my client."

"It's up to you," Willie said to Marion. "I'm sure I can get more alimony, but I don't think Harvey will budge on the stock unless we hit him with everything we've got . . . "

Marion hugged Willie. "Then do it. I don't care about the money . . . I'll have more than enough for the rest of my life no matter how this case turns out. I want my father's company back. I want to win, Willie, and I think you do, too."

Willie did. The following morning she launched her surprise attack. As Harvey approached the courthouse, she had Kusack serve him with notice of a second suit – charging

386

that he'd breached his fiduciary trust and demanding return of the stock along with $10 million in damages.

Willie watched with pleasure as Harvey turned frantically to his attorney and began shouting and gesturing wildly. Photographers began snapping photographs and reporters pushed forward with questions. Jessup hurried his client into the courthouse, trying to fend off the press with a terse "no comment."

Within the hour he called for a recess and cornered Willie in the corridor. "What's your bottom line?" he asked. "What will it take to close out both suits today? Right now?"

"Yesterday you could have settled for what we asked for in court," Willie said. "Today it'll cost you five million more . . . I can prove your client salted away at least that much. Tomorrow . . . shall I go on?"

"No." Steven Jessup was subdued. He appraised Willie for a long moment. "You look like a beautiful woman, but you think like a shark. Harrigan lost a real prize when you left."

"No," she said, "you've got that wrong, Steve. I just try to outflank the sharks and protect my clients from getting eaten up. Shall I draw up the necessary papers?"

As Willie sat down to prepare a bill for the matter of Silverstein vs. Silverstein, she realized that she and Marion had never discussed a fee. Though a percentage of the settlement surrounding the Marco stock might well have been reasonable, Willie felt she couldn't ask it now. Instead she simply multiplied the hours she'd logged by $150, the sum Harrigan and Peale had charged for her services – and added Kusack's investigative fees plus expenses. The total came to just under $100,000.

The size of Marion's settlement and the hint of malfeasance was enough to feed the gossip columns – and to stimulate wild speculations in the business press.

"Ignore it," she advised Marion. "Don't talk to reporters,

don't give them anything new, and soon they'll get tired of rehashing stale information."

But when Willie picked up a *Village Crier* and turned to Nick's column, she found it impossible to take her own advice. Alongside the picture of Nick's smiling face was a headline that made her own face darken with anger: "Can a Woman's Heartbeat Dictate the Beat of the Street?" The story that ran under it made her livid:

"After a string of success stories, Marco Enterprises saw its corporate stock take a nosedive this week. The reason? Not a rise in grape prices or a truckers' strike – it was a divorce between Marco's CEO, Harvey Silverstein, and his wife of thirty-odd years, Marion. This reporter wonders if we're seeing a strange new phenomenon, where a dying marriage can trigger a hemorrhage of the body corporate.

"By all accounts, CEO Silverstein built a mom-and-pop operation into an industry giant. Yet now his failures as a husband have clouded his success as a corporate animal. Is this the beginning of a trend? Will General Motors or IBM be next?

"Will the beautiful attorney-crusader, Willa Dellahaye, emerge as the Clarence Darrow of divorce litigation? Are we hearing echoes of the Scopes Case and witnessing a new evolution of Woman?"

Willie crumpled the paper and threw it into the wastebasket. She dialed Rossiter's number and let her anger spill out. "How could you write that stuff?" she demanded. "How dare you take something I care about and sensationalize it with cheap satire? I thought you were my friend, Nick, but *this,* this is really low . . . "

"Are you done?" he asked quietly, when she slowed down. "I don't see it that way, *Miz* Dellahaye. I don't tell you how to do your job, and I don't see that our friendship gives you license to tell me how to do mine. Your case was news, and that's what I write about, lady. And just for the record, if you expect me to show up for dinner tonight, I think you owe me an apology–"

"Owe *you* an apology? Of all the nerve . . . you can just

forget dinner and everything else, *Mr.* Rossiter." Sputtering with indignation, Willie hung up the phone.

Men! she thought. You couldn't trust them even if you weren't in love with them.

9

Overnight Willie became a star. The matter of Silverstein vs. Silverstein had all the ingredients adored by the media – money and power and a touch of scandal. And a beautiful heroine, the lawyer, photographed with one arm thrown protectively around her client's shoulder, the other raised in an angry fist – provoked by an overly aggressive reporter – a hallmark image to capture the public imagination.

Willie's phone began ringing incessantly with the first wave of newspaper stories and hadn't stopped ringing since. The demand for her services, which began with a few of Marion's friends, grew suddenly into an epidemic of women who had read her name or seen her face on the six o'clock news.

Some were wealthy, others were not. What they all had in common were unhappy marriages. The word of mouth was that Willa Dellahaye was different, that she wasn't part of the old-boy legal network where two lawyers would sit down over lunch and work out a settlement that was convenient for them. Willie would fight – with a vengeance. And suddenly it was as if women who were afraid to fight for themselves now saw Willie as their champion.

At first she tried to see them all. She tried to give them hope. And they in turn fed her indignation with stories of hurts and disillusionments and betrayal – and her expertise in the social and emotional wreckage that accompanies the failure of love.

At first she welcomed the chance to help, but soon she was overwhelmed and flooded by wave after wave of unhappiness. It was clear that she'd already outgrown not only the space she shared with Acme Insurance, but also the possibility of being a one-woman law firm. Yet hiring associates and staff, leasing office space, and buying furniture would take the kind of money she simply didn't have. Over and over she figured and refigured numbers on her pocket calculator. But the only sensible message she got from the bottom-line figures was that she was in no position to say "yes" to all the women who needed her – and would have to limit her cause to a few, like Marion, who could pay her operating expenses.

As Christmas drew closer, Willie worked furiously, trying to clear her desk and to postpone what could be postponed. She had promised to spend the holidays with Mama, and that was a promise she needed to keep.

When Marion called to invite her to lunch, Willie tried to beg off. "I'd love to see you again," she said, "but I'm swamped. Could we make it after New Year's?"

"It's about your bill," Marion said. "I want to talk to you about it . . . but not on the telephone."

Willie agreed to meet Marion, but the call made her anxious and apprehensive. What was the problem with her bill? she wondered. She'd tried to be fair, even at her own expense. What else did Marion expect?"

The lunch crowd at La Cote Basque was sleek and glamorous in a quiet, understated way. Conversation was conducted in low, well-bred tones and even the sound of silverware against dishes was subdued. Little packages from Fifth Avenue jewelers and Madison Avenue boutiques were tucked neatly under chairs and tables, a discreet reminder of the holiday season.

Willie gave the maitre d' Marion's name and watched his face brighten with recognition. The beautiful young woman with the tawny skin and strawberry blonde hair was *somebody*.

He led Willie past a well-known talk-show host to a choice table in the center rear of the restaurant. Willie stared in disbelief. The woman who rose to greet her with a hug was stunningly, strikingly different from the sad, unhappy woman she'd met a few short months ago.

"Marion! You look terrific!"

"Don't I though?" Marion laughed, enjoying Willie's surprise. "This is what fifty-five can look like if you feel good about yourself. It also helps if you have a charge account at Elizabeth Arden."

It did Willie's heart good to see this new Marion, with her beautifully tinted pearl-gray hair, her smooth, beautifully made up complexion, her regal, confident bearing.

This was how she'd hoped Ginny would be after the divorce from Neal, but somehow it hadn't happened, at least not yet.

"I feel like smoked salmon and champagne to start," Marion said. "A bottle of Cristal. How does that sound?"

"It sounds like you really know how to celebrate," Willie said.

"I forgot how for a long time," Marion said quietly. "Make sure you don't ever do that, Willie . . . it's an awful waste of life."

Marion's advice had a clarion ring to it, but Willie wondered if she'd ever really learned how to celebrate. She'd always been too busy fighting, and even when she won, her moment of triumph was all too brief – and then it was on to the next battle. She could almost envy the exhilaration that Marion seemed to be feeling now. "What will you do next?" Willie asked. "Travel?"

Marion smiled like a woman with a secret. "I was hoping you'd ask. I'm going to run Marco Enterprises. As chairman of the board."

Willie stared again at what Marion had become: a butterfly emerging from a cocoon, full of color and surprise. "You're firing Harvey?"

"Not on your life," Marion laughed. "Harvey's too valuable to let go . . . at least until I learn more about the company. Then we'll see . . . "

"Good for you!" Willie exclaimed. "I can't tell you how much it means to see you happy . . . making a new life for yourself."

"I was unhappy for so long, it became a habit," Marion said. "I was afraid to leave because I couldn't see what was on the other side. But now I feel I can do what younger women talk about. I know I can have a career and"– she smiled – "I even feel I'm ready to love again. I couldn't have done it without you, Willie . . . "

The words warmed Willie. She sipped her wine and thought: *This* was what success was about. Making a difference, helping women when they couldn't help themselves.

"But your bill's way out of line," Marion said suddenly.

Willie was stunned. "But Marion," she protested, flushed with embarrassment, "I only . . . "

Marion shook her head. "Let me finish," she said, taking a cashier's check from her handbag. "I won't let you accept a penny less than this, and I don't want to hear any arguments."

Willie looked at the numbers on the check – $500,000, half a million dollars – and saw what she'd believed was out of reach: an office and a staff and the chance to open her doors to anyone who needed her, rich or poor.

"This is like an answered prayer," she said softly. "I can't begin to thank you enough . . . "

"You deserve it . . . and more. Merry Christmas, dear Willie," Marion said, handing over a red leather box from Cartier's. Inside was an oval-shaped antique gold watch circled with diamonds.

"Oh, but you shouldn't have," Willie protested. "It's beautiful, but I couldn't possibly take a gift like that from you, Marion. Please take it back, honestly . . . "

"It's too late to take it back," Marion said, turning the watch over. On the back was engraved: "To Willie, For being the daughter I never had, Affectionately, M.S."

Willie was moved to tears. "Thank you," she said shyly. "I'll treasure it always, but really, you shouldn't have . . . "

"Of course I should have," Marion said decisively. "Now you'll always have the right time – and a reminder that you can call me whenever you need a friend. I mean that, Willie . . . "

Marion's mood of celebration should have been contagious. Hers was a story with a happy ending. A beginning, really, after leaving a marriage littered with broken promises. Yet somehow her serene and smiling face seemed to reproach Willie – with how miserable and unhappy Ginny had sounded the last time they'd spoken. Heavy workload or not, Willie resolved to fly out to Palm Springs immediately.

After Willie left the restaurant, she deposited Marion's check in her new – and, heretofore meager – corporate account. Now the firm of Willa Dellahaye, Esquire, was solvent and off to a flying start.

She asked the bank manager, who was attentive and respectful as he had never been before, for some stationery and a stamp. She sat at his desk and wrote a check of her own – in the sum of $49,000 – to Jedd Fontana. She added a brief note: "Paid in full." Yet even as she wrote the words with a righteous flourish, Willie wondered if what was between them could be so neatly concluded.

A luncheonette on Lexington Avenue was a far cry from La Cote Basque, but that was where Betty Lockwood had asked to meet Willie. In her rehearsal clothes, down ski jacket, and long woolen muffler, Betty looked like an ageing waif.

Willie explained that she had done exhaustive research and found no precedents that would support Betty's case. "The most radical thing the courts have done is recognize common-law marriages in some states – which isn't going to help us. We'll be breaking new ground," Willie said. "It's time that the courts recognized alternative lifestyles – but that doesn't mean they will. We have to convince a judge that an economic contract existed, that promises were made to you and subsequently broken. I have to warn you, Betty, this would be an uphill battle even if you and Margo were straight."

"I don't know if I can afford that," Betty said, biting her lip nervously.

"I can," Willie said. "If you have the heart to fight this

out, I'll take you on as a *pro bono* case. I think it's important to bring the issue of unwritten contracts, made by two people who live together, into the courts. Some-body has to start somewhere – and if we win, we'll both be famous in the law books."

Willie left the luncheonette wishing there were some-thing more she could promise Betty Lockwood. The dancer owned no companies, had no wealth, yet she, too, had invested all she had to give, with the understanding that she'd be taken care of in return. Willie believed with all her heart that anyone who did that deserved better than to be cast off like a piece of outgrown clothing.

For the first time in her life, Willie had a clear, fully drawn mental picture of herself – as a woman who defended those who had been wounded by love, who had been disabled, disadvantaged, or otherwise hurt. Though she found it hard to trust the value of love, she was a strong believer in its power to cause pain. She felt like a professional soldier who knew too much about the horrors of war – and far too little about the joys of peace.

10

"I'm terribly sorry," the man said as he jostled Willie's arm, reaching for a leather suitcase on the luggage carousel. "I seem to get clumsy whenever I'm rushing."

"That's okay," Willie said with a smile. She had noticed him during the connecting flight from Los Angeles to Palm Springs. He was tall, rather distinguished looking, with even, regular features and crisp brown hair cut close to the head. He was wearing a dark business suit, suggesting that he, like Willie, had begun his trip in a colder climate.

Now he lingered at her side, until her bag appeared on the carousel. "Allow me," he said, and retrieved it for her.

She thanked him and turned to leave the terminal.

"Can I give you a lift?" he asked. "I have a car waiting outside."

Willie hesitated briefly, then decided no harm could come of a brief ride with an attractive stranger, and accepted the offer with thanks.

"I'm Greg Temple," he said, extending his hand with a smile.

"Willie Dellahaye."

They were met outside the baggage area by a uniformed driver who escorted them to a Lincoln stretch limousine. During the ride into town, Willie told Greg that she was a lawyer from New York and that she was in Palm Springs for the holidays.

"Then we belong in the same club, counselor," Temple laughed. "I practice in Chicago . . . I'm here on business – and hopefully a little pleasure, too." Temple went on to mention fellow lawyers they might know in common, but Willie shook her head. "Wait a minute," she said. "You probably know the head of my old firm . . . *everyone* knows Harrigan . . . "

"Francis Aloysius?" he laughed. "You're right. Not only do I know him, we even crossed paths – or swords – once."

"Who won?" Willie asked.

He smiled. "I'd have to say it was a draw. My clients wouldn't settle for any less."

They traded a few Harrigan stories, and as the limousine pulled up to Ginny's house, Temple asked if he might take Willie to dinner one night.

In New York, she might have said "yes," but here, Willie explained, she intended to devote all her time to Ginny.

"I'm staying at the Royce," Greg said, giving Willie his business card. "Just in case you change your mind."

From the moment Willie rushed into her mother's arms for a tear-drenched reunion, she could see how much of herself Ginny had lost and how aimless her life had become. Her delicate childlike beauty had begun to blur with age and disappointment, and the amber eyes that had sparkled with fairytale hopes now seemed dull with resignation.

The house Ginny had rented after her settlement from Neal had a musty aura of neglect. It was a sprawling hacienda-style ranch, complete with swimming pool, well appointed and well furnished by owners who had moved to Europe. The furniture was dusted, the floors and carpeting cleaned by the Mexican housekeeper who lived in the small guest cottage, yet the place had an uninhabited, almost abandoned feeling. The kitchen was clean and tidy, but the refrigerator and cupboards were empty of all but the most basic staples.

There was no hint of the holiday season in sight – not even a Christmas card. Of all the places Ginny had lived, this luxurious rented house seemed somehow the poorest. She lingered, rather than lived here, unable to move forward or to get back.

I'll change all that, Willie resolved as she prepared salad and canned soup and served it on trays in the living room. She lit the logs in the fireplace and snuggled down on the Mexican rug beside her mother. But when Willie tried to draw Ginny out, to get some sense of how she might help, the answers were vague and distracted. She shifted the conversation to her own life, but soon realized that there was little to tell outside of work that revolved around pain and unhappiness.

Fatigue finally took Willie to bed, where she lay awake making plans for tomorrow. Filled with purpose, her sense of mission in full bloom, she was sure if she could only find the right key, she could free Mama of the listless defeatism that had robbed her of vitality and purpose. She fell asleep imagining Ginny looking as sleek and optimistic and happy as Marion did now.

In spite of the six-hour time difference, Willie awoke early and put some coffee on to brew, feeling as if she'd brought the kitchen to life when the aroma filled the room. She scrambled some eggs and made cinammon toast, which she cut in triangles and arranged on a pressed-glass plate. She picked a few wildflowers from the overgrown garden, put

396

them in a small silver vase and carried a breakfast tray into Ginny's darkened bedroom.

"C'mon, sleepyhead," Willie said brightly, dropping a kiss on her mother's forehead, then opening the blinds. "Time for breakfast."

Ginny squinted against the light, looking disoriented and a little bewildered. She smiled as Willie's face came into focus. " 'Morning, baby. What a pretty tray."

"Cinnamon toast, just the way you like it – and good strong coffee."

Ginny picked at the food.

"What time do you go into the boutique?" Willie asked. "If I come along and help out for a while, maybe you could play hooky today? We could have lunch and do some shopping . . . "

"Honey, that sounds wonderful," Ginny said, her face brightening. "But let's not bother with Silver Screen today. My salesgirl Meg can take care of the place. I just want to enjoy having my little girl with me."

The streets were just beginning to fill up with holiday shoppers as Willie parked her mother's Cadillac off Palm Canyon Drive. The sound of Christmas carols coming from a music store stirred a sudden nostalgia in Willie for those all-too-brief moments when it seemed all might be right with her world. Now it was up to her to make that happen for Ginny. "Come on, Mama," she said, slipping her arm into Ginny's, "let's have us a great Christmas!"

For the next few hours they strolled along the Drive like children, stopping in one elaborately decorated shop after another, buying whatever took their fancy – a small Christmas tree, evergreen wreaths trimmed with red ribbons, boxes of brightly colored ornaments, candles in the shape of snowmen, stockings filled with candy, tapes of Christmas carols.

The day was balmy and dry, and when they got hungry, Willie chose an outdoor café in a small arcade. Remembering

Marion's advice about celebrating life, she ordered a bottle of champagne. *Mama needs that,* she thought, *even more than I do.*

She was about to raise her glass in a toast to Mama, when her chair was bumped from behind, causing her wine to spill.

"I'm terribly sorry," a deep voice apologized. "Here, let me help . . ."

When Willie looked up from mopping the spill, she saw that it was Greg Temple, the man from the airport.

"We have to stop meeting like this," he laughed.

"Let me guess," she laughed along. "You're in a rush, right?"

"Right . . . but now that I've run into you again, so to speak . . ." Greg stood beside the table, making no move to leave, so Willie introduced him to her mother.

"She can't be your mother," he said. "Your beautiful sister, maybe, but not your mother."

When Willie saw Ginny light up, just the way she used to at the club when an attractive man flirted, she invited Greg to sit down.

"I'd love to," he said, "if I didn't have an important meeting with a client. But I'm going to a Christmas party tonight . . . would you both like to join me? I'm sure I'd be the envy of every man there . . ."

Ginny looked like a child offered a rare treat, so Willie didn't hesitate. "We'd love to," she said and gave Greg the address.

Whether it was Temple's brief presence, the prospect of a party, or the second bottle of champagne he'd ordered for Willie and her mother, the lunch took a decidedly festive turn.

When they left the café hand in hand, becoming part of the holiday spirit that filled the streets and arcades, Willie thought she could see more spring in Ginny's step, more energy in her face.

In an exclusive boutique filled with fine jewelry, Willie spotted a pair of topaz earrings set in gold. She held the green stones against Ginny's cheek. "They almost match your eyes," she said tenderly. "Let's make them an early present, and you can wear them to the party tonight. Merry Christmas, Mama." She kissed Ginny right there in the store, and for a moment they were as they had been years ago, bonded and strengthened by their love for one another.

"My turn," Ginny said, laughing as she pulled Willie along the street and into another shop. She pointed to a white suede jumpsuit in the window, "Size six," she told the salesgirl. "It's for my daughter. She's a lawyer . . . she came all the way from New York to see me."

The pride in Mama's voice warmed Willie, yet made her somehow sad because Ginny had somehow forgotten to be proud for herself.

"Look," Willie said after they'd left the store, "we're only a block away from Silver Screen. Let's stop by now . . . maybe I can give you some ideas for generating new business. We used to be a pretty good team, remember?"

"I remember, honey," Ginny said. "You always stuck by me, no matter what."

There seemed to be a kind of plea in her mother's words, and when Willie crossed the threshold of Silver Screen, she realized with a shock that Ginny's stories about being tied to the business had been just that – stories.

Like Ginny's house, her boutique had an abandoned quality. There was little evidence of new designs. The merchandise had lost its sassy freshness and the displays that had once been bright and original now seemed tired and listless. The salesgirl reading a magazine seemed surprised to see Ginny, as if her presence in the shop was rare and unexpected.

The sight of Mama's faded fantasy sickened Willie. There was more to Silver Screen's decline than the divorce from Neal. Ginny had stopped caring, given up the dream that had nourished her a long time ago. Could it be revived, Willie wondered, or was it dead? And if so, how could she help Ginny find another dream?

Cautiously Willie walked around the shop, the young salesgirl trailing in her wake, looking through the stock and trying to formulate a plan for a new beginning. Ginny sat quietly on a satin chaise, as if she were waiting for Willie to tell her what she already knew, that she was a failure at anything she tried.

Willie sat beside her, draping an arm around her shoulder. "Maybe what we need here is a consultant," she said, "to advise us in what direction to take the business. I met someone like that while I was working for Harrigan . . . he has a terrific reputation. Let me call him tomorrow . . . let it be a Christmas present. I'll bet he can—"

Ginny shook her head. "What's the sense in throwing good money away, honey? My stuff was just a fad . . . a joke . . . and now it's over."

"It doesn't have to be over unless you want it to be," Willie urged. "Maybe Silver Screen started out as a fad, but if you think about it, I know we can come up with some new ideas . . . something you'd enjoy."

But Ginny's face refused to shed its resigned expression. "Don't waste your time or your money, baby. It's no use."

"Mama, why are you like this?" Willie asked in desperation. "Why won't you even try?"

Ginny looked like a scolded child. "I'm sorry, honey, I guess I've been down in the dumps so long . . . "

Willie remembered how Marion had described unhappiness as a habit – and felt a sudden surge of guilt for living her own life while Ginny's had been foundering. "I'm sorry, Mama," she said. "I had no right to talk to you like that. If you don't want this place, we'll figure out what to do with it later."

They left the gloom of Silver Screen and emerged into the sunshine, and though the bright promise of the day had turned out to be a lie, Willie fought against the sadness that had once again overtaken her mother. She drove to a nearby supermarket, where she heaped a cart with fruits and vegetables and enough meat and chicken to fill Ginny's empty freezer.

When they got back to the house, Willie tried to recapture the holiday spirit that had vaporized so suddenly. All right, she thought, Mama was in worse trouble than she'd imagined, but if she stuck by her, took care of her, they would pull through the way they always had before. She put the Christmas music on the stereo. She hung the wreaths and persuaded Ginny to join in festooning the windows with tinseled garlands. "Isn't this fun?" she said brightly. "Maybe we can have a couple of people in later this week. We could ask the neighbors . . . and what about Laura? It would be fun to see her again."

"Laura doesn't work at the club anymore," Ginny said quietly. "Last I heard she got married and moved to Sacramento. It's like I keep telling you, honey. I've got nobody, no friends, nothin' . . ."

"You have me," Willie said, taking Ginny's hands in her own, determined to cut through the shroud of desperation that had wrapped itself around her mother. "And I'm not leaving as long as you need me."

Ginny gave her daughter a look of naked despair and began to cry. "It's no use, honey," she sobbed. "I try and try, but nothin' turns out right."

Willie held her mother close, as she'd done so many times before, searching herself for words of comfort and hope. "It will, Mama," she said, "it will, just give yourself a chance. You're still young, and you have so much going for you. Who knows," she added, in spite of her own prejudices, "maybe you'll even meet a nice new man . . . "

These last words triggered a fresh burst of sobbing. "Oh, baby, that's what I've been trying to tell you. Nobody wants me anymore, nobody . . . "

"I can't believe that," Willie said soothingly, stroking her mother's hair. "I know how special you are . . . any man worth his salt would know it, too."

Ginny shook her head. "I love you for saying those things, baby, but I know different." There was a silence and then she began a long, halting recital – a story of her desperate search for love, of pickups in bars and brief moments of respite from loneliness, of men who passed through her life and then went away, cheating her of money and confidence and hope.

Willie listened quietly, trying to make some sense of

what her mother's life had become. "Mama, listen to me," she said finally. "Maybe you've been having such bad luck with men because you're so down. Those men you took up with . . . they're the ones who are worthless, not you. Can't you see that? Come back to New York with me. Sell the business . . . we'll be together, just like in the old days. Say 'yes,'" she entreated. "It'll make it better for you, Mama . . . "

Ginny looked into her daughter's face. "What would our life be like if I did that, honey?" she asked quietly.

"We could get a bigger apartment," Willie answered quickly. "I'll take care of you . . . you'll meet new people, we can take vacations once in a while . . . travel together. Wouldn't you like that?"

For a moment Ginny's face relaxed, and it seemed she might agree. And suddenly her expression shifted, as if she'd closed the door that had just been opened. She shook her head. "No, Willie," she said, her voice stronger. "You've always taken care of me, just like you were the mother instead of me. It's time you stopped that and lived your own life."

"But, Mama," Willie argued, "I want to . . . I need to make sure you're okay."

"I can take care of things on my own, honey. Like I told you, it's time."

Willie couldn't quite read the expression on her mother's face, but it seemed somehow more resolute than peaceful. "Okay," she said, "if you have some ideas of your own, that's fine. But if you change your mind, if things aren't working out, remember . . . I'm always there for you."

Ginny nodded, and though she didn't say a word, Willie felt almost enveloped by the love that shone through the eyes that were still wet with tears.

Though Mama had declared her intention to handle her own problems, Willie felt no less protective. As evening – and Temple's Christmas party – approached, she ran a bubble bath for Ginny. Later, while Ginny applied her makeup, Willie sat on the bed and watched the ritual, just as she had in childhood. When Ginny pulled one dress, then another, from her closet, asking "which one do you like best, hon?" Willie voted for a striking beaded emerald-green gown that gave color and sparkle to her mother's fair skin and blond hair.

Then Willie hurried through her own shower and makeup, as if she wanted Ginny alone to look special tonight. She slipped into a simple floor-length white knit and went to tell Mama she was ready.

Ginny was standing over the bathroom vanity, Willie's new watch in her hand, reading the inscription, a strange expression on her face.

"It's a Christmas present from a client," Willie offered. "A special client."

Ginny nodded. "It sounds like you have everything you need in New York," she said, "even a lady who wants to be your mother."

"Oh, Mama," Willie protested, "that could *never* be. My work's in New York, that's all. I have the best mother anyone could want. We're a team, and that's how it's always going to be." She touched her mother's cheek tenderly and made a silent wish – for whatever would give Ginny the happiness that had eluded her for so long.

11

The chauffeur held open the door as Willie and her mother stepped into Greg Temple's limousine. Greg had lavished compliments on both women and seemed now almost to be reading Willie's mind – and being particularly attentive to her mother.

"Do you come to Palm Springs a lot, Greg?" Ginny asked, as she accepted a glass of chilled wine from the bar.

"That depends," Greg answered, "but I'm always here at Christmas time. My client gives one helluva party every year . . . flies in all his business associates, a couple of big

403

bands, and the champagne flows all night long. And this year, it's going to be really special, now that I've met the two most beautiful women in town."

Willie was only half listening to the conversation, but as she looked out the window, she saw the car turn into a private road. "Where did you say we were going, Greg?" she asked sharply.

He gave her a quizzical look and answered: "To a Christmas party . . . at Sam Fontana's house."

Willie went pale. "I . . . I don't think I can go after all, Greg . . . "

"I don't understand," he said. "Why not?"

"Oh, honey," Ginny intervened, her face clouding with disappointment, "don't be that way . . . we got dressed up . . . and Greg here, he doesn't want to go alone . . . "

Willie gave in. She would handle her problems with the Fontanas, rather than spoil Ginny's evening.

The limousine drove up to the big iron gate, which swung open after Greg gave his name. The sprawling mansion was brightly silhouetted against the navy blue sky, light pouring from every window. An enormous Christmas tree stood on the front lawn, blazing a bright welcome to the arriving guests. Such a beautiful setting, Willie thought, remembering how awed she'd been when she'd first glimpsed the splendor and power of the Fontanas. That was before she'd known that they were a law unto themselves, handing down a legacy of corrupted power from father to son, along with the heritage of wealth and luxury.

As Willie stepped out of the limousine, she saw the governor of California – and not far behind him, a well-known recording star. As a child, she'd been impressed by the man who could command guests such as these; now she was merely repelled.

The mansion was already crowded, the party well under-way. White-jacketed waiters circulated with silver trays of hors d'oeuvres and glasses of champagne. Socialites, entertainers, politicians, men and women who somehow belonged to Sam Fontana's personal club danced in the enormous center gallery, under a canopy of evergreen garlands and white helium balloons, to the music of a Peter Duchin orchestra. In each of the adjoining rooms, a massive buffet had been set up, along with tables and chairs where the guests would later dine.

Willie looked through the sea of glittering evening clothes. She'd probably have to face Sam Fontana – and his son – before the night was over, and she hoped she could get it over with soon.

Ginny, on the other hand, was wide-eyed and excited about being at the legendary Fontana party, a place to which even her marriage to Neal had never taken her. When Greg whirled her onto the dance floor, she seemed as fluttery as a teenager.

Funny, Willie thought, how grownup and old she often felt in the face of Mama's childlike ingenuousness. And how often she'd wished she could give Ginny some of her own defensive armor, some protection from being so vulnerable and so easily hurt.

When the dance was over, Greg returned, but without Ginny. "Where's my mother?" Willie asked.

"Some guy stole her away," he laughed. "Not that I can blame him. Not only is she beautiful, she's a great dancer, too. Would it be out of line," he said after a brief hesitation, "to ask why you didn't want to come to this party?"

"No," Willie answered, "but it's too complicated and too personal to get into right now. Would it be out of line," she countered, "to ask what you do for Sam Fontana?"

Greg laughed, a little too heartily, Willie thought. "Now *that* is complicated – and confidential, as you well know. Let's just say I handle some of Sam's business ventures in the Midwest."

Willie nodded. She hadn't really expected Greg to say much more, especially now. After years, decades actually, of doing as he pleased, several of Sam's "business ventures" had come under a fair amount of public scrutiny lately. There had been a tax investigation of a corporation in Boston, and a federal inquiry into the practices of a

Fontana-held Miami bank, prompted by an anonymous allegation of money-laundering. And even in his home state of Montana, where Sam had virtually ruled without challenge, there had originated a wire-service story suggesting that the unions had been kept out of Fontana construction companies by intimidation and violence.

Yet Sam endured, Willie reflected, and, judging from the lavishness of this party and the stellar quality of his guests, continued to prosper.

"If you're uncomfortable here," Greg said, moving in a little closer, "we could go somewhere else after an hour or so . . . Sam won't mind as long as I've put in an appearance."

"I don't know, Greg, let's just see how it goes," Willie answered cautiously, not wanting to spoil Ginny's evening.

"If it isn't the elusive Willie Dellahaye . . . " The voice was silky and sensual and heart-stoppingly familiar.

She spun around. It was Jedd Fontana, just as he'd appeared in so many of her fantasies. Tan and handsome, his dark hair slicked back, a crimson tie and cummerbund set against the creamy silk of his pleated tuxedo shirt, Jedd looked more like a Velasquez prince than the heir apparent to Sam's tawdry empire.

"Hello, Jedd," Willie said, trying to sound casual.

"Greg . . . it's good to see you again . . . glad you could come. How long have you known Willie?" Jedd asked, sounding equally casual.

Greg looked as if he'd been asked a question to which there was no right answer. "Willie . . . Miss Dellahaye . . . and I met yesterday," he replied stiffly. "She and her mother were kind enough to come with me to your party." He tugged at his tie like a nervous schoolboy. "If you'll both excuse me," he said, "I'd better pay my respects to Sam." And then he was gone, without so much as a backward glance in Willie's direction.

"Dammit, Jedd, look what you do to people! A grown man – and he's afraid of you!"

Jedd gave her a lazy smile. "But you aren't afraid of me, are you, Willie? Would you like me to put the word out that

406

Temple can have a clear field with you?" His manner was teasing, but his dark eyes were sending messages she couldn't quite deflect.

She glowered at him, but took the hand he held out and a moment later was swept in his arms onto the dance floor. They didn't speak for a time; Willie simply melted into Jedd's body. It was easier to find fault with him from a distance, but close up, it was hard to concentrate on all the reasons why she should ignore the quickening of her pulse.

"I knew you'd turn up sooner or later," he murmured against her ear. "And now that you're here, I won't let you slip away so easily."

She wanted to contradict him, to call him arrogant or cocky, yet it was hard to argue with what she was feeling – that when they came together, it was as if they were two interlocking pieces of the same puzzle.

They danced one dance after another, and Willie felt as if she could never be tired, as if she were as light as a feather in Jedd's arms. Finally he asked, "Would you like some supper? I heard tell the stuffed quail's terrific."

"Let me check on Mama first," Willie said. "I want to make sure she's having a good time."

"My pleasure. I've always liked your mother. She's a lot less snobbish than you are," he teased.

They found Ginny on the edge of the dance floor, flushed and smiling and showing Greg how the Lindy Hop was done back in Belle Fourche. "Hi, baby," she said, pausing for breath. "Me and Greg are gonna catch the late show at Cecil's. Do you want to come along – or maybe you want to stay here?" she asked, casting a meaningful look in Jedd's direction.

"Willie's staying," Jedd said, giving Ginny a conspiratorial wink. "Have a nice time," he added, smiling at Greg, as if he were granting permission.

He pulled Willie away before she could tell him he had no right to speak for her – and almost ran into his father. "Hi, Dad, remember Willie Dellahaye, don't you?"

Sam nodded. "I never forget a beautiful woman," he

said. "Welcome to my home, Miss Dellahaye. I see you've made good on your ambition. I've heard interesting things about you."

Willie looked at the man who had once made her feel she wasn't good enough for her son. His wavy hair was grayer, his midsection stouter, yet Sam Fontana hadn't changed. He exuded the same powerful presence, but now she met the dark eyes that belied the welcome and the flattery. "I've heard interesting things about you, too," she said.

Sam smiled. "Still a fighter. That's a good quality . . . in a lawyer." He turned to his son. "I need to talk to you, Jedd . . . there's a problem with the shopping center in Miami . . . "

Jedd hesitated. "Not now, Pop," he said, in a voice almost as commanding as Sam's. "Willie and I are just about to have supper."

Willie unconsciously held her breath, waiting to see how Sam would handle this challenge to his authority. But his expression didn't change, and he merely smiled again and said: "Later, then . . . we don't want to keep a beautiful lady waiting."

Jedd led Willie to a corner table and summoned a waiter. "We'll have the Oysters Rockefeller and a chilled Chardonnay. Later . . . the quail and a bottle of the '67 Lafitte from my wine cellar." The food appeared almost instantly, as if even the temporary help knew it wouldn't do to keep a Fontana waiting.

"When did all that happen?" Willie asked. "That business with you and your father."

"What business?" Jedd asked innocently.

"As I recall," she said crisply, "he called the tune and you danced to it."

"Only in your mind," Jedd said. "I love my father, Willie, and we've always been close – just like you are to your mother."

"But you work for your father."

"I work *with* my father now. You know, Willie," he said quietly, "one of these days, you'll have to stop playing

Scarlett to my Rhett." When she didn't answer, he asked: "Can you give me one really good reason why we're not together?"

Seeing Sam again had reminded Willie all too clearly of her reasons. "We're still from two different worlds, Jedd – even more now than when I was a kid. You Fontanas make your own rules, your own values—"

"Not good enough, Willie," he cut in, fixing her with a clear, steady gaze. "Not anymore. When two people want to be together, they find a way to make it happen. They build bridges over their differences. Or they let them be. I don't think this is about me anymore . . . I think it's about you. What are you running away from?"

Jedd's question cut right to the heavy, nameless fear she'd carried for as long as she could remember. She shook her head as if to say "stop."

"Tell me you don't feel the same things I do," he pressed. "Tell me you don't remember how good we were together. Say you don't want me and I'll never bother you again."

Willie couldn't say the words. Memory flooded her senses as if it had been yesterday that she'd lain in his arms. And though she'd never been able to reach out and embrace Jedd with all her heart, it was unthinkable to never see him again.

"Good," he smiled, "now we're getting somewhere." He stood up and held out his hand. "Let's go."

"Go where?" she asked.

"To somewhere real, away from all this plastic sunshine. Somewhere white and beautiful, just you and me. Say 'yes,' Willie, because I won't ask again . . . "

Willie rose from her chair and took his hand, unable to deny the longing his presence evoked. Jedd was like a drug, teasing and tantalizing, a promise of something more intense and exciting than mere earthly pleasure. She wouldn't have sought him out, but now that he was here, she couldn't turn away.

Jedd excused himself to make a phone call and when he returned he was carrying a long sable coat. "Here," he said, draping it over Willie's shoulders, "you'll need this tonight . . . let's hope my sister doesn't miss it."

A car was waiting in the driveway, and Jedd bundled her into it. She nestled into his shoulder as the car sped into the night, not stopping until they reached the airport.

"Where are we going?" she asked again, as they boarded a small jet with the name "Fontana" painted in black letters on the side.

Jedd laughed and shook his head. "Don't you ever get tired of being earthbound, Willie? I already told you all you need to know."

They arrived at Fresno airport in a light rain. A four-wheel-drive Jeep picked them up and they drove for more than an hour, until the rain became snow and the highway fed into a mountain road, winding upward, and in the heavy darkness they could see the majestic peaks of the Sierra Nevadas.

The Jeep stopped in front of a massive log and stone lodge. A welcoming light shone from behind the paned windows and white smoke curled upward from the chimney.

The front door was unlocked, and when they walked in, Willie saw a spacious yet cozy room with a beamed ceiling, a roaring fire in the fireplace, a tray of sandwiches on the coffee table and a bottle of champagne chilling in an earthenware cooler. "I feel like Goldilocks," she said, "but who lives here?"

Jedd came up behind her and slipped his arms around her waist. "Fontana executives on retreat. But tonight," he said softly, "we live here . . . just us." He kissed the back of her neck, his breath like a caress, melting the frosty reserve that protected Willie from love but not from pain.

As they warmed their hands in front of the fire, she felt as if Jedd's words were true, that tonight the real world and everyday rules were far away and there was just the two of them, a man and a woman. Icicles tinkled like wind chimes outside, and the wind had a soft crooning sound as it dusted the snow against the windows, wrapping them in a thick, cottony blanket.

When Jedd held out his arms, Willie went to him without

hesitation, meeting his lips, feeling the warmth of his body flow into hers. When his tongue pressed against her teeth, her mouth yielded readily, inviting him, tasting his sweetness as it mingled with hers.

And then he was everywhere, kissing her eyes, her nose, her bare shoulders, his hands tugging at her clothes, seeking what was hidden. She reached behind to help him, finding the zipper and releasing it, letting the gown fall to the floor. The heat from the fire inflamed her skin, her breathing ragged as she pushed the jacket from his shoulders and pulled the studs from his shirt.

They sank down on the white fur rug in a tangle of limbs, flesh melting eagerly into flesh. Jedd's touch was sure and certain; no one had known her so instinctively and so well. As he rounded the contours and valleys of her body with his hands, it was as if he were sculpting her, creating undiscovered desires. Mind gave way to consuming feelings and a hunger for more.

Bathed in the glow of the fire, Willie was like a golden goddess, her hair tumbled around her face, her expression dreamy, eyes half-closed, seeing only Jedd's nearness. As he caressed the smooth curve of her breasts, her nipples rose to meet his fingertips.

He groaned as her hand closed around his penis, guiding it inside her. He began to move, slowly at first, then harder, pushing and probing, as if he were searching her very core. And from somewhere deep inside her, hot molten sensations began to shimmer. Her eyes shut tight, as a desperate wave of longing arched her back, lifted her higher. Arms and legs wrapped around Jedd tighter and still more, as if she would draw him into her, consume him with her need. Somewhere from a distance she heard herself moan, then cry out as the heat erupted, shaking her limbs, blinding her with its intensity.

Willie opened her eyes and looked at Jedd, who was stretched out on the rug, one arm thrown over her waist, the other gracefully extended. Naked, he was like a statue, smooth bronze skin and tightly muscled body. The fire was

411

dying now and when she burrowed against him for warmth, he smiled and held her.

"You're cold," he said tenderly, and with a strength that surprised Willie, he scooped her up in his arms and carried her into a bedroom decorated in shades of forest green, with rustic oak furniture. He tucked her into the four-poster bed and covered her with a down quilt. Then he returned to the living room and brought back the champagne, and two glasses.

"You'll spoil me," she said with a smile as she took the glass he offered and sipped the sparkling wine.

"I want to . . . I've always wanted to, Willie. See what you've been missing?" His fingers touched her cheek lightly, and she wanted him close to her again.

She flung back the covers and drew him down beside her.

"Now?" he laughed. "Don't I even get to drink my champagne?"

"Later," she said, taking the glass from his hand and putting it on the bedside table. She kissed his mouth, then buried her face in his chest, licking his nipples, catching them between her teeth until they stiffened into fierce, hard points.

With tongue and teeth, she traced a downward path along his body. She took his hard phallus in her mouth, tasting the salty juices of her own body as she teased him with her tongue, licking and sucking until she felt him tense and quiver. She raised herself and straddled his belly, pushing her swollen clitoris against his penis until he slid inside her. She rode him hard, head thrown back, sweat drenching her skin as she strained for release. He cupped her buttocks, fingers probing until she gasped and stiffened and collapsed on his chest with a deep, shuddering sigh.

The morning began with sunshine and lovemaking, slow and lazy and without urgency, as if they had all the time in the world to touch and explore and discover one another.

Then Jedd brought Willie breakfast in bed, and when she marveled at the fluffy eggs and good strong coffee, he said, "Another of your prejudices, right? Jedd Fontana, the rich kid who can't boil water . . . admit it, that's what you thought."

"You're right," she laughed, "that's exactly what I thought."

After breakfast they searched through the amply filled wardrobes that held a variety of heavy winter clothing. They bundled up in parkas and ski pants and ran outside like children, pelting each other with snowballs and rolling around and laughing until their chests hurt.

Willie sat up in a snowbank. "I still don't know where we are. Is it still a secret or are you going to tell me?"

"I'll show you," he said, taking her by her hand. They walked along the mountain trail until they reached a sign that said: "Welcome to Yosemite National Park." The park was virtually deserted, except for the rangers on duty. The majestic beauty that greeted their eyes made them silent: the granite face of El Capitan rising almost 4000 feet from the glacier-gouged valley, its summit silhouetted against puffy white clouds and a brilliant blue sky. Ancient redwoods, more mighty than city scrapers; majestic canyons and roaring waterfalls.

The air was sharp and cold and deliciously clean, and this world seemed bright and new, as if it had all just begun. Willie remembered the day she and Mama had stood atop a mountain with Webb and Laura, looking down on the valley and what would be their new life. So many beginnings since that day, different and yet the same, as if Willie had been moving and growing but somehow going round in circles.

The time she'd shared with Jedd was almost like a dream, yet it gave Willie a curious kind of peace to be no longer fighting what had been since she'd first seen him. No one had touched her as he had, and she thought, probably no one else ever would.

"I've imagined being here with you," he said huskily, "and now that you're here, I can't imagine it without you." Willie snuggled up against him, but said nothing.

If only it were that simple, she thought, if only there were nothing but this place and the two of us, I could stay here

413

forever. But tomorrow was Christmas Day, and it was time to get back to Mama – and to all the realities of her life.

Numb from the cold, they ran back to the lodge. "You start a fire," Willie said, "while I make us some tea."

"I have a better idea," Jedd said, pulling her into the bathroom which occupied the entire back wing of the house. Under the skylight was an enormous Jacuzzi, set against a thermopane window, which made the snow outside seem close enough to touch.

Jedd flicked a switch and the water in the tub began to pulse. Clothes were flung on the floor and Jedd and Willie jumped into the warm, bubbling water, splashing and playing.

Jedd began to sponge Willie's body, almost with a woman's gentle touch; it was nearly erotic; yet for a rare moment Willie felt like a child, being bathed and cared for by a loving parent.

Jedd wrapped Willie in a white bath sheet and carried her to the big oak bed. She thought they might make love, but he simply held her for a while and stroked her hair.

"Marry me, Willie."

The words startled her. They hung in the air for a long moment while Willie tried to imagine what it would be like to fall asleep beside Jedd every night, knowing that he was no more than an arm's reach away. That she could imagine, but the rest of it – the sharing of a life where Jedd became more and more like his father – was like a blank page, empty and somehow frightening.

"I can't," she said, her voice barely above a whisper.

Jedd stared, disbelief clouding his dark eyes. "What do you mean, you can't? Willie, you and I . . . we've been as close as two people can be."

"Jedd," she said, "I can't deny it anymore – not even to myself. I'm fascinated with you, enthralled. Nobody affects me the way you do – nobody ever has, perhaps ever will." She looked away from his hopeful eyes. "But I don't respect you or what you stand for. We can't spend our lives like . . . like this. I've seen what happens when two people

414

don't agree on what's important. I saw my father and mother turn into enemies, trying to destroy each other." She could see them now, even, Mama as she had looked after being beaten by Perry. She turned back to Jedd, anything to shake off that sordid vision of the past. "I won't let it happen to me, Jedd – to us. I just can't."

The muscle in his jaw tightened, as if her were struggling hard for self-control. "I'm not your father, Willie, and I've never wanted you to be someone else. All I want is you – as is."

She started to turn away again, but he seized her forcefully by the arms. "Listen to me, Willie. I won't ask you again. You'll have to meet me – if not halfway, then somewhere along the line. We belong together . . . I've always known that. I just hope to God it's not too late when you see it, too."

The trip back was quiet, like passion spent. It was as if Jedd's proposal had completed yet another circle for Willie. If she couldn't marry him . . . perhaps that meant she could marry no one.

It was nearly dawn when she let herself into the house. She was glad that Ginny was still asleep and that she wouldn't have to explain what she herself didn't quite understand.

Willie's Christmas gift to Ginny was a weekend at the Palm Desert Spa. She hoped that the pampering and cosseting would keep her mother interested in taking care of herself. The spa was small and exclusive, located in what had been a private estate, accommodating only thirty or so "guests" at a time. Willie and her mother shared a room, and each morning they were awakened at seven with a breakfast of fresh orange juice, coffee, and bran cereal. Next came a brisk three-mile walk around the estate grounds, followed by a whirlpool bath and a swim in the Olympic-size pool.

Clear broth and whole wheat toast were served poolside, and after a fifteen-minute rest, there were aerobic exercises and yoga stretches for the remainder of the morning. The afternoons were devoted to such sybaritic luxuries as Japanese or Swedish massages, herbal wraps, facials, and pedicures. Dinner was served early on an outside terrace and most of the guests were in bed before ten o'clock.

Though Willie had booked the weekend with Ginny's welfare in mind, she found to her surprise that her body responded, like a parched plant to water, to the spa's physical ministrations. Like the time in Jedd's arms, it reminded her of what she usually ignored, that while she might drive herself like a machine, she had a physical self that hungered for care and attention.

The days passed quickly, and for a time she and Ginny were like girls at camp, giggling about the rules and regulations, groaning when the exercises were too demanding – but enjoying every moment.

On their last evening, as they both sat up in bed, sipping caffeine-free herbal tea, Ginny asked: "Aren't you gonna see that Fontana boy again before you leave? He's had a thing for you for the longest time, honey, and I figured . . . well, I figured after the other night that you were finally gonna give him a chance."

Willie looked into her mother's eyes, which seemed misty with longing. "I guess you could say I have a thing for him, too, Mama, but I can't see myself making a life with him. We'd be fighting all the time about things . . . important things . . . "

"Like me and your father used to fight, is that it, honey?" Ginny asked softly. "Maybe it's my fault and Perry's that you didn't have a good home life, but it's your turn to do better now, Willie. I don't mean to hurt you, baby, but when it comes to men, you think more like a judge than a lawyer. Everybody comes with problems, but if you don't want to go through life all alone, you just have to take your chances and do the best you can . . . "

"But how can you feel that way after all the trouble you've had with men?" Willie asked.

"Like I said, there's no way to know about trouble ahead of time, honey," Ginny answered, "and you're probably gonna get mad at me for saying this, but I'll take my chances with trouble over bein' lonely anytime . . . "

Willie went to sleep with Ginny's words echoing in her ears like a lullaby. There seemed to be a key in what Mama had said, a key that might unlock the secret feelings imprisoned inside her and set them free. How odd it was, she thought, that with all Mama had suffered, she still talked so easily of taking chances with men, while Willie could only think of reasons to stay away from the one man she'd never been able to forget.

All too soon the holidays were over. "Go on back to New York, honey," Ginny urged. "I don't want you hanging around here on my account. I'll be okay. Like I told you, it's time I took care of myself."

Mama did look better, Willie could see that, and she seemed to be in better spirits. But though there was pressing work waiting in New York, Willie felt a strange reluctance to leave in spite of Ginny's reassurances. It was as if by letting her go, Mama had drawn her even closer, with a bond that could never be broken.

12

Winning became a habit for Willie. As long as she knew her cause was just, she rarely counted the cost or weighed the risks. Her clients' enemies became her enemies; her clients' friends became Willie's supporters. Betty Lockwood's case brought Willie a fair share of both. The notion of a female homosexual marriage was grist for the tabloids; a lawsuit involving broken promises allowed the media to exploit and sensationalize the story under the guise of reporting the news.

As Betty's attorney, Willie was censured by a Catholic bishop and an orthodox rabbi and bombarded with hate mail, attacking her as "pervert-lover" and damning her to eternal perdition. The attacks bewildered Willie no less than did the invitation to speak at a gay rights conference, and the fan letters praising her support for "true sexual freedom"– for she saw her cause as justice and not a stand for or against homosexuality.

Willie pleaded Betty's case eloquently. She hammered home the point that sexual orientation was not the issue, that she wasn't asking payment for sexual favors. She argued that Betty had invested time and talent and energy in her lover's career and general well-being, and had been promised she'd be taken care of in return. Willie asked for a cash settlement of $75,000 and weekly payments of $300 for five years.

Though she supported her case well, with documents and witnesses, the court balked at validating a live-in relationship – and a homosexual one at that. It ruled that Betty had indeed served Margo in more than an emotional and sexual capacity – but awarded only $20,000 for her years of service.

When the ruling was announced, Willie remembered Matt's admonition on the importance of timing when it came to social issues. She was sure that one day the courts would do better by people who lived together without benefit of marriage, whether they were straight or gay. And although the ruling was a moral victory, Willie felt as if she had somehow let her client down.

"I'm so sorry," she said to Betty. "I wanted you to have more for all those years—"

"Don't say another word," Betty interrupted. "You've been great. It felt good to have my say, instead of just slinking off and disappearing like Margo wanted me to. Anyway," she added with a little smile, "the publicity's made me sort of famous. I've had a couple of job offers . . . and a publisher's willing to give me forty thousand dollars to do a book. That's better than retiring to the old actors' home, and I owe it all to you, Willie."

Willie was glad there were some bright spots in Betty's future, but she came away from the trial with her sense of fair play bruised – and her crusading spirit afire. She spent her zeal writing for five nonstop hours. The result was an article called "Get It in Writing," published by *The Reader's Digest* – counseling women to get for themselves protection the law didn't provide, by drawing up notarized agreements that spelled out each partner's financial responsibilities.

The case generated a fresh wave of new clients, and the article added another dimension to Willie's career, creating a demand for her services as a lecturer and authority on separation and divorce.

Living up to her own success pushed Willie into yet another cycle of movement and change. She found a suite of offices in a midtown tower, this time with room to grow, hired a decorator to furnish it, then sublet half the space to a freelance publicist. She hired a receptionist and two associates, Pamela Belzer, a recent Yale graduate, and Margaret Crown, who'd worked her way through New York University at night.

Time, as Willie had known it, began to blur – and when it re-formed again, it took on different shapes and meanings. Weeks, months, seasons, became defined by her clients' lives and their most pressing needs – how long it would take to get a restraining order against an abusive husband, how quickly she could release a wife from a marriage that had been a mistake, how much room there was to eat and sleep between satisfying the demands of her clients and the complicated bureaucracy of the court system.

Willie lived the work wherever it took her. There should have been little time to think of anything else, for wasn't that how it was supposed to be for anyone dedicated to a cause? And yet there was always the odd moment – looking outside her window on a glorious day, hearing a love song on the radio, indulging a fantasy before sleep – when some part of Willie, the woman who lived inside the crusader, would whisper softly, "But what about me? Don't I count, too?"

*   *   *

Regina Shepherd came into Willie's office fighting mad; all five feet and ninety-eight pounds of her were bristling with indignation. "I paid all the bills," she said, pounding Willie's desk emphatically, "rent, food, even Jack's med school tuition. I worked double shifts, took care of his apartment – and Jack, too. I typed his papers and filed his research grants. And what do I get for all this?" Regina paused for dramatic effect.

"I'll tell you what," she continued. "I get 'thank you very much, Regina, but while you've been busy turning into a drudge, I've met someone who isn't too tired to have fun.' And when do I get this?" Regina paused again. "I get it just when Jack's practice begins to bring in some money. I don't think he should get away with that."

"Damn right, he shouldn't!" Willie's blue eyes had begun to iridesce with what Harrigan had called "the wrath of righteousness." She'd heard stories like Regina's before, of young wives giving up their own ambitions, working at jobs rather than careers, investing their all in a husband's education – only to be left behind after the career was launched.

These stories infuriated Willie, as did the system of justice that allowed a husband to walk away with a graduate degree worth hundreds of thousands of dollars without fairly compensating the woman who had paid for it. In Willie's eyes, that was as bad as the emotional damage done to discarded women, who came to her feeling used and worthless, and all too ready to take whatever crumbs their husbands offered.

Regina Shepherd was different. She wasn't willing to act like a loser or to become a silent statistic. And no matter what the courts had done in the past, Willie felt instinctively that she and Regina could make a fighting – winning – team.

She looked through the financial documents Regina had laid on her desk. "There isn't much in marital assets," she said. "I don't suppose you've overlooked anything . . . ?"

"You suppose right," Regina answered, her black eyes flashing indignantly. "Not unless you count the equity in

Jack's office equipment – and his new Mercedes. We always talked about buying a house, but we're still renting – and don't think that wasn't part of his master plan!"

Willie nodded sympathetically. Whether or not Jack Shepherd had a master plan was beside the point. The bottom line was that there was no property to divide, no investments and not much of a bank account. Thanks to his medical degree, Jack would have all of those things – and soon – while Regina, who had dropped out of medical school to earn money as a lab technician, was supposed to start over with next to nothing.

Willie couldn't give back those lost years, but she could fight for a settlement that repaid Regina's sacrifice with something more than the bitter taste of regret.

"I'll have to talk with Jack's lawyer first," Willie said. "It's my guess he'll offer alimony based on Jack's present earnings. It's also my guess he'll hit the ceiling when I make my counter-offer . . . "

Regina leaned forward eagerly. "What are we going to ask for?"

Willie smiled. "We're going to say 'yes' to the alimony *and* we're going to ask for a cash settlement based on the value of Jack Shepherd's medical degree."

Regina shook her head in bewilderment. "But I just told you . . . Jack doesn't have any cash. How . . . ?"

"Let him take out a loan," Willie said crisply. "Banks love to give doctors credit. Jack owes you for his degree, Regina, and I mean to make him pay that debt, even if I have to take your case all the way through the court system."

Regina considered what Willie had said. "If you can do that," she said slowly, "maybe you should know that Jack's research involves a new pregnancy test. I heard him say it was better than anything on the market now . . . but if he's holding off on marketing it until after the divorce, he can keep whatever he makes, can't he?"

Willie thought for a moment. "I don't know. But if he's sitting on something of value, and if there's a way for you to have a share, trust me, Regina, I'll find it."

When Regina left her office, Willie felt like a thorough-bred at the starting gate, keyed up with anticipation and eager to run the race. This case could make a difference, not just to Regina Shepherd, but to so many women like her. The courts had finally recognized that wives had a dollars-and-cents value – and Willie meant to push the limits of what they were owed.

She put one of her associates to work on researching precedents and then called Larry Kusack and asked him to run a thorough check on Dr. Jack Shepherd.

"The usual?" Kusack asked.

"The works," Willie answered. "His finances, his girl-friend, right down to what kind of shaving lotion he buys, if that'll help us get a better settlement."

Kusack sighed. "It's a shame, Willie. You're a good lawyer, but with all due respect, it's a damn shame people can't just sit down and work out something that's fair without calling in lawyers to slug it out."

"No offense taken, Larry, but the women who come to me didn't marry decent guys like you." Remembering that Kusack's ex-wife had been in the hospital for a hysterec-tomy, she asked, "How's Sally?"

Kusack sighed again. "It's hard on her, Willie. I feel so bad that I can't cheer her up. She doesn't want to have any more kids . . . hell, there isn't even anyone she wants to marry. But she keeps saying her life is over."

The words sent a shudder through Willie. "Don't let her believe that, Larry," she said urgently. "Do whatever you have to do, but don't let her think that." The moment she hung up, Willie flipped through her card file, dialed the number of Robert's Florist, and ordered a dozen roses for Sally Kusack.

Impulsively she ordered another dozen for Ginny, with a card reading: "Just because I love you. Hugs and kisses, Willie."

In spite of Ginny's insistence on handling her own problems, Willie still phoned regularly. But now the calls had a different quality. Mama rarely complained and seemed to be more at peace. When she announced she was selling Silver Screen, Willie felt a twinge of regret at the passing of yet another dream, yet thought perhaps the move might be a step forward.

About her personal life, Ginny rarely made mention, but she spoke often of a volunteer job she'd taken, teaching pattern-making and sewing at a Catholic shelter for unwed mothers. More than once Willie had told Mama how proud she was – and Ginny accepted the compliment, assuring Willie there was no need to worry.

Willie's intercom buzzed. "Nick Rossiter to see you," her secretary announced. "He's not on your calendar . . . he says he's a friend."

Willie made a face. Some friend, she thought. After their argument, he'd dropped out of her life, and being right, she hadn't gone after him. "Show him in," she said at last.

"Long time, no see." Nick greeted her jauntily, and surveyed the office with wide eyes. "I see you've come up in the world . . . pastel wall, a staff . . . I'm impressed. A lot's happened since we lost touch."

"Did you expect me to stand still, waiting for a call?"

Nick gave her a tired smile. "No, Willie. You'll never stop going places." The steam went out of his repartee, and he slumped into the chair in front of her desk. "This is a professional visit, kid. I need a divorce."

Willie stared at the man who'd said he didn't want emotional baggage. "A divorce? When did you get married?"

"Couple of months ago . . . in Vegas," he mumbled. "I went out there to soak up some atmosphere for Sean McDowell's latest case. It turned out to be a short story, Willie. Too much drinking, maybe too much loneliness. Sharon was dancing in the chorus at Caesar's. She was pretty and she was fun and we ended up in a wedding chapel at four in the morning – and now I have a hangover that won't quit."

Willie didn't want to hear any more. "Sorry, Nick," she

said, "you've come to the wrong place. I don't clean up hangovers."

"Just like that?" he demanded, an angry edge to his voice. "You don't even want to hear about it?"

"Look, Nick," she said, "you married some poor woman, and now you want to dump her. Find yourself a lawyer who thinks it's okay to do that."

Nick didn't move from his chair. "You know, Willie," he said quietly, "maybe the issue here is you. You think you've made yourself into the white knight you never found. Running around saving women in distress . . . Christ, I told you once and I thought you heard me, women don't have a monopoly on hurting."

Willie softened. Rossiter had his faults, but he'd never done her any real harm. "Okay, Nick," she said, "I'll listen to your story, but I'm not making any promises . . . "

"Let's just say it was a case of mistaken identity. I thought I was marrying a playmate; Sharon thought Sean McDowell came with a bankroll that wouldn't quit. She's almost picked me clean, Willie – and now she says no divorce unless I sign over the royalties from the next book. Does it make me a bad guy if I don't think that's fair, counselor?"

Willie didn't think Nick was a bad guy, not compared to some she'd met in her line of work – but she couldn't quite see him, or any man for that matter, as the victim of a woman's wiles. She had felt he was the kind of man who could hurt a woman who loved him – yet in fairness, she couldn't know for sure if the second Mrs. Rossiter fell into that category.

For Willie, the heart of the matter was this: She could not imagine using her skills against a woman, yet Nick had been a friend and he was asking for help. "All right," she said, "do you remember when we had our fight? You said you wouldn't tell me how to do my job. Well, I can't do your divorce, Nick, I just can't. But I will turn it over to one of my associates – and I'll look over the papers myself, just to make sure everything's in order. That's my best offer, and I hope it's okay."

Nick was quiet for a moment and then he nodded his agreement. "Does this mean we're friends again," he asked with a smile, "even if you disapprove of me?"

"Under those conditions – yes, we can be friends again."

"Does that mean you might be glad I'm available again?" he asked, half joking.

The question made Willie think of Jedd – and she knew that she and Nick would not be lovers again. One dead end in her life was enough. "It means I'm glad we can be friends again," she answered. She pulled over a yellow pad, and picked up a pencil. "Now answer a few questions for your lawyer . . . "

"There's no such thing as having it all," Faith Spaulding declared bitterly. "And whoever made *that* myth up and sold it to women should be shot."

Willie listened. She'd become an excellent listener over the years, and this client had a story Willie hadn't heard before.

Faith Spaulding might have been a magazine-cover success story. Tall and sleek, with blunt-cut black hair and discreet makeup, she had a challenging and well-paid career as vice-president of a successful "boutique" advertising agency. Faith also had a six-year-old daughter and a husband who had supported her every goal and ambition.

"Jay was in my corner until I got my last promotion," Faith said. "He even joked about how great it would be to have a wife who could afford to keep him in style. When we bought our BMW, Jay made a point of telling the salesman it was my money that moved us up from a Honda . . . "

"And then?" Willie prompted, knowing there had to be a poisoned apple in Faith Spaulding's personal Eden, else why would she be here?

"Then Jay started to notice what wasn't happening in his life and his career – and blaming me for it. My hours are crazy, and I travel a lot. Jay teaches at a junior college . . . he has some control over his schedule. We agreed

425

that he'd be home for Jennifer, our daughter. Then Jay got passed over for the chairmanship of his department because he couldn't put in the extra time.

"He said the promotion could wait, he said our marriage and our daughter were more important, but *something* happened, Miss Dellahaye. We were living in a great apartment and we had a beach house in Southampton. Jay got to spend the whole summer there with Jenny, while I commuted on weekends. But 'the good life,' as he called it, seemed to matter less and less. Jay started taking verbal potshots at me, especially when we were entertaining clients – and when I tried to talk to him, he said it was my imagination. We stopped making love and he started accusing me of having affairs. Finally I couldn't stand it anymore; I made the mistake of insisting on marriage counseling."

"The counseling didn't help?" Willie asked.

Faith shook her head. "Jay wasn't looking for help. He was looking for someone to blame for what wasn't happening in his life. I was shocked at what came out of his mouth . . . all that frustration and anger. It was like I was the enemy and he was just waiting for the chance to say how I'd taken away his manhood and how much he hated me for it."

"Your husband wants a divorce, then?" Willie asked.

"My husband wants me dead," Faith answered bitterly. "I want the divorce. I can't live with all that resentment and blame."

"I'm sorry," Willie said, feeling the failure of Faith Spaulding's dream, as if it were personal, just the way she always did. It *was* unfair, just as Faith had said, to believe in what the women's books called "options," to reach for them, with a mate's support – and then have him turn on you, just when it seemed that having it all was possible. "If Jay won't contest the divorce, then all we have to do is iron out the custody and financial arrangements."

"That won't be so easy," Faith said quietly.

Willie waited, while the woman who sat across her desk struggled to say what was on her mind. "Divorce is never

426

easy," she said encouragingly, "but I'll do my best to make it . . . "

"You can't," Faith said in a choked voice. "You see, when I give up Jay, I'll have to give up Jennifer, too . . ."

"No way!" Willie exploded. "No matter what kind of threats Jay is making, I'll make sure . . ."

"You don't understand," Faith broke in, her face a study in misery. "This has nothing to do with Jay." There was another long silence. "It's me," Faith continued, her voice barely above a whisper. "I never realized while I was busy congratulating myself . . . because Jay made Jenny's lunches and drove her to school . . . I didn't realize that they were becoming a family and I . . . I was becoming somebody who brought a big paycheck home." Now the tears were flowing freely from Faith's eyes. Willie got up from her chair and put her arm around her client's shoulders in a silent gesture of comfort.

"Jenny would die if she had to leave her father," Faith said hoarsely, her perfect makeup streaked with tears. "He's the one she turns to and needs. I can't take that away from her, and I can't stay home and be just a mother. It's breaking my heart, Miss Dellahaye, but I don't know what else to do . . . "

Fight, Willie wanted to say — but against what? Like so many of the women who came to her, Faith had been seduced by illusions — by choices that had seemed real and had turned out to be shadows. Remembering all the years she and Ginny had stuck together against the rest of the world, Willie felt the price of Faith's failed illusions was far too dear for any woman to pay. "Maybe you can take a leave from your job," she said, almost pleading, "spend time with your daughter, find a way to be together . . . "

But Faith seemed not to hear, as if somehow she had already passed sentence on herself — for the crime of daring to want more than a woman should. She instructed Willie to meet with Jay's lawyer and to work out a fair property settlement and a schedule of child support payments.

After Faith left, Willie pressed her fingers against her

427

throbbing temples and tried to massage the pain away. There were still clients to see, and she needed to be alert and ready. But sometimes, on days like this, it was as if the pain they brought into her office invaded her very soul, and it was all she could do to keep from being overwhelmed by the unhappiness she had made her life's work.

Nothing changes, she thought wearily, rich or poor, young or old, weren't they the same? Dreaming and hoping – and then paying and paying.

13

COURT SAYS PAY, DOC SAYS NO WAY!

The headline said it all. Thanks to Willie's eloquent arguments, the court had ruled that Jack Shepherd owed his discarded wife half of his medical license – and set the price at $50,000.

Moments after the landmark decision, Shepherd's attorney had held a press conference on the courthouse steps, attacking Regina as "the classic woman scorned" and arguing that Jack should not be "indentured for the rest of his life" simply because he had fallen out of love with the woman he married.

"You can bet we'll appeal," he said, "and we'll show the court what a grave injustice has been done today. I speak for all men," he added piously, "when I say there must be limits put on the price of a woman's disappointment."

The little speech, reproduced in every newspaper and replayed on the evening news, had made Willie see red, but the years had taught her to curb her righteous indignation. But just a little. She'd been reprimanded by judges for pushing the limits of courtroom etiquette – and had even been cited once for contempt, cooling her heels

428

in jail for five hours until Pam Belzer had arrived to bail her out.

The reprimands and the stiff fine hadn't banked Willie's driving passion. At heart she was the same little girl who had cried out against injustice in a small-town courtroom. But she had learned how to use her righteous indignation in the service of her clients. And she had learned that fighting fire with fire was often better than simply crying in the wind.

If Jack Shepherd was hoping to get public opinion – at least the male contingent – behind his appeal, Willie would do the same.

She buzzed her secretary and instructed her to say "yes" to all requests for interviews and talk-show appearances. Then she called Nick Rossiter. "Do you plan to write about the Shepherd case?" she asked.

"What's it to you?" he countered, affecting a tough-guy tone. "Are you gonna bust my chops again if I don't say 'may I?' "

"No," she laughed, "not this time. I've learned my lesson, Nick. A man's gotta do what a man's gotta do. But I'm asking a favor . . . "

"Shoot."

"If you are planning a column on the case, wait until after tonight."

"Sounds interesting. Will you ply me with liquor and seduce me into writing something nice about the noble Regina? Because if you are, I can probably be had, counselor."

"Why, Nick," she gasped in mock horror, "I wouldn't *dream* of compromising your journalistic integrity. And I don't want you to write anything *nice* about my client – but I do hope you'll write something fair about the issues . . . "

"'Fair' meaning the way you see them?"

There was a silence on Willie's end. "Okay," she said finally. "Maybe I deserved that. All I'm asking is that you listen. I'm giving a talk at the New School tonight. Just show up . . . I'll buy you dinner later."

429

"Aha, I knew it! You *are* trying to bribe me. Here's my best offer, Willie – I'll show up and I'll listen. And *if* I decide to write something, I'll call it how *I* see it – fair enough?"

"Fair enough."

Thanks to a full-page ad in the *New York Times* prominently featuring Willie's picture, the auditorium of the New School for Social Research was filled to capacity for the lecture on "Divorce in America – A Woman's Perspective." The crowd consisted mainly of women, mostly in their thirties and forties, with a light scattering of men.

There was an appreciative murmur from the audience when Willie took the podium. She was simply dressed in a dark-blue business suit that dramatically framed her striking natural beauty.

"Perhaps some of you have read about my most recent case," she began. "Perhaps you put the story aside, thinking that Regina Shepherd's problems have nothing to do with you. If you did, you may have made the same mistake Regina did: believing that divorce happens to other people.

"Take a look at the woman sitting to your right," she instructed. "Assuming you're both married, the odds are that one of you will find yourself in a divorce lawyer's office long before 'death-do-us-part.'" Willie paused to allow her words to sink in.

"And if *that* statistic doesn't make you think, try this one on: in the year following a divorce, a woman's standard of living generally falls by seventy-three percent – while a man's typically rises by forty-two percent during the same period." Now there was a deep, rumbling murmur from the audience.

"It's time women took their heads out of the sand and faced the tough reality that marriage has changed – and that you must change with it – or risk some devastating consequences. Some of you may feel it's unromantic to think about divorce until it's staring you in the face. I say it's unromantic to wake up and find yourself impoverished, socially, emotionally, and financially. I say that you can protect yourselves – just as you'd protect yourselves against heart attacks and strokes – by knowing the risk factors and acting accordingly, instead of waiting until it's too late."

As she warmed to her subject, Willie's blue eyes glowed with the fire of conviction. "Women can no longer afford to submerge themselves in marriages that can be broken at a husband's whim. You need to keep your identities, socially, emotionally, and financially – so that if or when divorce comes, you have the resources to survive as whole human beings."

Willie spoke for almost an hour, describing the plight of America's "new poor" – middle-class women abruptly impoverished when their middle-class marriages broke up. The crowd was silent, almost spellbound as she spoke, and when she was finished, a flurry of hands went up immediately. Willie pointed to a youngish woman dressed in blue jeans and a western shirt.

"Miss Dellahaye, you say we should keep our financial identities – but how do I manage that when my husband and I need two paychecks to stay afloat?"

"One way is to maintain your own credit cards," Willie answered promptly. "Not as Mrs. John Smith, but as Mary Smith. Keep your own checking account, and use it to pay some bills – so that you'll have a credit history. Keep records of your earnings and how they're used. When you make any big purchases, like houses or apartments, make sure your name goes on the deed."

Another hand shot up. "What happens when we stop working and take time out to have a baby?"

Willie had a ready answer. "Make sure it *is* a 'time out.' Keep your job skills alive and don't lose touch, so you'll have something to go back to when you're ready. If you're just beginning a career, choose companies with liberal maternity leaves – and possibly child-care facilities. And when you decide to become a mother, make sure you don't become your husband's financial ward. Insist on keeping those credit cards and checking accounts going, whether or not you're working."

An older woman stood up. "I read about one of your big cases, counselor, where you got some rich woman a lot of money. But what if we're not rich and we aren't married to rich men? How do we get a decent deal if there's a divorce?"

"Make sure you always know what your family's net worth is . . . That means how much insurance you have, how much is in the bank, what your home's market value is, and where every penny you jointly own is invested. Find a lawyer who knows the value of getting as much as possible up front. The sad truth is that fewer than twenty percent of ex-husbands keep up their alimony payments, so whenever you can, get property or cash or investments, rather than a promise to pay in the future. If your divorce settlement does include alimony, make sure it's protected with an insurance policy – so you won't find yourself suddenly destitute if something happens to your ex-husband."

A voice from the back of the auditorium challenged Willie: "Isn't it true that lawyers like you encourage people to fight because you make more money that way? Why don't you tell people they can save a lot of money if they keep it friendly and use one of those do-it-yourself divorce kits?"

Willie winced inwardly at the accusation, but she knew there was some truth in it. "I can't defend the entire legal profession," she answered. "Some lawyers do escalate marital battles because it means bigger fees. And it's true that some people can work out a fair and friendly divorce between them. Those people don't show up in my office. I see women who tried to keep it friendly – and found their savings accounts cleaned out and their safe-deposit boxes emptied before they could turn around. Remember, the man you're divorcing can be very different from the man you married. I say: If divorce is on your mind, see a lawyer before you mention the word out loud." Willie looked at her watch and said she'd take one more question.

"How do we find a good divorce lawyer, counselor – in the Yellow Pages?"

432

Willie laughed. "I don't recommend that, though you could get lucky. Your best bet is word of mouth – find someone who did a good job for a friend or relative, and chances are you'll be well taken care of, too."

As Willie left the stage, a dozen or so women crowded round her, each with a question or a story to tell. And though she saw Nick waving from the back of the auditorium, Willie couldn't walk away from anyone who asked her help. She took a handful of business cards from her wallet and gave them out, pausing when she came to a shabbily dressed young woman holding a child by the hand, a little girl about eight or nine. Just about the age Willie had been when she'd first learned the meaning of the word "divorce" – a word that had shaped and colored almost every moment of her life.

"Call me," she said to the group, but looking into the young woman's eyes. "Tell my secretary you were here tonight and she'll give you an appointment. If you need a divorce, I'll—"

"I already got a divorce," the woman blurted out, "but what you said before . . . it happened to me. I'm working two jobs and I can't make ends meet. I can't afford a big-shot lawyer like you . . . "

Willie drew the woman aside and scribbled her private number on the business card. "Call me tomorrow," she said, "and don't worry about my fee. We'll work something out, I promise."

And as she walked away, the beginning of a plan formed in her mind. The city must be full of women like the one she'd spoken to, suffering and scraping by because they couldn't afford first-rate legal skills. And while Willie had never turned away anyone who asked her help, she knew that many women would feel as Ginny had so long ago, that they would have to settle for shoddy representation because they were poor.

She would change that, Willie resolved. Most law firms handled an occasional case on a *pro bono* basis, for the public good and without charge. But now that her firm was prosperous and successful, she could do more. She

433

would hire more staff and establish an entire *pro bono* division, dedicated to helping any woman who was victimized by an unhappy marriage or impoverished by an unfair divorce.

"About time," Nick said when Willie finally joined him. "Didn't anyone tell you that guys don't like to be kept waiting?"

"No," she said, "but feel free to educate me."

"Maybe I will . . . but after I get the dinner and drinks you promised."

They went to a small Italian restaurant on Bleecker Street. "I was impressed," Nick admitted between mouthfuls of pasta. "You made a good case about women coming out on the short end of divorce. But there's something more to it, the way you talked to those women about marriage and divorce . . . something about you, Willie. I always figured some guy did a number on you and you never got over it. Am I right?"

"Not tonight, Nick," she said with a smile. "I'm supposed to be persuading you that Regina Shepherd deserves what she got in court – and more. Remember?"

He shook his head. "If you wanna talk, you gotta listen sometimes, Willie. Maybe I will scribble a word or two on behalf of your noble cause. But I just wonder if you know how you came across tonight. It's one thing to let women know what the score is – but you made it sound like getting married was in the same league as chain-smoking and putting away a quart of gin every day. Maybe you see it that way, but maybe when two people start a life together, they're just making an act of faith."

"That's quite a speech for a tough guy," Willie said. "Maybe you still believe in love – and fairytales and Santa Claus and leprechauns—"

"I do," Nick said solemnly. "And you know why? Because if you don't leave room in your life for those things to show up, counselor . . . they never will."

434

14

The cherry trees were laden with buds on the brink of blooming, and Willie was just hours away from what could be the biggest triumph of her career. Tomorrow morning she would stand before the highest court in the land and argue the case of Shepherd vs. Shepherd for the last time.

Yet as her limousine crawled through the late-afternoon Washington traffic, Willie's mind filled up with yesterdays. Washington was Matt Harding's city, and she couldn't help but wonder what life might have been like if she and Matt had married.

Clear-headed and practical though she could be, Willie had never really let go of this one "might-have-been." Emotionally she'd resisted considering all the practical reasons why a marriage with Matt might have been difficult, thinking only that it could have meant an end to loneliness. A real home, a child – always a daughter in Willie's fantasies – who'd be raised strong and independent, confident of love and free from fear.

What was Matt thinking now, Willie wondered, and how would he feel tomorrow when she stood before him? Would he feel the nagging tug of regret? Willie hoped so; it didn't seem fair that she alone should be the custodian of their memories.

The limousine pulled up in front of the Willard Hotel. Quickly she checked in and settled herself in a spacious suite overlooking Pennsylvania Avenue and with a commanding view of the White House.

She arranged on the bed the hundreds of pages of legal documents that had gone into the Shepherd case – a case that had, she once joked, almost become a career.

Jack Shepherd had won his appeal by successfully

arguing that his ex-wife had no right to mortgage his entire future. The judge had agreed, stating that Regina had no right to seek unreasonable compensation for performing the duties of a good wife and that awarding her a portion of Jack's medical license would perpetuate "the childlike dependency of women which our society and our courts have sought to banish."

Willie's response was quick and angry: gender discrimination, she said. Now she had to convince Matt and his colleagues – and to persuade them that Regina's share in Jack Shepherd's future prosperity was not charity, but a rightful debt that should be repaid.

Taut and tensed for combat, she drilled and rehearsed until the words were etched on her brain. All she needed now was a light supper and a good night's sleep.

Nostalgia took Willie to Sorvino's, one of Matt's favorite places. The small restaurant was not very crowded, and there were no familiar faces, no landmarks of another time. Even the menu was different. Willie ordered a glass of Orvieto and some angelhair pasta in a light cream sauce. Because she hated eating alone in restaurants, she always brought something to read.

She turned the pages of the *Washington Post*, thinking she might find some mention of Matt, but there was only a paragraph on the Court's calendar buried in the metropolitan section.

For a long time after their last meeting, Willie filled with apprehension whenever she saw the words "Supreme Court" in a headline, dreading the moment she'd read the story of Matt's death. And after a while, when the moment never came, relief mingled with resentment over the empty nobility that had cheated her of mate and lover and family.

Once Willie had seen Matt's picture in *People* magazine, alongside an elegant woman described as the chairperson of some benefit or other. Staring at the photo, she had felt a surge of anger, though there was no mention of a personal relationship.

His old friend John Martin Gibbs had died a few years

ago, and since then Matt's opinions had taken on some odd colorations. At times they echoed Gibbs's conservative views; often they seemed simply eccentric, as if he had given up the pure liberalism Willie had admired. "Life's about change, kid," he'd once said. "It's about confusion and growth – and without that, the best mind in the world is just a muddy, stagnant pool." Matt certainly practiced what he preached, Willie reflected, recalling his declarations of love.

"*Signorina?*" Willie looked up from her paper to see a waiter hovering at her shoulder. "The gentleman over there wishes to offer you a drink. May I bring you a cognac or a cordial?"

A few tables away, an attractive man of about thirty-five caught her eye and smiled, but Willie was in no mood to exchange conversation or anything else with a stranger tonight. She smiled and shook her head, pointing to her watch to soften the "no."

As Willie walked toward the hotel entrance, she noticed a black limousine parked nearby. It can't be, she thought, taking in the Supreme Court crest on the door. But when she stopped at the reception desk to check for messages, a uniformed driver approached. "Miss Dellahaye?" he asked.

"Yes?"

He handed her a plain white envelope. Quickly she tore it open. The handwriting on the note was bold and strong, the words few and to the point. "My good sense must have deserted me, I know – but I must see you." The note was signed "Matt."

It was as if a key unlocked a Pandora's box of emotions that had been tucked away but not forgotten. Willie had been prepared to face Matt in court, but this – this was too personal. And crazy – a meeting between a lawyer and a judge the night before an appeal. The newspapers would have a field day.

For a long moment, Willie stared at the note, weighing

wisdom and common sense against something that was over but not forgotten. She got into the car.

How different my life might have been, she thought as the car sped toward Georgetown. Matt's love might have made a difference, taught lessons far better than the one he'd given on a cold autumn night.

Coming back now felt like a pilgrimage, like seeing a piece of her life replay itself. As the car rounded the circular driveway, she could see Matt standing in the doorway, tall and ramrod straight as always, silhouetted in the light.

"Willie." He said her name softly, almost reverently. Then, more casually: "It's great to see you again, kid."

"You're looking very well," Willie said stiffly, with an edge of accusation. "And this *is* crazy."

He grinned mischievously, like a small boy caught in a prank, and led the way into the familiar book-lined study. A fire was burning brightly in the fireplace; two glasses and a decanter had been set out. Without asking, Matt splashed some brandy into the crystal balloons and handed one to her. In his jeans and cotton knit pullover, he looked rugged and boyish, playing the same scene that had warmed so many nights for Willie.

"Nothing's changed," she said quietly.

"You have," Matt said, staring openly. "You were always beautiful, but now . . . you're everything I knew you could be, strong and proud and accomplished. I'm proud of you, Willie. You followed your dream and made it happen."

Yes, she thought, taking a small sip of her brandy, I made one dream happen – the only one that survived.

Almost as if he could read her mind, Matt said: "You're angry with me . . . I felt it the minute you arrived. Go ahead, Willie, take your best shot. I owe you one."

"Damn it, Matt! I loved you," she erupted passionately. "We're both still here, and we could have had all this time together! Why couldn't you just trust what we had? Did you really believe it was all for the best when you took my chance for happiness away?"

438

Matt opened his mouth to speak, but a grimace of pain contorted his face. He gripped the arm of his chair and closed his eyes – and Willie was suddenly frightened.

She rushed to his side and gripped his hand. "What's wrong? Matt – do you need a doctor? Is it your heart?"

The pain passed, and though Matt was visibly paler, he managed a jaunty smile. "It's nothing, kid – just a little twitch." He took a sip of brandy. "Sure, I've had my share of regrets, Willie. What man in his right mind wouldn't? But you'll just have to believe that what happened between us *was* for the best."

Willie didn't believe that, any more than she believed the pain she'd seen in Matt's face was "just a little twitch," but she was afraid to risk upsetting him with an argument. "Why did you send for me tonight?" she asked. "It would have been safer tomorrow . . . "

The mischievous grin returned. "I couldn't be sure you'd see me after tomorrow."

Willie took the bait. "Does that mean you're planning to vote against me?"

"Judges don't plan their decisions without hearing the evidence, Willie," Matt chided her. "But no matter how I vote, remember I'm never against you. I've tracked your career every step of the way. You're as fine a lawyer as I knew you'd be . . . "

Willie waited for the "but" to follow.

"My only concern," he continued, "is that wonderful single-mindedness of yours. I love your passion and determination, all the more as time has diluted mine. But I hoped you'd learn that the law can be a dangerous and consuming lover."

"Is that why you brought me here tonight," Willie demanded, "To give me a lecture?"

Matt laughed. "You look like a little girl about to stamp her foot. If I were twenty years younger, I'd take you over my knee for that – but I'm afraid the fun of it would kill me. Do you remember," he asked, "when you were clerking for John Martin Gibbs? Remember that case you wanted so much to be heard?"

"I remember," Willie said, not knowing where Matt was leading.

"Remember how I warned you about the danger of using your personal passions to define your pursuit of the law?"

"I remember," she said impatiently, "but what—"

"Hear me out," Matt ordered. "From what I've seen you've never really made that distinction. Now you've done what every lawyer dreams of . . . you've taken one of your personal causes and gone the distance . . . "

"But this one isn't just my cause," Willie protested. "The issues are important, and they *are* timely . . . "

Matt shook his head. "You know we can't say another word about this case. I know it's important to you. What matters to me is that you learn the lesson – because I won't be around to teach it again. I want you to be a whole person, not just a . . . a law machine."

"And if I am?" Willie asked defiantly, the words wrenched from her heart. "What about the lessons you *did* teach me? My God, I trusted you, Matt! Don't you know how hard that is for me? Don't you see that it would have made a difference if you'd married me? If you hadn't taken your love away?"

Matt's face went ashen, but he struggled for control and answered quietly, "I do love you, Willie, I've never stopped. I've learned some lessons, too. I did what I thought was right – and sometimes, all that gets you is being right. Let me give you that one, Willie, it's gospel and I've paid for it."

Willie listened without gladness as she looked into the gray eyes that had once glowed with promises of love. Matt's pain didn't take away her own – or bring back the "might have been" years she'd mourned.

Maybe I could have changed his mind. The thought came to Willie with a shocking clarity. All her life she had fought and argued for what she believed. Yet when it came to her own happiness, she had let the man she loved send her away without a fight. And all she had to show for

440

that easy surrender was a feeling of waste. A lesson even harder than Matt's.

"Thank you," she said quietly, accepting the regrets that were all Matt had left to give. "I'll try to remember everything you taught me." She paused, everything said, yet not wanting to leave him. But finally they both knew their time was over.

"I guess you ought to be leaving," he said.

She nodded.

They walked to the door slowly, drawing out the last minutes together, sharing a silent mourning for a moment that had passed. Matt put his arms around Willie and hugged her close. Briefly, she laid her head on his chest and felt the steady beat of the heart that had betrayed them both.

As Willie left the Georgian house and went out into the spring evening, Matthew Harding leaned hard against the doorframe. With a great effort he steadied himself and reached for the wheelchair concealed by a pair of thickly branched ficus trees.

Letting go of the pose he'd sustained with nothing more than pride and determination, Matthew Harding slumped into the chair and was transformed in a matter of seconds into an old and tired man, left with only a dream of a beautiful woman whose adoring eyes had made him young.

Ascending the marble staircase of the Court building, the final forum for appeal in the American judicial system, Willie felt a profound sense of awe. For two centuries the Court had interpreted the Constitution and decided issues affecting the rights of every American citizen, rich and poor, condemned prisoners and presidents of the land.

That she was here told Willie her cause was timely, for of the five thousand or more cases submitted to the Court each year, fewer than two hundred are heard. She had filed her brief as required and now she had approximately half an hour to present her oral argument.

441

"Knock 'em dead," Willie said under her breath, as she walked past the guard at the door and into the courtroom, which was open to the public and members of the press.

Amidst the majesty and power of her surroundings, Willie sought Matt's face, fixing on it as a dancer takes her bearings. If I can convince him, she thought superstitiously, I can convince them all.

"It has been said," she began, "that America is in the midst of a divorce revolution. We can bemoan the breakdown of families and the losses in human terms. But as the institution of marriage becomes less than a lifetime contract, it becomes crucial to recognize the change in the laws which govern divorce.

"We must put a monetary value on the investment made by partners who channel their talents and energies into promoting the economic well-being of their partners – with the clear understanding that they will share in the fruits of this partnership. Jack Shepherd said 'yes' to the support and investment his wife made. Now he says 'no' to repayment, denying that the sacrifice of her own career was anything more than a performance of her wifely duties. For a state court to support that view, to characterize Regina Shepherd's fight for justice as 'childlike dependency,' is clear gender discrimination.

"I ask this court – the protector of our fundamental human rights – to protect Regina Shepherd's investment, *and* all similar investments by spouses of either sex. The court cannot give my client back the years she labored on her husband's behalf. But the court can rule that she does indeed hold a rightful claim – a mortgage, if you will – against Jack Shepherd's medical degree.

"We are not seeking, as Dr. Shepherd claims, to punish him for the lapse of his affections or the failure of his marriage. We ask only that he share, as is proper, with the woman who made his career possible.

"In today's world, emotional commitments between spouses may be a matter of conscience. I ask the court to rule that economic commitments are real and tangible and will be upheld. I ask the court to set aside the discriminatory

442

ruling based on gender stereotype – and not on hard socioeconomic realities. To do otherwise will devalue the marriage bond to the point of worthlessness."

Nine old men of the court listened with impassive faces as Willie pleaded with all the passion and skill at her command. Even Matt's expression told her nothing. With every fiber of her being, Willie believed that her cause was right, that the welfare of thousands of women depended on convincing the court to see the issues as she saw them.

Yet she knew all too well that Justice could be not only slow, but also shortsighted. Indeed, life had taught her that too often Justice – as surely as love – could be absolutely blind.

Two weeks passed – not an uncommonly long wait for a Supreme Court decision – before Willie had her ruling. Eloquent though she had been, she did not carry the entire court with her arguments. Yet the outcome, all that really mattered, was five votes to four in Regina Shepherd's favor – with Justice Matthew Harding casting the deciding vote.

Joy and gratitude filled Willie's heart, as she said a silent "thank you," not only to Justice, but to Matt, who had, in his own way, said that at last, the time for what she believed in had come.

Book V

Judgment

1

New York City: Today

The first sound Willie heard was the fear in Sofia's voice, then her own name, urgently whispered. And then a moment of dead silence.

Willie's grip tightened on the cold black telephone receiver. "Sofia? Where are you? What's happening? Talk to me . . ."

"He's found me . . . I heard voices in the hall . . . speaking Arabic. I don't know what to do. Help me, Willie . . . please."

Willie murmured sounds of reassurance, her mind darting from one possibility to another. She had been certain Sofia would be safe in her suite at the Waldorf Towers, registered under another name. "Are you sure they're Seif's people?" she asked. "Has anyone talked to you or tried to get in?"

"No," Sofia answered her, her voice now a breathy whisper. "But I'm sure they're Seif's men. They left a minute ago, but they'll be back, I know it."

"Listen to me," Willie commanded. "Stay away from the door. Call security and tell them you heard intruders outside your door. Then call your brother. Get Harry to stay with you until we go to court."

"Harry's not here," Sofia wailed, "He's in Chicago selling some jewels for me. He won't be back until tonight. I'm all alone . . ."

"Not for long," Willie said crisply. "Fix yourself a stiff drink, keep your door locked, and give me time to get some reinforcements."

But what kind? Willie wondered after she hung up. She

447

could call the police and say that her client – an American citizen – was being threatened and harassed. She had done exactly that a week ago, when three of Seif's flunkies had followed her and Sofia from Willie's office to Lutece and stationed themselves outside while the two women lunched and planned Sofia's divorce.

When the police arrived, the men had produced diplomatic passports, insisted their presence was innocent, and threatened to file a complaint with the State Department. In spite of Willie's angry protests, the police could do nothing.

Just before they left, one of the officers had taken her aside. "Do yourself a favor and don't mess with these diplomatic types, counselor," he said. "Just between us, these guys are a royal pain in the NYPD's butt, and unless we catch them doing something a lot bigger than loitering, we can't touch 'em."

If the police couldn't help protect Sofia, then who would? Willie asked herself. The answer was clear – and not to her liking. Someone who didn't care about diplomatic immunity or any other niceties. Willie didn't know anyone like that, but she knew someone who did.

She dialed Nick Rossiter's number. "I need a favor," she said without preamble. "And fast." The urgency in her voice left no room for the usual banter.

"You got it," the newsman answered.

"One of my clients is in bad trouble," Willie explained. "I need what you call 'muscle' to keep her from getting hurt."

"Call the cops," Nick said promptly. "It's cheaper and—"

"The cops can't help," she said impatiently. "I wouldn't be asking if I had a choice. I don't care what it costs. Just do it – now."

"How many guys do you need?" Nick asked.

Willie thought for a moment. "At least two, maybe three. I want them right now, Nick – as in this minute. Can you do it?"

"I'll try." There was a pause on the line. "Willie," he said, "you've always played by the book, and this sounds

448

like something that could get dirty. Are you sure you know what you're doing?"

"Yes. Get back to me fast, Nick . . . I'll wait for your call."

I should have done this from the beginning, Willie thought. Ever since Sofia had slipped away from her bodyguard Fawzi, losing him in the rabbit warren of private rooms at Elizabeth Arden's, they had barely managed to stay ahead of Seif's long and powerful reach.

Willie had believed she could hide a lone woman in this city of nine million, keep her out of sight until the divorce case was before the court. But she hadn't reckoned with Sofia's needs.

After living like a virtual prisoner for so long, she behaved like an unruly child, rebelling against Willie's instructions to stay indoors and to see no one but her brother. More than once – as Willie learned after the fact – Sofia had persuaded Harry to take her to the theater or to a restaurant. Maybe Seif would have tracked her no matter what precautions were taken – but now there was more than a "maybe" to deal with. Seif's men were on Sofia's heels, and Willie would have to find a way to make them back off.

She stared at her telephone and willed it to ring.

Willie didn't know what she'd expected – maybe heavyset men wearing bad suits and attitudes to match. Nick's "referrals" were on the large side, and their clothes were not impeccably tailored. But their attitude was that of schoolboys, waiting for a teacher to explain an assignment. They introduced themselves as Ralph, Jack, and Billy, then stood "at ease" in front of Willie's desk.

Briefly she explained the situation. "I don't know what kind of protection we'll actually need," she added. "Maybe no one will bother my client if you're there. I don't want you to start any trouble, but if someone tried to hurt Mrs. al-Rahman in any way . . . "

The three men nodded, almost as one. Willie started to

write a check, but was politely reminded that cash was the preferred method of payment. "Take the check for now," she pleaded, "and I promise to cover it by tomorrow. Please."

Fifteen minutes later, Willie was knocking on Sofia's door. When no one answered, she tried the knob. The door opened. The luxurious suite was empty. A half-full glass sat on the coffee table, alongside an ashtray brimming with cigarette butts. On the couch was a pair of black satin mules and an open magazine.

Willie ran into the bedroom, the three men close behind, as she checked the closet and dresser drawers. They were still filled with Sofia's things. But where was Sofia? There was no trace of a struggle, no sign that the door had been forced.

Willie silently cursed herself for not coming the minute her client had called. Now Sofia had vanished, and heaven only knew what kind of danger she was in – or if she was still alive.

"Counselor . . . over here." Willie went into the bathroom. Sofia's cosmetics lay in a jumbled heap on the marble vanity, as if they'd been hurriedly used and discarded. Ralph picked a crumpled matchbook from the pile and opened it. The matches had been torn away. Inside, on the gray cardboard, drawn with a crimson lipstick, was a crude picture of an airplane. Ralph held it out to Willie.

"They're taking her back to Jeddah!" she exclaimed. "We have to stop them. Come on – they can't be that far ahead of us. Hurry."

As the black limousine hurtled toward Kennedy Airport, Willie looked at her watch, tapping her fingers impatiently on the car telephone. After wasting precious minutes arguing with the control tower, she'd learned that Seif al-Rahman's private jet, the *Hayat*, had filed a flight plan for Jeddah and was waiting to be cleared for take-off.

"Can't you hold them?" Willie pleaded. "My client's on that plane, against her will. If you let them take off, there's no telling what will happen to her."

450

"Sorry, ma'am," the control tower supervisor replied, "unless we get orders from the police, we're not authorized to interfere. Federal Aviation rules . . . "

"Rules be damned!" she exploded. "I'm talking about a woman's life! Look," she said, reining in her temper, "I know it's not your fault, but I'm on my way . . . all I'm asking for is a little time. Can't you find a way to help me? God knows I've been stuck in your traffic jams myself. You don't have to say anything to the pilot. Can't you just let someone else take his turn? Please . . . "

There was a moment's silence. "I'd like to help you, ma'am, but I just don't know. How long till you get here?"

"Fifteen minutes, tops. Please," she begged.

"I can't make any promises," the man said, "but the traffic *does* look a little heavy right now."

Willie hung up the telephone. "Hurry," she urged the driver. "Just don't get us stopped." She turned to the three men in the car. "If the plane's still there, we have to find a way to board. Any ideas?"

Ralph looked to his companions and then back to Willie. "Listen, counselor," he said, "if you want us to get on, we'll get on, just as long as you're not too fussy about how we do it." He opened his jacket, revealing the butt end of a revolver as he produced a leather billfold. Inside were some official-looking documents. One identified Ralph Dawson as an agent of the Federal Bureau of Investigation, another identified the same Ralph Dawson as detective, second grade, of the New York Police Department.

Ralph lightly touched his shoulder holster. "This is legal," he said, "it doesn't cost you extra. But these, the phony ID, that's risk, and in my business, risk costs extra."

Willie struggled with what he was saying. A licensed gun could be legally drawn by a bodyguard in protection of his client. Maybe. But heaven only knew what might happen if these men tried to storm the *Hayat*. Impersonating a policeman or a federal agent was illegal for any reason – and Willie was an officer of the court, sworn to uphold the law.

Never in all her career had Willie done or sanctioned

anything remotely illegal. But right now, she couldn't see any other way to save Sofia. "Use the ID," she said – and prayed that the guns wouldn't be necessary.

As the limousine drew closer to the private runway, Willie could see the sleek silver jet that bore the al-Rahman crest, a two-headed falcon in flight. The doors to the plane were closed. "Stop here," she instructed the driver. "It's better if no one sees me."

To Ralph, she said: "Keep it simple. Say you're after Sofia. Say she's wanted for questioning . . . smuggling, tax evasion, anything . . . but get her off that plane."

Willie crossed her fingers and held her breath, as she watched Ralph lead the other two men toward a mechanic in gray coveralls, flash his bogus identification, and gesture toward the jet. The mechanic shook his head doubtfully and walked away, into a workmen's shed.

He returned with another man. Ralph repeated the ritual, and Willie prayed that no one would think to call the police or FBI. A few minutes later, she saw a set of boarding steps being rolled toward the plane. She watched with a grudging respect as Ralph and his companions walked up the steps, slowly and deliberately, as if they had every right to board and search a private plane.

The door opened. Willie's heart sank when Fawzi appeared. He wouldn't be so easy to deceive, she thought. And sure enough, he was shaking his head and gesturing forcefully. Ralph waited calmly, not moving a step, and then pointed inside the plane. He produced another document from his pocket, allowing his jacket to flap open and reveal his weapon.

"Oh, my God," Willie gasped as Fawzi reached into his own pocket. She gripped her armrest and held her breath for a long frightened moment until Fawzi's hand reappeared, holding only a paper of some kind.

Ralph glanced at it, shook his head, and pointed once more into the plane. And then miraculously Sofia appeared. It was all Willie could do to keep from rushing out of the car, but she forced herself to stay out of sight and to wait.

Ralph took Sofia by the arm, as if he were taking her into custody, and walked slowly down the steps, just as if he had every right to be there. And in spite of herself, Willie was impressed by the cool professionalism of the men she had hired to do what the law could not have accomplished.

"It's all right," Willie said over and over again, soothing her terrified client as the limousine sped away from the airport. "He can't touch you now, Sofia. These men will stay with you round the clock. It's going to be all right."

Sofia nodded mutely, but her body was rigid, her eyes wide with fear, as if she were still on the plane, awaiting her husband's brand of justice.

"What happened?" Willie asked finally, as the car drew closer to the city.

"It wasn't my fault," Sofia choked out. "I tried to do what you said, but I was so frightened. And right after you hung up, Fawzi was outside my door, talking to me and saying how I'd never get away from Seif. He said you were only a woman and couldn't protect me. He said Seif would forgive me if I went with him, but this was my last chance . . . "

Willie nodded knowingly. In her years of practice she had seen this kind of thing before – a wife being drawn to the spouse who abused her, clinging to the very person she needed most to escape. Just as Mama had done for so long.

Yes, Sofia's moment of weakness was understandable – and now it was up to Willie to make sure that Seif would never again exploit that weakness.

Armed with a cold, consuming fury, Willie stormed the offices of the law firm of Rogers, Bannister and Stevens, pushing past receptionists and secretaries until she faced the senior partner, Philip Bannister.

"Kidnapping's a federal offense, counselor," she said, "and not even your client can get away with that."

Bannister looked at Willie with a patrician air of

disbelief. As head of a distinguished and rather staid firm that counted a former U.S. senator among its partners and various members of royalty among its clients, Bannister was clearly unused to outbursts of this kind. "Come now," he said, smiling, "kidnapping is an ugly word, Miss Dellahaye. As I understand it, my client simply wanted an opportunity to speak privately with his wife. There's no law that prohibits conjugal conversation, is there?" he asked rhetorically. "My client informs me that he was seeking to reconcile with Mrs. al-Rahman – and that he genuinely regrets any misunderstanding that ensued."

"Misunderstanding, my foot," Willie snapped. "My client was in fear of her life – and with reason."

Bannister sighed. "Really, Miss Dellahaye, professional courtesy notwithstanding, if you insist on creating an international incident, I may have to remind you that trespassing on the property of a Saudi national is also illegal.

"May I suggest," he added in a conciliatory tone, "that the interests of both our clients will be best served if we put this unfortunate matter behind us and proceed to the business at hand . . . a speedy divorce. Perhaps you and I might meet in the next few days and try to work out an agreement . . . "

Willie heard both the threat and the hint of a deal. And tempted though she was to launch a personal vendetta against Seif al-Rahman, she wasn't at all sure that was best for Sofia. Though Willie had surrounded her with enough security to repel a full-blown terrorist attack, Sofia was still jumpy and apprehensive. More than anything, Willie felt, she needed the reality of a divorce and the chance to begin a new life.

"I have a restraining order prohibiting your client – or anyone in his employ – from coming within a thousand yards of Mrs. al-Rahman," Willie said. "Do I have your word that the order will be respected?"

"Of course," Bannister said smoothly. "I've been empowered to act on my client's behalf in this matter, and I

454

can assure you that we will proceed according to the letter of the law."

Willie left Bannister's office as abruptly as she had arrived. The assurances of a man of his stature had to mean something, she told herself, even if his client was not to be trusted.

As she had done for the past few days, Willie closeted herself in her office, building a seamless, solid case that would knock Bannister off his patrician wing-tip shoes – and make him more agreeable when it came to negotiating a settlement. "No calls," she instructed her secretary. "I'm out to everyone except Sofia al-Rahman."

Willie intended to do her negotiating from strength and that meant being prepared to go to court. She reviewed her list of witnesses, which included a noted surgeon who would describe in horrifying detail the surgery that had brutalized Sofia's body – and a distinguished psychiatrist who would testify that she had been emotionally maimed as well.

Bannister's assurances of goodwill notwithstanding, Willie had filed a petition requesting the court to freeze Seif al-Rahman's American assets, pending the outcome of the divorce action.

She checked her watch, wondering if Sofia was awake yet. Willie had made a practice of talking to her several times a day, assuring her that all was well and that she would soon be a free – and very wealthy – woman.

She picked up the phone and started to dial Sofia's number at the Waldorf Towers when she saw her own private line light up. She buzzed her secretary on the intercom. "No calls," she repeated.

"It's a Mr. Hobson from the State Department, Miss Dellahaye," her secretary said. "I tried to take a message, but he says it's urgent and insists on talking to you now."

"Put him on," Willie said, wondering what business the State Department had with her.

"We have a problem, counselor," the caller said after identifying himself.

Willie caught the word "we" and sat up at attention.

"It's our understanding that you're representing a Sofia Baldwin in an action against Seif al-Rahman," the voice continued.

"That's correct," she said crisply. "May I ask what your interest is in this matter?"

There was a long silence. "Our interest, in a nutshell, counselor, is a matter of national policy. Seif al-Rahman has been, shall we say, invaluable to this department in the past. Without breaching security, I can tell you that at this moment, he's assisting our government in some very delicate negotiations in the Middle East . . . "

"Why are you telling me this?" Willie asked.

"Because, counselor, we would like you – and the request is unofficial – to back off."

"Back off?" she repeated. "Are you saying my client shouldn't get a divorce because of some secret goings-on in the Middle East?"

"Feel free to get all the divorces you want," Hobson replied, "as long as you don't harass Mr. al-Rahman. And if you'd like an example of what I mean, I'll tell you that we don't look kindly on your attempt to freeze his assets in this country. I hope that as a patriotic American citizen, you'll take what I'm saying in the right spirit . . . "

Willie's anger rose to the surface. "I'm as patriotic as you are, Mr. Hobson, but what you're suggesting sounds to me like intimidation. What if I don't back off?"

There was another silence. "I don't think you understand me, counselor. As of this morning, Mr. al-Rahman has been appointed economic attaché to the Saudi Embassy. That makes him a foreign diplomat in good standing. Your petition to freeze his assets will be denied on those grounds – and his diplomatic immunity will protect him from any fancy legal maneuvers you may have up your sleeves. Take my advice and settle this quietly, counselor. It will be better for you and your client."

Willie could scarcely contain her anger and frustration. In

spite of all her careful preparations, Seif al-Rahman had found yet another way to elude and thwart her.

Now what? she asked herself, knowing that if she faced Philip Bannister across a bargaining table, he'd be holding all the cards – and she would be like a supplicant, begging for whatever crumbs he cared to throw her way. Even if she went to court and won, she feared it would be a Pyrrhic victory if there was no way to collect what was rightfully Sofia's.

Willie's head began to throb, but she tried to ignore the pain. More than ever, she needed to mobilize, to get past this setback and formulate a new strategy. But how, when it seemed the government of the United States had a vested interest in protecting Seif from all the legal means at her disposal?

She opened the thick file that Kusack had supplied on the al-Rahman business interests in the United States. Slowly she went down the list of companies Seif had dealt with in the past, not knowing exactly what she was looking for, but simply hoping to find something, anything that would work to her advantage instead of his.

Suddenly her attention was riveted by a single name: Fontana Enterprises. Seif al-Rahman had done business with Sam Fontana – and knowing what she did about both men, Willie began to think of a possibility that once would have seemed to her unthinkable.

Willie called Sofia immediately. "Have you ever heard your husband mention a Sam Fontana?" she asked.

"He's a friend of Seif's," Sofia answered promptly. "They've known each other for years, and when Fontana Enterprises wanted to build two hotels in Saudi, Seif was their local partner. We entertained Sam in Jeddah a couple of times, and Seif often visits him when he's in the U.S. on business. Why are you asking?"

Willie wasn't ready to tell Sofia that their case had suffered a massive setback – and that she now had only a slender hope of reconstructing it. "It's nothing for you to worry about," she said. "Let me follow through on a hunch I have, and if I come up with anything, I'll be in touch."

After she hung up, Willie looked at the telephone on her desk, knowing what her next step could be, yet hesitating to take it. For years she had known – and scorned – the seamy side of Sam's business. Now, when all the legal niceties had failed her, when it seemed she couldn't defeat a man as powerful and well connected as Seif al-Rahman, she found herself on the brink of a course she'd never taken before: win at all costs, even if it meant getting down into the mud, using the kind of edge Sam Fontana used – and asking Jedd Fontana to help her.

Willie placed a call to the corporate headquarters of Fontana Enterprises in Butte, Montana. But when she asked for Jedd, a distant, impersonal voice informed Willie that Mr. Fontana was in the Dominican Republic, supervising the construction of a new Fontana resort. "This is urgent," Willie insisted, refusing to hang up until the voice supplied a number where Jedd might be reached.

Two hours later, Jedd's silky voice was on the line. "What is it, Willie?" he asked, genuine concern in his voice. "You've never called me before . . . are you in some kind of trouble?"

"I need to talk to you, Jedd . . . but not on the phone. When will you be back in the States?"

"Not for at least two weeks. Dammit, Willie, now you've got me worried. Can't you give me a clue?"

She hesitated. "I can tell you this much," she said. "I'm not in trouble, but it's important that I see you. If I fly out tomorrow morning . . . "

"Not tomorrow, Willie," he said. "I'm meeting with the Minister of Tourism all day. Get here by evening and I'm all yours."

Evening . . . and then the night. She would be all his, too, she thought, if they met by starlight. "I'll be there the next day, early afternoon," she said.

There was a pause, as though he'd understood the significance of the schedule and was wondering whether to try getting her to change her mind.

"Whenever you come, Willie," he said finally. "I'll do whatever I can to help."

458

Would he? she thought after hanging up. Asking Jedd to do a favor that involved his father's business – perhaps even his personal interests – might be testing Jedd too much.

Or perhaps that was exactly what she needed to do. Perhaps she was only seizing an opportunity to test his feeling for her in a way that she had wanted to do for as long as she had known him.

2

Willie landed at the airport near Puerta Plata on the north coast of the Dominican Republic. Her American passport smoothed her way through customs. The sunshine and balmy breezes, and the strolling musicians outside the terminal, completed the welcome.

She'd left New York in a cold, sleeting April rain and now as she shed her coat and allowed the warm breeze to caress her skin, she felt a small easing of the tensions that had become a part of her daily life.

Jedd had offered to meet her, but she'd declined. Now she almost regretted her stubborn independence when the car her secretary had arranged turned out to be an elderly Chevrolet that looked as if it were held together by nothing more than the confidence of its driver, who'd plastered the interior surfaces of his vehicle with photos of José José, Barbra Streisand and Julio Iglesias.

Mercifully the ride was a short one, for what the vehicle lacked in shock absorbers, it made up for in enthusiasm on the part of the driver. When she arrived at her destination safe and sound, she paid the fare and asked the man to wait.

Willie's hotel was one of the many that had sprung up on the north coast of the island, which contrasted sharply with the overbuilt honky-tonk atmosphere of Santo Domingo.

Her suite fronted the ocean and what had been until recently virgin beach, unmanicured and still dotted with palm trees and shrubs. She spent a brief moment on the terrace; it had been a very long time since she'd relaxed or enjoyed the fruits of her success. And even now, in a place that was beautiful and serene, Willie couldn't let go and just be a part of it.

Quickly she showered and changed into a white cotton jumpsuit and a pair of open sandals. She brushed her long blond hair into a ponytail, applied a bit of lip gloss, and was out the door.

As the old Chevrolet bounced along the dirt road, Willie saw a sign that a new Fontana hotel and casino would open next spring. She got out of the car in front of a trailer that appeared to be a temporary office. Inside was a young woman sitting at a typewriter, striking the keys to the beat of the Rolling Stones.

Willie asked for Signor Fontana. "He's expecting me," she added. The girl nodded and waved a hand in the direction of the beach.

Willie made her way along a narrow pathway, through a half-cleared forest of palm trees and beach grass. Off to one side, a steel-girded skeleton dotted with workmen rose a dozen stories skyward. Straight ahead, a bulldozer pushed against a pile of boulders. Shouting orders to the driver was Jedd, hard-hatted and shirtless, wearing only a pair of khaki shorts, his bronze body gleaming with sweat under the afternoon sun.

The sight of him made Willie's skin tingle, just as if he'd touched her, and she had to remind herself that she was here to help a client – a woman who'd been bewitched by a man's wealth and power – and not to fall under Jedd's spell again.

She called out to him several times before he heard her over the noise. And then he ran to her, covering the distance between them with an athlete's easy grace.

"Hi," he said, placing a kiss on her forehead. "Just give me a minute to get cleaned up."

Willie had always thought of Jedd as a kind of pampered playboy, but in this setting, he seemed as tough and strong as the men who worked beside him. As she watched him casually sluice the day's grime off under a makeshift outdoor shower, she felt the heat rise in her own body, and she looked away.

Jedd ducked into a construction shed for a few minutes and came out wearing khaki trousers and a T-shirt imprinted with the Fontana Hotel logo, his dark hair glistening and wet. "You have my undivided attention," he said to Willie. "I'm flattered you came all this way to see me . . . are you sure it's only business that brought you?"

She looked into his eyes. "My work means more to me than 'business', Jedd. But yes, I'm here only because a client is in trouble – and I think you can help me help her."

He smiled, his confidence undampened by her answer. "Come on," he said, taking her hand, "let me show you around. Even a missionary needs to relax once in a while . . . "

As they walked along the beach, Jedd pointed out where the buildings of the new resort would stand. "The main hotel's at the center," he said, "and along the surrounding hills, we'll have low-rise condominiums, built in the Spanish style. We're working with a terrific local architect, so this place won't look like every other new hotel. The recreational complex is off to the south . . . two swimming pools, eight tennis courts and a championship golf course. To the north, we'll build the casino—"

"Just what the world needs," Willie cut in, "another gambling casino, but then you Fontanas have never been particular about where your money comes from."

Jedd stopped in his tracks and swung round to face her. "There was a time when I would have taken that hook, Willie. I might have said that 'we Fontanas' aren't so different from you, that we have our dreams and fight for what we want, that we make mistakes – but sometimes we do things that even you might approve of. But I'm not going to do that – and you know why? Because I'm waiting for you to figure that out for yourself."

Jedd started walking again and Willie followed. Why did she always bait him? Willie asked herself. Even when she was here to ask his help, she couldn't seem to stop herself.

As she hurried to keep up with his long, easy stride, she glanced at his face, so aristocratically impassive in profile. She had seen laughter and anger, desire and even love in that face, but now it was closed against her. "I'm sorry if I made you angry," she said finally.

A hint of a smile tugged at his mouth. "That sounds like a lawyer's apology, Willie . . . scrupulously unsatisfying. But I'll take it . . . for now."

As the beach curved inward, Willie saw a thick cloud of gray smoke coming from a bank of palm trees. "Look," she said, "something's burning over there."

"I hope not," Jedd laughed, "or you'll miss the best food on the island." As they approached a crudely constructed cantina set back from the beach, Jedd said, "Come on, let me buy you lunch." He led her to a single rough wooden table and a pair of rush chairs. The makeshift bar consisted of a tin cooler; outside, two young boys were cooking fish over an open fire.

The proprietor beamed when he saw Jedd, greeting him like an old friend. They spoke in Spanish, and Willie understood that Jedd was asking about the man's wife and children and not much more.

Jedd turned to Willie and said, "Miguel's menu is limited, but whatever he serves was swimming in the sea no more than an hour ago." He translated his words for Miguel, who became even more expansive.

"Si, Señor Fontana, hoy tenemos mero y cangrejos," Miguel explained, spreading a threadbare but clean cloth on the table. "Algo a beber?"

"Dos cervezas, por favor," Jedd replied.

Another surprise, Willie thought. In her mind's eye, she'd always imagined Jedd surrounded by luxury, yet he seemed as much at ease in this simple cantina as he'd ever been at the best places in Palm Springs.

She started to explain why she'd come, but he stopped her. "Not now," he said. "Let's just enjoy this beautiful day and Miguel's excellent cuisine."

Willie realized she was quite hungry, and when the fish was set before them on thick earthenware plates with slices of fresh lemon, she dug right in, thinking she couldn't remember when food had tasted so good. The icy beer straight from the bottle was perfect with the tender, succulent grouper and the delicate sweet crabs.

Jedd watched her with a smile. "Do you know what I like best about you, Willie?"

"What?" she asked, wiping her chin with the back of her hand.

"Well," he drawled, "you're beautiful and smart – but that's not it. And you can be a real pain in the neck – but that's not it. What I like best is that you need me. And you know why?"

"I'm sure you're going to tell me . . ."

"Because I'm not intimidated by that chip on your shoulder . . . and because I can show you how to enjoy life . . ."

She almost said "but there's more to life than enjoyment," yet as she finished the last of her food and looked out onto the blue-green waters of the Atlantic, feeling sated and content, she realized how few her moments of pleasure had been – and how intensely felt her time with Jedd always was. The thought made her nervous, drawing her in dangerous directions.

Once again she started to tell Jedd why she'd come, and once again, he held her off. "Just a little longer," he said. "I've saved the best part for last."

He paid the bill and spoke to Miguel's boys, who scampered away and disappeared into the foliage. They returned about ten minutes later with two horses, a russet-colored gelding and a white stallion.

Willie reached for the white horse's reins, but Jedd shook his head. "Take El Rojo," he said. "He's partial to beautiful women, and he'll do exactly what he's told. The stallion has a mind of his own, and I think you'd have a problem with that."

"Shut up," she said pleasantly, swinging onto the red horse's back and riding into the surf, feeling a sudden exhilaration as the salt spray and cool breeze hit her face. The horse had a steady gait. When Willie squeezed his flanks, he went into a smooth, easy canter, unlike Jedd's, who was tossing his head and fighting to break into a gallop. "What's the matter?" she called out, laughing. "Can't you handle a little difference of opinion, Jedd?"

"I can handle anything," he called back, the muscle in his arms tensing, as he shortened the reins against the animal's powerful neck, and in a little while the horse stopped fighting and matched his pace to the gelding's.

"I'm impressed," Willie said.

"Don't be. Sometimes El Blanco gives and sometimes he throws me the hell off. We're friends anyway . . . just like you and me, Willie."

For a little while, Willie didn't think of why she'd come here; didn't think at all, as she became one with El Rojo's rhythmic rocking, the shimmering water and blue sky around her. It felt so good to simply breathe the tangy air and be caressed by the breeze.

The sun was just beginning to sink to the horizon when Jedd turned his horse and galloped away from the beach. Willie followed, through a clearing and up a winding mountain trail, upward until they reached a ridge overlooking the beach.

Together they watched the sun streak the ocean with ribbons of orange and red and finally purple. As the light faded, the air seemed to come alive with night sounds, the humming of insects. Somehow Sofia al-Rahman and New York seemed very far away, and Willie couldn't bring herself to speak of what Jedd called "business" at this moment. "Thank you," she said quietly. "It's been a beautiful day."

"You're welcome," he said, reaching over and taking her hand. "I just wanted you to know what you've been missing."

When they returned to the construction site, Jedd swung off his horse with a single graceful sweep, then held out his hand to help Willie dismount. He led her back to the trailer, which was now deserted, flipped on the lights, and sat down. "Okay," he said, "you have my undivided attention. How can I help you?"

"I need information," she said, "for my client."

"What kind of information?" he asked, his dark eyes wary now.

"My client's married to a man who does business with your father. His name's Seif al-Rahman . . . "

Jedd's nod was noncommittal. "My father does business with a lot of people."

"But Seif al-Rahman's not 'a lot of people.' He's a very rich, very powerful man. He joint-ventured the Fontana Hotels in Saudi Arabia. His wife tells me that he and your father are friends, that Sam's visited their home in Saudi."

Jedd's expression was unreadable, and Willie could see that she would have to tell him more before he would respond. Briefly she told him the story of Sofia's marriage – and of the problems she'd come up against in seeking her client's freedom. "I'm stumped, Jedd. I've tried to fight al-Rahman by the book, but every time I think I have him, he pulls another trick and outmaneuvers me."

"But why come to me?" Jedd asked. "If you think I have any influence with the State Department . . . "

"No," she said, shaking her head, "that isn't it. If you know Seif al-Rahman you know what kind of man he is." She took a deep breath, and she could feel herself blushing as she came to the point. "I was hoping you might have access to some information . . . something I can use as leverage against him, something that would make *him* back down . . . "

In the dim light of the trailer's single lamp, she could see the shock on Jedd's face. "Wait a minute," he said. "Am I hearing right? Is this the Willie Dellahaye I know and love talking about blackmail? The same woman who gave me hell because maybe, just maybe, my family doesn't always do things by the book?"

"All right," she said quietly, "you've made your point. I know what I'm asking isn't very nice, but I'm dealing with an evil man, Jedd, and there doesn't seem to be any other way to fight him."

"But if I gave you what you wanted," Jedd said slowly, "then I'd have something on you . . . "

"That's right . . . you would," Willie answered simply.

Jedd was silent for a moment. "What you're asking, Willie . . . is it just to help your client, or is there something about me . . . about us . . . you want to know?"

Willie met his eyes with a level look. "Helping my client is always my first priority, Jedd."

Jedd stood up and paced the tiny trailer, stopping at the window, his back to Willie. "Assuming the information you need exists – and I'm not saying it does – giving it to you would mean betraying a friend of Pop's," he said finally. "Ask me something else, something I can do."

Willie struggled with her pride, reminding herself that she'd come here to help Sofia and couldn't go back empty-handed. "Jedd, I told you that helping my client was my first concern and I mean it. Her husband has mutilated and humiliated and terrorized her and now it looks like he'll get away scot-free. Please help me . . . "

Jedd turned and gave her an odd smile. "I'd like to help you, Willie, but what you want is impossible."

She stood up stiffly. "Then you can go to hell," she said and walked out of the trailer without looking back.

I should have known better, Willie told herself, yet even after she returned to New York, she was still angry and beyond that, disappointed. For all his declarations of love, Jedd had refused her – and for what? Out of the same misguided family loyalty that had gotten between them so many times before.

I don't need his help, she told herself. It may take longer, but I'll get what I need. She called Larry Kusack and told him to run an intensive personal investigation on Seif al-Rahman. "I want dirt, Larry," she said bluntly, "the uglier the better – something that would embarrass his government into disowning him . . . "

Kusack gave a low whistle. "That's not the kind of thing we usually do, counselor." There was no reproach in his statement, only a question.

"Special case, Larry," she said. "I've just learned that 'by the book' isn't always good enough, not when the other guy makes his own rules."

For the next two weeks, Willie dodged Philip Bannister's calls and his attempts to set up a meeting. There was no point in showing up simply to concede defeat, and if she stalled for time, maybe Kusack would come through for her, as he had done so often before.

Meanwhile, keeping busy was easy, for her caseload was heavier than ever before. And though she cared deeply about each and every one of her cases, there were days when they almost seemed to blur, when she needed an extra moment to remember exactly what needed doing and for whom.

Time seemed to be shrinking, for while she often stayed at the office past midnight, she never outpaced the work or even caught up with it. She didn't care that she hadn't taken a real vacation in ages, but what she wanted to do – and soon was spend four or five days with Mama.

They talked on the telephone at least once a week, yet ever since Ginny had declared her independence, Willie felt the need to be with her even more than she had in the days when she'd acted as parent to her mother. Ginny would be old one day, she now realized, and time would not stand still, not even for a career as consuming as the one Willie had chosen.

Yet while she pushed herself to complete work that never ended, Willie was feeling the strain of marking time with Sofia's case, a case she was afraid she would lose. She became more demanding of her associates, as if making everyone else work harder would somehow make a difference.

Though Willie had always prided herself on the morale in her firm, she began to hear, for the first time, complaints about the heavy caseloads and the need for more help. And when Pamela Belzer brought the subject up at a staff meeting, Willie's composure cracked. "If you wanted a nine-to-five job, you picked the wrong place," she snapped.

Pamela's response was in keeping with her cool, clear-headed work style. She simply got up from the conference table and walked out of the room. The remainder of the staff sat in embarrassed silence, and a shamefaced Willie called the meeting to a close.

She apologized to Pamela immediately. "I had no right to speak to you that way," she said, "especially in front of the rest of the staff."

"Apology accepted," Pamela answered, "but there's something I've been wanting to say to you for a long time. I take my work seriously and I've never been a nine-to-fiver. I just happen to believe that I'm entitled to a life, as well as a career. If they're one and the same for you, that's fine, but if you make that a condition of my employment here, then let's shake hands now and part company. I respect you enormously, Willie, but I have no wish to be your clone."

Willie was stunned. She'd heard one of the clerks refer to her as a slavedriver, but it never really occurred to her that a capable and valued partner could be dissatisfied to the point of leaving. Yet now she remembered how often she'd marched into Harrigan's office, full of frustration – and in precisely that state of mind. Had she been as insensitive as Harrigan to the needs of those who worked for her? Willie's sense of fairness struggled with her belief that anyone who practiced law ought to be as dedicated as she was. Finally she said: "I respect you, too, Pamela, and I don't want to lose you. If you feel my demands have been unreasonable, perhaps it is time to hire more associates."

When Willie went back to her office, she found a bulky manila envelope on her desk. It had been delivered by messenger and was marked "Personal and Confidential." There was no return address.

Inside was a newspaper clipping, a brief story datelined Palm Springs, on the death of a local call girl under mysterious circumstances. It stated that the police had investigated rumors of a wild party she'd attended on the estate of Sam Fontana – but had found nothing to connect Fontana or any of his guests with the death.

With the clipping was a collection of photographs, obscene

pictures of Seif al-Rahman, indulging his perverted appetites on the bodies of several young women. In one picture, one of the women was wearing a black hood over her head. Her hands were bound and there was a heavy choke collar around her neck. Willie felt a frisson of horror as she realized she could be looking at al-Rahman's private snuff scenario, a sadomasochistic sex game that had gone too far.

Willie's revulsion gave way to a feeling of triumph. What she had in her hand was circumstantial evidence. It might not convict Seif al-Rahman of murder in a court of law, but it was a weapon against which he had no defense. If she threatened to turn this material over to the *New York Times*, or to any major newspaper, Seif would know she had the power to destroy him in Saudi Arabia. The puritanical Wahhabi government might look the other way when its leading citizens kicked up their heels abroad and indulged in a little drinking and gambling – but a world-wide sex scandal would cost al-Rahman the royal connections on which he'd built his business empire.

And it was Jedd who had made it possible, she was sure of that. He had helped her after all, and in a way that couldn't have been easy for him – as people who cared for one another did.

If Philip Bannister was surprised by Willie's eagerness to meet, he didn't show it. Nor did he gloat over the enormous advantage he believed to be his. In the polite, evenhanded way that had won him a reputation as "a gentleman's lawyer," he began outlining Seif's terms for a divorce – and a settlement that would leave Sofia nearly penniless.

Willie listened politely and then shook her head. "That isn't what I had in mind, counselor. Take a look at this package and we'll start again." She shoved the envelope of photographs across the walnut conference table and waited while Bannister inspected the contents.

To his credit as a professional, Bannister neither blanched nor betrayed any sign of emotion. And when he spoke, his voice was strong and even. "This is interesting material, counselor. You could make a case for divorce on the grounds of adultery, but I don't—"

"I wasn't thinking of using it in a court of law," Willie cut in. "What I had in mind was something else. Since Mr. al-Rahman proposes to impoverish my client, I was thinking she might earn a few dollars by selling this material to the newspapers. It would make interesting reading in Saudi, don't you think? I'm sure the royal house would be fascinated to see how Mr. al-Rahman spends his leisure time in the west . . . "

Bannister opened his mouth as if to argue – and then thought better of it. He stared at the beautiful young woman who smiled sweetly across the conference table. "May I ask your terms?" he said finally.

Willie wrote a number on a piece of paper and passed it to Bannister. He looked at it and then rose from his chair. "If you'll excuse me," he said, "I will need to consult with my client by telephone."

"One more thing," Willie said. "I want him to waive his diplomatic immunity on the issue of freezing al-Rahman assets until the settlement is paid."

Bannister was gone for a brief quarter hour. And when he returned, he said simply, "My client agrees to your terms. I'll have the papers drawn up today and messenger them to your office."

Willie stuffed the photographs into her briefcase and bade Bannister good day. As she left the offices of Rogers, Bannister and Stevens, she realized that Philip Bannister had failed to shake her hand.

3

Willie gripped Sofia's arm and hurried down the court-house steps, one hand shielding her eyes from the blinding glare of flashbulbs and strobe lights.

"How does it feel to get a fifty-million-dollar gift, Mrs.

al-Rahman?" one reporter shouted out.

"That was no gift," Willie shot back. "That was war reparations – and, to my mind, it would have been fairer if Mr. al-Rahman had been left as bankrupt financially as he is morally."

The reporters shoved their recorders closer, hungry for more newsworthy quotes.

"Is it true your husband ran orgies for American politicians?" another piped up. "Is it true you've signed a movie contract?" somone else shouted out.

"No more comments," Willie said as she pushed forward, struggling to stay close to Sofia's bodyguards, who had formed a human wedge to cut through the crowds of reporters and curiosity seekers.

Sofia waved to the crowd, stunningly beautiful and triumphant in her victory over the man who had brutalized and maimed her, but Willie felt limp and spent and almost claustrophobic as she fought her way through the crush. Though her cases often made headlines, she still hated the sensationalism that focused more on the titillating details of her clients' private lives than on the issues of fairness and equal rights.

A limousine awaited in front of the courthouse, and when they finally reached it, Willie bundled Sofia inside, then took a seat beside her.

"It's finally over," Sofia said with a sigh. "But when I think of what could have happened . . . "

"Don't. What matters is that you're free," Willie said reassuringly, though in truth there had been moments when she'd been terrified that she'd lose Sofia to her husband's vengeance. Willie had run into vindictive husbands, angry husbands, but none had been so powerful, none with a reach so long as Seif al-Rahman.

Yes, Willie thought, she had won a good victory, in spite of his power and wealth, and her fee for this case would be enormous, more than enough to carry a hundred *pro bono* clients. Yet the victory felt somehow tarnished by the dirtiness of the fight.

" . . . and I can't thank you enough," Sofia was saying.

"I'll be staying in New York. If there's anything I can do for you, anything at all, just ask."

Funny, Willie thought, how many of her clients expressed similar sentiments, and many even remembered her with cards and gifts at Christmas . . . but except for Marion Silverstein, they had all become closed case files. There were many clients, too, Willie had found, who would just as soon forget her along with the painful history they'd shared.

It was a little after five when the limousine dropped Willie in front of her office building. She went through the revolving doors, thought about the messages and demands that awaited her – and then turned around and went outside again. Not today. No more of the problems that sometimes made it seem her world was made of nothing but broken hearts.

She walked aimlessly for a few blocks, feeling like a child playing hooky, but with nowhere to go and no one to play with. After a while, she realized how tired she was. She stepped into the cool, air-conditioned anonymity of the first bar she saw, found a corner table, and ordered a scotch.

Fatigued as she was, the alcohol hit her system like an anesthetic. Through a kind of haze, she heard her name mentioned. She glanced up and saw Sofia's likeness on the television set above the bar.

"Do you believe that?" a man in work clothes said. "This dame got fifty million bucks. I'd like to meet the broad who's worth that much."

"Yeah," the bartender laughed, "that's why I'm still single. Used to be women took you for better or worse. Now if you don't watch out, they just take you, period – straight to the cleaners."

There was a time when Willie would have gotten up, marched over, and given the men an instant education, but now the ignorant remarks just depressed her. No wonder men and women couldn't get along, she thought. When they weren't busy mating, they seemed to be natural enemies who didn't even speak the same language.

472

After two more drinks, what was even more depressing was the fact that there appeared to be no end to the war between the sexes. She had built an entire career protecting women from their mistakes. She had eased pain and suffering, she had made legal history more than once, yet she had also traveled roads she'd never meant to travel.

Once Willie had believed it was enough to know what was right and fight for it, cleanly and fairly and by the book. Yet she hadn't known then what it would be like to face opponents who made their own rules.

She had rescued Sofia from degradation, probably had even saved her life – and she had won the highest divorce settlement in American history.

Yet she herself had broken the law to accomplish this. Perhaps a judge would have deemed her action justifiable, had it come to light. What bothered Willie was knowing she would do it again – and not knowing where her boundaries were any more, where she'd draw the line.

It was an unsettling, almost frightening place to be.

The call came just as Willie was getting ready to go to lunch.

"Take a message, Lettie," Willie told her secretary, who stood in the doorway, waiting for her to pick up the telephone.

The secretary shook her head. "I'm sorry, Willie," she said in a strained voice that matched the expression on her face. "I'm afraid you'd better take this call now . . . "

Willie gave her a worried glance, then walked back to her desk and reached across to pick up the phone.

The caller was male. "Palm Springs Police Department," he said.

Willie's heart lurched at once. From some deep well of intuition, she knew the rest of what she would hear before it was said. She barely listened, scattered phrases passing between a thousand memories of moments – chances, perhaps – that could never be relived.

"Last night . . . your mother . . . sorry . . ." and finally, the awful, irrevocable word "dead."

473

She braced herself against the desk, struggling against the heavy numbness that paralyzed her as the room started to whirl and spin.

When she opened her eyes, she was lying on the leather couch in the office, surrounded by sympathetic faces. For one merciful, disoriented moment she had no idea how she'd gotten there or why her secretary and partners were standing around looking at her.

"I'm so sorry," Pam Belzer murmured, taking Willie's hand. "Is there anything I can do?"

And then Willie remembered. The concern on the faces around her brought the awful reality back. She could hear the policeman's voice again . . . and then her imagination began to hurtle down its own track. Imagining Mama alone . . . desperate . . . so hopeless that she couldn't go on another second. If only she could have been there—

Willie sat up abruptly, almost as though she wanted to run to Mama now—and then the dizziness hit her again.

"Shall I call a doctor?" Pam offered.

"No," Willie choked out, forcing herself to stand. "I have to go . . . Mama needs me." She fled the office like a woman possessed, her only thought to get to Palm Springs. Was it possible there had even been a mistake—that Mama was alive? No, of course that was too much to hope. But, with an urgency that came out of some subconscious need to believe that the clock could somehow be turned back, the irrevocable undone, she needed to find out what had happened . . .

Hurry, Willie kept telling herself as she packed a bag, but her movements felt heavy and dreamlike, as if she were trapped in a body not her own. And when she was finally on the plane, she had no recollection of how she got there.

In the cold, antiseptic atmosphere of the county morgue, with a police sergeant standing at her side, Willie identified the mortal remains of her mother. Except for a dark bruise on one side of her face, in death Ginny looked as peaceful as a sleeping child.

"Mama," Willie whispered, touching her mother's cheek

gently with trembling fingers. The skin was cold and unyielding, beyond feeling and beyond hurt, but Willie lingered, encapsulated in shock.

"Ma'am?" The officer took Willie's arm and steered her outside.

"How?" she finally asked. "How did . . . it happen?"

The policeman hesitated for a moment. "The housekeeper called us at eight a.m. Your mother had been dead for about four hours. Overdose of tranquilizers. She'd been drinking, and we didn't find a note, so the medical examiner's calling it an accident . . . "

The silence that followed was gentle, but the meaning behind it was not. Slowly it penetrated the numbness that was holding Willie together. Mama had killed herself. But why? Had it been a terrible accident – or had she really wanted to stop living?

"Ma'am . . . "

"Yes?" Willie turned pain-glazed eyes toward the officer.

"I'm sorry to trouble you at a time like this, but I'd like you to come back to headquarters with me."

"Why?"

There was another hesitation. "We need an identification on some jewelry. We think it might belong to . . . the deceased."

Willie shook her head in bewilderment. "I don't understand. Why aren't you sure? If you found it with her—"

"Just come with me, ma'am," the policeman interrupted. "I'll fill you in on the way."

As they drove to the police station, the sergeant explained that Ginny had not been alone on the last night of her life: the housekeeper had seen her return home around midnight with a man.

A sick feeling came over Willie as she remembered the bruise on her mother's face. "Are you saying my mother was robbed?" she asked in a strangled voice.

"We don't know," the officer answered. "We picked up this guy on a drunk and disorderly. He's got a half-dozen priors . . . small stuff. Anyway, he had a diamond pin and some earrings on him. We figured they were stolen, but he claimed that a lady friend gave them to him. He wouldn't give us a name until we told him he was looking at a felony rap. When we told him the lady was dead, he cracked. I'm real sorry to have to tell you this, ma'am, but it seems your mother picked this character up in a bar and took him home with her. He says he asked her for money, and when she didn't have much on her, he slapped her around and took the jewelry. We talked to the housekeeper and the bartender, and they say . . . "

The officer's voice droned on, telling a story that was unbearable for Willie to hear. Mama, alone and friendless, living lonely days and empty nights, watching television in the barren luxury of a big, empty house or going to bars to pick up strangers.

As Willie remembered all the times Mama had assured her that everything was fine, all the bright conversations about her volunteer work, the brave, noble lies, she felt a sharp, slivering pain in her chest, as if her heart were breaking into a million pieces.

When the sergeant showed Willie the jewelry – the diamond and jet clip Mama had worn the night Silver Screen had been launched, and emerald earrings that had been an anniversary gift from Neal – she began to tremble with rage. These pieces that had once made Ginny's eyes sparkle and dance with pleasure had been taken from her, along with her confidence and her self-respect.

She made the necessary identifications and left the police station in a blind haze of grief and sadness and guilt. The phrases "might have been" and "if only" raced through her mind like a fever. "I should have known" tortured Willie; "how could I have known?" gave her no peace.

She checked into a nearby motel, unable to face the house that had never been a home, but just a way station between Mama's broken marriage to Neal and her death.

Willie was hot and tired and grimy, but she felt as if she could neither rest nor do all the things that needed to be done. She looked into the mirror over the dresser and saw

476

the image of a stranger. Dull eyes, an expression of ineffable pain, the face of a displaced person.

She shed the suit she'd worn to work a lifetime ago and cooled herself under the shower. She reached for a towel and started to shiver, though the room was warm in spite of the air-conditioning. She pulled the coverlet from the bed and wrapped herself in it.

There was a knock on the door.

"Yes?" she called out. "Who is it?"

"I'm the manager," a woman's voice answered. "Can I come in?"

Willie opened the door to admit a gray-haired woman carrying a plastic bucket of ice and a bottle of club soda. "Excuse me," she said shyly. "I thought you might like a little something to cool you off, the weather being so warm . . . "

"Thank you," Willie said, reaching for her purse.

"Oh, no," the woman said hastily. "That's not necessary, honest." She set the bucket on the nightstand, but made no move to leave.

"Was there something else?" Willie asked, making an effort to focus and wishing that the woman would leave.

She hesitated, biting her lip. Finally she spoke. "You're Willa Dellahaye, aren't you . . . the lawyer? I saw you on television. You did wonderful for that sheik's wife."

Willie smiled modestly.

"I don't want to bother you, honest. My husband would have a fit if he knew I was visiting a paying customer. But when I saw you come in, I thought it was like a sign. 'God sent her,' I said to myself."

Willie knew what was coming. But she didn't have the strength to help anyone now – not even herself. Nor the courage to stop the woman from speaking.

"It's my daughter," the manager continued. "She's married to a hard-drinking man and she suffers something awful. I took her in with me, but Larry said if she didn't come home, he'd fix it so's she'd never see her little boy again. He means it, Miss, and my girl knows it. Isn't there something you can do for her?"

477

Willie looked into the woman's tear-filled eyes and felt as if she were being pulled into a whirlpool of anguish and worry and fear. She tried to speak, to say that there were protections and remedies for her daughter, but the words wouldn't come. She felt the warm rush of tears in her own eyes, the pounding beat of her heart and an awful sense of childlike helplessness.

The woman looked at Willie with alarm. "Good heavens, Miss Dellahaye. Are you all right . . . ?"

Willie swallowed hard and took a deep breath. "I'm just tired . . . I . . ."

"Oh, gosh, and here I am bothering you. I'm sorry, Miss, I'll let you get your rest." The woman retreated, shutting the door behind her.

Willie huddled into the bed and closed her eyes, waiting for the panic to subside. An hour passed, then two, and then it was night, quiet and cold and lonely.

Had it been like this for Mama, she wondered, this trapped feeling, this dreadful paralyzing heaviness? Could someone die of too many lonely nights? Of being too scared and too tired to try anymore?

"The Lord is my Shepherd, I shall not want . . . "

Willie sat in the tiny funeral chapel, a single mourner dressed in black, her beautiful face ravaged by tears, saying her last good-bye. As they had been together against the world so often in life, it was just the two of them now. Except that Mama wasn't really here in the bronze casket. And Willie was alone as she never had been before.

The chapel was full of flowers, two wreaths from the law firm and the rest from Willie. A Unitarian minister intoned the Twenty-third Psalm. Willie had chosen it because it seemed fitting for a lost child, a prayer promising comfort and peace. Yet for her there was neither comfort nor peace. She had never had the chance to hold Mama, to beg her to stay.

Willie tried to focus on the minister's quiet voice, on the words of the psalm.

478

" . . . yea, though I walk through the valley of the shadow of death . . . "

A silent rage welled up in Willie's throat, choking and burning because it had nowhere to go. It wasn't good enough to blame the drifter who had hurt and robbed her. It was unbearable to think that someone so worthless had destroyed the one person she had loved without reservation.

Finally the brief service was over. As Willie walked out of the chapel, head bowed, numb with grief and pain, someone reached out and touched her arm. Willie looked up, her eyes clouded with tears. For a moment it was difficult to focus.

Then she saw it was Jedd, standing at the door of the chapel. The look on his face was so sincere that it unlocked the last bit of control that had kept her together. She put her head down on his white shirt and wept as if she would never stop.

"I'm so sorry, Willie," he murmured over and over again. And somehow she believed him. Of all the people she and Mama had ever known, only Jedd Fontana was here.

"How did you know?" she asked finally.

"My sister was taking a vacation in Palm Springs. She saw the story in the paper and figured I'd want to know. I haven't spoken about you to Sam very much, but over the years I've mentioned you quite a few times to Sis . . . Soon as I got her call, I flew out. Willie . . . is there anything I can do for you?"

"Just stay with me," she whispered. "I don't want to be alone."

It was Jedd's strong arms that held Willie as she stood on a grassy knoll and gently laid a single rose on the bronze casket. And it was Jedd who steadied Willie when her knees buckled as she tried to walk away.

He took Willie back to the rented house, unlocked the door with the key she'd silently handed over. She walked in slowly, searching for her mother's presence, trying to hold on to the sense that Ginny hadn't gone away forever.

The house was spotlessly clean, and there was little trace either of Ginny's life or her death.

"Willie . . . maybe you should rest a little and let me take care of things. Just tell me what you want done," Jedd offered.

"No. I want to see Mama's things . . . touch them. It's all I have left."

In a desk drawer, she found Ginny's will, a simple document made a year before. It left a scholarship fund to the Catholic home – "for deserving girls with talent and dreams" – and everything else to Willie.

She searched her memory, trying to remember if anything had happened then, anything that would lead her mother to make a will. But all she could think of was a visit Ginny had made to New York. Willie had taken several days off from work and taken Ginny to the best restaurants and the most popular Broadway shows. And when it was time for Ginny to go back, Willie had urged her to stay. "I have such a big apartment now, Mama," she'd said. "You'd have your privacy, and . . . "

"It isn't my privacy I'd worry about, honey," Ginny had said. "I'm real proud of you, Willie . . . you deserve the best." Had Mama known even back then that her hold on life was fragile and tenuous? Had she chosen to die alone rather than be a burden to her only child?

Willie began to cry again. Oh, Mama, she said silently, it didn't have to be that way. I would have taken care of you forever, if only you'd stayed.

Jedd held her quietly, stroking her hair until the tears subsided. Then he went into the kitchen, made a pot of tea, and sat with Willie until she drank a cup.

He followed when Willie went into Ginny's bedroom, as if he knew that this would be the hardest part of all. Almost reverently, Willie sorted through her mother's dresses, pulling out the ones Ginny had designed to take back with her to New York. The rest, she decided, could go to the home for unwed mothers.

As she came to a chiffon negligee trimmed with marabou,

Willie smiled in spite of her pain. "This one is really Mama," she said tenderly.

Jedd nodded, as if he knew exactly what she meant.

In an old battered box that seemed incongruous with the luxury of Ginny's bedroom, she found a picture she hadn't seen in years, of Mama with Perry, his arm draped over her shoulder.

She showed it to Jedd. "Mama was happy then, I can see it in her face, happier than I can ever remember." And suddenly Willie realized that if Fate had been kind to Ginny, it would have allowed her to live out her days with her high-school sweetheart, protected from realities she couldn't handle and with her fairytale dreams for company. Virginia Dellahaye had never belonged anywhere else but Belle Fourche. Broken into little pieces and driven away from the only place that was really her home, she had lived like a stranger . . . and searched for love among other strangers.

How long and how hard I've fought against that legacy, Willie thought. And how far I've gone to avenge it.

"You know," she told Jedd, "you were right about me. If I've been running away from you, it isn't just what you do and who you are. It's me. Maybe this is what I've been afraid of," she said, pointing to the photograph. "She loved him, Jedd, you can see it, and if he'd shown her a little understanding . . . "

Jedd touched her cheek. "But I'm not your father, Willie, and you aren't your mother."

"I know," she said. "When you sent me those photographs, when you helped me with the al-Rahman case, I realized you understood . . . "

"I don't want to talk about that," Jedd replied.

"Why not?" she argued. "I know how hard it must have been, and . . . "

"Because whether or not I helped you is beside the point," he said quietly. "I love you, Willie; nothing means as much to me as your happiness. And that should be enough. You can't change me from what I am, so take me *as* I am. Because if you go on looking for some kind of perfection as an answer to your father – to what he did to you and your mother – you're going to have as little chance to find love as she did."

Willie lay on the living room sofa, half drowsing in the crook of Jedd's arm, watching the flames flicker in the fireplace and thinking of all the kindnesses he'd shown her today. He had worked by her side all day, held her when she needed him, and made himself inconspicuous when she needed a moment of privacy. Without fuss or fanfare, he'd prepared a light supper and coaxed her to eat.

She knew she could fall asleep now; she was too drained to do anything else. It was a strange feeling, she thought, to come to rest in the arms of the man she'd fought against for so many years.

The following morning Jedd drove Willie back to the motel. She collected her things and went into the manager's office to settle her bill. "I want to apologize for the other day," she said to the woman. "I'm sorry if I didn't seem concerned . . . "

"That's okay," the woman said. "A famous person like you . . . you must have more important things to worry about than people like us."

"No," Willie cut in, "that isn't it. Everyone's important. Your daughter needs help, and I'll see that she gets it. As soon as I get back to New York, someone from my office will call you."

The ride to the airport was brief and quiet. "Thank you," Willie said, "for everything. Having you here . . . it helped so much. I . . . I hate to say good-bye."

Jedd leaned over and kissed her lightly. "Then don't." He ruffled her hair affectionately. "You'll probably be hearing from me sooner than you'd imagine. I may be needing a good lawyer sometime soon."

"What do you mean?" she asked.

"We'll talk later. Now get going before you miss your plane."

"Jedd," she persisted. "Are you in trouble . . . ?"

He smiled. "No more than usual."

"Then tell me—"

"Another time," he said. "If you'll give me one . . . "

The stewards announced the last call for boarding and reluctantly she backed away.

Only when she was on the plane, looking down at the clouds, did she completely understand what Jedd had meant. Always before she had rejected him because of what he was, the things he did. Now he was letting her know that the legacy of his family had put him in a position to need her help. He loved her – she believed that as never before. But still, he had not changed.

But had *she* . . .? Was she ready to love him in spite of what he was – had always been?

4

The people around her tried to be kind, but their constant gestures of support only increased Willie's sense of help-lessness and loss. Her junior partners urged time off, offering to carry her caseload, but the prospect of solitude seemed more frightening than restful.

For a time, habit took her to the office every day, even earlier than usual. She tried to throw herself into her work, as she had always done in times of trouble or pain, but now this remedy only filled the hours without easing the pain. Yet as she struggled, Willie felt as if she had lost not only Mama, but somehow herself, too.

She saw clients, she went to court, but she felt like an impostor, like the ghost of Willie Dellahaye, who used to care passionately for each and every case she fought. It was as if she was dead inside, and what she did was empty and meaningless, too.

She worked like a sleepwalker, staring into space, often forgetting what she had said or done within the space of a few hours. Yet she avoided going home until well past midnight, for her nights were tortured with nightmares.

The landscapes were always the same – mountains and deserts – and the dreams would always begin with her and Ginny in Ben Cattow's old truck, fleeing from something terrible. The truck would break down in a desolate spot and Willie would get out to look under the hood. Then Mama would be gone and Willie would be left alone, crying. She'd wake up, pillow drenched with tears and sweat.

She found it impossible to eat, and without nourishment or rest, her slender body became gaunt, her face all hollows and sharp planes, like a Modigliani painting. It was as if all the underpinnings of her life had fallen away, leaving her anchorless and rudderless. For so long she'd thought of Ginny as dependent, yet now Willie realized how much she'd counted on her mother just being there. Mama had been the driving force, through every change and every new beginning. Now there was only the legacy that had turned Willie into an instrument of vengeance. Where and how would she start again?

One evening, as she sat at her desk, trying to decipher notes she'd taken on a new case, she found to her horror that she had written nothing that made sense. Feverishly she tried to remember what the client had said, to reconstruct the meeting they'd had only a few days before. Her work had been the one thing Willie could count on, the remedy for pain, the antidote to loneliness, and without that, she would have nothing. But the harder she tried to focus, the more sluggish her thinking became.

Defeated, she left the office and told her driver to take her to Beekman Place.

The lights in Marion Silverstein's new townhouse were on, and Willie hoped that Marion would be alone. She rang the bell. A moment later Marion appeared, her smile of welcome like an oasis.

"Willie," she said warmly, "what a pleasant surprise! I've been meaning to call you . . . " Then she took a close look at Willie's face. "What's wrong, dear?" she asked.

"My mother died," she blurted out.

"I'm so sorry," Marion said, taking Willie's hands and leading her into a pastel-colored living room that still smelled of paint and fresh upholstery. She poured two glasses of sherry from an antique decanter and sat down beside Willie. "Tell me, Willie," she said.

The story of Ginny's death tumbled from Willie like water from a dam, her old prideful independence lost in a desperate need for solace.

"But why didn't you come sooner?" Marion asked.

"I didn't think of it," Willie answered truthfully.

"Dear Willie," she said, "why do you isolate yourself so? You help so many people . . . why do you feel you have to face everything alone?"

Because of Mama, she thought, because Mama trusted everyone and everyone let her down – even me.

"I should have been there," Willie said tearfully. "I could have saved her. She kept telling me she was all right, but of course she wasn't. I should have known . . . "

"Her life wasn't yours to save, Willie," Marion said with quiet firmness. "You aren't God and you aren't responsible for everything that happens to the people you care about. I know how much you loved your mother. I can only imagine how she loved you, how close you were. I'm sure her heart would break if she saw you torturing yourself."

"That's just it," Willie said, her voice ragged with emotion. "I'm not sure of anything any more. When I was back in Palm Springs, I started to feel I didn't even know Mama the way I thought I did. If I had, I could have—"

"But you loved her," Marion cut in, "and that's all you could have done. You gave her so much just by loving her. You saved her as much as she'd let herself be saved." Marion took Willie's hand and pressed it between hers. "If you're feeling confused now, maybe that's not such a bad thing. I felt that way for months after I left Harvey . . . it goes with change, Willie. Don't fight it . . . maybe change is what you need. And stop punishing yourself for your mother's unhappiness. A life of penance is for saints and martyrs . . . is that what you want to be?"

Willie smiled at the image.

"That's better," Marion said approvingly. "Now I think you need a friend. I want you to stay here until you get back on your feet. Let me help you the way you helped me, remember?"

Willie nodded. It was a relief to stop struggling, to feel childlike and helpless. It was a relief to give up loneliness and to surrender to Marion's confident ministrations.

For the next two weeks, she stayed in the Beekman Place house, sharing Marion's new life. Everything in the house reflected Marion's impeccable, gracious style and energy. The guest room in which Willie slept was feminine, yet strong, decorated in bold shades of burgundy and gray, furnished with English antiques and strewn with vases of fresh flowers. Compared with Willie's luxurious but sterile bedroom, the place felt like a haven, a shelter from loneliness and bad dreams.

And because she had somewhere to go, she began to leave the office early, to look forward to the dinners prepared by Marion's cook and beautifully served in the airy dining room overlooking the formal garden.

Later, they would talk for an hour or two, and for the first time Willie aired her feelings about Jedd. Where once Willie had given Marion counsel and hope, now it was Marion who offered guidance and conviction. "It's time to let the past rest, Willie," she said. "One way or another, we all have to come to terms with what our parents were. I tried to be just like my mother because she and my father were so happy. But Harvey wasn't my father, and I simply ended up becoming a shadow to a man who used me.

"You went the other way," Marion continued. "You saw your mother's unhappiness and based your whole life on being different. You've spent years gathering 'evidence' to support a distorted view of what the relationship between a man and woman can be. This Jedd sounds like a man who cares for you, yet you've found one reason after another to make him 'wrong.' That's fine if you truly want to be alone – but I don't believe that's a choice you've really made. I think you've cut yourself off by default, because you're afraid to repeat your mother's mistakes. And I think the cure you've chosen is worse than the risks you've worked so hard to avoid. People don't die of broken relationships,

Willie. But they *can* wither away for lack of love. Think about that now, while there's time to have it all."

Taking advice had never been Willie's strong suit, yet Marion seemed to be a living example of "having it all," just as she'd once predicted. As chairman of the board, she played an active role in Marco Enterprises, her lifestyle was rich in comfort – and there was a new man in her life, a cosmetics executive almost a dozen years younger. Judging from Marion's serene glow, the relationship was a happy one, and when Willie was included in one of their evenings together, she couldn't help but notice how vivacious and alive Marion seemed in her "boyfriend's" company.

"Aren't you afraid it won't last?" Willie later asked.

"I think about that sometimes," Marion admitted, "but I'm happy now and I'm having fun. What's the alternative?"

What indeed? Willie asked herself, remembering all the times she'd pushed Jedd away.

Gradually Willie's senses came alive again. Under Marion's tutelage, she began to understand the meaning of living in the present, to see the difference between savoring a meal in pleasant surroundings and in good company – and consuming a sandwich, alone, to assuage hunger. Or the difference between Marion's sensual, comfortable home and the sterile luxury of her own apartment.

And as Willie began to feel again, her interest in work revived, too. Not in the same driven way, but with a sense that she was fortunate to have a career and skills that could make a difference to so many people. She began to look forward to the national conference on matrimonial law, to the chance of speaking out on the inequities of divorce, even to the prospect of jousting once more with Francis Aloysius Harrigan.

At last, she thanked Marion for nursing her back to health and, with some reluctance, returned to her apartment at the Pierre.

On her first day back at work, Willie saw the story in the newspaper. It was a wire-service piece on the sudden disappearance of a Montana state official, Farley Jeffers, who had left his home, his wife, and his five children on a Sunday morning and not returned. The wife called the police on Sunday night, after finding a note that said: "Please forgive me. I have no choice. I hate what I've become and there's no turning back."

The wife told the police that her husband had been withdrawn and moody for some time, but she did not know why. She also said that on the previous Friday, her husband had met for several hours with "someone from Fontana Enterprises" and come home in a depressed state, saying "things have gone too far."

The story stated that the man had withdrawn all the funds from a sizable bank account and was seen by one witness at the airport in Butte. It closed: "When reporters asked police chief Harker if the disappearance might be connected to wrongdoing on the state level, Harker replied: 'I doubt it. We will investigate, of course, but I'm confident we'll find that this is purely a domestic matter.'"

There was a companion story, headlined "Who Runs Montana?" along with a picture of Sam, laying the corner-stone for a Fontana-built office building in Helena, the capital. The article was written by a Greg Heywood and described Sam as "an old-fashioned robber baron" who built an empire on flagrant disregard of the public good. It criticized the "see-nothing, do-nothing" stance of both regulatory and law-enforcement agencies and quoted an unnamed source as saying: "Sam Fontana has made personal employees of elected officials, not only in the state of Montana, but wherever Fontana Enterprises does business." It concluded: "There are those who feel, as this reporter does, that it's the job of the fourth estate to penetrate the shadows and smokescreens that have hidden and protected the real Sam Fontana under a cloak of respectability."

Willie's first reaction was concern for Jedd. Could this have anything to do with his remark about needing a good lawyer? she wondered. Though she had thought the worst of Sam for a long time, Willie had finally allowed herself to see how good and decent Jedd could be. He had told her she didn't have to make Ginny's mistakes, but how far would his own misguided loyalty to a father without scruples take him?

She reached him with a call to Fontana corporate offices.

"Jedd, I've been reading the papers. This is the trouble you were talking about, isn't it? How bad is it?"

There was a long silence. "I told you before . . . no more than usual."

"That's not an answer," she pressed. "I want to help . . . "

She heard what might have been a chuckle, but it was strained. "Isn't that a switch, Willie? For as long as I've known you, you've never missed an opportunity to let me know how much you disapprove of me and what I do. Why would you want to help me?"

Because I love you, she almost said. But somehow she couldn't. Jedd thought love made everything possible, and she wasn't sure of anything any more. "We go back a long way," she said, "and if you need my help, I'm here."

"Thanks, Willie," he said, his voice husky with emotion, "but this isn't the first time that people have come after the Fontanas. It'll blow over, you'll see. Pop gives himself an edge whenever he can, but whatever they're saying, I know it isn't true."

Wake up, Jedd, she wanted to say, wake up before he takes you down, too. "Are you so sure?" she asked. "Loyalty is one thing, but blind loyalty—"

"Back off, Willie," he interrupted. "Like I said, I appreciate your concern, but nobody knows my father the way I do. We'll handle what needs to be handled . . . and then you'll be hearing from me."

But Willie couldn't leave it at that. She followed the newspapers carefully, and curiously enough, it was in Nick Rossiter's column that she next saw mention of the Fontanas. Titled "An American Tradition," the column was full of insinuations and innuendoes, not Nick's usual style.

"America has always had its robber barons," he wrote, "the Goulds, the Vanderbilts, the Rockefellers – men who founded dynasties and grew rich on business practices that were neither altruistic nor ethical. Sam Fontana has followed in this American tradition. His hand has been behind profit-making ventures that are questionable, to say the least, yet thanks to his vast wealth and power, he has managed to leave few fingerprints. But this is the age of the computer, and we now have the means to find fingerprints where none before appeared. I predict that the disappearance of Farley Jeffers will turn out to be the first step in Sam Fontana's personal Watergate."

Willie called and invited Nick to dinner.

She arranged to meet him at Café Americano, a pleasant, out-of-the-way Tribeca restaurant that would be quiet until later in the evening. She started to make small talk, then stopped.

"Nick," she said, "I need some information. The piece you wrote about the Fontanas . . . it sounded like you knew more than you were saying. Am I right?"

Nick responded with a raised eyebrow and a grin. "What gives?" he asked. "I've never known you to be interested in big business, legit or otherwise. Unless . . . don't tell me the Fontana girl's getting a divorce?"

Willie shook her head impatiently. "There's no divorce that I know of. Can't I ask a simple question without being on a case?"

"Come on, Willie," Nick said. "I'm a newsman, remember? I smell more than idle curiosity here. Off the record, what's your interest?"

Willie debated silently. What she felt for Jedd was not something to share with Nick, yet she owed him some explanation. "I've known the family since I was a kid," she said finally. "Please . . . tell me what's going on."

Now it was Nick's turn to hesitate. "If you're friendly with those people," he said, "you're not going to like this. Greg Heywood's an old buddy of mine . . . we started out together on *Time* magazine . . . he took an investigative team out to Montana. He trailed that guy who skipped . . . Farley Jeffers . . to the Bahamas. Turns out he's been taking payoffs from Fontana Enterprises for a couple of years. When he wanted out, Sam's boys said 'no way.' Jeffers is scared, and Greg convinced him that the way to save his own skin was to blow the whistle on Sam. Greg's a real bulldog, Willie. He always gets what he's after – and what he's after here is a Pulitzer Prize exposé. The Fontanas may own the state, but when Greg's stuff gets into print, the U.S. Attorney is sure to move. Satisfied?"

Willie nodded, her heart heavy. She had no doubt that Sam deserved whatever Justice dealt him.

But Jedd . . . ? Did he deserve it too?

5

"Your next appointment is here," the secretary's voice came over the intercom.

Willie asked for a few minutes to complete a phone call to an opposing lawyer with whom she expected to arrange a settlement. It was getting easier to stay out of the courtroom these days. Her record alone was enough to make many lawyers decide that it was better to avoid giving Willie a chance to express her righteous anger in front of a jury.

At last she buzzed Lettie to show in her next visitor.

She was astonished to look up and see Suzanne St. Clair coming through the door.

"Suze . . . it's great to see you!" Willie opened her arms to embrace the old friend she had not seen in several years, their friendship a victim of Willie's consuming schedule. "But why on earth did you call here for an appointment? We could have had dinner or . . ." The look on Suzanne's face stopped her in midsentence. "Oh, dear. Don't tell me you and Jim are getting divorced?"

Suzanne gave the ironic smile Willie remembered so well. "Never fear, *that* piece of business was taken care of two years ago. It was a dull, routine divorce . . . nothing like those cases of yours I've read about. I wouldn't have imposed it on you."

"It wouldn't have been an imposition," Willie said. "But, then, what *is* the problem . . . ?"

Suzanne took a cigarette from her purse, lit it, and took a long, deep drag. "I'm dying, Willie."

"Oh, my God, Suze . . . "

Suzanne smiled and waggled her cigarette. "I should have given these up years ago, but there it is . . . not much point now."

Willie reached out and held her friend's hand. "Tell me what I can do to help. Whatever it is . . . "

Suzanne closed her eyes for a moment, and for the first time Willie saw pain in her face. "I got custody of the children in the divorce. Now Jim wants to take them away from me . . . "

"Bastard!" Willie spat the word. "He can't do that!"

Suzanne shook her head, as if to throw off Willie's anger. "It isn't like that, Willie. Jim's a decent man. He didn't fight me for custody during the divorce and he's tried to be a good father to Trish and Bobby . . . "

"Then why?" Willie demanded.

"He wants to take them now, as soon as possible, so they . . . " Suzanne faltered, then pushed on bravely: "He thinks that the experience of staying with me will be bad for the children – to have them see me get sicker and die, you see, he thinks it's something they won't get over . . . " Now the words came in a rush: "I've tried to talk him out of it, but he's so scared himself, he just can't hear. We're so close, the three of us. We need each other. If I were . . . gone, they'd understand being taken away, but not now, not like this. Help me, Willie, please help me keep my children."

"Just try to stop me," Willie said fiercely. "Just let *anyone* try to stop me."

For a moment the old sparkle came back into Suzanne's face. "You're some piece of work, Willie . . . I'm glad things turned out well for you." She looked intently into her old roommate's eyes. "They *did* turn out well, didn't they?" The question was almost a plea, as if Suzanne needed to believe, even as her own life was slipping away, that someone else's dream had come true.

Willie wrestled with the truth for just a moment. "I'm doing what I was meant to do," she said, "and what I want to do now is help you, Suze. It's going to come out right. We'll make it come out right – together."

Suzanne smiled again. "There's just one more thing," she said quietly. "I don't have any money, Willie. I wouldn't be able—"

"Do you think I'd take a penny from you?" Willie broke in. "But what happened? Your family . . . ?"

"What happened to the Parkman fortune? Good old George." Suzanne said, her voice edged with resignation. "True to form all the way. You remember, Willie, don't you? According to George, our job was to marry well, some 'nice young man' who'd take care of us. Well, I did it, but the joke was on me. Old George got caught between the bulls and the bears, and what was left, he divided among my brothers. So here I am, looking for a handout from an old friend."

"It's not a handout, Suze. It's a chance to pay off an old debt. I only wish I could do more . . . "

For the next few weeks, Willie said "no new cases" to any and all who requested her services. Suzanne would have her best, her undivided attention, she vowed. It wasn't enough, Willie knew that, not when a miracle was what Suze needed, but it was all that was in her power to give.

Though she usually assigned research to clerks or associates, Willie did her own this time, not wishing to trust any part of Suzanne's welfare to someone else. She spent dozens of hours reviewing child custody cases in every state of the union. She read articles on cancer in medical journals and interviewed psychologists and specialists in oncology, looking for expert witnesses with impressive credentials who could give strong, credible testimony to support her case.

So engrossed was she in helping Suzanne that she almost

swept the crudely lettered envelope off her desk, along with the daily ration of "fan mail" – some hateful, some full of praise – into the basket she had marked "Later." But something caught her eye. The South Dakota postmark and then the name in the corner, an echo from the distant past. Elmer Hawkins . . . one of Perry's old cronies from the Lucky Nugget. She tore it open and began to read:

Dear Willie,

Maybe you don't remember me, but I feel like I still know you because Perry talks about you all the time. And with the way things are, I figured you being the only family he has, you might want to help him out. What happened, Willie, is last week the new Sheriff took Perry in for vagrancy and all because he had a little too much to drink and fell asleep in the park. Perry would've stayed in jail till kingdom come, but me and the missus posted bail and took him in. He had nowhere else. Ever since that cabin of his burned down, your pa has been living like a drifter with no place to call home. I know there was bad blood between him and your ma, and maybe that all rubbed off on you. But he's your pa, and it don't seem right that Perry should end up so bad off. So that's why I wrote.

Yours truly,
Elmer Hawkins

P.S. Do not tell anyone of this letter because Perry is a proud man.

The letter touched old scars and awakened a confusion of emotions. She felt for Perry's plight, but Willie couldn't forgive him for what he had done to Mama. Not now, not while the memory of Ginny's suffering was so tender and fresh.

She called Larry Kusack. "I have a job for you," she said. "I want you to go to a small town in South Dakota . . . Belle Fourche. I'll give you a letter of credit you can take to one of the local banks. Tell them you want to set up a lifetime trust for someone . . . anonymously."

"Who's the beneficiary?" Kusack asked.

She hesitated. "His name's Perry Dellahaye. He's . . . my father."

There was a moment of silence, then Kusack said quietly, "I'm not going to ask any questions, counselor. But if you ever want to talk about it, remember . . . I'm a father, too."

Bless you, Kusack, she thought as she hung up the telephone. She had done what she could, and maybe one day, forgiveness and peace would come, too.

Not for the first time in her career, Willie regretted the notoriety her work had brought her. Normally a hearing of this kind would have commanded only some small notice in the local press, but because Willie Dellahaye, Esquire, was representing the plaintiff, she became part of the news.

One of the Connecticut papers called her a carpetbagger; the other unearthed the fact that she and Suzanne had once been classmates and described her presence as a "mission of mercy." Willie didn't care what they said about her; she prayed that the publicity wouldn't adversely touch Suzanne.

In the weeks since she'd taken the case, Willie had become more and more concerned about Suzanne's health. Always high-strung and high-spirited, Suze now smoked more than ever, tension and anxiety constantly etched in fine lines around her mouth. Her slender body, once graceful and lean, now seemed painfully fragile; her beautiful clear skin was pale and almost transparent, while her dark brown eyes glowed with an unnatural brightness.

"It's going to be all right," Willie promised over and over again, struggling against her own feelings of inadequacy, knowing the best she could do was to make what remained of her friend's life bearable.

*   *   *

The hearing began with brief opening statements by both attorneys. As the petitioner, James St. Clair presented his side first. Under questioning by his attorney, he explained his reasons for seeking custody of his children. "I have nothing but the highest regard for my ex-wife Suzanne," he said, "and I'm truly sorry that she's ill. I simply want to spare our children an ordeal that could mark them for life."

"Do something," Suzanne whispered, tugging at Willie's sleeve. "He sounds so damn convincing . . . "

Willie shook her head. Trying to discredit a man like Jim St. Clair might backfire. She decided to let his testimony stand.

The opposing attorney produced character witnesses, relatives and neighbors who testified that Jim St. Clair was a solid, respectable citizen and a loving parent. Willie neutralized the testimony by getting the witnesses to describe Suzanne in much the same terms.

Next came Jim's expert witness, a child psychologist from Cornell University. Underneath the conference table, Suzanne's icy hand grabbed Willie's when the doctor testified that the children would be better off if they were protected from the worst of their mother's illness. He recommended custody for Jim, with liberal visitation as "the most humane solution for all concerned."

"Don't worry," Willie whispered, as she stood to begin her cross-examination.

"Dr. Kingsley," she said, "your credentials as a child psychologist are impressive indeed. Can you tell me exactly how many cases of this type you've seen in your practice?"

The psychologist cleared his throat. "That's a difficult question to answer, counselor. As you can imagine, no two cases are exactly alike . . . "

"I understand," Willie said reassuringly. "Let me rephrase the question. How many similar cases have you seen in your practice? Ten? Five? Even one? Or could it be that this is the first of its kind? Remember, Dr. Kingsley, you are under oath . . . "

The man fidgeted and shifted in the witness box. "If you

require a precise answer, counselor, I'd have to say that this was the first, though I have . . . "

"Thank you, doctor. Would it be fair to say then that the opinion you've expressed is based on theory?"

"Yes, but . . . "

"Thank you, doctor. No more questions."

She winked at Suzanne, who managed to smile.

But on redirect, the psychologist explained that he had treated children who had been traumatized by the death of a parent.

Then it was Willie's turn again. She produced her own psychologist, who said the children would feel guilty and abandoned if they were taken away from their mother now.

"Dr. Edelstein," Willie said, "I'm going to ask you exactly the same question I asked of the plaintiff's expert witness. Have you ever had a case of this type in your experience?"

"No."

"In other words, your view comes from the same information given to Dr. Kingsley. It is an opinion, am I right?"

"That's correct."

After a lunch break, Willie produced her second and final expert witness, the chief of staff at Memorial Sloan-Kettering Center for Cancer Care.

"Dr. Farber," she began, "you've examined my client and reviewed her medical history. Based on your considerable experience, what is your prognosis?"

"The more experience I have, the less I'd care to generalize, counselor. I've seen patients die who should have lived and I've seen total remissions with no medical explanation whatever. All I can say with certainty is that Suzanne St. Clair is seriously ill and that there's the possibility she may have no more than a year or so of life."

"The will to live, that's important, is it not?"

"Yes, it is. I've seen patients prolong life for years simply because they want so badly to live."

"But Suzanne has more than willpower in her favor, does she not, doctor? Are there not, as we speak, new drugs and therapies being developed and used effectively on patients with her condition?"

"Yes, that's true, though I'd have to be conservative in my optimism regarding new therapies."

Jim's attorney cross-examined. "Dr. Farber, would you describe for me the course of an illness like Mrs. St. Clair's."

Willie could feel Suzanne tremble as the oncologist listed symptoms . . . "extreme weight loss" . . . "inability to digest solid food" . . . "lapses in mental faculties" . . . "periods of extreme pain." She felt a consuming hatred for the cruelty and ignorance that would expose someone as good as Suze to this kind of torture.

She sprang to her feet when Jim's attorney was through. "Dr. Farber," she said, "what you've described is a worst-case scenario, is it not?"

"Yes."

"And in fact, if my client were to be in such a condition, she would no longer be at home caring for her children but in a hospital, isn't that so?"

"Yes, I would say so. Definitely."

"Thank you, doctor."

Jim's attorney gave a brief, sympathetic summation, expressing compassion for Suzanne and emphasizing that this action was being taken only in the best interest of the children.

Willie knew that this was the operative concept in all matters concerning minor children. She knew that she could not win merely by eliciting the judge's sympathy for Suzanne, who looked pale and quite ill now.

Willie stood in front of a crowded courtroom and spoke out, her voice strong, her bearing confident:

"Suzanne Parkman St. Clair is my client. She has also been my friend for nearly two decades. She is a fine and decent human being. Suze and I went to law school together . . . such a long time ago. She gave up her chance at a career to marry and have children. Her family is Suzanne's life, and she stands before you today pleading that her family not be taken away. To be ill is not a crime. I beg you not to punish Suzanne by imposing a burden she cannot bear, the loss of her children.

"We've heard it argued today that it is in the best interest of those children that they be removed from their mother. I say this is a monstrous idea, well intentioned perhaps, but monstrous in its implications. Are we to teach children that illness is a reason to abandon someone we love? Are we to teach them to turn away in times of trouble?"

Willie's voice broke, tears streamed freely from her eyes, but she went on:

"This should be a summer season for Suzanne, a time of watching her children grow, a time of looking forward – to the harvest of her love and devotion. But winter came early to my friend Suzanne. I beg of you . . . allow her to give the gift of her final season, however long it may be, to her children."

The judge was out less than an hour. Willie gripped Suzanne's hand tightly as he began to speak. "The court cannot in good conscience remove minor children from their mother without compelling reasons. The petitioner has presented no such reasons; therefore I must find for the respondent, Suzanne Parkman St. Clair."

"Thank you, oh, thank you," Suzanne cried out, her thin, pale face transformed with joy, and Willie marveled that someone so gravely ill could be so happy. She wiped the tears from her own face, and embraced her old friend.

It had been a long time since she had tasted such sweetness in one of her victories.

6

The day began like any other. Almost. The weather was springlike; sunshine streamed through the French windows and the plants on the terrace glistened with morning dew.

Willie did her exercises and showered, then took her

room-service breakfast onto the terrace, a spacious expanse of brick and wrought iron where a hundred people might be comfortably entertained – but never had been. Lingering over her coffee, she watched Fifth Avenue and Central Park come to life with joggers and cyclists and early commuters. In the aftermath of Suzanne's illness, Willie had felt for the first time that mortality might be waiting almost anywhere. She had made an effort to slow down and "enjoy the wildflowers on the side of the road," as Matt had advised so long ago.

And the slowing down made Willie notice what she had managed more often than not to ignore. She had a career that would be the envy of any law student; a law firm that commanded respect; beauty and talent that had been publicly lauded; a palatial apartment in the heart of the world's most exciting city.

Yet today, on her thirty-eighth birthday, she was all alone. A scattering of gifts had been delivered with her breakfast – a silver martini pitcher, a case of Dom Perignon champagne, several lavish floral arrangements, and a set of Baccarat brandy glasses – all from business associates and clients.

Only one package had any meaning. An envelope from Cheryl Vinnaver, who had been Cheryl Mason, later Cheryl Hardwick, and was now Cheryl Trevino. She'd sent a photograph of her current family; a husband, three children, and two stepchildren. "You may be chicken," the inscription read, "but I mean to keep on trying until I get it right."

The picture filled Willie with an odd nostalgia. She couldn't remember actually being happy during those Palm Springs days, when she and Cheryl had been "the oddballs." But if not happy, hadn't they at least believed in the power of their own good intentions?

They were still oddballs in a way. Cheryl had made a career of searching for the love neither Malcolm nor her elusive father had given. And Willie herself, it seemed, had made a career of proving that such a search was futile.

More than ever she thought of Jedd, of what he'd been to her and all he wanted to be. He had warned her once about

500

waiting too long, yet ironically now it was Jedd who seemed to be lost in a limbo of Sam's making, a web of evil and corruption he still couldn't see. Was it too late, she wondered, to open a door that fear had sealed shut when she was too young to understand?

Willie's mood was pensive and shaded with gray when she arrived at the office. The cries of "Happy Birthday" that greeted her, the bouquet of tulips her secretary had left on her desk, seemed a reminder that her life was bounded by the business of Dellahaye, Belzer and Crown. Lettie Bowden, her secretary, presented Willie with two other items. The first was a cardboard sign that said: "Divorce is Forever." Once, she might have cynically agreed with the gallows humor, but today, marking another year in her own journey toward forever, she craved something richer and sweeter than cynicism.

The second item was a newspaper article circled in red, a report that after a steady rise for almost two decades, the divorce rate in America had finally leveled off. Willie smiled as she read it – and wished with all her heart she'd see the day when her business declined.

Her newest client, however, seemed to fall into the "Divorce is Forever" category. Charlene Barlett said she was twenty-eight, but she looked about sixteen, with a little girl's voice and child's face framed by scraggly blond curls. She was already a veteran of both marriage and divorce.

She had been divorced for five years and had been awarded child support until her youngsters reached eighteen and alimony until she remarried. "I guess my ex figured I'd get another husband and he'd be off the hook," she said plaintively. "But I didn't want to do that to my kids, I didn't want to bring in a stranger and make them mind him . . . "

Willie nodded her approval, remembering how hard it had been to handle Neal's presence in her life, even though she'd been a young woman.

"Paul – my ex – got married a couple of years ago . . . his new wife has three kids, and I guess she got tired of watching the money go out for me and mine . . . Now Paul is taking me to court to take my alimony away, Miss

Dellahaye," she said, sniffing tearfully. "He's got a nice house and a new family, and he's trying to take the bread out of my mouth."

"On what grounds?" Willie asked sharply, already angered by what she was hearing.

"He's trying to say that my boyfriend Andy and me are living together like . . . you know, like man and wife. But it isn't true," Charlene sobbed.

Willie gave her a glass of water and waited until Charlene calmed down.

"I can't live like a nun," Charlene continued. "I'm a woman, and it feels bad to be alone all the time. Me and Paul aren't married anymore . . . is it fair that he snoops on me and plays dirty tricks just so he can get out of paying what he promised me?"

"What dirty tricks?" Willie asked.

Charlene blew her nose loudly. "About a year ago, he hired a guy and tried to set me up, you know, so he could say I was living with somebody. I got wise to him, but now he's trying again . . . "

Willie was livid. Of all the issues she'd ever championed, the impoverishment of divorced women and their children was the one she cared about most. It was bad enough that alimony and child support payments were often pitifully inadequate. Bad enough so many husbands didn't pay – and got away with it when ex-wives had no money for rent or food, let alone expensive litigation. Now this one was trying to use the law to victimize a woman who was little more than a child herself – because it was no longer convenient to meet his responsibilities.

"I'm just going to ask you one question," Willie said. "Would a court have any reason to think your boyfriend was, in fact, taking your husband's place?"

Charlene blushed. "If you mean, do we sleep together . . . ?"

"No," Willie said sharply, remembering the days when an abandoned wife had no choice but to live like a nun – or else lose everything. "You have every right to a private life, as long as it doesn't harm your children. What I mean is,

502

does your boyfriend pay bills, buy groceries, that kind of thing?"

Charlene shook her head. "Andy takes me out a couple of times a week, when I can get my mom to sit with the kids, but that's about it."

"Then you'll be fine," Willie promised. "I won't let you lose that alimony, no matter what it takes."

Charlene Barlett left the office smiling, and that, Willie thought, was probably the best birthday present of the day. One of the best moments of her career had been the day New York had passed a law she'd lobbied hard for, the State Office of Child Support Enforcement. It gave private lawyers like Willie the right to garnishee the wages of fathers who were delinquent in their child-support payments. It was a step in the right direction, and so was the computer system that tracked them, but it wasn't enough, especially in big cities, where defaulting fathers could still lose themselves.

A man like Paul Barlett, Willie thought . . . I can make an example of him, set a precedent that would discourage other men from trying to dodge their responsibilities. As a first step, she ordered a thorough investigation into his life and his finances. "This is a rush job," she told Larry Kusack. "My client goes to court in two weeks, so I need the ammunition fast."

"When will it all end?" Kusack sighed rhetorically.

"I don't know," Willie said. "Maybe when people do what everybody talked about in the sixties . . . make love instead of war."

"From your lips to God's ear," he chuckled.

Shortly after lunch, Pamela Belzer ushered a pair of female law students into Willie's office. "Here they are," Pam said, "the best and the brightest from my alma mater. I've wined them and dined them, and now they want to meet the legendary Willie Dellahaye."

So soon? she thought. Was it already time for another graduating class, another courtship ritual between promising students and Dellahaye, Belzer and Crown? "I'm delighted to meet you," Willie said. How young they are, she thought, how eager and ambitious they look. "I assume Pam's reviewed our compensation package for first-year associates . . . "

"Yes," one of the women replied, "the pay scale's competitive with other firms in the city. But we have a question, Miss Dellahaye . . . "

"Ask away."

"We've heard you represent only women in divorce actions. Is that firm policy – and do you impose it on associates?"

Willie had to think for a moment. How could she explain what had brought her – no, driven her – to the career choices she'd made? "It's true," she said, "that my clients have been women. Call it personal policy, if you like, but no, I don't impose it on associates." Then she added, "I like to think of Dellahaye, Belzer and Crown as a law firm with a conscience. We do more *pro bono* cases than any firm in the state, maybe the country, and if our clients tend to be women, that's because they have the greatest need of good representation. Does that answer your question?"

Willie caught the look the two women exchanged as Pam bustled them away for a tour of the firm's offices; it was the kind of look she and Suze would give each other when "old George" spouted his chauvinistic worldview. Could it be that they'd somehow misunderstood what she was trying to say? Surely, as women, they'd want to be of service to their own sex . . .

Willie spent the next few hours working on her speech for the conference on matrimonial law. If she had a single ambition at this point, it was to undermine and expose the current divorce law for what it was – a boon to men.

As the clock inched toward five o'clock, Willie decided she didn't want to go home and do what she'd done her last two birthdays – read briefs and go to bed early.

She called Nick. "Can I take you out to dinner?"

"Looking for a shoulder to cry on?" he asked, a strange edge to his voice.

How did Nick know it's my birthday? she wondered. "I

504

don't know that a birthday is anything to cry about," she said, "but let's say I'm not thrilled about it."

"Birthday?" Nick echoed. "I thought . . . haven't you read the papers today, Willie?"

"I haven't had a chance. What's in them, Nick?"

"Some news about your friends, the Fontanas," he answered bitterly. "Greg Heywood's disappeared. His car was found wrecked at the bottom of a canyon just outside of Butte. He's presumed dead. The local cops are trying to stonewall and call it an accident . . . but it doesn't take a genius to figure out who's responsible."

"No . . . it can't be," Willie protested, her voice barely a whisper. What Nick suggested . . . it was horrifying. Sam was thoroughly crooked, she was certain of that, but might he go this far? And would Jedd be his accomplice in something as awful as murder?

"Believe it," Nick said grimly, "because every reporter I know does. Sam Fontana made a big mistake. He may have gotten rid of one man, but he didn't kill the story, not by a long shot. Reporters can be like cops, Willie. Somebody hurts one of our own, we'll go after him. I'm flying out to Montana myself. A team from the wire service is taking Greg's notes to the U.S. Attorney's office there. We're gonna get on their backs and make so much noise, they won't have any choice *but* to nail Sam Fontana. Sorry I can't make dinner," he said just before hanging up, "but happy birthday, anyway."

Willie sat stunned at her desk as the last of the day faded outside her window and lights came on in the city. A part of her wanted to face Jedd and demand the truth. And a part of her accepted it already.

She had no real doubt about what Nick had said – and that Sam Fontana deserved whatever Justice had in store for him. But Jedd . . . did he deserve to go down with his father simply because he'd been too blind to see the corruption that had surrounded him all his life? Willie's heart cried out "no."

Her hand reached for the telephone – and froze in

505

midair. Would she be betraying Nick's trust if she shared the information he had given her?

Then Willie remembered that Jedd had once been faced with a similar question – and that he had chosen to help her. Could she do less, now that Jedd's world was about to come tumbling down?

She placed the call, and when she heard his voice on the line, she wasted no time on small talk. "Listen to me," she said urgently. "I've just heard about Greg Heywood's death. I'm sure there's going to be an investigation, a big one. Sam's gone too far this time, and you can't go on pretending any of this is going to blow over, not now . . . "

"Are you still on my father's case, Willie?" he asked, his voice edged with anger. "I know you don't like him, but I've told you more than once: he'd never do half the stuff he's been accused of . . . never."

"Jedd," she said softly, not wanting to argue, "this isn't about your father, it's about you. Regardless of what Sam's done. I know *you* couldn't be part of it. I want to help you, the way you helped me . . . "

There was a hesitation, and then he said quietly, "Thanks for the thought, Willie, but if your fee includes betraying my father, I can't afford it."

And then the connection was broken. Damn you, she thought, damn you for being so stubborn and proud – and so loyal to a man who doesn't deserve it. But as Willie put the receiver down, her eyes were filled with tears.

7

"Is this it, Larry?" Willie asked, unable to hide her disappointment. "That's all you could find on Paul Barlett?"

A grin creased Kusack's plain face. "If I didn't know you better, Willie, I'd say you wanted me to manufacture some dirt. His credit rating's not too good, but the man looks to be okay otherwise. Good husband, hard-working employee and, according to the neighbors, a good father to his stepchildren."

"If he's such a good father," Willie snapped, "he wouldn't be trying to hurt the mother of his own children."

"If you say so, counselor. But if the pieces don't fit right, maybe a few are missing. I don't want to tell you your business, but maybe you want to talk to your client again . . ."

"I know all I need to know," Willie insisted. "The man's trying to weasel out of his responsibilities and I'm going to nail him."

But after Kusack left, she did call her client. A male voice answered, then summoned Charlene to the phone.

"Charlene," she asked, "can you tell me the name of the man your husband hired to set you up?"

There was an intake of breath. "Gosh, Miss Dellahaye, I was so upset, it went right out of my mind. I think it was Bob something."

Damn, Willie thought, her disappointment mounting. "Let me ask you something else," she said. "How many times has your ex missed his alimony payments?"

"Well," Charlene said, "he's all the time calling and saying he's short of money . . . and his checks are late *lots* of times . . ."

"But he's never actually missed a payment?" Willie finished.

"No . . . gosh, you're getting me scared. Why are you asking all these questions?" Charlene whimpered. "You promised I wouldn't lose my alimony, Miss Dellahaye, you promised . . ."

"I know," Willie said, "and I always keep my promises."

But after she hung up, she couldn't help wishing she had more to bring to court than her own skills and experience.

The issue was crucial, and she was bound and determined to win.

As Willie's limousine turned onto Forty-second Street, she was surprised to see the crowds and reporters gathered in front of the Grand Hyatt Hotel. Must be a slow day for news, she mused, for a conference like this didn't usually get more than perfunctory coverage in the press. What a break, she thought – a chance to focus national attention on a problem she cared deeply and passionately about.

But as she stepped out of the car, she was jostled and pushed by several women carrying picket signs, and as she struggled to regain her balance, she was stunned to see that the signs bore her name. "We Don't Want the Bad Old Days, Dellahaye!" and "Go Away, Dellahaye!"

"Get back in your fancy limousine and go home!" one woman shouted – and the crowd took up the cry. "We don't need a millionaire's lawyer here!" another called out. "What do you know about women like us?"

Before she could say anything, a reporter shoved a microphone under her face. "I hear you're coming out against the reformed divorce law, Miss Dellahaye, that you're against no-fault divorce and equitable distribution. How do you justify that position?"

Willie felt like Alice in Wonderland. "Justify?" she repeated. "What are you talking about? I've always . . . " Her words were lost in the sound of cheering and applause. And then he appeared – Francis Aloysius Harrigan – on foot in his man-of-the-people guise, walking down the street, shaking hands and distributing smiles like a politician running for office.

He took charge of the crowd as if he owned them – and he probably did, Willie suddenly realized. With his own reputation up for scrutiny, the Silver Fox wasn't above this kind of theatrical dirty trick. Any doubt that she'd been set up vanished when he deftly maneuvered himself in front of the television cameras. "Ladies and gentlemen of the press," he began in a stentorian baritone, "I hope no one here is questioning the principles of this dedicated attorney. Let me assure you that although Miss Dellahaye and I often disagree on methods we are as one when it comes to the principle. We both want what's best for America's women and children, don't we counselor?" Harrigan turned to Willie.

"My record speaks for itself," she said. "And if anyone really wants to know what I'm for or against, come inside and listen." She left Harrigan basking in the glow of his celebrity, dishing out the double-talk he did so well.

"Thanks a lot, Francis," she muttered to herself, just as she had in the days she'd worked for him, as she pushed open the hotel doors. Some things you could always count on, and Harrigan's need to be right was one of them. He had brought her here to make a fool of her, not to permit an honest examination of "his" divorce law.

Francis was in rare form, Willie thought. His opening speech was a masterpiece compounded of hot air, smoke screen, and pure theft; she saw at once that he meant to neutralize her arguments by pre-empting them.

"As president of the Matrimonial Bar and chairman of this conference," he began, "let me be the first to say that our present law is imperfect. The legal profession is, alas, made up of human beings, fallible and imperfect. Like everyone else here, I deplore the disintegration of the American family and the terrible impact of divorce on women and children. However, I submit to you that the solution lies not in reviving old divorce statutes or even in new legislation, but in education. America's women have fought valiantly for equality. Now our society must teach them to be self-sufficient, so they may *be* equal with men in marriage and in a court of law . . . "

Willie was appalled by the murmurs of agreement, the applause that followed Harrigan's address. Couldn't these people see behind the high-sounding buzzwords?

Her dismay grew as Harrigan presented one hand-picked speaker after another to rubber-stamp his views. A sociology professor said it was true that many divorced women found themselves living substandard lives or dependent on welfare – but described the condition as "a necessary growing pain of a society in transition."

A judge proposed annual seminars – along with salary increases – for members of his profession "so we may have

509

the time and opportunity to study the needs of a changing population."

A Texas sheriff pounded the podium emphatically and insisted that "good law enforcement is the answer to all your problems. In the great state of Texas," he said, "we've always had a high regard for our women and children. Maybe our divorce laws are no better or worse than anybody else's – but ours have teeth. We don't have welchers in my district, and you know why?" He paused, while the audience whistled and cheered. "Because I throw 'em in jail – that's why! Let me tell you, folks, there's nothin' like a week or two in jail to get a fella to do right by his family."

Willie smiled in spite of her impatience. The sheriff had a point, she conceded – and Harrigan had been clever to invite him, even if he knew as well as she did that the "Texas solution" was highly unlikely in places where the police and the jails were already burdened by more serious crime.

The conference broke for a two-hour lunch. After that, the delegates streamed back, sated with food and drowsy with drink, rustling and shifting in their seats as the afternoon session got underway. As the hours passed and Willie waited and waited for her turn to speak, she realized that Harrigan's final trick was to exhaust and saturate the audience before she'd even opened her mouth.

Finally, at a quarter to five, Harrigan introduced her. "Ladies and gentlemen," he said, "I've saved till last this beautiful lady – a protégée of mine, I add with pride – for a very particular reason. We've heard excellent recommendations today, which will no doubt be implemented in time. But meanwhile, until we reach that Utopia of perfect laws that protect all people and harm none, we can only be grateful for attorneys like Willa Dellahaye, who have a direct line to the Deity and the readiness to show us the way . . . "

There was a ripple of laughter as Willie took the podium, flushed with indignation over Harrigan's mocking introduction. She spied a group of delegates leaving the back rows and working their way toward the exits. She put her

510

notes down and called out: "Hold it! Just stay where you are! I know you're tired, but give me just a few more minutes – please. I've listened to the same do-nothing, chicken-and-egg talk you've heard all day. My reaction is like Mr. Bumble's in Dickens's *Oliver Twist*: If the law doesn't protect the people, then the law is an ass.

"No matter what any of you have heard, I don't advocate a return to the bad old days when getting divorced was next to impossible unless you were rich, when adultery or mayhem, real or fabricated, was the only way to leave a marriage. But in making divorce simple, we've taken away the one thing an unwanted wife had: leverage to negotiate. And in its place we have something that sounds good on paper – equitable distribution – and left it up to judges and lawyers, who are still primarily male, to decide what's 'equitable.'

"We've done a terrible injustice to middle-class women who have made a career of marriage. When the career is taken away, they're left without skills and resources. If they're lucky, half of the family home is usually what they're awarded, which in real life, ladies and gentlemen, translates to an appalling decline in the standard of living.

"Mr. Harrigan's generous introduction to the contrary, I have no road map to Utopia. I have questions I beg you to consider in the name of Justice. We – the legal profession – have created a generation of 'new poor.' I ask what you will do about them."

The applause began slowly and then built, as delegates rose to their feet, cheering and whistling like a crowd at a baseball game.

"Nice recovery," Harrigan said approvingly as Willie walked past him to leave the stage. "But do you really imagine it will make a difference?"

She stopped and looked him in the face. "I don't know, Francis," she said simply. "I do know the law needs people like me to keep people like you honest."

511

8

"We meet again, Wonder Woman," said Bud Hodge, leaning over the conference table where Willie sat with Charlene Barlett. "But I must say I'm surprised you'd take a case like this. I thought you had a few principles."

"I'm not surprised to see you," Willie countered. "You were always a sexist, Bud. This case should be right up your alley."

Bud opened his mouth as if to speak, then shook his head and went back to his client.

Seeing her old rival again, remembering how he'd tried to undermine her at "Ring and Wait," how he'd beaten her for the *Law Review* editorship at Harvard, made Willie want to win all the more. From the list of Bud's witnesses, she could see that he had no more hard evidence in this case than she did. It would be her skills against his, Charlene's word against her ex-husband's – the good guys against the bad.

Bud's case opened with Paul Barlett, a diminutive, soft-spoken man whose manner somehow reminded Willie of Larry Kusack. She brushed the image aside and reminded herself that Kusack was a decent man who took care of his ex-wife and children. "Mr. Barlett," Bud began, "will you tell the court in your own words why you're asking for relief from further alimony payments?"

"Well, it seems to me, my ex-wife is living with a man, and it doesn't seem fair that I should have to support them."

"Objection!" Willie was on her feet in a flash. "Petitioner has yet to substantiate the fact that my client cohabits with anyone."

"Sustained," the judge agreed.

Bud tried another question. "Will you tell the court why you agreed to pay alimony until your ex-wife remarried."

"Objection!" Willie was up again. "What's relevant here is that the petitioner did agree to pay, not his state of mind."

"Sustained."

By actual count, Willie raised eighteen objections during Barlett's testimony, most of them technical – and most of them sustained. And try as he would, Bud couldn't manage to get more on record than the fact that his client was having a hard time making ends meet.

Bud did manage to produce two neighbors who testified that Charlene's boyfriend could be seen at her home "seven out of seven days a week." The testimony disturbed Willie, but she countered it with technicalities, getting the neighbors to admit that no one could actually prove he lived there.

When it was her turn, Willie produced rent receipts for a furnished room that the boyfriend kept – and then put Charlene herself on the stand. Dressed in a pink dress with a white Peter Pan collar, Charlene looked like a girl on her way to Sunday school. She sobbed as if her heart would break, describing how she struggled to live on what her ex-husband paid.

"I want to get a job, your honor," she said tearfully. "I've been studying typing and shorthand from books, but what with two little ones at home and my health not being so good, I just haven't been able to . . ."

Willie caught the flicker of sympathy in the judge's expression. She pushed for more in her closing statement, arguing that Barlett's case was based on convenience, rather than cause. "Your honor," she said, "my client has freely admitted she has a relationship with a man. We no longer live in the dark ages, and that in itself is no reason to deny her the support to which she's entitled. To grant Paul Barlett relief in this action would be to further erode the slender security that divorced women have. I beg the court to uphold that security."

The judge agreed, framing his decision in almost the same words Willie had used, saying "we no longer expect an adult woman to live like Caesar's wife in order to receive payments specified by her divorce decree."

A cry of anguish rang through the courtroom. Willie turned to see a young woman, Paul Barlett's second wife, clinging to her husband and weeping.

Willie turned back to her own client, but the words of congratulation stuck in her throat; the expression on Charlene Barlett's face wasn't one of peace or even gratitude. It was that of a Cheshire cat.

A grim-faced Bud Hodge marched over to Willie and roughly grabbed her arm. "Always on the side of the angels, aren't you, Willie?" he said sarcastically. "Thanks to you and the parasite who hired you, a decent man is going down the tubes. The only really bad thing Paul Barlett ever did was to marry that scheming bitch . . . and I for one don't think he should have to pay for that mistake the rest of his life. This one's going to appeal, Willie, free of charge, and I'm going to win, I promise you. By then Paul Barlett will probably be in Chapter Eleven, right along with his wife and two kids, but I know you won't let a little thing like that disturb your conscience, counselor. After all, he's only a man . . . " Bud released her arm and walked away.

But his words echoed in Willie's head and wouldn't go away. There had never been any love lost between her and Bud, but he had never attacked her personally.

Later that night, as she tried to sleep, she began remembering little details. The fact that Charlene couldn't name the man her ex-husband had allegedly hired to set her up. The way she said she'd never wanted to inflict a stepfather on her children, yet the man she was with seemed a fixture in her life.

She remembered Paul Barlett's face when she'd cut him off repeatedly, whenever he tried to say something damaging about his ex-wife. That was her job, she told herself, to protect her clients and to do her best – but it had always been a point of honor for Willie never to take a case she didn't believe in – and now . . .

The nagging doubts didn't go away, not the next day or the one after that. Willie did something she had never done before. When her driver arrived to pick her up for the daily trip to the office, she gave him Paul Barlett's Riverdale address instead.

It was a hot, humid day, and as Willie pulled up in her limousine, Barlett was in his shirtsleeves, loading boxes from what had been his home into a van outside.

"What are you doing here?" he demanded harshly.

Willie swallowed hard. "I'm still looking for the right verdict," she said.

"A little late for that," he said flatly, though something flickered in his eyes.

Willie stood her ground, ready to face Barlett's anger in her need to find the truth.

Finally Barlett mopped his brow with a handkerchief and said, "You may as well come inside."

The living room was stripped nearly bare, and Barlett motioned for Willie to sit on the only chair. "Hearing what you just said . . . It isn't easy. Did you mean it?"

"Yes."

"Then you may as well hear what you didn't let me say in court."

Willie winced at this reminder of how well she had done her job.

"I met Charlene when she was sixteen. She'd dropped out of high school to take a job as a waitress in a fast-food restaurant. I used to have lunch there and we got friendly. We'd been seeing each other a few months when she told me she was pregnant. I believed her. We got married and it turned out there was no baby after all," he said with a mirthless smile.

Willie felt almost physically ill as Barlett went on, describing a wife who'd seen marriage as a ticket to a life of leisure, who'd seen to it that she'd become pregnant just when he began talking about divorce.

"After our twins were born, I couldn't go through with it. I stayed for a couple more years, but finally I just couldn't take the laziness and the lies. I wanted out, and I gave Charlene everything she asked for. To tell you the truth, I figured she'd land some other poor sucker pretty quick. I guess she figured different . . . that she'd live off me forever. I paid and I paid, and when I saw how I was cheating my wife and my family, I figured it was enough, that Charlene could get a job and work for a change, like my wife has had to do since the day she married me."

And when Paul Barlett finished, Willie knew instinctively that he'd been telling the truth. She remembered the time she'd accused Bud of stealing her notes – and how she had been wrong then. How terrible it would be, she thought, if after all these years it turned out that Bud had a better sense of justice than she did.

"It isn't enough to say I'm sorry," Willie said, "but if I don't tell you that I was wrong, I'd be a worse loser than I am . . . "

Barlett shook his head. "This may sound crazy, but thank you for coming. At least I know you didn't just do a job on me . . . you know, all in a day's work . . . and then walk away and forget about it."

"No," Willie said, "I don't plan to forget about you, not ever. But Bud Hodge is a good lawyer . . . and I can promise he won't be facing me on appeal. I wish you luck," she said and left the house.

As her limousine pulled away, Willie looked back. In the driveway were stacks of boxes and a small tricycle. The scene stabbed at Willie's heart, forcing a remembrance of the day she and Mama had been turned out by the Sheriff, their meager belongings cast aside by uncaring men.

Be careful, Matt had warned her more than once, about being blinded by passion. Everyone who cared had warned her, and now she felt like a character in a Greek play, undone by her own unseeing pride. She had known what was right, she had always known.

If Charlene Barlett had been a man, I'd have been more careful, she thought. I would have seen the holes in her story, I would have looked harder for the truth. But Charlene was a woman, and Willie realized that she'd been guilty of a double standard of justice and all too ready to see every woman as a victim and every man as a perpetrator. All her life she'd nursed a very different kind of image, of a man as a taker, destroyer. But Paul Barlett hadn't been that kind of man. He'd been giving and kind and she had punished him for it.

She had built a life and a career on getting even – when love would have made a difference, taken away the anger, opened her heart. It was the lesson Matt had tried to teach once; it was the lesson Jedd had begged her to hear. Perhaps if she had let herself love, she would have been saved from the blind anger that had made her do a terrible thing.

Enough, she said, and no more. Jedd was right and she needed to talk to him – and more important, to hear his side of the story she'd heard from Nick – now, before another precious moment of life slipped away. But when she phoned the corporate headquarters of Fontana Enterprises, she was told that Jedd could no longer be reached at this number.

Frantically, she dialed the Fontana ranch, hoping to find him there, but when she asked the housekeeper to put Jedd on, the voice that answered was Sam's.

"I was trying to reach Jedd," she explained, "but he isn't at the office and I didn't know where else to try."

"He isn't here," Sam said. "I don't think he'll be back." There was a cold and frightening finality in the statement.

"But where then . . . ? For heaven's sake, Sam, please tell me . . . has something happened to Jedd?"

"You know, Willie," he said, just as if she hadn't asked the question, "you and I should be natural enemies. But I respect you . . . and Jedd, I know he cares for you. It's no secret, you aren't what I would have picked for my son, but now . . . "

Willie could hear Sam taking a deep breath.

"Now, Willie," Sam went on, an edge of defeat in his voice, "he needs you more than he needs me. If you care for my boy, stand by him, Willie."

"What's happened, Sam? Tell me . . . "

"Let Jedd tell you. Go to him, Willie. He's up at the state capital . . . at the U.S. Attorney's office."

Abruptly, Sam disconnected.

Now Willie was terrified. Was Jedd under some kind of

517

indictment? Her mind raced through possibilities, none of them good. She called the U.S. Attorney's office in Montana, but though she pleaded and badgered a receptionist and an aide, she was told that no information could be released on an ongoing investigation: "You'll have to wait for the press conference tomorrow morning, just like everyone else."

That was all Willie needed to hear.

There were no commercial flights available for hours, so she chartered a small plane to make the flight to Helena. The trip was bumpy and a summer storm forced the pilot to cut his air speed, but Willie was scarcely aware of the rising and falling of the plane – or even of the thunder and lightning that crashed around her. Don't let me be too late, she prayed, without knowing what too late might be.

The press corps had turned out in record numbers in the auditorium of the State House. There was, for them, no bigger story than the murder of one of their own in pursuit of a story.

Willie maneuvered through the crush of people and equipment, and near the front of the auditorium she spotted a familiar face – Nick Rossiter. "What's going on, Nick?" she asked, too anxious to bother with greetings or small talk. "I heard they were holding Jedd Fontana."

Nick stared at her for a long time. "So that's it," he said finally. "I always knew there was more to the story . . . "

"Nick, I promise you'll know everything there is to know . . . on the record or any way you want it . . . just tell me, what are they holding Jedd for?"

"You've got your facts wrong, Willie," he said. "They aren't holding him. The press convinced the U.S. Attorney's office to put out a warrant on Fontana Enterprises records . . . the works. Turns out Sam decided this might be a good time to retire to Palm Springs. Permanently. Once his son got a good look at what he was inheriting . . . my sources tell me he came forward voluntarily, with the names of the men who did the job on Greg Heywood – and a lot more. The authorities seem to be satisfied Jedd Fontana had nothing to do with the murder. I'd guess they're a lot more interested in cleaning up the state than in nailing him for what his father did. That's all I know, Willie, scout's honor."

"Thanks, Nick," she said, giving him a grateful hug. "You're a good friend . . . I owe you."

"Just remember that next time I need a divorce," he said with a grin.

She broke away and pushed through the crowd, stationing herself near the door through which Jedd would pass. And then it opened. He was flanked by two plainclothesmen, but he looked so alone, tense, tight-tipped, as if every movement caused him pain.

"Jedd!" she called out. "I thought you might need a good lawyer," she said, holding out her hand. "I knew you wouldn't ask."

Jedd's face lit up when he saw her. Ignoring the reporters, he took Willie's hand, and led her back to the anteroom. "You were right," he said. "It wasn't nearly as simple as I thought. When I got a good look under the surface, behind the expensive corporate offices and the fancy accounting, when I saw how deep the dirt went, you were there whispering in my ear every minute. I wouldn't be here if it weren't for you . . . "

"I didn't want you to turn against your father," she said.

"He turned away from me, Willie, when he made choices I couldn't live with. Fathers don't always think about us when they make decisions . . ."

"No," Willie said. "I know something about that, too."

"Stay close to me," Jedd said urgently. "I need you now."

"Every step of the way," she promised, meeting his lips with a kiss. "It's taken us too long to find each other," she murmured, "and from now on, we travel together."

And she was not far away when he went to stand alone before a battery of microphones. There was still pain in his face, but from where she sat, he had never looked quite as handsome to Willie as he did now.

"I've always been proud to be a Fontana," he said

huskily, "proud of the heritage that's been handed down from father to son in my family. We settled this state when it was wilderness, we helped build it and make it great. But the wilderness days are history." He glanced over to Willie before he went on, as though acknowledging her part in having given him the words that came next. "This is no time for the rule of the gun or frontier law. It's a tragedy that my father didn't realize that sooner. The era of his kind of man . . . let's call them the grandees . . . is over."

When he was finished, Willie rushed to his side.

"Are you representing Mr. Fontana?" a reporter called out.

Jedd answered before she had a chance. "Let's just say she's the leader of my defense team."

Willie looked up at him and smiled. Realistically, she knew there would have to be a number of expert lawyers to untangle the kind of problems that Jedd was facing.

"This case is a little out of your line, isn't it, Miss Dellahaye?" a reporter called out.

"It may be something new for me," she said, as she slipped her arm through Jedd's, "but no . . . this isn't really out of my line, not at all."

She looked up again, and her eyes met his. For all the thousands of times she had looked into those dark eyes, she had never been able to read their message so clearly.

Whoever was listening, when she spoke again it was to him, only to him. "As a matter of fact," she said softly, "I'm right where I belong."

BRENDA MCBRYDE

HANNAH ROBSON

Hannah was twelve when she watched her mother
battle with death in agonising childbirth. That day she
swore no man would ever put her through such
horror.

Years of thankless toil on her father's bleak North-
umbrian hill farm have left her unafraid of hard work.
She determines to support herself and never be at the
mercy of a man. Setting out alone into the world, she
encounters kindness and friendship, but trouble dogs
her footsteps. In the bustling commercial life of the
port in Newcastle, Hannah's courage and quick intelligence are at last rewarded. But it is only the pain of
near-loss that will free her heart to love.

A triumph of a book – about a woman whose sparkle,
humour, resilience and passion will not be sup-
pressed.

'*Hannah Robson* is a memorable story of a strong-
minded and delightful girl and woman. A book full of
a kind of gritty warmth which gave me enormous
pleasure from the first page to the last.'

Rosemary Sutcliff

'I enjoyed *Hannah Robson*. Hannah *is* unusual, her
decision to opt out of lady's maiding and so gain
independence was interesting – raised the novel
above the normal historical romance.'

Margaret Forster, author of LADY'S MAID

HODDER AND STOUGHTON PAPERBACKS

BELVA PLAIN

HARVEST

Iris and Theo Stern seemed to have it all; a secure marriage, four attractive children, a beautiful house filled with lovely things as well as the respect that came from Theo's work as one of the country's top surgeons.

But one outsider, Paul Werner, knew better. Watching over them with anguish, he knew of Iris's frustrations, Theo's wandering eye and affections. He saw their eldest son, Steve, bright and sensitive, beginning to rebel against the values and beliefs of his family.

But above all he knew the secret that lay buried at the heart of the Stern's seeming security and happiness. The secret that could destroy everything . . .

'Belva Plain writes with such warmth and compassion about family life that you'll enjoy every minute of this book'

Annabel

HODDER AND STOUGHTON PAPERBACKS

ELIZABETH ADLER

PRIVATE DESIRES

The enthralling story of a passion that leads to heartbreak and tragedy.

Half-Egyptian, half-French, Leonie is born into poverty and hardship.

Exotic good looks and a fierce fighting spirit lead her to a very different life of wealth and luxury in turn-of-the-century Paris — until her fateful encounter with a cruel and powerful man whose obsession becomes her destiny . . .

HODDER AND STOUGHTON PAPERBACKS

ELIZABETH ADLER

PEACH

'A long, fast romantic read . . . one of the best'
The Mail On Sunday

Peach de Courmont and Noel Maddox.

Two people born on opposite sides of the world, at opposite ends of the scale of fortune. Two people who were destined to meet — and destined to love each other . . .

Moving from the slums of Detroit to residential Boston, from the glamorous Riviera to Paris and the peaceful English countryside, PEACH is the enthralling, heart-stopping story of their love.

HODDER AND STOUGHTON PAPERBACKS

RONA JAFFE

AN AMERICAN LOVE STORY

Sophisticated, compulsive, passionate ... the ultimate love story of our age.

Four very different women, each in love with the same man. He is Clay Bowen, superstar producer, irresistibly seductive, incurably unfaithful.

Real women in the glamorous media world where only success and power are respected, AN AMERICAN LOVE STORY is a saga of obsession, betrayal and survival.

LAURA is the prima ballerina he married for show and has driven to the edge of mental collapse.
NINA is the daughter who will risk everything for his love and attention.
SUSAN is the fiercely independent writer for whom he has become a near-fatal addiction.
BAMBI is the deviously ambitious companion of his mid-life crisis years.

'Bowen is one of those men you love to hate'
Sunday Express

'Jaffe is one of the best'
The Sunday Times

'A best seller'
The Observer

HODDER AND STOUGHTON PAPERBACKS

JESSICA MARCH

OBSESSIONS

As long as she could remember, beautiful Niki Sandeman had been fighting back. Fighting against the stigma of illegitimacy. Fighting to redeem the legacy of her glamorous but ill-fated mother.

Now she is engaged in the most perilous fight of her young, defiant life.

The challenge is to beat at their own game the arrogant, powerful Hyland dynasty — her own family, which has always refused to acknowledge her. The prize is control of a mighty business empire.

But if she wins in business, she may lose in love. Only if she can break free from her own hunger for recognition and revenge will she be able to give her heart to the one man who can mean more to her than any of life's obsessions.

HODDER AND STOUGHTON PAPERBACKS

ELIZABETH ADLER

TEMPTATIONS

For every woman with a need to be healed, a need to be loved, a need to be saved.

The Oasis.

Once she had been the international jet set's most glittering cover girl. Throwing herself into an ecstatic whirl of love affairs, fueled by the most potent pleasure drugs of an era of abandon, Stevie Knight had emerged as a rare survivor from her generation's dizzying, devastating trip into decadence. Survived because she was as strong as she was beautiful.

Now, America's richest and most glamorous women come to The Oasis — the haven she has set up in the New Mexico desert. There they are helped to overcome their addictions, repair their shattered lives.

But even as she uses all her strength and her hard-won insights to help her clients, Stevie is facing her own greatest challenge. She has fallen in love with a passion greater than any she has experienced before. Fallen in love with a man who demands a commitment she is too proud to make, who demands the one thing to which she has never surrendered. Surrender itself.

HODDER AND STOUGHTON PAPERBACKS

MORE ROMANTIC FICTION AVAILABLE FROM HODDER AND STOUGHTON PAPERBACKS

JESSICA MARCH

☐ 52808 1 Temptations   £5.99
☐ 53949 0 Obsessions   £4.99

RONA JAFFE

☐ 55830 X An American Love Story   £4.99

ELIZABETH ADLER

☐ 41369 7 Peach   £4.99
☐ 39460 9 Private Desires   £5.99

BELVA PLAIN

☐ 54290 4 Harvest   £4.99

BRENDA MCBRYDE

☐ 55350 2 Hannah Robson   £3.99

All these books are available at your local bookshop or newsagent or can be ordered direct from the publisher. Just tick the titles you want and fill in the form below.

Prices and availability subject to change without notice.

HODDER AND STOUGHTON PAPERBACKS, P O Box 11, Falmouth, Cornwall.

Please send cheque or postal order for the value of the book, and add the following for postage and packing:

UK including BFPO – £1.00 for one book, plus 50p for the second book, and 30p for each additional book ordered up to a £3.00 maximum.

OVERSEAS INCLUDING EIRE – £2.00 for the first book, plus £1.00 for the second book, and 50p for each additional book ordered.
OR Please debit this amount from my Access/Visa Card (delete as appropriate).

Card Number ☐☐☐☐☐☐☐☐☐☐☐☐☐☐☐☐

AMOUNT £ ....

EXPIRY DATE ....

SIGNED ....

NAME ....

ADDRESS ....